What She Will Become

What She Will Become

An Alex Bell Mystery

SUSAN THISTLETHWAITE

RESOURCE *Publications* · Eugene, Oregon

WHAT SHE WILL BECOME
An Alex Bell Mystery

Resource Publications
An Imprint of Wipf and Stock Publishers
199 W. 8th Ave., Suite 3
Eugene, OR 97401

www.wipfandstock.com

PAPERBACK ISBN: 978-1-6667-0081-7
HARDCOVER ISBN: 978-1-6667-0082-4
EBOOK ISBN: 978-1-6667-0083-1

05/25/21

The two lines from the Edwin Rolfe poem, "Little Ballad for Americans—1954," are quoted by permission (January 12, 2021) of Cary R. Nelson (crnelson@illinois.edu), who holds the copyright.

Robert Frost, "The Gift Outright," public domain, January 1, 2019.

To all those who resist tyranny

"Such as she was, such as she *would* become, *has* become, and I—and for this occasion let me change that to—what she *will* become."

> —ROBERT FROST at the Inauguration of John Fitzgerald Kennedy as President of the United States following the reading of his poem, "The Gift Outright," an ode to American exceptionalism first published in 1942.

Student, student, keep mouth shut and brain spry—
Your best friend Dick Meriwell's employed by the F.B.I.

> —EDWIN ROLFE, "Little Ballad for Americans—1954"

CONTENTS

PREFACE AND ACKNOWLEDGMENTS

The decade of the 1960s has both formed and deformed our present moment. Assassinations, struggles for racial equality, a deadly and deceptive war in Vietnam, a drive to land on the moon, nuclear stand-offs, and other huge events defined those years as perhaps the most tumultuous in American history for a long time.

Until now. The first decades of the 21st century can easily match the 1960s for turmoil.

These two eras are closely related. Both the horrible and the hallelujah moments of this current time have been, I believe, to a great extent seeded by the 1960s.

The politics of fear born out of the anti-Communist fervor of the 1950 post-WWII era also has played an enormous role in shaping this country. I had not sufficiently realized, however, until I began the research for this book, that the "Red Scare" of the 1950s had morphed into the "Lavender Scare," that is, the persecution of LGBTQI persons as security risks, by the 1960s, and that conception was, I think it is fair to say, promulgated, and perhaps actually created, by J. Edgar Hoover. The idea that the body politic was "unsafe" unless heterosexual, white, and male became imprinted on this society in that time. The persistence of that physical and political construct continues to this day.

I decided to begin this novel at the beginning, so to speak, on Inauguration Day, 1961. Camelot would meet catastrophe in only three years, and there would be riots and love fests in the succeeding years.

This is a work of fiction, however. There are historical figures who come on scene briefly such as both John and Robert Kennedy, as well as Phil and Katherine Graham. While these were real people, what they say and do in this novel is completely fabricated. One exception is J. Edgar Hoover. I have taken the scene in this novel, where Mr. Hoover testifies at a congressional hearing, directly from a video of him doing so and the words he speaks in that chapter come from that video. That link is included in the bibliography of books and articles I have consulted for the historical portions of this novel. The two characters in Greenwich Village, Ed Francher and Rev. Howard Moody, are also not fictional and some of the dialogue I attribute to them comes, in paraphrase, from *The Village Voice*, the famous local paper edited by Francher to which Rev. Moody contributed articles. Senator J. William Fulbright likewise was a real person, and his statements at a fictionalized hearing are again paraphrases of his views on the Cuban embargo. Fidel Castro's speech to the U.N. is excerpted from the original.

The rest of the characters are entirely fictional, as is the structure of the State Department as I describe it. The main character, Alex Bell, and her Hungarian immigrant family, are very, very loosely based on my own Hungarian immigrant family who worked in sweatshops in the Garment District in New York City in the early 20th century.

I want to thank my supportive family. As always, their love makes me feel I can attempt anything, and believe me, writing an historical novel was quite a reach for me.

I need to thank Rev. Jane Fisler Hoffman again for her careful reading of all the chapters and her critiques and suggestions all through this process. I must thank Dr. Cheryl Townsend Gilkes for nearly forty years of friendship and for her careful advice about the choices for music, and the order of the music, for a jazz funeral. I must thank Dr. Mary Hunt who has also read the manuscript and endorsed the book. Mary says, of my novels, "I'm a fan!" and that cheers me on so much.

I would also like to thank all the dogs who have lived with us over the years. Life is richer with dogs. Their personalities collectively helped form the character of Miss Bea.

Who is Miss Bea? You'll see.

PROLOGUE

A cloth bag went over his head and the darkness was absolute.

He tried to yank it off, but his arms were grabbed from behind. Questions were shouted at him.

He shook his head no, and blows rained down on his body. More questions. He shook his head. More pain.

I was so stupid was his last coherent thought before a fist broke his nose. His head rocked back as another punch broke his cheekbone. Then another punch came higher on his face. His head snapped back and a bone in his neck broke.

His brain gave up before his body.

I

SUNDAY, JANUARY 22, 1961

Alexandra Zsófia Bel ran down Canal Road in Washington, D.C., past where that waterway joined the Potomac River. Her breath blew out steady, even clouds of ice droplets that were whisked away as silently as her snow muffled footfalls by the bitter wind off of the gray, racing water. She was running along this barely plowed road because the footpath along the very edge of the water, where she normally ran, was still impassable from heaps of snow and ice. Two days before, this self-absorbed city had been forced to a halt by a thick, white onslaught. A relentless eight inches of an uninvited, southern blast had treacherously attacked a town with, up until then, only the transfer of power and inaugural parties on its collective mind.

The Army Corps of Engineers had been marshalled to repel this icy assault on the tony inauguration of John Fitzgerald Kennedy as the 35th President of the United States. They had managed to plow the major streets, but they had not yet completely cleared all the secondary roads. It was safe enough to run here so early on this particular Sunday morning, as most of Washington was sleeping in after what one Washington reporter had called a "gilt-edged, mink-lined, silk-hatted, 100-proof" celebration.

That was not for Alex, as she liked to be called. She had spent the night hidden in her small apartment and was cold sober on this frigid dawn. Not for her the celebrity-packed Washington scene. She was out running before sunup to quell her mounting fear. She hoped to sneak in to this powerful city and appear to fit in, but she was as wary as a feral cat hiding in the bushes, starving but waiting until dark to venture out.

She had good reason to be afraid. To get to Washington, D.C., to get a job in a Senator's office as she had, Alex had needed to become someone else. She had added an "l" to her last name so she could go from the Hungarian immigrant "Bel" to the oh so British "Bell." She used "Sophia" as her middle name if pressed, but mostly confined it to an "S." She told no one who her mother and aunt, her only living relatives, actually were, and more than that, what they actually did.

She ran on, ignoring the pain in her empty stomach. When Alex was worried, she couldn't force herself to eat. And now she was nearly petrified. She shared this with her little dog, Miss Bea, who was running ahead. Miss Bea was the only living soul in whom Alex dared confide.

"I'm scared, Miss Bea," Alex said.

Miss Bea ran on, having heard this lament for the last couple of days. "She'll get over it," Miss Bea said to herself. "She always does."

Miss Bea had been a stray that Alex had found in a ditch, thrown away like so much trash, on the side of another snowy road. That road had been in a semi-rural area in Michigan last winter where Alex had been trudging along as a volunteer on the Kennedy campaign. She had spotted the little, nearly frozen puppy, scooped her up, rubbed her vigorously with her mittens, and then, seeing that the pup was breathing, stuck her inside her warm wool coat and kept on going to canvas the next house. Alex had named her Bea because she looked like a beagle with mink brown head, floppy ears and a sleek, dark copper coat. The pup stayed on the small side as she grew, but sleekly muscled. Alex had come to think there was some Jack Russell mixed in. Bea, it turned out, was a strong personality, and she had acquired the "Miss" by force of will.

Miss Bea pulled ahead, unhappy at being on a lead. She bent her dark, quivering snout to the plowed road. Not a lot of smells Miss Bea noted, but with her beagle nose she was always able to follow a scent, even in the worst conditions. They were now closer to where the canal joined the river and, even with the ice skimming the water, there were always good smells there.

Alex saw Miss Bea's lack of attention and made her point again.

"No, seriously Miss Bea, this is nothing like what I've tried before. Working for a Senator. Suppose they investigate me? Worse, suppose they investigate my family? I've worked so hard and it could all go to pieces on me before I even get started."

Miss Bea lifted her head for a moment, and Alex was pleased she had finally gotten her attention. But Miss Bea wasn't listening to Alex, she was on a scent.

"What is that smell?" Bea wondered. She pulled to the side of the road and put her nose up as high as she could, taking in the drifting odor coming from the other side of the big mound of snow plowed to the side of the road. "Meat? Maybe, though rotting." Miss Bea turned her head directly toward the smell and perked her ears, trying to better trap the odor. "Rotting meat for sure," she thought, "and a little sweet too." She pulled hard on the lead to get to it.

"Come on, Miss Bea," Alex snapped with some impatience. "We're on a run here. Try to concentrate."

Alex was much stronger than she was, and when Alex tugged on the lead, Miss Bea bowed to the inevitable and ran on.

And that was how both Alex and Miss Bea ran right by the corpse covered with snow down by the bank of the river opposite the misted shape of Roosevelt Island.

* * *

It was late, but Alex couldn't sleep. She got up and walked quietly around Miss Bea's basket. The little dog was snoring lightly, one paw over her nose. Miss Bea was tired from their long run in the snow. So was Alex, but she was too keyed up, too worried about starting her new job the next day to fall asleep.

Alex went in the kitchen area of the small apartment, pulled out a little sauce pan and some milk from the apartment's battered refrigerator. She hadn't been able to eat any dinner, but perhaps she could get the milk down, she thought. She heated it slowly on the electric stove. Slowly was the only way the stove heated anything, and only two of its four, ring burners worked. And it, and the refrigerator, were astonishingly pink, at least where the finish had not chipped off. In the New York tenement where Alex had grown up, and where her mother and aunt still lived, the refrigerator was an ancient, white box with a hood on top that wheezed and whirled if asked to make a little ice. The appliances in her DC apartment were decades newer, but Alex had shaken her head at the idea of pink in the kitchen.

The milk finally gave off a little steam. Alex poured it into a chipped mug and sat down on the rickety chair by the window, gazing at the empty, frozen street below. She blew and sipped and thought. Then she suddenly jumped up, put her half-full mug on the small coffee table in front of the sagging couch and dug under the sink for a screwdriver she kept there. She carried the tool to the front hall closet and knelt down. She pushed a couple of boots and a battered pair of shoes out of the way and unscrewed a panel off the wall of the back of the closet to reveal a hidden compartment she'd made when she'd first moved in. She took out a shoebox from the small space, carried it over to the sitting area and put it on the coffee table. Then she moved her milk over, not wanting any spills to get on what was in the box. But she didn't open it right away.

Alex's previous life was in the box. It held many of the same things she held inside, things she had changed to become someone else.

She noticed the top of the box was dusty, and she got a rag out of the kitchen and dusted the cardboard lid, but still she didn't open it. She folded her long, thin legs under her and sat on the floor by the low table, contemplating the box.

Finally, Alex snorted, impatient with herself, and she opened the box, took out the contents and placed them carefully on the table. The photographs were on top. A couple of the pictures were getting yellowed, she observed, as though these images were from a far-off country in an ancient land. Nothing to do with her. Except, there was her aunt, her gnome-like, tiny figure appearing larger because she was standing on a wagon. Her thin arms were spread to the sky in a gesture Alex knew, from many years of experience, was one of outrage. Gathered around the wagon were men and women with gaunt faces, wearing layers of thin and ragged clothes. They were gazing at her aunt who, for all her shrunken size, was a powerful speaker. There must have been hundreds. Alex put it aside and picked up the next photo. It was of four women in dark coats and cloche hats with large placards pinned to their chests. "Strike! Local 76" was written in large, black letters. The two center figures were her mother and her aunt. Her aunt's bent frame was nearly hidden by the placard. Her mother was very thin, but at least a foot taller than her sister. Her mother smiled up at her, her sweet, long face animated. She couldn't help it. She smiled back.

There were no photos of her father who had died when she was a baby, or so she had been told. "He no like his face shown like that," her aunt had explained when she'd asked to see a photo of him. There wasn't even a wedding photo, or one that had survived.

Two thin, metal discs pinned to a long ribbon slid off the pile and on to the floor. Alex looked down at them and then picked them up. "Stand Up for America Wallace for President" was printed in red and blue on a white background on the political buttons. The white ribbon had "New York Delegate" embroidered in red thread on it. That's right, Alex remembered. Her mother and her aunt had both been Progressive Party delegates to the Philadelphia convention in the summer of 1948 when Henry Wallace launched his presidential campaign. Wallace had run on a platform of desegregation, equality for women and national health care. His campaign had been sunk by accusations that he was a Communist. Alex had stayed with Mrs. Bronstein, their neighbor across the hall, while her mother and aunt had traveled to Philadelphia. They had been so happy, Alex remembered. They had thought change like that could really happen. She sighed.

Alex's birth certificate was next, with her real name. Alexandra Zsófia Bel. There it was. She sat back on her heels. Should she change her name legally and not just keep adding an "l" and translating her middle name into English? Something to think about. Oh, but if her aunt in particular ever found out, there would be hell to pay.

She saw another paper stuck to the back of the flimsy copy of the birth certificate. She gently separated the papers and, speaking of hell, she thought, looked at her baptismal record from the Hungarian Catholic Church on East 82nd Street in Manhattan. An ornate script spelled out *Szent István Római Katolikus Magyar Templom*, St. Stephen of Hungary Church in English, and Alexandra Zsófia Bel and the date. She shook her head at the idea that her passionately socialist family had gone to a Catholic church so that a priest could sprinkle water on her baby head. She put both papers aside.

Socialist Workers Party flyers were next and stuck to one was another button. "Democratic Socialist Party" it said in bold red, not yet faded. A clenched fist decorated the center.

And then Alex reached the union material. International Ladies Garment Union Workers flyers and buttons. Dozens of them. And here was another ribbon, this one folded and creased. "National Child Labor Committee" was printed on this white ribbon in black, the circle symbol for abolishing child labor below it. Another convention, another delegation. That time, only her aunt had gone, she thought, as Alex had been very young. At least, that's what she'd been told.

Below that were Alex's high school grade reports. All A's. She smiled. She had almost never slept in high school she'd worked so hard. And there was the telegram, offering her early admission to Smith College with a scholarship. I should have that one framed, she thought, but she put it back on the pile.

Alex placed her grade reports and the telegram back in the box and then added her birth certificate. But what about the rest? Should I destroy it, she wondered.

She sat back on her heels again, thinking. She took a sip of the now cooled milk and grimaced. Then she felt Miss Bea come up next to her and sit, her ears cocked and an inquiring look on her face.

"I know, Miss Bea. We should be sleeping."

Alex had made up her mind. She'd keep the box. She was not that person any more, but she could not bear to let that past go. She carefully piled all the items back in the box and took it to the front hall closet where she wedged it in the small space at the back. She fitted the wooden cover she'd made from a tea tray over the hole and carefully screwed it back down. Then she put the boots and shoes back and stood up.

When she came back, Miss Bea had her paws up on the coffee table and was finishing off the cooled milk.

"Not bad," Miss Bea thought, licking her jowls.

Alex sighed.

"Come on, Miss Bea, let's try to get some sleep." And they both walked into the bedroom, got into their beds, and immediately fell asleep.

* * *

While Alex and Miss Bea slept, the temperature dropped to single digits and a light snow fell. The slightly thawed corpse stiffened again and the white shroud over it deepened.

2

MONDAY, JANUARY 23, 1961

Miss Bea sat facing the faded wallpaper that covered the walls of Alex's bedroom. The paper had once shown bunches of red flowers tied with ribbons, but now these pictures reminded Bea of soup bones with a little rotting meat attached. But Bea was not interested in the wallpaper right that minute. She was interested in making her displeasure known.

"Come on, Miss Bea, don't be like that," Alex said as she pulled a dress back over her head, placed it carefully on the bed with another discarded dress, and reached for a white, Peter Pan collar blouse instead. Better go with the suit, she thought. The safer choice. Senator Madeleine Carpenter, Alex's new boss, always wore suits. And pearls. Three strands. Wear the suit, skip the pearls. Don't want to fall into parody, Alex thought as she checked her hose for ladders. No. They were good.

Alex looked at Bea's stiff little back and sighed.

"I had to cut our run short. I'll make it up to you tomorrow."

Miss Bea did not move. She was very good at this, and the key was not to show you were even listening.

"Well, I had to have a lot of extra time, so that's that. It takes some doing to turn me into one of them, and I didn't want to mess up. First day, you know."

Bea continued to look at the faded wall.

Alex went over to the closet and took out a dark, maroon suit. It was beautifully tailored, like all her dressy clothes. The label might not say "Givenchy," but the cut and the shape did. That was because Alex had tried on the original at Bonwit Teller, the famous department store in New York

City, and then carefully copied it in her own bedroom. All her good clothes were made by her, or by her mother or her aunt who were skilled garment workers and who had taught her to do exquisite tailoring. All her good clothes were modeled on the best designers.

Her mother and aunt, as well as her deceased father, had all immigrated from Hungary and landed in New York City's garment district as teenagers where they still worked in terrible conditions. No wonder they organized to get unions, Alex thought, thinking of her midnight foray into her hidden shoebox.

But I am becoming someone else, she thought as she smoothed her hands over the jacket of the impeccable suit as it lay waiting on the bed.

Alex had wanted to become someone else for a long time now, ever since she'd been a young teenager. She wanted to become a true American and some immigrants, like Hungarians, were not. That realization had hit her like a slap in the face one day when she, her mother, and her aunt had been a little uptown and out of their own neighborhood. They had been turned away from a store that didn't serve "Hunkies," the racial slur for Hungarians. She had promised herself she wasn't going to suffer the shame of being turned away from stores any more. Or turned away from anything. She wanted to fit in.

Little by little, Alex had changed, and she'd changed even more than adding an "l" to the name on her birth certificate. She'd changed how she looked. Her eyes were green, and unfortunately not the light green of the British, but the deeper green of her central European ancestors. A flick of dark blue mascara was the best she could do there. Her dark brown hair was something she could change and so she had dyed it blonde, enduring her aunt's rages at that. "So, the dark hair of your ancestors you must hide? We not good enough for you?" her aunt kept ranting. Her mother had not said anything, but Alex knew she had been hurt.

But she had persisted, the memory of being refused entrance to a store a constant ache like a bad tooth. She had put lemon juice on her face to lighten skin that was too dark, and every day she spread a thin coating of zinc oxide for protection from any sun exposure. With her grueling work in high school, she had gotten to Smith College. And all the time she'd been at that posh school, she had studied them, the girls who were actually blonde, actually white, and actually Protestant. She had especially studied the way they acted. They were who she wanted to become.

Alex had graduated a semester early from Smith with top marks, and with her degree in government in hand she had applied early on for the Kennedy campaign. She had been hired by Robert Kennedy, his brother's campaign manager, and she realized right away her job was to look like a pretty, young, white Protestant girl. She went door-to-door, calling on other white Protestants and telling them how wonderful John Fitzgerald Kennedy was and how his form of Catholicism was really practically Protestant. But she'd gotten sloppy, she remembered with dismay.

She had been outside a lot, and she had forgotten sometimes to wear a hat and spread on the sun-protective zinc oxide. Worse, she had not lightened her skin religiously. She stared in her bedroom mirror, but she was transported to a dingy hallway in the Grand Rapids campaign office where she had heard the drawn out, Boston a's and rolled r's of the candidate himself. To her dawning horror, she had realized the candidate and his brother were apparently discussing her.

"If thaat young woman is a Praatestant, Ahmmm J. Edgar Hoover," Jack Kennedy was saying, his distinctive, Boston-accented voice coming out an open door.

"Look, Jack," his brother had replied in his far more clipped and rapid way, rushing over his vowels like they were in his way. "Drop'it. Those white-bread Protestant types love her, so they love you. Lots of good reports."

"Well, those eyes, and those cheekbones, and the cuh-lah of her skin, oh mai mai, there's no real whitebreaad there. But a lot of aasests, and Ah do mean the aass part."

"I said drop'it, Jack," Bobby had snapped back. "Too hard to get volunteers as it is."

The next day, Alex had asked for a transfer to eastern Ohio to be closer to her "sick mother." She'd tried to be out canvassing whenever the candidate was in town, and she'd never forgotten again to keep her face and hair as light as she could make them.

She trembled a little from the memory and then tried to shake it off. She focused on her reflection in the mirror, eased the frown from her forehead and carefully applied the layer of the white, sun protection cream on her nose and cheeks. She let that dry for a few minutes while she checked her pale nails. They were okay. She checked her roots. No brown line yet, but she'd need to touch up her hair this weekend. Then she carefully put on her precious Max Factor pale foundation. Another brush of the dark blue mascara, very pale pink lipstick, and she was done.

She peered critically at her image and patted her cheeks that were now a little too pale under her makeup. Yes, she was a light brown-skinned child of Central European immigrants and an atheist Catholic. But that wasn't the worst. She knew she would be in really big trouble if they knew about her fake name along with her family's socialist activities. That would read secret "Commie" in the Kennedy books.

I can't get sloppy again, Alex thought. She continued to gaze in her mirror, counting back from 100 until her breathing slowed. She looked exactly as she wanted to look. She glanced at her half-full cup of coffee, sitting on her dresser. It was all she had fixed herself for breakfast this morning, but her stomach was rejecting even that. She took the cup with the remaining coffee into the little kitchen, dumped it out and then washed the cup and put it on the drying rack.

She went back into her room, got a hat, gloves, her exquisitely tailored, belted navy winter coat, and she pulled on her smart, black leather boots. On her and Bea's short run, there had been about an inch of new snow. She tucked her low-heeled pumps into her bag, and she turned to speak to Miss Bea one more time.

"I promise, Miss Bea, we'll go for a long run tomorrow morning. I'll just get up earlier."

Bea remained facing the wall, but she was content. She had now decided on her revenge. There were those fuzzy slippers Alex liked so much, and she'd seen one peeking out from under the bed. "Just a few bites," she thought. "One has to be disciplined about this kind of thing. Just make a statement."

And then Miss Bea heard the front door close, and she turned to the bed.

* * *

"So you went to Smith College?" Senator Madeleine Richards Carpenter asked, her well-modulated voice flowing out of her discretely lipsticked mouth. The pale pink on the Senator's wrinkled lips nearly matched the shade Alex had chosen.

"Yes, Madam Senator," Alex replied quietly, and correctly, having studied up on the form of address Senator Carpenter preferred .

Senator Carpenter smiled, pleased, her round, regular features pulling upward into a nice smile, a friendly smile and, Alex suspected, a very practiced smile. Her signature pearls were in evidence, surrounding a high-collared blouse in a very unfortunate yellow, a Tweety Bird yellow that clashed with the faded, chartreuse wall color of this older part of the Russell Senate building. And neither of the tones flattered the Senator's pasty white skin, and really, Alex reflected, her skin is very white. It contrasted sharply with her helmet of suspiciously uniform brown hair.

"I attended Wellesley College," the Senator was saying, sounding a little like she was practicing scales. "Some might say," she continued, "not all that different from Smith. We Seven Sisters need to stick together." She nodded her head in assent with her own comment, and Alex noted that her hair did not move at all.

Alex took a moment to look down at her lap, feigning shyness. This was something she had learned from the young women she had carefully observed at Smith. They had used that technique with the professors at the school and then laughed about it after. Alex saw how well it worked to charm the teachers into giving them better grades than Alex thought they had earned. So she had copied them. But she was glad her aunt could not see her now.

"Yes, well, Madam Senator, I am honored to be on your staff and I will do the very best job I can," she said to her lap and then looked up with a tremulous smile.

Senator Carpenter nodded her hair helmet, picked up a pencil and made a little notation in what was clearly Alex's file.

Then she cleared her throat.

"You can see," and she pointed with the pencil out the door of the small, private office where they were sitting, "I don't have one of the bigger suites. Stands to reason, as I have only been here two years. You will take the desk out there to the right, closest to the main office door." Another pencil point.

Alex turned in her chair to look at that empty desk, though she'd passed it, and another empty desk further back in the room, when she'd arrived. A third desk was occupied by a middle-aged woman with frizzy, graying hair, who was stuffing envelopes. A raised counter, with a desk behind it, was at the very back. That perch belonged to Alistair Bentley Carrington, Alex had been informed by pompous Alistair himself when she'd arrived. His whole, upper-class name was written out on a name plate with "Senior Legislative Aide to Senator Carpenter" below. Not content with having Alex merely read his title, however, he'd announced the whole thing through his nose when she'd introduced herself and said she had an appointment with the Senator. Alistair had already adopted the President Kennedy haircut, closely cropped sides and longer, controlled shaggy top. On Alistair's narrow head, however, the height of the longer hair on top made him look a little like a large, Airedale terrier. His unfortunate, pointed ears added to the Airedale look.

Probably Yale, not Harvard she'd thought as she'd acted impressed by Alistair, his title, his nose and his hair.

"I'd like you right there as the first face someone sees when they enter," the Senator continued. "You have such a ladylike appearance, it will send a very good message to visitors and staff alike. We are ladies here," the Senator said firmly, fingering her pearls.

I wonder if Alistair knows that, Alex said to herself and had to look down at her lap again to hide a smile.

"Your job will be to answer the mail my constituents send me and include little tidbits about my life here in Washington. I get a lot of letters, especially from women in my home state, and they like that personal touch."

"Oh, I will like to," Alex started to say, but she was interrupted by a very loud "Meow!"

Alex, already on edge, started.

"Oh, don't be alarmed," Senator Carpenter said with a soft laugh. "That's just Fluffy," and she reached down under her desk and brought out one of the largest and ugliest cats Alex had ever seen. Fluffy probably weighed 30 pounds. Fluffy glared at Alex from the comfort of the Senator's arms.

"What a beautiful animal," Alex lied as Fluffy continued to glare. The huge cat had mounds of gray hair and yellow eyes. Alex made a mental note never to let Fluffy and Miss Bea meet. It would be a fight to the death.

"Yes, he is, isn't he, the handsome thing," the Senator crooned. "He was my husband's pet and now he is very devoted to me." She dropped her voice. "We're not really supposed to have pets in Federal Buildings, but my colleagues overlook my little indiscretion knowing how much comfort Fluffy gives to a widow."

"How nice," Alex said, unable to think of anything else to say.

"Besides," said the Senator, her voice losing the hint of baby talk, "my constituents love Fluffy and ask about him all the time. He's worth thousands of votes to me, I'd say," and a very shrewd look came over the round, grandmotherly face before she bent her head and nuzzled Fluffy. Fluffy looked grim.

Alex contemplated the Senator cuddling Fluffy. Alex knew she needed to have the Senator's support if she were to move up in this office, to say nothing of moving up in government. Better flatter Fluffy, Alex thought.

"Madam Senator," Alex began in a soft voice, "If you think it is a good idea, I should mention Fluffy in the replies to your constituents, I mean the ones who ask about him, certainly, and even quote Fluffy's observations on this magnificent city. That could then lead in to your contributions to our government."

The Senator stopped cuddling Fluffy, placed him on her lap where he glowered over the desk at Alex, and he looked at her again with narrowed eyes. For a moment, Alex wondered if she'd made a mistake, but then the Senator spoke.

"Oh, my dear, what a wonderful, wonderful idea, and what an asset you are going to be to my office!" Senator Carpenter actually clapped her hands. Fluffy didn't like that sound over his head, and he hissed a little. The Senator ignored him and went on praising Alex.

"That's just the kind of thing many of my constituents like to hear from me. I just can't wait to read what you will write. So good. So very good."

Alex just smiled. Apparently having even such a paltry idea was a novelty in this office. Well, she thought, probably here in Washington as a whole.

This won't be hard, she thought while continuing to smile at the Senator, though Fluffy did seem to get she wasn't smiling at him, and he scowled at her, his yellow eyes in slits. Too bad for you, Fluffy, Alex thought. I like writing fiction, and I'm good at it. It will be good practice, Alex reflected, as she had concluded, as a government major in college, that most of what was written in political life seemed to be basically fiction.

"My, I'm so glad you like my idea. I can't wait to get started," she bubbled as she gathered her bag, hat, and gloves and stood up.

The Senator put Fluffy back down under her desk into what was likely a cat box there. There was a muted growl. The Senator stood up.

"So, so happy you are one of my team," she said, reaching over the desk to shake Alex's hand.

"Thank you, Madam Senator," Alex said, taking the offered hand. It was so smooth and soft Alex had a little trouble holding on to it. Fortunately, the Senator let go almost immediately, and Alex inclined her head, not too much, but just with a hint of a bow and walked out toward the desk that would be hers.

Alistair, whom she assumed had eavesdropped on every word through the open door, gave her a condescending look that drew his long face even further down.

You better not look at Fluffy like that, Alex silently warned Alistair as she sat down with relief in the desk chair and placed her bag and other items in an empty drawer. Fluffy has claws. Well, she thought, so do I.

Alex reached over for a stack of mail piled in the inbox of the desk she'd been given.

Come on, Fluffy, let's meet your fans, Alex thought and stuck the letter opener into the first envelope. She cut it briskly. The tearing paper made a satisfying sound like the paper was yielding to her.

She scanned the first constituent letter and when she saw the word "Fluffy" with a little heart drawn after it, she sighed with satisfaction. This could work.

As Alex read the constituent letter, she pondered how to create Fluffy's voice. *He's protective of the Senator, of course, and, really, of the people of her state,* she mused. *He's not going to have a cute voice. That's got to be pretty clear. Otherwise, how to justify that mug of a face he has?* Alex laughed to herself, continuing to construct Fluffy's character in her head. *Why,* she realized, remembering Fluffy's face as he had glared at her, *he looks a lot like J. Edgar Hoover. I wonder if he's hiding any dangerous ideas,* she reflected as she drew a clean sheet of the Senator's stationary toward her, rejected a BIC ballpoint and picked up a fountain pen.

According to her family and their socialist friends in New York City, Hoover was the most dangerous man in the country. *Well,* Alex reflected, *Fluffy probably could be dangerous, but no reason to reveal that.* Alex grabbed for her imagination and concentrated on the Fluffy character. *Fluffy should know the ins and outs of Washington and be very smart. After all, he'd been smart enough to land in a Senator's office. Twice.* As Fluffy's profile began to take shape in her mind, Alex started to write.

"I bet you're surprised that I'm writing to you," she penned in a rounded cursive.

* * *

Alex walked tiredly up the three flights to her apartment. There was little light on the stairs as their cheap landlord put in the lowest watt bulbs and only a few of them. The 14th Street bus had been packed, and she was tired from her long day of watching her every word and gesture.

She managed to get her key in the lock after several tries in the dark hall and pushed the door open. Her roommate Gwen wouldn't be back until tomorrow. She had stayed with a cousin so they could go to the inauguration together.

Alex flipped on the light and saw the carnage.

"Oh, Miss Bea! How could you?"

Her beautiful, fuzzy mule was in pieces in the middle of the front hall.

"I did get a little carried away," Bea admitted.

3

TUESDAY, JANUARY 24, 1961

A gray mist rose from the wide and racing river, chunks of ice tumbling and breaking on the partly submerged rocks. Not a good idea to fall in here, Alex thought as she and Miss Bea ran along their usual trail, down by the Potomac River. There was a well-trodden footpath and the snow on it was packed down, but treacherous, especially in the pre-dawn dark. Streetlights from Canal Road above gave some light, but Alex used a flashlight to illumine the path and to see Miss Bea who was off leash and trotting ahead.

The previous day's slush had turned to ice in patches overnight. Day-time Washington temperatures had stayed above freezing since the President's frigid Inauguration Day, but the nights had dipped down.

Alex didn't speak, giving Miss Bea the silent treatment after the slipper incident, but she was talking to herself in her head, running over ideas about how long it would take her to move up and become a legislative aide herself.

Miss Bea didn't register she was getting the silent treatment. Her nose was down, and she had picked up that same delicious scent she had smelled from the road above on their last run. The smell was much stronger down here by the river than it had been up on the road.

Bea sped up as the intensifying aromas drew her on like a magnet.

"Miss Bea, slow down!" Alex shouted as she picked up her own pace to keep the little dog in sight. It really was treacherous here, and if Bea slipped down toward the river, Alex might not see her.

"Here!" Bea said to herself as she left the path and started to dig in the snow closer to the side of the river. "Yes, yes, definitely it." She dug harder, her small paws working hard, snow flying up to be blown away by the wind off the water.

"Miss Bea, stop! What are you doing?" Alex cried out as the circle of light of her flashlight revealed the furious efforts of the dog and the raging river just beyond.

"I knew it. I knew it," Miss Bea told herself as she reached the source of the smell and dug her nose right in. Even frozen, the flesh gave off a dozen different aromas that Miss Bea's beagle nose drew in like it was dog ambrosia. As it was. Miss Bea raised her head and gave a howl of triumph.

"Oh, Bea, what did you dig up there?" Alex panted as she carefully navigated her way over to the excited dog, expecting to see a dead fish. She grabbed Miss Bea's collar and pulled her back from the object and shone her flashlight on it.

Then she crouched down to get a better look, dread filling her chest. Fingers. Pale, ragged, human fingers protruded out from the center of the snow where Miss Bea had been digging.

Alex barely registered Miss Bea's enraged efforts to get free of her restraining hand and back to her find.

"Mine. Mine," Miss Bea was howling.

"Oh, Miss Bea," Alex said. "This is awful."

Alex still squatted, now cradling the squirming dog under one arm and using her teeth to pull off the glove on her free hand. It was revolting, but if there were any chance this person were alive she had to check. She brushed away some snow over the wrist, but it took her only a second to register the flesh was frozen solid. A dead body.

Alex sat back on her heels and considered just running on. From her mother and aunt, and really the whole New York immigrant community where she had grown up, she had learned to fear the police with their fat bellies and their uniforms and badges that made them think they could do what they wanted with you. And they could. She had pretty much made up her mind to just keep on and never come this way again when a shout from above nearly stopped her heart.

"Hey you, down there!" A deep male voice was calling out and a bright light picked her out. "What's goin' on?" The voice cut through the freezing air. Accusing voice. Typical. She could see a flashing light on the top of a car on the road. Damn it.

Alex stood up, continuing to hold the squirming Miss Bea under one arm, while she shone her own light up the snowy slope. She summoned her sweet young woman voice and called out.

"Oh, no, no. I'm not okay. It's awful, just awful. My dog found something here, and I think, I really think, it might be a body. A frozen person." She let out a long sob on the last word, pitching it loud enough that the guy above could hear.

"Now, now, don't get excited, Miss," the deep male voice called, now a little gruff. "We'll be right there."

Alex heard a car door slam and boots crunching on snow. "Shit," she heard one voice say. "Watch out. Ice under the snow." The crunching boots came closer.

Alex climbed back up the slope to the path and pulled off her dark, knitted cap, letting her blond hair spill out over her shoulders. Blonde hair always worked. She shook her hair out and then bent her head as though overcome, but really just to let the two approaching figures get a good look at her fair hair curling around her face.

"Now, now, Miss, we're here. It's going to be okay," said the deep voice cop as the two of them approached.

Alex raised her head to look out at them from under her wet lashes. It was a big help to be able to cry at will. She made sure to hunch her shoulders and tighten her arms around Miss Bea as though seeking security from the little dog.

Bea, however, was not going along with this. She growled. She was not going to share her prize with these guys. She wiggled again, and Alex bent her head once more, but this time to hiss into Bea's still perked ear.

"Knock it off, and there's a butcher bone in it for you. With lots of meat."

Miss Bea thought it over and then stilled. "A bone with meat is really tasty," she reflected, and Alex was always as good as her word.

Alex again raised wet eyes to the two officers.

Tall and short, no fat bellies, she thought, though their bulky, wool, winter uniform jackets hid a lot. Alex's tailor-training had her automatically registering the poor fit of the dark clothes. Both men seemed to still be in their twenties. The tall one was white, though now really red in the face from climbing down to the river. The other, the short one, was a thin, light-skinned, Negro man who seemed less winded by the climb down.

"Officer Harold Richardson," tall said, quickly holding out something that might have been an I.D. and then just putting it in his pocket.

"Officer Edgar Thomas," the young, Negro officer said, holding out an I.D. for a little longer than his partner. He had a nice voice, and he put out a hand to give Miss Bea a pet. Miss Bea, now having been bribed, shook her ears in an endearing way.

"Good doggie," Thomas said.

"Oh, brother," Bea thought.

"So now what do we have here?" asked the deep-voiced cop, now identified as Richardson, looking down toward the little pile of snow Miss Bea
had made, and the fingers sticking out along with the bit of the wrist Alex
had exposed. And then they could all see that the snow was mounded up in
body-shaped pile.

Alex looked away and shuddered, and she didn't really even have to
fake it.

Summoning her scared young woman voice, she breathed, "My little
dog must have smelled something and dug into the snow. I had just had
time to see the fingers," another shudder, this one, truth be told, also not a
fake, "and thank heavens you called out to me."

Alex, still holding Bea under one arm, took out a tissue from her
pocket and gave a ladylike sniff.

Richardson gestured to Thomas, and he bent to examine the fingers
without touching them.

"Yeah," Thomas said curtly, standing back up. "Looks like a man's
hand. It's frozen, but there's signs animals had fed some before he froze up
solid. Few days, I'd guess."

Alex felt her stomach turn over, and she turned away, crossed the path,
and sat down on the snowy slope on the other side.

"Just breathe, young lady," tall cop's deep voice advised from behind
her.

"I'll call it in," he went on, addressing Thomas. "You get her information." He unhooked a radio unit from his belt and raised an antenna. "Hope
this damned thing works in this freezin' cold." The radio crackled to life and
he walked a ways down the path to talk into it.

Alex's mind felt fuzzy. Pull it together, she reminded herself. Negro or
white, these are cops. Don't let your guard down."

Thomas crouched down next to where Alex was sitting on the cold
ground.

"Now, Miss, I need to get some particulars from you," he said, and he
took out a small notebook and pencil. Then he seemed to realize he couldn't
write with his big gloves on, and he pulled one off and stuck it in the pocket
of his heavy coat.

"Certainly, Officer," Alex said softly after he finished these maneuvers.
She had waited so he would be looking at her, and she then gave him a brave
smile. It was one of her best, and Thomas could not seem to help returning
it.

"Name and address?" Thomas asked.

"Alexandra Bell," Alex replied, spelling out her last name with the added l, and then she gave her address. She dug in her pocket and brought out the small wallet she always carried when running. She showed Thomas her Washington D.C.driver's license that was on one side, making sure to tilt it so he'd see her Congressional I.D. that served as her pass into the Senate office building in the opposite plastic window.

He bit right away.

"You work at the Senate?" he asked, shining his light on the red, white and blue I.D.

"Yes, I do," Alex said, lowering her eyes modestly. "I am an assistant to Senator Madeleine Richards Carpenter."

"Well, well," said Thomas, writing that down.

"Oh!" Alex said, her alarm not entirely feigned. "I have to let the Senator's office know I will be late. I just started working there, and I don't want to make a bad impression. Oh, my. How can I do that?"

Miss Bea gave a small snort, but otherwise did not comment.

"Now, don't you worry," Thomas said soothingly. "We can radio to Dispatch, and they'll get a message to the Senator's office."

"Oh, but they don't have to know about all this, do they? Couldn't you just send a message I've witnessed an accident and have to give a statement? Please?" Alex accompanied this with a tiny hair toss as she gazed up into Officer Thomas's eyes beseechingly.

He coughed.

"Actually, Miss, that's all we can say." Thomas looked at Alex more sharply, his dark brown eyes narrowing. "Unless you know something about this you're not telling me?"

Damn. A mistake, Alex thought. She'd have to go full out stupid blonde.

"Know something?" she breathed, looking up again. "About what?"

Thomas was not buying it.

"About who that man was and what he's doing on the side of the river in the snow?" Thomas paused, "And what were you doing out at this ungodly hour, anyway?"

"Well, officer, to tell the truth," Alex said, raising her voice to the next level, up to her little girl, confiding voice. "I just hate it, but I have to do exercise pretty much every day or I just can't keep my girlish figure, you know? I mean, don't tell anyone, but I just can't keep away from whipped cream and chocolate."

Thomas harrumphed a little, but he wrote the drivel down. Then he looked up with interest.

"So did you run this way yesterday? The day before? See anything? We need to know when this body got here."

"Oh, no, I didn't, sorry," Alex said, trying for a "I'm such a bad girl" kind of touch. "Too much snow recently. This was my first day out in a while. I really should have, you know, but I didn't."

Miss Bea, drowsing a little in Alex's arms and dreaming of her bone with meat on it, raised her head. "I definitely smelled that three days ago," Bea recalled, and then she returned to the bone reflection.

* * *

The sun had risen like a spotlight behind Alex's shoulder and was piteously illuminating the scene down by the river. More officers and emergency personnel had arrived, and the snow was being brushed carefully off of the prone body.

She had found a fairly flat rock to sit on instead of the cold ground as she had been curtly told "Wait!" by Thomas. He had a streak of nice, however, that being a cop had not entirely extinguished, and he had gone up the slope to his police car to get her a blanket out of the trunk. He'd placed it over her shoulders. The blanket smelled distinctly of horse, and Miss Bea had waked up and taken some offense, woofing a little with irritation. Bea had seen horses on their warmer weather runs, and she had been frightened by their immense size and their superior manner. Miss Bea became aggressive when frightened, and she had barked at the first horse she had seen. The horse had not even looked down at her, and that had irritated her even more.

Alex misunderstood Miss Bea's woof, and she had stood up and taken her for a short walk on her lead. Alex readjusted the blanket so it was folded on the rock, and she could sit on it, and Miss Bea had settled down again to sleep on Alex's lap. She was now dreaming of biting a big horse on its stupid, skinny leg.

There was a stir among the cops clustered around the corpse, and they came to attention as a big man strode up. Here was the big stomach Alex had been expecting, though a very well-tailored overcoat did its best to hide the bulk of the wearer. Watch out for this one, Alex thought, and she shifted Miss Bea into her arms and stood up.

Big man had a big voice, and it carried to Alex as he bent down to look at what had been uncovered of the body.

"Ho, ho," he chuckled, and he stood back up and slapped the cop nearest him on the back.

"One of the sphincter boys, eh? Well, this'll be a quick one." He paused, looking down at the body and growled, "God damn perverts. Gotta root'em all out. One less to worry about."

Then Thomas spoke to him quietly across the body and gestured toward Alex. Big man turned and looked at her.

Showtime, Alex thought and pulled her knitted cap back off. This big, stupid jerk would be just the kind to get distracted by blond hair and a girly voice.

Thomas came around to the side of big man, and together they approached. Thomas looked distinctly ill, but he was working to hide it.

"Detective Peter John Hicks," big man introduced himself in his big, loud voice.

"Miss Alexandra Bell," Alex replied. "How do you do?"

"How do you do?" Hicks guffawed to Thomas. "She acts like it's a god-damn cotillion. You know what a cotillion is, Thomas? A parade of young white girls. Outta your league," and he laughed again.

Alex took this in but gave no sign of being offended. Thomas just continued to look sick. German, she was thinking as she looked up at Hick's enormous, round, ruddy face framed by what she could see of his light brown hair under his fashionable fedora. No, she corrected herself, more likely Dutch, noting his height and the way he carried his big frame as though he owned everything. Just like the rich, Dutch businessmen of New York City. Rude like they were, and, like them, he wore money on his back and head. That had to be a custom-made hat as well.

"Miss Bell discovered the body," Thomas contributed, looking even shorter next to Hicks and very pinched in the face. "She was running here along the river earlier this morning."

"A little cold to be out running, isn't it young lady?" Hicks said, frowning down at her.

"I like to stay fit," Alex said, focusing her eyes on the slope of Hicks's top coat.

Mistake, Alex thought in the next second as Hick's icy blue eyes narrowed. I let him get to me. I need to fix it, she thought.

"As I told the officer here," Alex trilled, assuming her little girl voice, "I have to exercise to keep my figure, you know?" She did a little hair toss as well. Not too much, just to catch the morning light.

"And actually it was my little dog here," and she held up the now awake Miss Bea who was still behaving herself, "who smelled something and led me over to it." She managed a very credible shudder.

"I see," said Hicks, and his florid lips turned up a little, but Alex didn't think it was a smile. It was more cruel than that. Then he looked over at the body.

"I would like you to take a look at the body and let me know if you recognize this, ah, gentleman."

"Oh, no," Alex squealed. "Do I have to? Really?" The revulsion wasn't an act, just the tone.

"Oh, yes, you really have to," Hicks said with a kind of satisfaction that made Thomas turn his face away. Then Hicks took hold of Alex's upper arm and led her toward the body.

His grip actually hurt. Alex went along quietly, but she was preparing to scream as soon as she saw the corpse. That, as it turned out, had been an excellent plan.

They reached the knot of people working around the body and several of the men stepped to the side so that Hicks could drag Alex up toward the head.

She looked down at the frozen face and screamed as loud as she could and pulled away so sharply that she caught Hicks off guard, and she freed her arm. She kept screaming while she ran across the path and back to where she had been sitting.

The frozen face showed some bruising, and it had been missing part of the nose and both eyes. The upper body was loosely covered with a woman's sheer evening dress, torn in places, through which Alex had seen more bruises. But that was not why she kept on screaming. She had recognized the corpse. It was Stephen Gray, a young Negro lawyer she had met in Ohio when her future roommate, Gwen, had introduced them. Gray had been working for the Kennedy campaign along with Gwen. Now, they were both at the State Department. He was Gwen's brother. She hugged Miss Bea to her and thought about vomiting. Gwen's only brother. Miss Bea whimpered and Alex released her grip a little. This was awful.

Hicks came up, stood so he was nearly touching her and loomed over her.

Miss Bea sensed a threat. She lifted her head, tensed her whole body and clenched her teeth, ready to bite if this big man tried to hurt Alex. And the big man stank. Her beagle nose was assaulted with the explosion of smells coming off him. "Whiskey," she registered. She knew whiskey from the campaign trail. But there was more. "Sweat, and something sharp and maybe sour under there too." Bea perked her ears and took a few more big sniffs. He smelled like her own puke mixed with that stuff Alex used to clean the floor that hurt her nose. Miss Bea didn't know that odd, putrid smell, but she'd remember it and remember this bad man. She let out a low growl.

Hicks ignored the dog and glared down at Alex.

"So, girlie, you know that guy?"

"No, no, no, no!" Alex said, not raising her bent head. "Disgusting, just disgusting." She decided now would be a good time for hysterics, and she burst out crying.

"I want to go home. I want to go home," she sobbed. Miss Bea knew they needed to get away from the bad man, and she did her part and started to howl. Hicks stayed by Alex's side, not moving or reacting to her shuddering sobs or to the howling dog.

He reached into an inside pocket, took out a packet of cigarettes, and took his time lighting one while he just stood there, looking at them. Then he turned and called out to Thomas.

"Get a car and take girlie here home and her little dog too," he said, chuckling as he walked away, smoke trailing after him.

Wizard of Oz joke? Alex thought, amazed. Hicks was a serious threat. Alex had smelled the whiskey too. But she had missed the sharp, sour smell.

Miss Bea had not.

4

TUESDAY, JANUARY 24, 1961

Alex fought her way across the gummy plastic covering the back seat of the police car that had brought her and Miss Bea home. When Thomas opened the rear door, she scrambled out, holding Bea in front of her. Thomas drove off as soon as she slammed the door. He clearly didn't want to linger, and Alex wanted him gone. Her neighborhood was just on the fringe of Georgetown, in the remnants of the much older blocks of still mixed race housing where even Negro cops were treated with suspicion, and white cops with downright hostility.

Alex put Miss Bea down and walked half a block to where she knew there was a phone booth. She hoped it had not been vandalized. Again. She needed to call Gwen right away and not give out any information to phones that might be bugged at the State Department. Gwen had said Stephen thought they were under constant surveillance, and Alex didn't know if that meant the phones too. There was nothing any of them would put past J. Edgar Hoover's FBI especially after the last few years.

Alex pushed hard on the bent, aluminum folding door and it gave enough that she could slide to into the filthy, plastic booth. It smelled like a public toilet even in this freezing weather. She sighed with relief when she saw that the call box looked to be intact. At least the handset was still connected and not pulled out. Alex dug out the change she needed, got a dial tone and called the direct number for Gwen's desk. She sighed with relief when she heard Gwen's soft voice. "Office of the Secretary for Political Affairs."

"Gwen. It's me. Go to an outside phone and call me back at this number." Alex read off the numbers on the scratched label below where it said Bell Systems.

"Hurry."

Alex hung up, not waiting for Gwen to reply.

Miss Bea, who had fit easily into the booth at Alex's feet, was busily sniffing the disgusting floor, its brown and yellow stains embedded into the cracked concrete.

Alex jumped when the phone rang.

"Alex, whatever is the matter?" Gwen breathed, her voice tense with anxiety.

"Gwen, I am so sorry to have to tell you this, but Stephen is dead. I think he was murdered."

"My Stephen?" Gwen gasped out the desperate question.

"Yes, Gwen. I'm so, so sorry."

"Oh, Jesus have mercy. Oh, no. Oh Jesus, no, no."

Alex could hear sobbing.

"Honey, listen. There's more but I don't want to say it over the phone. I think you should go back to the office. Make some excuse and come home as soon as you can. Okay?"

"Yeah, yeah, okay, but Alex, you have to tell me. Who did that to my brother?"

"I don't know, Gwen, but we'll need to be the ones to find out because I can tell you I don't think the police will lift a finger to find his killer. Just come. I'll tell you it all."

Alex heard a giant sigh and then a small, "Yes," and Gwen hung up.

She pulled the grimy phone booth door open and breathed the outside air with relief. Miss Bea was reluctant to go until Alex said the magic words.

"Let's go get your bone, Miss Bea. The butcher at the end of the next block should have some meaty bones."

"A deal's a deal," Miss Bea agreed.

Alex also bought a ham hock from the butcher to make a thick bean stew for Gwen. She would need the sustenance. And, Alex thought, we need some wine. So she stopped in the little grocery and got a bottle of a cheap red.

* * *

Miss Bea was established in the bathroom with her meaty bone. Alex had covered the cracked tile with some old newspapers to keep the floor clean.

When they'd moved in, she and Gwen had attacked the grimy grout in the old bathroom together until it was clean. She didn't want the mess from the bone to undo all their hard work. Alex had blanched a little when Bea had pounced on her bone with gusto, and she saw the blood on the newsprint. A front-page photo of President Kennedy's top-hatted head had been quickly obliterated with blood and fat from the bone. She had shuddered and shut the door to keep Miss Bea and the blood in there.

Alex looked at the clock. Unbelievably, it was barely noon. Well, that was a good time to call the Senator's office, she thought, as she bet Alistair took his lunch right at 12. At 12:05 she rang the direct line.

"Senator Madeleine Carpenter's office, may I help you?" The nasal, midwestern tone of Mrs. Anderson, the gray-haired envelope stuffer, greeted her.

"Oh, yes, oh, that's you, isn't it, Mrs. Anderson? Thank heavens. It's Miss Bell." Alex put just the slightest tremble into her voice.

"Oh, Miss Bell, we are so glad to hear from you. The police called and. . ." Then the phone was muffled for a second.

"Miss Bell, here's the Senator. She was just passing my desk on the way out. She wants to speak to you."

"Miss Bell, are you alright? The police called and said you had witnessed an accident." The Senator's choral tones flowed over the wire to Alex.

"Oh, ma'am I'm alright but I don't mind telling you, it was awful. I have never seen a dead man before and my, my, it just made me so sick at heart. Terrible. Terrible sight."

"A dead man, you say?" The Senator's voice sharpened. "My goodness. Do you know what happened?" Alex could practically hear the Senator saying, "and will it affect this office?"

"I have no idea what happened, ma'am. I imagine it was some kind of accident, truly, but I have no way of knowing. I wasn't there when it actually happened. I'm very sorry not to be at the office."

"Now, now," the Senator said, the tension gone from her voice. "Don't think about that. Just rest and you can get back to work tomorrow. And I'm sure Fluffy misses you."

"Oh, the darling. I miss Fluffy too," Alex lied, glancing at the bathroom door behind which Miss Bea was demolishing her bone to be sure she would not be overheard.

"Thank you, Madam Senator, for your consideration," Alex said. The Senator said something equally sappy, but Alex didn't listen to it as the key was turning in the lock. She said good-bye and hung up.

The door opened slowly, like the person on the other side of it was unsure whether they wanted to enter. Alex had time to cross the room and be ready to fold Gwen into a hug. But as her roommate came in, she just walked past Alex, her normally smooth, coffee-with-cream face blotchy and her reddened eyes unfocused. She was wearing a dark watch cap pulled down low over her ears and her old, cloth coat not even buttoned up correctly. She just walked rigidly to the faded couch like it gave her pain to move and sat down on the edge.

Alex quietly shut the door and, after looking at Gwen sitting unbendingly on the couch, her coat and hat still on, she went to the kitchen and put the kettle on to make hot tea for Gwen and herself. While the stove laboriously heated the water, she sat at their small table, thinking about what she knew about Gwen and Stephen.

She had met Gwendolyn Augusta Gray on the Kennedy campaign trail in Ohio. Gwen had graduated from Howard University two years before and had worked in a Washington law firm as a secretary. She'd quit to join the campaign. Gwen's job was to reach out to the Negro community, as Alex's was to get the white Protestants on board for Kennedy.

They had gotten to know each other riding in the old, green Chevy van that "Mike," the campaign coordinator for northern Ohio, drove to cart volunteers around to their designated campaign territories. All the rest of the volunteers were white when Alex joined them after Michigan, and as she stepped on to the rickety van for the first time, she saw they had managed to arrange themselves so there was no room for Gwen in the front seats. Gwen was sitting by herself in the back gazing at her gloved hands in her lap.

Despite Alex's efforts to project an image of "I'm a white, Protestant girl," she knew deep down she didn't want to totally become them with their mass of prejudices. She just wanted to look like them and be accepted like they were so she could get ahead in government. But in her heart she was too much her mother and, truly, her aunt's child. The sight of Gwen sitting alone in the back of the bus, her narrow shoulders squared under her old, cloth coat, was more than Alex could stand. "What is this, 1954?" she muttered to herself as she moved resolutely down the aisle.

She had grown up in and around 42nd street in lower Manhattan where not only the Hungarians, the Poles, and other Central Europeans, especially Jews, lived and worked in the garment industry, but also with more restrictive immigration laws, the Negroes and the Puerto Ricans that had moved in for the jobs. Every day the streets and the sweatshops were a mix of races, languages and religions, and that was fine with Alex. What wasn't fine with Alex was prejudice. As she had moved down the aisle of the swaying bus for the first time to take a seat next to Gwen, she had muttered again to herself, "once a socialist always a socialist, just don't tell anybody." She'd sat down and smiled at her new seatmate.

Gwen didn't say much at first, but soon, as they bounced along to-gether each day on the van that seemed to have no shock absorbers what-soever, they would tell each other the stories of the people they had talked to about Kennedy and the especially awful responses but turning the stories into jokes. "I'm never going to let the Pope run this country, you hear, young lady? You should be ashamed of yourself. Get off my porch." "What do you think that white boy is gonna do for us, you reckon? Nothin'. Purely nothin." But the very worst comments they kept to themselves. Gwen's step-father was a Baptist preacher, Alex had learned, and Gwen could work that into almost any conversation with a prospective Negro voter for Kennedy, con-veniently dropping the "step" part. "Well, ma Daddy, the Reverend Johnson, always says. . ." And then Gwen would make up some appropriate Daddy-saying for the occasion.

Alex had realized that Gwen was making up Daddy-sayings as she went along when Gwen had told her two Daddy-sayings on successive days that contradicted each other. Alex had teased Gwen about that, and she'd laughed and said, "I wouldn't dare tell them what the Reverend really says!"

In Akron, Gwen, as the only Negro volunteer, was asked to duck down on the bus as the coordinator didn't even want to be seen driving her through all the white neighborhoods. Since the seedy hotels where the campaign had reserved rooms for the volunteers were segregated, Gwen had had to come in the back door after everyone had gone to their rooms. Gwen and Alex had started rooming together then, and they kept it up as they were moved east to Cleveland and the racial balance shifted. Gwen tolerated Miss Bea, and Miss Bea returned the favor.

That's when Stephen Gray had joined them, and he had followed the volunteers in his own car from town to town until the election. He was working on voter registration. Late one night the three of them met up in a hotel that happened to be Negro-owned where Stephen was staying. They sat in the dimly lit lobby on battered chairs, drinking some horrible, sweet red wine Stephen had gotten and talking over their days. Then Stephen had noticed a scratched, upright piano against one wall. He'd just gone over to it, sat down and played some wonderful, intricate jazz. Alex couldn't help but notice his long, slender fingers as they rippled over the keys, the same fingers Gwen had. The shabby lobby had pulsated with sound. They hadn't noticed the older Negro man in the baggy, salesman's suit sitting in the corner until Stephen stopped playing, and the man had stood up and applauded. Then he'd gone down the hall and disappeared. Stephen had walked Gwen and Alex back to their hotel that was a few blocks away. Alex went in the front and then let Gwen in the back. Acid burned in Alex's stomach every time they had to do this, but Gwen gave no sign this was anything but what she expected. Alex had been turned away from one shop as a young girl, and the injustice still festered in her. What was it like for Gwen to live with that every day? Alex knew she shouldn't ask.

Kennedy didn't win Ohio, as it turned out. Stephen got Gwen a job as a secretary at the State Department where he was a staffer in the Office of the Legal Advisor. The campaign offered Alex the staff job in Senator Carpenter's office that she had been told would start the Monday after Inauguration Day. Alex went home to her aunt and mother's apartment in New York after election day and was planning to take a bus down to the capital to hunt for a place to stay. Gwen had called her there, saying her roommate had "just up and left" and did Alex want to share her apartment? Alex jumped at it when she heard the rent, packed her bags and after Thanksgiving got on the bus to Washington, Bea tucked in a carryall, and moved in with Gwen.

The shrill sound of the kettle startled Alex out of her reverie and she quickly shook some tea leaves into the pot, added the water and brought it over to the little coffee table in front of the couch. She went back for two chipped mugs and the sugar tin.

Gwen sighed deeply and pulled her fingers down her face, the same beautiful, long fingers her brother had, Alex thought sadly. Then she shivered as the pale, frozen fingers of Stephen's dead body flashed in front of her eyes. She shook her head to clear it.

Gwen pulled off her cap and let it fall on the couch as she sat back. She kept her coat on.

"Gwen, I'm so, so sorry," Alex said quietly.

Gwen gave a jerky nod, but kept her eyes down, looking at her lap, or more likely, looking inward.

Alex poured the tea into a mug, added three teaspoons of sugar, stirred it slowly and held it out to Gwen. For a minute, Gwen just stared at the mug, but then she took it and cupped her hands around it, the steam rising in the cool air of their underheated apartment.

Silently, Alex poured her own tea, took a little sip and waited.

Finally, Gwen put down the undrunk tea, looked up and said, "Tell me."

Alex didn't say anything for a moment, wondering how to begin.

Just tell it all, she thought, and she did, starting with her run, Miss Bea's digging in the snow, exposing the fingers, the cops seeing her from the street up the slope, and then she stumbled.

"Gwen, there was this detective, and then, well, they had uncovered more of the body from under the snow, and he grabbed my arm, pulled me over and forced me to look. I saw, I saw it was Stephen but I didn't say. I just screamed and pulled away."

"That's not all," Gwen said flatly, wrapping her arms around herself, bracing for another blow. "Is it?"

"No. No it's not." Alex took a sip of the hot tea, welcoming the pain in her throat as it scalded, a foretaste of the pain her words would cause Gwen.

"He'd been beaten, Gwen. I saw bruises on his face and his chest because, well, because he was wearing what looked like a torn, women's evening gown, and the detective, he'd been snickering before he dragged me toward the body. He called Stephen a name and said something about not needing to investigate 'this one' all that much."

"What name?" Gwen asked in that same flat voice, as if it were all the noise she dared make.

Alex hesitated.

"What name?" Gwen repeated, her voice toneless.

"Sphincter boy."

"So what'd you think about that?" Gwen asked, her eyes now on her cooling tea sitting on the little table.

Alex put her mug down beside it, leaned forward in her chair, putting her trembling hands on the scarred surface. She knew what that meant, but it didn't matter to her. What mattered was that Stephen had been killed, and filthy cops were laughing at him.

"Look, Gwen, I know that type of cop. They're all alike. They beat my aunt and my mother and other people on picket lines all the time. That detective, he smelled like whiskey, Gwen. At dawn. He reeked of it, like they do. They're bullies, they're lazy, they're drunks, and they're haters. Whoever killed Stephen knows what DC cops are like, what all these big city cops are like, and they dressed Stephen up like that after they killed him so the big, stupid cop wouldn't even investigate."

Alex stopped, out of breath from her tirade. She realized she had clenched her hands into fists, and she was drumming them on the table. She had remembered her gentle mother and her pugnacious aunt both with cut lips, moving slowly, trying to hide that they were in pain after they had come home from marching with their placards. But one time she had seen more when she'd accidentally opened the bathroom door and her mother was undressed. Her mother had been looking in the mirror. Alex had been 10 years old. Her mother had seen Alex in the mirror. "Now, now *kisbaba*, you go on now. I am fine. You go on," she had said through her cut lip. Her mother had called her "baby" in Hungarian, but Alex knew she'd not been a baby since that day. She had backed out of the bathroom, her small fists in her mouth, frightened by the blooms of purple and yellow and red all over her mother's stomach and breasts. So Alex knew the cops aimed to hit women strikers on their breasts and stomachs.

Alex carefully opened her fists and looked down at the table, struggling for control. She looked up at Gwen and was startled to see a little smile on her face.

"Girl, you are somethin', you know. You try hard to look like that little Shirley Temple kid, and you're really Sugar Ray inside."

Then Gwen's face sobered.

"Alex, you knew Stephen, but you didn't know him." Her thin shoulders shook a little, and she hugged herself as she whispered in a shaky voice, "Stephen my brother. My brother."

Then she sat up a little straighter, fighting for control.

"You know a little about my step-daddy now, preacher and all. He rode Stephen hard, tryin' to 'get the sissy' out of him. Now, the music was bad enough, especially after he'd been, oh, about fourteen first time and he'd just hopped on buses and gone to Harlem, to some of our real Daddy's musician friends, and he'd learned that jazz. Mama had told him not to play it 'cept when the Reverend was out of the house. But still and all, Stephen he just wasn't the Reverend's idea of a man. Mama is strong, so the Reverend didn't dare lift a hand against Stephen, but he rode him, he rode him hard. Lots of scripture, shouted over and over. Stephen he didn't so much as go to that college out in California. He plain escaped."

Gwen broke down completely, and her hands covered her face as she rolled backwards and forwards on the couch.

"Oh, Mama, oh Mama. I got to tell Mama."

Alex just went over to the couch and put an arm around Gwen who curled forward, wracked with pain.

Alex thought about what Gwen had told her. Didn't change anything. That pig of a detective wouldn't lift a finger to find out who had murdered Stephen.

Gwen sat up and shook off her coat.

"I gotta go wash my face and then call Mama. Tell her just I'm comin' for a visit. Can't break her heart over the phone. And my aunt and my sister. Gotta tell them too. Oh my, oh my."

She was up and off the couch before Alex thought to react.

"Oh, Gwen, wait. Miss Bea is in there and. . .."

Gwen gave a little scream as she opened the door to the bathroom, and Miss Bea stood up and displayed her bloody nose and jowls.

"Oh, Lord, oh my Lord, what has that dog gotten into now?"

Gwen tolerated Miss Bea, but mostly just referred to her as "that dog."

Alex hustled forward and explained as best she could while Gwen just stood there. This had been one shock too many.

"Sit down for a minute, Gwen, and I'll clean up."

"It was an excellent bone," Miss Bea contributed while Alex wiped her jowls, and then hastily crumpled up all the bloody newspapers and stuffed them into a paper bag for the incinerator. Then she picked up the nearly clean bone and placed it on top of the refrigerator.

Miss Bea eyed the chair pulled out from the little kitchen table, the small counter and the height of the refrigerator.

"Piece of cake," she thought and went to her basket in Alex's room for a much needed rest.

Alex followed and shut the bedroom door to give Gwen privacy for her phone call.

Even though Alex didn't really believe in God, Gwen did, so she whispered a little prayer.

"God be with them," she said. And then added sternly, just in case there really were a God and he was listening, "You'd better be."

5

WEDNESDAY, JANUARY 25, 1961

Alex unlocked the door, and she and Miss Bea entered the silent apartment.

Gwen had been up and ready to leave when she and Bea had gone out for their pre-dawn run. It took a solid six hours by bus to get to Petersburg, Virginia from Washington. That was a long time to be alone with the pain of loss Alex thought as she shut and double-locked the door.

She felt a tug on the leash and realized Bea was trying to lick her paws. She reached down, grabbed the struggling dog and carried her into the kitchen to wipe off the Vaseline jelly she always rubbed on Bea's paws to prevent cracking before they went out for winter runs. It had to be cleaned off immediately or Bea would lick it off along with any salt and dirt from the path and then vomit.

"Hold still!" Alex commanded as the dog tried to get a paw in her mouth.

"But it's so delicious," Miss Bea protested with a whine.

Alex had just let Miss Bea go when they were both startled by a loud knock on the door.

"Police! Open up in there!"

Miss Bee started barking furiously. "I know that man's voice. That's the awful man who took my find!"

Alex grabbed Miss Bea and whispered in her ear. "Be quiet, Bea. Very quiet."

Miss Bea heard the fear in Alex's voice and stopped her barking.

"Okay," Bea said to herself. "But I will bite if they try to hurt you."

34

"Who is it?" Alex asked in her sweetest voice.

"Police! Just open up!" a guff voice barked, sounding remarkably like Bea.

"I think you are who you say, but could you hold your badge up to the little peephole so I can be sure," Alex said, allowing her voice to go a little higher, conveying a young woman who is a little scared.

"Oh, for Christ's sake," muttered the deep voice, and a badge appeared and disappeared in front of the peephole.

It was the tall cop who'd come when she'd found Stephen's body. Richardson.

"Oh, Officer Richardson," Alex said warmly as she opened the door. "I didn't know it was you." Richardson's long face was either red with anger or with the exertion of climbing up the flights of stairs. Probably both, Alex thought. Then she saw Richardson was not alone. "And Officer Thomas," she said, smiling at him as well.

"Hello, Miss Bell," said Thomas, a smile lifting up his thin lips.

"Thomas, we're not here to smile and wave," Richardson snapped and then turned to Alex.

"Look, lady, you need to come downtown with us right now. Detective Hicks wants to ask you some questions."

"Now?" Alex asked, genuinely dismayed. "I can't do it now, I have to get to work. Could I come at five, let's say?"

Richardson cocked his head toward his partner and gave him a wide grin. "She really does think this is a social occasion, Thomas. Amazing." He turned back and glared at Alex.

"Just come on, girlie," he snapped, and he reached out to grab her by the arm. He pulled his hand back as Miss Bea bared her teeth.

"Get rid of the mutt or we'll take it to the pound and get it put down," he said angrily.

Alex believed he would have Miss Bea killed. She turned without speaking, carried her little dog to her bedroom and shut the door on an outraged Bea.

As she walked back to the door, she fought to control her anger. Be the sweet girl, she lectured herself, be the sweet girl. It was hard. Centuries of Hungarian Magyar warrior ancestors protested in her veins.

Well, one thing was for certain, Alex vowed as she crossed slowly back to the open door. She would not go see that awful Hicks without her armor of beautiful clothes.

She opened the door wider and gave a smile and a full arm welcome gesture worthy of Mrs. Cleaver on that TV show a couple of the young, white women on the Kennedy campaign would flip on in their hotel lobbies.

Alex had sat with them a couple of times and been amazed these college-educated women had actually chosen to voluntarily watch the insipid Cleavers. There had been no TV in the apartment where she'd grown up.

"Officers, just come in, come in will you? Let me fix you each a cup of coffee or tea. I will put on something suitable, get my bag, and be right with you," Alex said sweetly, stifling the Magyar urge to go find a sword to deal with this invasion.

"Look, I said. . ." Richardson began.

"Come on, Harold. What's the diff? I could use some coffee," said Thomas walking past him into the apartment and glancing around.

"Oh, what the hell, sure," Richardson said, and he followed. Alex knew why Thomas had agreed. He was clearly the smarter of the two, and he'd seen a chance to look around her place. Richardson was a little slower to catch on, but she could see him get the picture from his narrowed eyes as he scanned the room. Alex was okay with that. She knew they would get no information from the sparse sitting room.

Alex crossed to the tiny kitchen, filled the kettle and turned on the best burner. She also filled a bowl with Bea's dog food and another bowl with water and put them to the side. She got out two cups and turned to her unwanted guests.

"Coffee or tea?" she asked while the kettle started to steam.

"Coffee, thanks," Thomas said.

"Yeah," Richardson said.

She fixed them instant coffee, got some milk from the wheezing refrigerator and carried it all on a tray to the tiny table in front of the small couch.

"I'll be right back," she said, smiling at both of them, though it hurt to unclench her jaw.

Alex quickly picked up Bea's food and water and hurried into her bedroom. She whispered to the still outraged Miss Bea who was standing rigid right behind the door.

"Yes, I know Bea, but you don't know that they would have killed you in a heartbeat."

"I would bite them first," Miss Bee vowed. She ignored the bowls Alex put down for her, and she remained sentinel by the door, her sleek little body rigid with outrage.

Alex quickly pulled on stockings and grabbed a navy blue suit and a cream blouse, an ensemble like she had worn to work on Monday, but a little more severe in cut. She stepped into her pumps, ran a brush through her hair and then opted for a black cloche hat with a black ribbon band and a small brim. She looked in the mirror. Suitable for a possible funeral, she thought. Then she turned, opened her top bureau drawer and took out several beautifully pressed, linen handkerchiefs. Hicks would bully her, and she would want to cry into dainty linen.

She grabbed her coat, bag and gloves and stepped out of her room, shutting Bea in again. She saw Richardson was across the room going through their small bookshelf under the window. Since it only contained a used encyclopedia and a couple of novels from her Smith English class, she didn't even comment. Thomas was gazing blankly at a women's magazine open on the little coffee table, and he was sipping his coffee.

Alex took that moment of their distraction to cross to their telephone and quickly dial the Senator's office.

"Mrs. Anderson?" she said, relieved, when she heard the motherly voice. "Yes, I am sorry to say I will be delayed today. Yes, that accident I came upon. I need to follow up." She listened for a second while Richardson turned and looked outraged. "Oh, the Senator is not in today? Well, I will be there as soon as I can."

At the word "Senator," Richardson's face had turned from outraged to stony. Good, Alex thought. He wonders if I have any power here in Washington.

"Shall we go?" she asked brightly.

Richardson only grunted, Thomas flipped the fashion magazine closed, and they all left.

* * *

"So, Miss Bell, do you know the penalty for lying to the police in an investigation?" Detective Hicks asked with a nasty smile, leaning back in his oversize desk chair. His large, round, ruddy face was glistening with sweat, though he'd taken off his jacket and rolled up his sleeves exposing hairy, meaty forearms. His huge stomach loomed large, and it was accentuated by an extra-long tie. Hicks probably imagined that the tie distracted from the beach ball sized bulge of his stomach. Instead, it looked like an arrow pointing out his huge belly. Both the tie and his wrinkled, white shirt had a glistening brown stain across them. Hicks had spilled some of his breakfast there, Alex mused.

She pulled her thoughts back to this dangerous moment, but continued to sit quietly, her gloved hands in her lap, looking at him.

"I have not lied to you, Detective Hicks," she finally said.

"Oh yeah, girlie? That faggot N***** you found by the river is the brother of your so-called roommate!" Hicks pounded a huge fist on the desk that separated them.

"I saw a disgusting corpse, Detective. Not a man," Alex replied with a little sob. "Really, it was horrifying," she sniffed and brought one of her linen handkerchiefs into play, dabbing at her eyes.

"That N***** wasn't a man, now sweetheart, was he?" Hicks jeered.

Alex kept silent with her head bent, still applying her handkerchief a little. The sound of typewriters clacking away outside Hicks's closed door seemed to be muffled, and the smell of carbolic covering up the sweat and vomit odors of the police station bullpen seemed to decrease as she focused her mind on taking back control from this typical bully.

"So the three of you do it together, do you?" Hicks went on making kissing noises.

"Really!" Alex said sharply, and she looked up. "That is very offensive and very untrue," she protested. "I have seen Stephen Gray exactly once, Detective, on the campaign trail for now President Kennedy. Gwen, his sister, is my friend, and she introduced us. That's it."

"Friend, huh?" Hicks guffawed, and he pulled a cigarette out of a box on his desk and lit it while he watched her.

"Yes, Detective," she said firmly, now meeting his eyes. "Gwen is my friend, and now we split the rent on an apartment. And you have no evidence of anything else because there isn't anything else," Alex said tersely. She was just barely holding on to her temper now.

"You givin' me lip, gal?" Hicks asked with a deep laugh that moved his belly in and out like a large bellows. Then he abruptly stopped laughing and raised the flat of the large, calloused hand not holding the cigarette, moving it slowly toward Alex across the desk. She kept an eye on it like she would keep an eye on a poisonous snake.

"You know, in New York, where I'm from," Hicks said through florid lips that he had wet with his tongue, "that pretty little lip of yours would already be bleedin' on that pretty, white blouse of yours while you cried for real."

Then he slapped that hand on the desk in front of her. Alex had been expecting it, and she didn't flinch. Hicks narrowed his eyes at her while he tapped his forefinger in front of her on the desk.

"Here where the government is all fags and lesbos you think we gotta play nice. Don't count on it."

"May I ask you a question?" Alex said, hoping to distract this raging bull a little.

Hicks pulled his hand back, took a big drag on his cigarette and leaned back again in his chair. His piggy eyes squinted at her through the smoke and then he shrugged.

"Sure, whatever. Ask."

"How was it determined that the frozen corpse was Mr. Gray? Was he carrying identification?"

"He was carrying nothin', girlie, not even all his parts if you get my drift." Hicks rocked forward and ground out his cigarette in an overflowing ashtray, watching Alex. She concentrated now on the sounds of the type-writers and the horrible smells and said nothing.

"So, how'd we know? Well, the pinkos and fags over at the State Department missed your Mr. Gray. Didn't show up where he was supposed to for a couple of days. Though how they'd miss just one of their N***** batty boys when they got so many, who the hell knows? Anyway, they missed one, called us, we had one, and it added up."

Alex looked down at her hands on her lap, holding the crumpled linen square. She felt real tears well up in her eyes. Somehow, Hicks's horrible words made Stephen's unspeakable death seem more real.

She could hear Hicks light another cigarette, but he said nothing for a full minute.

"Get the hell out of here, girlie," he barked. "I know where you live, and I can get you if I want to."

Alex stood up. Her legs felt like they were filled with water, but she clenched her muscles and forced herself to remain upright.

"Good-bye, Detective," Alex said in her best Smith College voice, and she looked down at him like he had just crashed a late afternoon sherry reception in his underwear.

Hicks grunted. He'd wanted her fear, and he hadn't gotten it.

Alex turned and left, glad her legs would carry her.

* * *

The cold hit Alex's face like the slap Hicks had threatened her with. She walked along the sidewalk lost in thought, heedless of the icy patches that still clung to the concrete.

New York, she thought. Her aunt and mother, and their labor friends, constantly complained about the corrupt New York cops. There must be dirt on Hicks, she realized.

The light at the corner changed, and Alex crossed Constitution and its many lanes paying little attention to the jostling crowd around her. The cars belching white smoke out of their tailpipes as they reluctantly waited for the pedestrians to pass were just a blur of dirty steel and shiny bumpers turned black by the slush.

I need to call my family, or better still, go see them, she thought. Getting the telephone installed in their tiny apartment had been a struggle. Her aunt and mother had only agreed when Alex went to college, and she'd argued she "needed to hear their voices" while she was gone. She really thought they needed to hear her.

Alex stepped carefully over a pile of dirty snow and reached the sidewalk. That Hicks is dangerous, I knew it when I saw him, and Gwen is probably even more at risk than I am, Alex reflected as the Senate office building came into view down the block. She knew that kind of cop would throw dirt and beat and bully his way to some kind of false arrest, and he'd target the Negroes first. They always did.

Alex finally reached the Senator's office at noon. It was locked, but she knocked, and Alistair opened the door.

When he saw her, his long, thin face broke into a smirk, but he said nothing to her. He just returned to his high perch desk and sat up tall like he'd just won a "Best in Class" ribbon at a dog show. He might even be perking his ears, Alex thought as she went to the closet.

She wearily hung up her long coat and placed her hat on the shelf above. She went to the inbox tray by the door and took the letters addressed to the Senator to her desk. She slit the first one open and started to read.

"Dear Senator Carpenter: Greetings from Eureka Springs! How is dear Fluffy? We miss him so much now that he is living in style in the capital of our nation. "

Alex sighed and picked up the fountain pen.

6

THURSDAY, JANUARY 26, 1961

A half hour run was pitiful, Alex thought as she dragged herself up the stairs.

"You call that a run?" Miss Bea thought, but she was just too stubborn to admit to herself how tired she was. She hadn't slept the whole, previous day worrying about Alex and that tall man with the mean eyes who'd taken her find on the path and then grabbed for Alex yesterday. Just remembering that made Miss Bea's teeth snap. She didn't even protest when Alex wiped her paws. She just lay down by her food bowl and closed her eyes.

Alex treated herself to a bath, using more hot water than they could afford. Dry and warm, she went to her closet and contemplated her choices. Her beautiful clothes announced the new person she had become even before she spoke, and she needed that support after the horrors of the last days.

After careful consideration, she chose a black, wool and silk blend sheath dress she had designed herself. The pencil skirt and long, fitted sleeves emphasized her long, slender frame. She was getting thinner by the day from not eating, but her stomach would not cooperate. She hoped it still fit, but she shook out the dress with pride. The skirt was narrow, but it was narrow by necessity. She had wanted a more flowing skirt, but the end piece of the fabric bolt she had fallen in love with could not accommodate it. So she had pared the dress design down as much as she dared. She adored the line of it and as she pulled up the side zipper and smoothed it over her hips, she was very relieved it still fit. The beautiful fabric seemed to mold itself to her frame without clinging. That was quality.

As a youngster, Alex had been dragged to many basements around 42nd Street by her Aunt Kitti. That was where partial bolts of high quality fabric could be found, stacked row upon row.

"Fabric is everything," her aunt would mutter over and over in Hungarian as her tiny, bent figure moved among the narrow aisles where the exquisite fabric roll ends were piled. Kitti would take her time, first rubbing the fabric between her thumb and middle finger. If it seemed to have promise, she would caress the cloth and then let it slide through her hand, assessing the potential drape. Only the natural fabrics like wool and silk would pass muster. Her aunt's muttered comments on the new polyester blends that were becoming more popular were also said in Hungarian, and Alex knew the swear words well.

At first, Alex had found these trips boring, but gradually she learned how to spot high quality fabric. In recent years she would go to the basements on her own. This wool and silk blend had been a real find. It had flowed through Alex's fingers when she had first seen it, and she had known, when she had finished a dress from it, that it would be a second skin. It would be the kind of protection of her new identity she sought from wearing beautiful clothes. She gave the dress a stroke and laid it carefully on the bed.

Today, however, she had chosen this stark, black dress as mourning for Stephen and for Gwen and her family. And, she thought gravely, for the grief still to come.

She adjusted the dress carefully around the collar and looked in her full-length bedroom mirror. It really should have a scarf at the neck, she reflected as she looked at her pale face and light hair floating above the dark silhouette. But no. There should be no softening, she vowed, and to emphasize her stark mood she pulled her long hair into a French twist and secured it with a black barrette. She nodded at her image, gathered up her outdoor things, gave the snoozing Miss Bea a pat and locked the apartment door behind her.

Miss Bea looked up drowsily as she heard the door close.

* * *

Where is everybody? Alex wondered as she entered what seemed to be an empty suite. The door had been unlocked, but Alistair's desk perch was empty, Mrs. Anderson was not at her desk, and the Senator's door was closed. The lights in that inner office did not seem to be on.

The Senator was probably at some political breakfast, Alex mused. She looked at the clock on the wall. Mrs. Anderson wasn't actually late yet. The odd absence, really, was Alistair. Yes, it was a little early, but Alistair had already crowed to her several times that "I am always early. Always have been. You have to be if you want to succeed." His long nose came in handy for the exaggerated New England accent he put on, she thought as he had inhaled and then practically wheezed the word "been" until it became a low, doggy snort. His canine image was now fixed in Alex's mind.

Alex hung up her coat again in the office closet and sat down, but before she'd even put her purse in her desk drawer, the inner office door was jerked open, and the Senator spoke to her from the doorway.

"Oh, good, very good, Miss Bell. So glad you're in early. Please come in, will you, right away?"

"Certainly, Madam Senator," Alex said quickly. She pulled a pad and pencil from her center drawer and hurried into the curiously dark inner office.

The Senator was all in orange today, Alex registered with a mild shock as her boss moved around her desk to take a seat. Her whole ensemble was a deep, almost pumpkin orange down to the orange-dyed pumps on her feet. The ever-present pearls had taken on a slightly orange hue from the jacket. No wonder the Senator hadn't needed to turn on a light. That astonishing shade seemed to actually glow.

Alex wanted Senator Carpenter, the only woman senator, to succeed in Washington so more women could follow. How could the Senator succeed if she was dressed like a pumpkin? Alex asked herself gravely. And it's not only the color, it's the poor fit, she thought as she watched the Senator move around her desk to take her seat. This was not good. Washington was changing. Jacqueline Kennedy was raising the level of style dramatically, and this outfit said anything but style.

Alex continued to reflect on how she might help the Senator realize that she needed to improve her style and thus her image in the Kennedy era. But she gave no hint of her thoughts as she stood politely before a chair. When the Senator reached the other side of her desk, she seated herself and gave Alex a very appraising look from her head to her feet.

"Miss Bell, that is a lovely dress, and you look most suitable," the Senator said approvingly. "And please do sit down."

"Thank you, Madam Senator," Alex replied, lowering gracefully onto a straight-backed chair and smoothing her already smooth skirt. Plant just a little seed, she thought.

"I do admire the style of our new First Lady, don't you, Madam Senator?"

"Why, yes," said Senator Carpenter slowly.

One did not get to be a Senator by missing cues, Alex reflected.

"Anyway," the Senator said briskly, clearly moving on, "I am going to need you to take on an important task this morning. Mr. Carrington is ill today, and Mrs. Anderson had already let me know she would be late this morning. I will need you to attend a Senate committee meeting for me and take very careful notes. I have to meet some very important constituents or I would go myself."

The Senator's voice was very matter-of-fact until she reached the words "important constituents." Then the lyrical lilt came back. Alex thought she knew where the Senate committee ranked in the Senator's view. But then the next words surprised her.

"Now this committee meeting is of great consequence, Miss Bell, and I will want to write home to my constituents about it. Very, very great consequence." She nodded her helmet of hair, and then she pulled a file folder to her and opened it.

"Now, I am sending you to just listen, and, as I said, take careful notes." The Senator squinted down at the file and pulled some reading glasses on a beaded chain that had been concealed in the front of the very ill-fitting, orange jacket. Alex winced a little as the fabric of the jacket sagged down even more, unpropped by the hidden spectacles.

I need to focus on the job here, Alex cautioned herself as the Senator was now tapping the file with a well-manicured fingernail.

"This is a meeting of the Committee on Foreign Relations. It is my most important committee assignment. It will be about our policy toward that dreadful Communist, Castro and what he has done to our American business interests in Cuba. And, of course, what we as the United States should do even more than we have."

The Senator looked up and this was no kindly-looking, grandmotherly woman in an ugly suit. This was a shrewd politician glaring at her.

"You know, of course, what I am talking about?" the Senator suddenly asked, her faded blue eyes narrowing and the wrinkles around her eyes deepening behind her glasses.

Of course I do, Alex thought. Alex's mother and aunt, and their friends, had thrown an all-night party when Castro's victory over the hated Cuban dictator, Batista, had made the news. Alex had been glad too. One less dictator in the world was always a good idea, but she privately had thought the fledgling Cuban revolution had no chance against the might of the United States looming over the tiny island.

I really cannot say that, Alex reflected, and she took a moment to pick the words the Senator would expect to hear from her loyal American staff person.

"Fidel Castro, correct?" A nod from the Senator. "He's that radical who overthrew the Cuban government and just stole all those American businesses and their property, right?"

"Absolutely correct. We can't have that sort of thing going on."

"No, certainly not," Alex said evenly.

"Now, just go to the committee meeting, take a seat along the wall and listen out for anything that might make prices go up for my constituents. President Eisenhower immediately slapped an embargo on Cuban goods, and our own President Kennedy has continued it. You'll hear that at the meeting I'm sure. That is, of course, absolutely right, but I have a commitment to keeping prices down for my constituents."

She paused and fingered her pearls.

"For the people of my state, it's prices first, but they're also not going to want Communists that close to our good ole U. S. of A. Why those Communists could just come over in little boats to our shores and just hop right on to the beach in Florida. We absolutely cannot have that."

The "that" was very emphatic, and Alex feared for the pearls as the Senator gave them a tug. But then she let go and picked up the file and waved it at Alex who stood and went over to the desk to take it.

The Senator didn't hand it to her, however. She waved the file up and down slightly as she continued.

"Take really good notes and then write them up as a draft of a letter to the people at home. We'll see how you do."

"Thank you, Madam Senator," Alex said sincerely. This was a big step up from writing notes from Fluffy. Of course, she thought as she watched the file move up and down and then stop, some fiction writing will still be necessary.

"I'll do the very best job I can," she said, and the Senator released the file to her.

* * *

The committee meeting was set for 11 a.m. in the new Senate Office Building across the street from the Russell Senate Office Building where the Senator had her office. This gave Alex a lot of time to digest what was in the file the Senator had handed her. It wasn't much, and Alex was surprised to find there were inaccuracies. Who put this file together? she wondered. Had it been Alistair, and if so where did he get his information, and worse, were the mistakes deliberate?

Alex certainly knew more than whomever compiled this file. She kept it in front of her but thought about Castro. She had seen him and heard him speak, first in his rollicking visit to New York City in 1959 when schoolchildren donned fake beards and were photographed with the romantic revolutionary. Alex smiled at the memory of the newspaper photos. And then, when Castro came to speak at the United Nations in 1960, she had come home for the weekend from the Ohio campaign trail at her aunt's insistence. Her aunt had said she and her mother wanted Alex to go with them to stand with signs outside Castro's hotel in support of the revolution. She'd reluctantly agreed, primarily to be on hand in case she had to bail them out of jail.

New York that weekend had been one long celebration for the socialists. Her family and their union and party friends loved Castro for thumbing his nose at the U.S. government. It started off on the first day when he stomped out of the uptown hotel where he had been scheduled to stay, claiming he was being harassed, and he and his entourage had left for the Negro-owned Hotel Theresa in Harlem.

So Alex and her family had taken the subway to Harlem with a lot of their labor friends and there had been many more in the streets outside the hotel. Her aunt had dragged her quieter mother right up to the front by the entrance. Alex had stood next door to the hotel in the shadows of a bar and grill, wearing dark glasses and a hat. She had been fearful of being photographed, and she had seen she had been right to worry. There had been dozens of cameras and not all, she'd suspected, belonged to reporters. Some of the crowd had even climbed on to the roofs of cars parked in the street. She'd glimpsed Malcolm X, the activist, as he'd arrived, and then, later that day, the poet Langston Hughes. Then the crowd swelled, and a lot of people were roughly shoved back by the New York police when Nikita Khrushchev arrived. When the Soviet Premier and Castro started to walk down the main street of Harlem together, Alex had left.

She waited for hours, but finally her mother and aunt came home. Luckily they had not been arrested, though in her aunt's case she thought it was probably not for lack of trying. Together they had listened on the radio to Castro's nearly five-hour speech at the U.N. He had ranted for a long time about the colonization of the countries of the Caribbean and Latin America by the U.S., and then he went on to describe the horrors of the poverty of the people of Cuba that he had found when he had taken over. The U.S., he had claimed, had taken "one thousand million dollars" out of the Cuban economy in ten years to enrich the wealthiest nation in the world. The American businesses in Cuba had pushed the people to the brink of starvation. None of that was in the thin file she had in front of her. In fact, the file made the claim that there had been "well-paying jobs" in Cuba before Castro overthrew Batista and the local economy had been "good." Not according to the Cubans she had known in New York, Alex thought, and she began to wonder if she should call these errors to the Senator's attention. But how would she explain how she knew? Better to wait until after the committee meeting.

Alex was jerked out of her reverie when Mrs. Anderson came in looking windblown and tired. Alex greeted her and then checked the clock. Ten-thirty! Time to leave. Even though the new Senate Office Building was right across the street from where Senator Carpenter's office was located, Alex knew nothing of its interior, and she feared she would get lost. She grabbed her hat and coat, put the pad and pencil in her handbag, and hurried out.

Once outside, Alex squinted in the glare thrown off the dazzlingly white, marble façade of the huge, new structure. She tried to avoid the patches of snow that remained on the center median of the wide expanse of Constitution while she dashed across the street.

Suddenly, the enormous building was cast into shade as she hustled around the corner, and she narrowed her eyes, looking for the entrance. The entrances were surprisingly small, and, she knew from having taken a tour when she first moved to Washington, opened into small lobbies. But the whole effect of this giant, flagrantly white building was intimidation, and Alex realized she was very intimidated.

Am I a fool for thinking I can change the machinery of this giant government? she wondered as she hurried up the entrance stairs. No wonder my family marches in the street. That actually feels like doing something. Yet Castro has made a huge change, she reflected as she used her shoulder to move the heavy, revolving door. But not without violence, she sighed to herself.

She pushed harder and practically fell into the lobby.

Alex showed her Congressional I.D. to the portly guard, the buttons of whose uniform jacket looked like they would pop off any second from the strain of covering his stomach. She noticed what looked like a coffee stain on the jacket, and she suppressed a shudder, remembering Hicks's stained shirt and tie pulled over his big stomach. The guard frowned at Alex, and he actually took her I.D. over closer to a big window to examine it. Really? she thought. Then he lumbered to a cardboard box on a shelf near the door and handed her a tag that said "Staff." It had a lanyard to wear around her neck. She asked for the location of the committee meeting, and the guard sighed deeply. He took a clipboard off the same shelf, and she realized his florid lips were actually moving as he read it slowly. I will be late, Alex thought anxiously, but she didn't fidget. She just stood there counting backwards in her mind from 100, the technique she used to calm herself.

Finally, the guard read out the committee meeting room. 209. Alex walked quickly to the elevators. She had wanted to ask directions to the women's cloakroom, but she didn't think she could stand asking the guard anything else. She hung the tag around her neck as the elevator ascended.

Alex consulted her watch as she stepped off the elevator that had moved a lot faster than the one in the Senator's office building. She had time to look for a cloakroom. She hunted up one corridor and then another, vainly looking for anything that would show her a women's cloakroom where she could fix her hair and leave her coat and hat. Nothing.

"Lost, honey?" a pleasant woman's voice asked from behind her.

"Just looking for the women's cloakroom," Alex said as she turned and faced an older Negro woman in a gray dress who was standing behind a rolling cart.

The woman chuckled, the lines in her face radiating out like a child's drawing of a sun.

"Top floor, ah course. Only one. Down at the end, left hall. Little, bitty, bitty sign. Good luck, child," she said still rumbling a little laugh as she moved down the side hall, flicking a cloth at the bottom of the tall window ledges.

Okay, maybe I still have time, Alex thought. She turned back to the elevators and pressed the button for the top floor. The elevator whisked her up, and she practically skidded down the left hallway. Little, bitty, bitty sign is right, Alex thought, as she passed the door and then had to backtrack. She quickly hung her coat on a hook on the wall of the small room and put her hat above on a shelf. She took a moment to smooth her French twist and freshen her pale lipstick and then hustled out.

She went back to the elevators and was swiftly taken back to the second floor. She slipped in the door of 209 just as a guard was about to shut it. The space was cavernous with a high, ornate plaster ceiling and gleaming wood paneling extending to meet it. A long table with padded leather chairs dominated the center. There were wooden chairs with leather seats ranged all along the walls, and she saw a couple of vacant ones across the room. The meeting had not yet started, thank heavens. She walked in as dignified a fashion as she could across the echoing room and practically collapsed into a vacant chair. She started to count backward from 100 to still her racing heart until a voice practically in her ear nearly stopped her heart.

7

THURSDAY, JANUARY 26, 1961

Alex looked up in alarm. The deep voice had spoken practically in her ear. She saw a dark-haired man had taken the chair next to her while she had been trying to slow her racing heart.

"I beg your pardon?" Alex asked in her best Smith College put-down voice. That was certainly coming in handy here in Washington.

"Oh, perfect. Just perfect," the dark-haired man chuckled. "What I said was 'Audrey Hepburn, I presume?'" and he turned his broad shoulders in the chair that was a little too narrow for him. "You look just like Hepburn in that movie where she plays a run-away princess. Except," and he studied her in a way that felt most uncomfortable, "you have Grace Kelly hair. Of course, she's an actual princess."

He put out his large hand. "Frank Scott, State Department, your Highness."

Alex thought about just ignoring this brash man with his too-wide shoulders that were pushing into her chair, and then "State Department" registered like an electric shock. What if this person had known Stephen, perhaps had even worked with him? Better reply, she decided, but keep the banter going.

"I have not given you permission to address me," Alex said haughtily and made no move to shake his hand.

"That's true," Mr. Scott of the State Department said with a wide smile, smoothly withdrawing his hand but remaining turned toward her.

Alex appraised him, ticking off his key clothing features almost unconsciously. Clearly a bespoke suit, probably cashmere with a single-breasted, sack jacket with narrow notch lapels, two buttons, white, crisply pressed Oxford shirt, French cuffs, what might be gold cufflinks, and a narrow silk tie. The shoulders would argue for custom-made, she considered, but what about the quality? The State Department didn't pay that well, she knew from Gwen, so perhaps Mr. Scott had family money.

He was wearing horn-rimmed glasses and looked a little like an extremely well-dressed professor, except for those shoulders. Alex continued to look at him without speaking, and he sat still under her scrutiny, a faint smile still playing around his full lips. His dark hair was a little too long, not only on the top like the President Kennedy haircut that was sweeping the city, but also on the sides. His longer hair did not completely hide a faint, jagged scar that ran along the left side of his forehead

"Alexandra Bell, assistant to Senator Carpenter," she said finally, giving him and his spectacular suit a nice smile and holding out her own hand.

"Okay," said Scott, shaking her hand, "but I prefer 'your Highness.'"

"Often, so do I," Alex said dryly as a gavel signaled the start of the committee meeting, and she heard a muffled laugh beside her.

Then they both stilled as a firm voice with a modulated southern accent called the committee to order.

Alex knew that voice belonged to Senator William Fulbright, a Democrat from Arkansas. Fulbright had stood up to the terrible Senator McCarthy in the worst years of the so-called "Red Scare," McCarthy's dreadful crusade against suspected Communists or their supporters. Or against innocent people, wrongly accused.

Her family had approved of Senator Fulbright, though they had wanted much more condemnation of that "change to italics," or "horrible man" as her mother would say softly in Hungarian when McCarthy was ranting on the radio. And it was true. McCarthy had been a horrible man, Alex thought.

The Senator was seated at the far end of the long, oval table around which eight other Senators were ranged. His head was bent as he apparently consulted some notes in front of him, and the high ceiling lights illuminated his forehead, made broader by a receding hairline. Alex knew there was a total of fifteen members of the committee, so that was good. Senator Carpenter would not be the only one who had missed this meeting. The rest must have sent staffers as well.

Alex hurriedly got out her pad and pencil and started taking notes in rapid short-hand. She had taken a class in short-hand when she had started high school but had quickly developed her own system. It was indecipherable to anyone else. That had been useful when someone had asked to "copy her notes" at school. So sorry, Alex had demurred.

A lot of grandstanding, Alex thought, as her pencil flew over her pad. The Senator from Florida, Spencer Harris, was particularly vocal about "securing our shores," and he said it over and over. Others harped on how if this "rag-tag band of cutthroats," another prepared phrase Alex thought as she wrote it down, "were not taken out immediately, all of Latin America could be lost to the damn Commies."

"Yes, damn yes," said another.

Raised voices giving clearly prepared statements went on for a while.

"Now, fellow Senators," Fulbright said firmly, cutting into the posturing.

"Here comes the real reason for this meeting," Frank Scott of the State Department whispered in Alex's ear.

"We do need to be concerned about what is happening in Cuba," Fulbright intoned in a pleasant, well-modulated tone after most around the table had made their statements, statements that would later be leaked to the press. "That is true, but any extreme action will only make a hero, or even a martyr of Mr. Castro. I believe we should widen our focus and recommend increased aid to certain Latin American countries. At the same time, we should deny aid to those who assist the Cuban regime. And, we must keep the embargo of Cuban goods, especially sugar, in place. "

"Well, Ah think that's a bit mild, Mr. Chairman, since prices on sugar have jumped and look to go high as a kite," drawled the Senator from Louisiana.

Alex gripped her pencil more tightly, prepared to catch every word of the exchange on what was Senator Carpenter's highest concern.

"Now, now, Senator Longstreet, U.S. sugar production is going up even as we sit here. You know that better than most," Fulbright replied evenly. The meeting settled down after that, and the foreign aid issues came into focus.

Fulbright brought it to a close soon after that, having gotten what he wanted from his committee. No rash actions on blockades, or worse, invasions would be supported. And, Alex thought as she reached for her purse to put away her pad, Fulbright looked at the total picture.

"Will you join me for lunch?" State Department Scott asked as he stood, and Alex realized how tall he was.

She was torn. Her letter for Senator Carpenter's constituents was already half-written in her mind, but she wanted talk to Scott and see if he had known Stephen.

"I must get back to the office and write this up for the Senator," she said truthfully, "but I could meet you for coffee at 5," she said.

"A drink perhaps?" Scott asked and suggested a place nearby.

"Coffee," Alex said firmly. "I'll meet you there."

Scott chuckled as he walked out beside her.

By the time Alex had crossed the street, she had most of the letter written in her mind.

"Dear Friends: I am so pleased to tell you that our patriotic American growers are standing up to the challenge of the embargo of Cuban sugar. Even as I write this, American sugar production is increasingly rapidly and that, I am assured, will soon stabilize prices. In addition. . ."

* * *

"Miss Bell, this letter is excellent, truly excellent," Senator Carpenter said warmly as soon as Alex had entered her office at her summons.

"Oh, Madam Senator, I'm so glad you like it," Alex said, using the same warm tone and seating herself at the Senator's gesture. She clasped her hands in her lap. "I found it a privilege to hear all the Senators and their views, Senator Fulbright in particular."

"Well, you have captured exactly what I want for the people of my state to hear," she said, tapping a piece of paper in front of her that looked like Alex's typed draft. "Of course they are worried about prices and what that rebel Castro could get up to, but you have written a letter that reassures them while also sharing the wisdom of our leadership. So, so good, really." Tap, tap, tap.

Was this the time to mention the errors in the file on Castro? Alex wondered. No, she thought. I haven't even been here a week. There's time. It's not like Castro and Cuba are going anywhere.

"So," the Senator continued, giving Alex a smile that was a little warmer than her practiced political smile. "I have made no changes, and I will give it to Mrs. Anderson to get out right away."

She paused, fingering her pearls and looking across her desk at Alex with that searchlight stare. The ridiculous pumpkin suit faded into the background as the Washington power player peeked out above the old-fashioned reading glasses.

Alex made an effort to continue to sit quietly. She was glad of her mid-calf length skirt as her legs were twitching a little from tension.

"I will give you more such responsibilities, Miss Bell, as you really are so intelligent and such a lady at the same time." She paused and Alex thought she was going to say more, but then she just said, "You may go."

"Thank you, Madam Senator, I will try to do the very best I can," Alex said quietly and walked out.

Apparently "lady" and "intelligent" were often considered antonyms here in Washington, she thought wryly as she walked over to her desk and sat down. Well, everywhere, really, she supposed, and she pulled a stack of mail toward her. Then she paused. There had been no more mention of her writing as Fluffy, and, in fact, no actual Fluffy in the office for several days that Alex could see. I'll drop that idea of actually writing as Fluffy, she decided, unless the Senator instructs me to do it. We intelligent staffers don't do that. Maybe Alistair could be given that responsibility when he comes back, she laughed to herself, and she slit the first envelope briskly.

* * *

Miss Bea will not be happy, Alex thought as she walked down Constitution a little before 5 p.m. toward the new restaurant and bar, "the Monocle," that Scott had suggested after walking her out of the meeting room.

Miss Bea had a turkey roasting pan with sand in the bottom as her dog bathroom for in between walks, but she didn't like it. She was clearly offended when it became necessary. Alex didn't like cleaning the pan either, but did it frequently because otherwise Gwen would wrinkle her nose and say, "What is that awful smell?"

From what Alex had heard, "What is that awful smell?" also described the state of the old bars and eating establishments, sometimes called Ptomaine Row, Mrs. Anderson had told her, that dotted the streets around the congressional office buildings. But maybe those gloomy Eisenhower years were passing, Alex speculated, as she came up to the quaint, two-story building painted a deep, yellowing cream, its forest green shutters and awning a pleasing color contrast. "The Monocle" was printed in curling script on the awning. Charming, Alex thought, and gave Frank Scott of the State Department points for selecting it. Not the smoke-filled, sleazy dive Alex had imagined.

Alex entered, and she was immediately greeted by a maître d' in a frock coat who asked if she were the "guest of Mr. Scott." Alex nodded, somewhat bemused. Not just a cup of coffee, she thought. The arm of the maître d's frock coat stretched out in the direction of what must be the women's lounge. Brushed cotton, Alex thought automatically, as the sleeve with the pointing hand passed by her. She left her things in the lounge and returned to the paneled foyer.

"Miss Bell," a deep voice greeted her as she paused, looking around.

"Hello, Mr. Scott," Alex said evenly. He was standing in a broad arch beyond which Alex could see a wood-paneled bar area with tables.

Scott walked over, took her arm and led her across the deep, burgundy pile carpeting to a table against the far wall. The room was crowded with almost exactly the same people who had been at the earlier committee meeting. As they crossed the room, Alex registered that she was the only woman there.

Scott pulled out a chair for her, and a waiter immediately appeared.

"Miss Bell, what will you take?" Scott asked in his bass voice, and now she could hear a the faintest trace of what she thought might be an accent. British? No, Scottish perhaps.

"Coffee," Alex said gravely.

"Scotch neat," he said to the waiter. Then he simply sat there, looking at her for a long time. She registered he wasn't wearing his glasses, but she said nothing. This was his party, she thought.

The drinks came, and he raised his glass to her. She lifted her coffee cup with the same gesture.

"I did not think you would come," he said after he had taken a long sip, his eyes never leaving her.

"Why not?" she asked. "I said I would."

"Do you always keep your word?" he countered with a faint smile.

"When I can," she replied and took another small sip of coffee.

That did elicit a rumbling chuckle.

"Well played, your Highness," he said and took another substantial sip of scotch.

"So, tell me about yourself," he said went on, leaning over the small table, both arms resting on either side of his drink. His arms were so long they almost reached her side of the table. She resisted the urge to pull back, looked him squarely in the face and then registered his light green eyes.

"You're from Scotland, perhaps?" she countered. "Light green eyes and just a hint of that burr every once in a while. Mr. Scott from Scotland?"

"My parents, actually," he said evenly. "They were born and raised in Edinburgh, but I was born here. Right over there, as a matter of fact, at the old Washington Hospital," and he gestured with his glass toward the window next to their table.

"And you? How did a princess like you get stuck in a congressional committee meeting?" he went on smoothly. Those light green eyes were twinkling, and he was smiling, but his tone was more serious.

Alex had too much experience giving nothing away, so she smiled and faked a light laugh.

"Yes, I too was born," she said. "Not much to tell about a young girl who goes to high school, goes to college, works for the Kennedy campaign and who has been an assistant to a Senator for a week. Pretty thin resume." Alex paused, trying to assess how that cherry-picked version of her life was going over, but Frank Scott's handsome face gave nothing away. He had stopped smiling though, she registered.

"Well, in for a penny, in for a pound," she thought and pressed on.

"What do you do at the State Department?" she asked.

"Okay. Sure. Why not? My short form biography is I went to Yale, both college and law school. Became a lawyer. Joined the military and ended up in the Army Office of General Counsel. Got recruited to the State Department as a special assistant in the office that liaises with the military." He took another drink, his eyes never leaving her.

Alex considered her next words very carefully.

"I had met a nice lawyer on the campaign for President Kennedy who was a lawyer for the State Department too."

"Was?" Scott asked quickly.

"Yes. Tragically, he was just found dead. Some kind of accident I assume, though I really don't know." She paused, taking a breath. "His name was Stephen Gray. Did you know him?"

"Yeah, yeah. Gray. I heard something had happened to him. Such a waste. Smart guy."

Scott raised a finger to signal the waiter.

"I'm going to have another scotch," he said. "You want something stronger? We could toast to poor old Stephen Gray, going out so young."

"I can toast with coffee just as well," Alex replied. She pointedly looked at her half-full coffee cup.

"To Stephen Gray," Scott said when his new drink had been delivered. "Hell of a guy," and he drank.

"To Stephen," Alex said quietly, and she raised her coffee cup to her mouth. She didn't take a sip though.

"So, you want to get something to eat?" Scott asked her after she put her coffee cup down. "Maybe head into the dining room? The food here is really good."

"Thank you, but no. I need to get home," she said and drank the rest of her coffee. She pulled some coins out of her purse and placed them on the table.

"That should cover it," she said and then glanced at his face. He was clearly trying to hide his irritation.

"I'll get the check," he said curtly and gestured again for the waiter.

"I like to pay my own way," Alex said firmly. She stood.

"Thank you for inviting me," she said, and walked at a brisk pace toward the women's lounge.

Frank Scott ordered another scotch and sat at the table, thinking, letting the buzz of Washington gossip flow over him, unnoticed. A thin, wiry man at an adjacent table ordered another Guinness. His instructions were to stay until Scott departed and then follow him.

* * *

Alex walked slowly back toward where she could catch the first of the buses that would ferry her north and then west. The stream of government workers had slowed to a trickle, and she knew the wait times for the buses would be longer. She shivered in the cold, damp air and berated herself for freezing up and practically running out on Scott.

Alex walked faster to warm up and thought about how personal questions put her so on edge. Yes, working here in the government was dangerous for someone with her background, but, she reassured herself, she was being careful. She knew she'd never learn anything about Stephen's murder if she just ran away when she felt a little cornered.

Suddenly, she saw her first bus coming down Constitution and broke into a trot. She caught it and even got a seat. The overheated bus smelled of sweat and steaming, wet wool, but she scarcely noticed it. She twisted her gloves like she was trying to wring water out of them. I have to try again, she thought. I can't let it scare me.

While the bus bumped along, Alex thought about Stephen playing music and Gwen shaking with grief. In her mind's eye, she saw the face of the handsome, laughing man bending over the piano keys. She forced herself to replace it with his battered, broken face and the torn evening gown with the exposed bruises. Alex sat up straighter. The real question was not just who had killed Stephen, but why had he been killed in that way? His body had looked like he had been tortured. For what? Just cruelty, or to throw off the hateful cops, or was there another reason? As the journey of four miles took up the better part of an hour, Alex ran those questions over and over in her mind.

Exhausted, she finally opened her apartment front door at nearly eight and walked in.

Gwen was sitting on the couch, her arms wrapped around herself, one cradling her breasts, the other her stomach. She had a spot of blood on her chin from a cut lip.

"Oh, Gwen," Alex said quietly, recognizing the signs. She threw her coat and bag on the kitchen table, came over and knelt beside her.

"Yes, they picked me up downstairs about, I guess now, maybe three hours." Gwen shook her head as if to clear it. "Some cops and a big, nasty, nasty detective. They took me, I done know, to some precinct house. That big one worked me over. Asked me about Stephen. I done know what they wanted, just to hit me it seemed, that big one."

Hicks.

Alex got up and went to her room, got an empty ice bag and a couple of aspirin. She chipped out some ice for the bag from their little freezer compartment, filled the bag and took it to Gwen.

"Hold this against your chest and stomach for a while." She placed it gently in Gwen's lap.

Then she went back, got out a bottle of wine and brought the aspirin.

"Take these, and then drink this stuff. It does take the edge off," Alex said simply. She knew what worked for this kind of beating. Then she went back and got a glass for herself, poured herself some wine and sat on the couch next to Gwen, not touching her. Touch was not what Gwen needed.

"They came after me as well yesterday," Alex said quietly.

Gwen looked over at her, horrified.

"No, not as bad as you. That Detective Hicks threatened to slap me, but he didn't," and she gave Gwen a short and highly edited version of her interview with the horrible detective.

Gwen sighed and leaned her head back on the couch.

"They don't care about Stephen, they just wanna put a notch in their belts."

They both sat there in silence.

Miss Bea came up and stood in front of Alex.

"I have had no walk and no dinner," Miss Bea grumbled.

But for the first time in the little dog's life Alex ignored her.

Miss Bea stood there for another minute and then went to Alex's closet. She got out her bone where she had hidden it after pushing it off the top of the icebox. It still had some gristle and a little dried meat on it. Miss Bea had not forgotten starving in her puppyhood, and she knew it was always best to have a little food hidden.

She was tearing at a stubborn piece of gristle when she heard Alex calling "Miss Bea, dinner." But she finished chewing the gristle first and then carefully put the bone in the back of the closet.

8

MIDNIGHT, JEFFERSON MEMORIAL

"*The Devil take it, it's freezing here. Couldn't you have picked a warmer spot than this damn Tidal Basin, like a meat freezer?*"

Sound of feet stamping.

"*Shut up. You are such a bloody berk. What did he find out?*"

"*Not much. I was at the next table, and I could mostly hear what he asked and what she said, but it was a bust.*"

"*A bust? That's your report? A bust? What did he say? What did she say?*"

"*He tried the usual 'oh, tell me about yourself' crap, and she gave him the brush off. But she did ask about Gray.*"

"*It took you long enough to get to that for Christ's sake. Yeah. So what did she ask about Gray?*"

"*She said she had met him workin' for Kennedy and wanted to know if Scott knew him.*"

"*She say why?*"

"*Said he was 'nice.' Sure, fag N***** is gonna be nice.*"

"*The little C*** lives with his sister, for crap's sake, so do the math. She could know something. We need to know. Did Gray tell her anything? Tell the sister anything? Find that out. Do what you have to, you hear?*"

"*What about the kid in the Senator's office? Do we hobble him again or let him come back?*"

"*Give it a couple days. Let's see if Scott sniffs after her again.*"

"*Sure. Fine. Whatever. That it?*"

"*Yeah. Bugger off.*"

9

FRIDAY, JANUARY 27, 1961

"No run again," Miss Bea thought as she ate her kibble. "There's a lot wrong." Bea had smelled the strong, sharp tang of blood on Gwen last night, and both Gwen and Alex had had a bitter smell in their sweat. They were afraid.

Miss Bea was afraid too. Being hungry again had been very scary to her. She stopped eating her kibble and looked up. Alex and Gwen were sitting at the little table, not paying attention to her. She took a big mouthful of the dry food and carried it in to Alex's closet. She deposited it carefully in the back corner where she'd hidden her bone, and she came back and did the same until the bowl was empty. She felt better after that and went to her basket. But she didn't sleep. She listened.

"I been beat before, honey, don't look like that. This ain't so bad," Gwen said to Alex in response to the way Alex was silently assessing her over her coffee cup.

Alex's own breasts and stomach clenched in response to Gwen's words, but she just kept silent as she had as a child. Still, she noticed things.

The skin around Gwen's eyes was puffy and dark gray, Alex thought. She didn't get much sleep last night. Well, I didn't sleep much either, Alex said to herself. And she reminded herself not to push Gwen about it. She knew Gwen well enough to know she would say what she thought needed to be said.

"Tellin' Mama was awful," Gwen said after a little while. "Purely awful." She bowed her head over her own coffee, and her eyes filled with tears. "Worse than tellin' my sister." She paused, but she didn't lift her head. "She and Stephen were never close, but she cried on the telephone. She said she couldn't take off work to come see Mama with me though."

They didn't hit Gwen in the face, Alex thought as she watched the tear slide down from the red eyes, over the dark valley beneath and then down the smooth cheek. They'd just hit her where it wouldn't be seen. Alex felt such a rush of rage she thought she could crush the old mug she was holding with her bare hands.

"What about the Reverend?" Alex asked the silent Gwen when she thought she could speak calmly.

"Oh, Lord, Lord, he made it so much worse for Mama. That ole. . ." Gwen paused, swallowing the word she wanted to use to describe the Reverend.

"Hard-headed, hard-hearted so and so?" Alex contributed.

"Yeah, like that. Just like that. And more. Anyway, he just flat out told Mama he wouldn't do the homegoing for Stephen. And he stood there in the parlor thundering mean things about Stephen, rollin' out Bible verses like he thought he was some kind of Old Testament prophet. It was awful. Mama stood like a statue in the middle of the room when he was sayin' those things. Just holdin' herself up straight and her insides hurting so bad. I went in while he was still just going on and on. I took her arm, walked her out right from under his nose. We pulled our coats on in the front hall, and we went out, out of that man's house while he was yellin' 'Don't you dare walk out on me.' We walked all the way to Mama's sister Ivy's house, clear on the other side of town. Mama's gonna just stay there a while." Gwen paused. "Aunt Ivy was real, real quiet when I told her on the phone, but she was oh, so glad to see Mama. Mama be better there."

Gwen finished off her coffee and sighed.

"I hope she stays there forever, I purely do."

"Want more?" Alex asked, gesturing at the empty cup.

"Yes, I think so. It helps my head." Gwen rubbed her head, her dark brown hair that was usually so neat flying every which way.

Alex got up and moved the coffee pot back on to the coil of the burner. She came back and sat across from Gwen.

"So, anyway, Aunt Ivy and Mama got to talkin', and they called my real Daddy's friends in Harlem, those men he used to play with in the clubs. They were all over doin' the homegoing at this church they sometimes play at there, and the preacher he's a good one. Knew my Daddy. They gonna do it next Sunday, after church." Gwen paused. "I mean, I think they can if Mama can get the body released and you know. . ." She trailed off.

"Let me know where and when, Gwen. I will come," Alex said firmly.

"Oh, really, Alex. You done have to do that."

"I want to, Gwen. And I can just take the bus up next Saturday, stay with my mother and aunt. I'll take the train over to Harlem. I just need to know the address and time."

Tears rolled down Gwen's face now, and Alex handed her a napkin. Then she silently stood up, picked up the hot coffee pot, brought it to the table and started to pour.

"Oh, and my Lord, I didn't even tell you what was at Aunt Ivy's," Gwen said suddenly, startling Alex into nearly spilling the hot coffee.

"What?" Alex said so sharply Miss Bea opened her eyes.

"What now?" Bea thought, scared a little again.

"Well," said Gwen. "You purely won't believe it."

"Gwen, really, what is it?" Alex realized her hand holding the pot was shaking a little, and so she put it back on the stove and sat down.

"Well, after that calling of my real Daddy's friends and all, Aunt Ivy goes into her bedroom and brings out a postcard that had been delivered a couple days ago. From Stephen."

"Oh my God, really?" Alex exclaimed. "What did it say?"

"Well, I got it. I'll show you. Wait a minute."

Gwen got up quickly and a grimace of pain flittered over her face. Alex saw it but said nothing. Gwen held on to the back of her chair for a minute and then straightened. She walked slowly to her room and came back with a shoe, already talking.

"When those cops came at me when I got to our building, I had it in my clothes, close to my heart. Like it was a little bit of Stephen." She sat back down with a sigh and put the shoe in her lap.

"They pushed me in the back of the police car so fast, I couldn't hardly think. But then, when they was driving, I slipped it out down my dress, and I stuck it in this shoe." Gwen lifted the shoe off of her lap and pulled gently at the insole. "This inside piece has been loose for a while, so I slipped it under."

She lifted out a folded piece of what looked like cardboard and carefully passed it over to Alex like it was so fragile it might shatter at any moment.

"It makes no sense to me, I swear. But it is his writin', that is for sure."

Alex delicately opened the folded cardboard, spread it out on the table, and read it aloud.

"Dear Aunt Ivy: Please give this postcard to Gwen as soon as you can. Give it to no one else, not even Mama. I am counting on you, Aunt Ivy. This is important. Love, your nephew Stephen."

Alex turned it over and looked at the address. Just "Mrs. Ivy Everett" and what she assumed was Aunt Ivy's address. She turned it back over and checked the postmark. Then she looked up at Gwen. Tears were clinging to

Gwen's lashes like they were afraid to fall. Alex swallowed and looked down at the postcard again.

Suddenly she gently tapped the card.

"This was mailed what was likely the day before he was killed. It must be important, but how?" Alex said and looked up. Gwen impatiently brushed the tears away and frowned at Alex.

"Don't know, but those crap cops would have taken it from me, that's for sure."

"Yes, well, you're right about that." Alex looked down at the cardboard rectangle again. It was a little worse for wear. It was creased where it had been folded in Gwen's shoe, and a bit of the writing was smudged. Alex picked up the card and walked over to the window. It was written with a fountain pen, not a ballpoint and the writing was elegant. She squinted at it. Only one smudge, really. Just the 'o' of 'love', in fact.

Alex came back to the table and put the precious card in the center of the table, away from their coffee cups.

Gwen stared at it.

"I think he was sendin' a message to me," she said. "Just like him. He liked to fool with things, make secret messages and so. Even from when we were kids. Musta come from havin' learned to keep secrets, especially from the Reverend." She sighed and then turned the postcard over.

"What about the stamp?" Gwen asked suddenly. She got up and put the kettle on one of the working burners.

Stephen could have written something under the stamp, Alex realized. She got up too, bringing the postcard over by the counter. They waited impatiently for the kettle to steam. When it did, Alex handed Gwen the card. She carefully held the stamp in the steam, and it started to peel off. It took a couple of shots of steam, but Gwen was finally able to peel it off smoothly.

They went back to the table and examined both the back of the stamp and the area on the card where it had been. There was no sign anything had been written on either one.

"Nothin'," Gwen said sadly.

"Well, still. You better hide it well," Alex said. "Maybe the words are a code. We need to figure it out."

She stood up.

"I need to change and get to work. You going in?"

"No," Gwen said slowly. "I'll call. They know."

Alex turned to go to her room, but Gwen's next words stopped her dead in her tracks.

"But tonight, Alex, we got to go to a party."

Flabbergasted, Alex turned back and just stared at the small, drowned-eyed woman looking up at her. But there was a change, Alex noted. Gwen now looked grimly determined.

"A party?" Alex asked in what she hoped was a neutral voice.

"Yeah. We gotta go to this house party Stephen used to go to some. Always on Friday. A lot of his friends go there. We need to ask some questions."

Gwen looked up at Alex like she was measuring her. It turned out she was.

"We gotta dress like men. I done it before, so I've got a suit. One of Stephen's should fit you. When you get home, we need to go by his apartment and let you try 'em on and pick one. And just pick one. You hear me? No time for sewing and all the stuff you do."

Alex nodded, though she privately thought wearing an ill-fitting men's suit would drive her slowly out of her mind.

Gwen sighed deeply.

"I done know if he hid anything in the apartment give us a clue," she went on slowly. Then to Alex's surprise, Gwen turned and looked over at Miss Bea who was pretending to sleep.

"Let's take that dog. She might smell somethin', somethin' the cops missed maybe. I'm sure they've tossed his apartment by now, but know'n that boy he had hiding places. Good ones."

Miss Bea opened her eyes and pricked up her ears, surprised that Gwen knew that about her.

"I do smell out things exceptionally well," she concurred.

But then Gwen looked away, and her narrow shoulders drooped as she wrapped her arms protectively around her chest.

"Oh, and cleanin' out that apartment. That's another thing." But then Gwen seemed to force herself to sit up straight and stand. She turned to look unseeingly out of the grimy window.

"But first, we gotta get a suit for you and get to this party. Nobody gonna find out who killed my Stephen but us."

Alex stared at Gwen's rigid body for a moment.

"Okay. Yes. We have to try."

Alex turned and walked slowly toward her room. As she put on another beautifully tailored dress, she thought about what it was going to feel like to wear a suit of the murdered Stephen Gray.

* * *

Stephen's apartment was not too far from where Gwen and Alex lived, so when Alex got home from work, they leashed up Miss Bea, bundled up in dark hats and coats, with scarves hiding their lower faces and hurried out. They walked quickly through the cold wind that blew sleet and trash at them in relatively equal portions.

Alex was grateful, as they pushed along the streets, that she'd had an easy day at work. The Senator had been out of the office, and Alistair was still sick according to Mrs. Anderson.

"When he called, he said he feels worse again, poor boy," she'd said sadly. Alex thought Alistair would have been mortified to be reduced to a sick kid in Mrs. Anderson's motherly voice.

So Alex had spent the day reading the letters from the Senator's constituents and penning replies that matched the tone and content. The majority were from women whom Alex guessed were close to the Senator's age. Some included recipes the writers thought the Senator would like and many referenced Fluffy. Alex sighed about having to write about Fluffy again, but she at least put him to work in her replies. Fluffy was becoming a legislative aide in his own right, Alex had mused. He was quite knowledgeable about how to lower taxes, at least for a cat.

Suddenly Alex realized Gwen had turned and was heading for a small entryway in a narrow, three story brick building that jutted up between a small market on one side and a barber shop on the other. Lights were still on in both, but the entrance to the brick building was poorly lit. Gwen quickly used a key and opened the inside door. Alex and Miss Bea hustled in behind her, and they silently began to climb the stairs.

"Third floor," Gwen said in a hushed voice. The smells of dinners cooking and the sounds of babies crying filled the stairwell. Bea kept her head up, catching the sounds and smells, but she didn't lag. Neither did Alex. Gwen's tension was saying all that needed to be said. Be quiet and hurry up.

They reached a landing, and Gwen used a second key to open an apartment door. They all hurried through, and Gwen immediately locked it behind them and shot the bolt. Then she turned and gasped.

What had once been a well-furnished though spare front room had been viciously searched. Broken lamps, torn seat cushions, broken picture frames, books and records were strewn on the floor. Many of the records were broken, likely stomped on probably by police boots. A record player was in a dozen pieces on a tilting side table that had one leg bent. And the worst, Alex thought, was what they had done to the upright piano. It looked like someone had taken an ax to it. They likely had. That was like seeing Stephen's broken body all over again.

Gwen stood frozen in the midst of the carnage, her gloved hands clasped in front of her. Then, without turning, she said in a low tone, "Let that dog off the leash."

Alex did as she was bid, stunned by the way the apartment had not so much been searched as attacked.

Miss Bea walked over to Gwen and stood next to her, looking up.

"Dog," said Gwen solemnly, "You use that nose. Find what Stephen had hid."

Miss Bea cocked her head and then trotted off down a side hall.

"Let's see if them suits is still in one piece," Gwen said with barely suppressed pain in her voice. Then she turned away from the broken room and followed Miss Bea down the hall.

Gwen went into a door on the right, and Alex followed. She snapped on an overhead light, and the brutalized bedroom came into view.

The mattress had been slashed and the pillows as well. Clothes littered the floor but mostly were not torn. Gwen didn't move, so Alex went past her and walked over toward a small closet and saw some men's suits crumpled on the floor. She bent and picked them up and carried them toward a chair that had been overturned but seemed in one piece.

Alex righted the chair, put the suits on it, shook out the jackets and pants one by one and examined them. They too had been stomped on, it seemed from the dirt on the wrinkled fabric, but there was only one jacket that was actually torn. And it was along a seam.

I can fix that easily, Alex thought, turning the jacket in her hands. The wool is good. It will steam out.

Suddenly she and Gwen jumped as Miss Bea started to howl. They left the suits on the chair and ran down the hall toward the sound. Miss Bea was in the bathroom and had her nose pressed against some old, painted wood paneling that ran along the wall opposite the commode.

"Here, here," Miss Bea growled. "There's a smell of something in here. Get it. Get it."

Alex bent and petted Bea while also whispering "Okay Bea. We've got it. That's enough."

"Open it," Miss Bea growled again but more quietly.

Alex sat down on the cold, uneven bathroom floor tile and pulled Miss Bea into her lap. Gwen left for a moment and came back with a bent, worn knife. She knelt down by the cracked, painted wainscoting and inserted the knife between where there was a wider gap between two of the wooden slats. There was movement, and the outline of a panel appeared. Gwen slid the knife in another, shadowy gap about 2 feet along the wall, and the whole piece started to move. She put down the knife and lifted the entire section away.

A black, leather suitcase was inside. Alex moved to help Gwen lift it out and then they put it on the floor.

Gwen snapped the clasps open and lifted the lid.

They stared at a velvet lined case that contained photography equipment. There was a camera, several, different size lenses, a flash, rolls of what must be film, some cords, and what looked like a collapsible tripod. There were also bottles of fluid and, in the lid, some white, textured paper in sheets.

Miss Bea walked up and gave the case a thorough sniff, especially the chemical bottles and the film.

"Vinegar and maybe cheese. That's what I smelled."

"Did Stephen take photos as a hobby?" Alex asked, looking at what must be a very expensive photography kit.

"Not that he ever said," Gwen said slowly, sitting back on her heels.

"Maybe some of his friends know," Alex mused.

"Let's go," Gwen said, snapping the case closed. "We'll take this and the suits and figure it out at home."

"Okay," Alex said slowly, but she was calculating where in their small apartment they could make another hiding place.

Whatever Stephen was doing with this equipment, he had hidden it well. They had to do the same.

IO

FRIDAY, JANUARY 27, 1961

Alex followed Gwen up steep, stone stairs that were sandwiched between two high, boxwood hedges. They were so thick and tall they nearly blocked out the sliver of moonlight above and the dim glow of the street-lights below. Looming above them in the gloom was a black door with a brass knocker. The carriage light above the door was unlit. Are we even at the right place? Alex wondered to herself. The tall windows on either side of the door emitted no light. Then she looked closely and saw there were heavy curtains on the inside.

They had walked the eight blocks to this brick house in Georgetown. Alex had clopped along in the too-big men's shoes, and she felt very un-comfortable in the ill-fitting man's suit she wore. Gwen had only given her a few minutes to tack up the sleeves and pants and press the best-fitting of Stephen's suits they had carried back to their apartment.

Alex had muttered to herself as she pressed the dark gray, fine wool suit. The fabric was good, but the fit would be far from perfect. Then she had carried the suit to her room, placed it on the bed, and closed the door to change.

"And be sure to wear your women's underthings," Gwen had called through the door as Alex was about to put on the suit. "If the cops stop us for wearing men's suits, it's not illegal to wear 'em if we have on women's underthings."

What? Alex thought with shock, and she stopped as she was about to pull on the pants. She hadn't even considered changing her underthings, and what would she wear instead? Stephen's underwear that was sitting in a bag in the hall? Revolted, she felt acid pool in her empty stomach, and she felt sick.

She sat down on the bed, her head in her hands. "I do not want to do this," she moaned quietly so Gwen would not hear. A vision of Senator Carpenter's face as she berated Alex for such conduct rose in front of her. "You are not a lady, Miss Bell," she imagined the Senator's pursed lips saying before she fired her. And then another image made her lift her head. She saw a vivid picture of Hicks hitting Gwen on her breasts and stomach, and then it merged with a vision of her mother's bruised and swollen breasts and stomach. She saw Stephen's bruised, frozen face and his torn and bruised chest. I have to do this, she said to herself. They can't be allowed to get away with beating and killing. She stood back up and slowly picked up the pants from the bed and drew them on. She realized her hands were shaking as she did up the zipper. She shrugged into the jacket and reached for the tie.

Alex turned and looked at herself in the mirror while she fitted the tie around her neck and looped it properly. Then she turned down the stiff collar, and a blond woman's head floating above a man in a gray suit came into focus. Idiotic, she thought. I'll be arrested the moment I set foot out the door.

Alex opened her bedroom door to discuss how absurd she looked with Gwen, but she kept quiet because she heard Gwen muttering to Miss Bea in the little galley kitchen. Gwen was likely looking for a hiding place for Stephen's photography equipment, but what was Bea doing with her?

Miss Bea was following Gwen around as she looked for a place to conceal the leather case because she was worried that her hidden pile of food and her bone would be uncovered. But Gwen had not gone into Alex's room. Instead, she had been examining the back wall of the galley kitchen where a cabinet concealed the fold-out ironing board. Alex had just used it to steam out the men's suit.

While Miss Bea watched with approval, Gwen removed the ironing board from the sliding hinges and lifted a fitted shelf from the bottom. She pointed a bright flashlight down the hole to examine the space she had uncovered. "It should do," she murmured. She picked up the case and pushed it down into the bottom of the cabinet. It seemed a tight fit, but then it disappeared as it slid in. She put the shelf back in, re-attached the ironing board, and closed the cabinet door.

"There," Gwen said with satisfaction, patting the cracking paint on the wood door.

"A good job," Miss Bea conceded. "But I can still smell it."

Gwen turned and saw Alex standing behind her looking grim.

"Look, honey," Gwen said, reading Alex like a book. "It'll be okay. I done this before. And here, I got this for you." Gwen turned and picked up a hatbox from the little kitchen table.

"Wear the wig to cover all that yellow hair and wear the hat. And don't you use that white paint on your face you put on all the time, you hear? Your color okay without that, kinda like that Rita Heyworth gal, sort of Spanish. No face powder, no nothin', just so you don't shout out white first thing. And here." Gwen held out a pair of smoke-tinted spectacles. "These'll hide those green eyes." Then Gwen had just handed her the box and the glasses, bustled to her own room and shut the door.

Alex and Miss Bea looked at each other in silence. Then Alex carried the hatbox and the spectacles into her bedroom.

Now, we're here, Alex thought as she gazed dimly up at the shadowy black door through the smoky lenses, her stomach clenching in fear. Alex looked at Gwen's back as she stood above her on the stairs of the Georgetown house, waiting for a response to her knock. The fast walk in the cold air had waked her up some. She felt less like she was in a bad, waking dream and more like herself, but she was also shivering and not just from the cold.

Since they didn't have men's overcoats, they had just worn the suits with hats, gloves and scarfs. Alex was chilled to the bone from the eight block walk up the hill to a better part of Georgetown from where their apartment was located, and she could see Gwen was shivering too. Alex discretely scratched over her ear, trying not to dislodge the itchy wig and fedora she was wearing. She focused on Gwen's back again and on how the suit jacket Gwen wore had a good five inches of extra fabric flapping down the center back seam. Awful, Alex thought.

Then Gwen banged the knocker harder, and Alex jumped a little. I'm worrying about the fit of that men's suit so I don't have to worry about what is behind that door, Alex reflected.

The big door opened, and a tall man stood silhouetted in a dim back-light.

"Gwen! Gwen. My dear. You came." He drew Gwen to him gently and folded her into an embrace. He was tall, Alex thought, as he loomed over petite Gwen. Then she realized he was looking intently at her over Gwen's head.

Gwen looked up into his face, and she said firmly, "Howard, this is my friend Alex. She was also a friend of Stephen's."

"Well, well," the man introduced as Howard said as he put out a hand to draw Alex quickly through the doorway along with Gwen. He shut the door firmly behind them and flipped on a light in the foyer.

The tall man called Howard was dressed in a soft, brocade jacket, loose-fitting trousers, and he had a soft, beige scarf at his neck that complimented his chestnut colored skin, Alex registered as she gazed up at him. He had black, close-cropped hair with a few strands of silver over his ears and some silver in his thick, black eyebrows, the eyebrows that were raised above the rim of his black-rimmed glasses. She realized he was assessing her as carefully as she was assessing him. Gwen remained wrapped in his arms.

"So, Alex. How did you meet Gwen and Stephen?" the man called Howard asked over Gwen's head, pinning her with dark eyes slightly magnified by his glasses.

Alex had not expected an interrogation the minute she arrived, but she summoned her "I work for a Senator" voice and answered gravely.

"We all worked for the election campaign of President Kennedy and I met them on the campaign trail." She paused, and then added. "Gwen and I share an apartment."

"Ah," the man called Howard said gravely, and he released Gwen.

"Let me take your things, and you can go get what I am sure is a much-needed drink." He held out his long-fingered hands to Gwen to take her scarf and gloves, and Alex took that moment of his distraction to take off the hat, keeping one hand on the wig to hold it still. Then she pulled off the scarf and gloves.

"Please follow me, if you will," he intoned in his deep voice, and he started down the hall toward a door at the end, placing their items on a table as he passed. Before he opened that door, he snapped off the hallway light, and they were very briefly cast into complete darkness. Then he opened the door, and light and music spilled in to the hall.

Alex blinked at the sudden brightness, and she saw what looked at first like a cocktail party scene from one of those old "Thin Man" movies. Her first thought was that she'd have been better off in her sophisticated black dress instead of an idiotic men's suit. But then, as her eyes adjusted to the light, she realized the differences. The people were mostly darker skinned, though some had a more beige hue like hers. Some wore men's suits like hers, and others were wearing black tie. Others had on cocktail dresses and, she realized, some had combined men's suit jackets with dresses or the other way around. It was disconcerting, Alex thought, because the clothes did not especially signal who was a man and who was a woman. But then she huffed a little laugh, thinking that was the same for both her and Gwen. There was a lot of head apparel too. Turbans, cloche hats with long feathers, and a couple of tiaras adorned some heads, and some had black fedoras like she had taken off at the door. I could have kept my hat, she mused.

Gwen was in the middle of a circle of people, and they were patting her back or hugging her, clearly commiserating about Stephen. Alex did not want to interrupt that. Gwen needed the comfort.

What I need is a drink, Alex thought firmly and looked for a bar or a drinks cart. She decided it was likely to be where a small knot of people were standing along a side wall. It's too bad it's so dimly lit in here, she reflected as she moved carefully around various chairs and tables. These glasses make it so hard to see. She carefully made her way across to the table without knocking anything over and picked up what looked like a martini off the cart. She took it to an alcove along the same side wall, sat down on an empty bench and took a big sip. She shuddered. Whatever it was, it tasted like medicine, but she took another sip and gazed around the room trying to orient herself.

She idly took another swallow while looking at the people and nearly choked. Directly across the room, by tall windows that were heavily curtained, was Officer Edgar Thomas. It really looked like his profile, a narrow face with milk chocolate skin and dark, curly hair. Alex squinted her eyes. No, really, it couldn't be, could it? The light was poor, that's all. But she narrowed her eyes and considered. This man was wearing a well-fitting, silver women's evening gown and some pearls. The profile must just remind her of Thomas. But then the figure turned, looked right at her, and she saw him full-face. It was Thomas. She raised her glass to hide more of her features, hoping her wig, glasses, and suit were enough disguise. Thomas's eyes slid past her. Good. He didn't seem to recognize her. Well, Alex mused as she took another cautious sip of the awful drink, I could just go ask him how the investigation is going. But that's so not a good idea. She swallowed but kept the glass up by her lips, thinking. No, not a good idea at all. But I'll ask Gwen. We might be able to use this.

"Hello, honey. Mind if I sit?" a smoke-roughened voice asked. It came from a stocky person in a kind of flowered tent dress who stood right next to her.

Alex started, spilling a little of her remaining drink on her lap. She looked up at the owner of the voice.

"I beg your pardon," she said coolly, the Smith College voice firmly in play.

A round-faced, squat person of at least fifty was smiling down at her, a cigarette in a black, jeweled holder held in one hand, a tall glass with amber liquid in the other.

"Say, that's pretty good, little girl," the person said. She sat down, transferred the black cigarette holder to her mouth and stuck out her hand.

"I'm Eleanor Mary Brown, but everybody here in this Yankee town calls me Brownie," she said, expertly speaking around the cigarette holder.

Alex shook the proffered hand, rendered speechless. She had not thought of a fake name to use. How stupid can I be? she said to herself.

Alex looked at Eleanor Mary Brown, who liked to be called Brownie, now sitting inches from her. She must be a woman, given her name, Alex thought, but what does she want with me?

Brownie took a drag on her cigarette, hissed the smoke out, took a big swallow of her drink and then doused the cigarette in the remaining liquid, retrieving her cigarette holder and putting it in a pocket hidden in the voluminous folds of her dress. The whole time she focused bird-like, beady black eyes on Alex. She put the glass and drowned cigarette on the floor.

"You work in Senator Carpenter's office, right? Alexandra Bell?" she asked leaning forward to peer more closely at Alex's face.

Alex went rigid with fear. She looked at the unblinking eyes fixed on her. This must be what is like to have a snake stare at you, mesmerizing you in preparation to strike, she thought.

"Now, now. Don't look like that girlie," Brownie said quietly. "I keep secrets. Lots of secrets. I mean, it's a secret I'm here too, right? No, don't you worry. I saw you at that Cuba committee meeting, asked around. Got your name. That's all. No bad wig can hide those cheekbones and," she actually used a blunt finger to pull the smoky glasses down Alex's nose, "those green eyes."

Alex felt sharp anger rise in her. She brushed away the insulting finger and stood.

"I do not know you, and I do not wish to know you. Good evening," she said firmly and turned to walk away.

"Now, now," the gravel voice said behind her said again. "Don't be afraid. I'm not here to rat on you to the Senator. I'm a columnist for the *Washington Tattler*. I want to know what you and that sister of Stephen Gray over there are doing here at Howard's party. What do you know about his death? There's a police cover-up in motion, and it smells to high heaven. I want to get at what really happened to him." The voice softened. "Stephen Gray was a fine young man."

Alex turned back and looked intently down at the lined, plump face topped with a riot of improbable red hair, but she remained standing.

"Do you have identification?" Alex asked sharply. "Why should I believe you are who you say you are? Everyone here is apparently someone else," she said, turning slightly and gesturing at the room. Then she looked down at Brownie, paused, and pushed the smoky glasses firmly back up her nose. "Including me."

"Well, you're not all cheekbones and eyes, are you, sweetie? Sure. I always carry some cards when I'm out and about, especially at parties like these." She reached down into the folds of her voluminous dress, pulled out a card, and handed it to Alex. There were four printed lines.

"Eleanor Mary Brown. *The Washington Tattler*. 1152 15th Street Northwest, Washington DC. Phone: 555-1207."

Alex pocketed the card and sat back down.

"What have you heard?" Alex asked, looking intently at Brownie.

"Look. Glad you want to talk, but I need another drink. Want something?"

Alex shook her head no.

Brownie heaved herself up and headed for the drinks cart. In no time, she was back with another tumbler of amber liquid. She sat down, took a big swallow and then laughed, her sagging cheeks lifting up as her mouth curved.

"What have I heard? Who's doing the interviewing here, kiddo? I wanna know what you know. That's what reporting is."

Alex sat up straight and looked at the piercing eyes peering out from a web of wrinkled skin.

"Nothing goes in the paper."

"Yeah, well, not yet anyway," Brownie acknowledged.

Alex frowned but said nothing.

"Okay. Okay. Not until you say so," Brownie conceded.

"The detective who is supposed to be investigating is named Hicks. I think he's just looking to blame anyone. He despises people like Stephen. Horrible man, and I know he's violent with suspects."

"Yeah. I know who Hicks is. Came from New York. Big man, big mouth, big fists."

Alex thought about what she should say. I'm not telling this reporter about what Hicks did to Gwen, she told herself firmly. One leak and Gwen could really be in trouble. Instead, Alex turned and looked for Thomas. He was still by the windows.

"You see that young man across the room, silver cocktail dress and pearls?" she asked after a moment, gesturing toward him.

Brownie put her new drink on the floor, fished in another cavernous pocket and pulled out some spectacles. She put them on and looked where Alex was pointing.

"Yeah."

"That's Officer Edgar Thomas. He was one of the first on the scene. I found the body, or rather, my little dog did. Then he came to Gwen's and my apartment with an Officer Richardson to pick me up so Hicks could threaten me. He doesn't seem to recognize me in this getup I don't want to get too close to him, though. But you need to talk to him. He'll know the status of the investigation. Such as it is."

"Okay, good tip. Call me tomorrow at that number on the card. We can have coffee, or better, some lunch. I can tell you what I learn, you can tell me more. I know there's a lot more."

"Okay," Alex said, getting up slowly. She turned to leave, but Brownie got up nimbly and made her jump by grabbing on to her sleeve.

"Oh, wait, honey. I want you to meet my husband. He made it." Brownie waved the hand that was not holding Alex and yelled in her deep, frog voice, "Yoo-hoo, Higgy!"

A short, round man turned and waved back, a cheerful grin on his plump face. He held up two fingers and turned back to the tall, string bean of a young man next to him and seemed to resume speaking.

"You're married?" Alex asked, trying not to sound as shocked as she felt.

Brownie huffed a deep laugh that ended with a cough.

"Oh, dearie, you don't know much yet, do you? Yes, Higgy and I are married. Have been for years since we met in New York at the beginning of the war. I was writing military press pieces, and Higgy was a military lawyer. He had to check my copy over, you know, to be sure that I wasn't giving 'aid and comfort to the enemy' by blabbing secrets. Anyway, helped us both to be married. You'll find that a lot with folks, especially ones our age. Higgy works for Adlai Stevenson, has for years."

"Stevenson, the presidential candidate?" Alex asked, interested despite her whirling mind. "The one whom Kennedy beat for the nomination?"

"That's the one. There's only one Adlai that counts, really. Kennedy has made him Ambassador to the U.N., though our new president had to be dragged kicking and screaming into that, I tell you. Higgy is mostly back in New York now. He must have gotten down here with the Ambassador. Adlai's home is here in Washington too."

Just then, "Higgy" turned and started to walk toward them. He was so short he moved in and out of view, but gradually Alex saw him clearly. He had a bulbous nose, a bald pate, and white hair sprouting from above his ears. His eyebrows that rose at the sight of Alex standing with his wife were coal black. His multi-colored, polka dot bow tie was enormous, a kind of flag from a happy-go-lucky country tied around his neck.

"The Mad Hatter," Alex thought, dazed. "Of course, that's fitting." Alex had been taken by her mother to see the Disney movie *Alice in Wonderland* when she was eleven. "That Queen, just like a boss on the floor!" her mother had commented sharply as they had walked out of the theater.

"Higgy, get over here, I want you to meet someone," Brownie croaked loudly.

"Okay, okay, Brownie. I'm coming," he chortled, and he bounced up to them on little feet. Alex was charmed and terrified all at the same time.

"Bruce Reese Higgenbothem, meet Alexandra Bell. Alex, this is my husband Bruce, but everybody calls him Higgy."

"Hey, Alex! So glad to meet you. What do you do here in the foggiest of bottoms imaginable?" Higgy said with a chuckle that moved his whole round body up and down, tiny feet to bald head.

This is the kind of moment when killing myself to get into a Seven Sisters school is all worth it, Alex thought.

"How do you do, Mr. Higgenbothem," Alex said formally. She hesitated to put out her hand since Higgenbothem had not done so when he introduced himself. Still a little at sea, Alex clung to social formality like a drowning young woman would cling to a life preserver. "I am pleased to meet you. I am a great admirer of Ambassador Stevenson. And yes, I work here in Washington. I am an assistant to Senator Carpenter."

Higgy actually danced a little on his bouncy feet and then threw his wife a kiss. He also had tiny hands, Alex noticed.

"Brownie, where do you find them?" he said joyously.

"Now, Higgy. Never you mind. Miss Bell and I will be able to do each other a lot of good. I wanted you both to meet, but now you run along. I see Charlie over there, and he seems to be refusing to breathe until you turn and smile at him."

"Charlie?" Higgy said, even more happily, though that hardly seemed possible to Alex. "Adlai will have kittens when I tell him Charlie was here." He whirled and bounced off, taking two steps before he shouted a "gladto-meetcha" over his shoulder at Alex and then kept bounding along, disappearing into the throng.

"So, Alex, that's Higgy. Anyway, call me at that number and we'll meet up. We can do each other a lot of good."

Alex just nodded, completely out of words.

Brownie patted her on the arm with her big hand, and Alex wondered if there would be a bruise.

"The Bambi look helps, you know?" Brownie said, seriously, peering into Alex's face again. "Men will kill themselves to tell you everything they know."

Alex said nothing, and Brownie nodded in the direction of Thomas.

"I better get over there before he leaves with that guy," she said and walked briskly away, expertly threading through the crowd. Alex realized

Brownie must have been keeping an eye on Thomas even as she had been introducing Alex to her husband.

Alex stared after her and then saw Gwen was looking at her. She gestured to the door. Gwen nodded, and they each headed that way.

Gwen stopped and spoke to their host, Howard, as she made her way across the room. Alex just stood along the wall and waited. She realized she was exhausted.

Howard accompanied Gwen, and he let them out the door after they had retrieved their things, shutting off the hall light before he opened it.

They picked their way carefully down the dark stairs and hustled down the street. The eight blocks were downhill, but still a huge effort in the cold.

II

MIDNIGHT JEFFERSON MEMORIAL

"So. Was it there?"

"Nothin'. Not a bloody thing. And that feckin' mutt went nearly crazy when it heard me picking the lock."

"Jesus. Was it another cock-up? Did you have to do for the dog? Crikey, that will give away the game. They'll move it."

"Whadda you take me for? I knew there was a damned dog. I threw a piece of drugged meat in when I got the door open a crack, but the stupid mutt wouldn't touch it. Good thing I also had a little left of that chloroform we used on the other job. Put a drop on a rag, cracked the door again threw it on the mutt's head. Out like a light."

"You sure you didn't snuff it? Don't want them to suspect. Not yet, anyway."

"I put it in its basket before I left. It was breathing. But hell, where'd they put the case? I saw 'em carrying it away from the fag's place, and it's not in that apartment. I looked everywhere."

"Bugger it all. Follow them. Find it."

12

SATURDAY, JANUARY 27, 1961, JUST AFTER MIDNIGHT

Miss Bea felt awful. She had just awakened in her basket and couldn't remember how she got there. She felt like she wanted to puke. "What is wrong with me?" she thought groggily. She shook her head and wished she hadn't. The room went round and round. Then she heard the door of the apartment open. Bad. There was danger, and, she shook her head again, a bad man. Danger. She struggled up on wobbly legs and staggered into the front hall, making low growls. Then she saw it was Alex, and she just lay down on the floor.

"Bea! Bea!" Alex exclaimed, seeing the prostrate dog. "What is wrong with you? Are you sick?"

Alex picked Bea up, carried her to the sofa and sat down, holding her on her lap. Gwen came in and shut and locked the door.

"That dog sick?" Gwen asked as she pulled off her scarf, hat, and gloves and put them on the table.

"I think so," Alex said slowly, cuddling Bea, alarmed by her lethargy. She felt her nose. It was cold, so not fever, but she could feel the little body shaking. She gently lifted one of Bea's jowls and checked her gums. They were too pale.

"Bad man," Bea thought, her head clearing a little. "The meat smelled funny. I didn't eat it. Then, then. . ." Bea shivered more. Then there was nothing. That scared her. The nothing was scary.

"Gwen, get me that blanket at the foot of my bed, will you? Miss Bea is shivering."

"Sure."

The blanket felt good, and Bea started to doze.

"Somebody's been here," Gwen said sharply, and Miss Bea lifted her head.

"Yes. Yes. Bad man."

"What do you mean? How do you know?" Alex asked quickly.

"When I hid Stephen's case, I had to use a chair to hold the ironing board. I pulled this chair out, and then I just left it over here by the wall when we were rushing to get going. I'm sure of that, and now it's pushed back under the table." She stood stock still for a moment, her hand on the chair back, thinking, and then she rushed to the ironing cabinet. "I gotta check. Oh, my Lord suppose they got Stephen's case and his postcard? I put it in the case to keep it safe."

Alex kept cradling the now sleeping Bea, but she stood up to watch Gwen remove the ironing board and lean into the deep cabinet, lifting the lower shelf away and shining her flashlight into the space.

"They didn't get it. They didn't get it. It's still there, way down at the bottom. It's black and hard to see, but it's there. I can touch it." She pulled the case out with a grunt, put it on the little table and clicked open the latches. She sighed with relief.

"All of it. It's here. Postcard too." She closed the catches and pushed the black case back down into the deep hole of the cabinet into the crawl space below. Then she fitted the little shelf in, lifted the ironing board back on to its hinges, collapsed it, and closed the cabinet.

"You think someone was here, though," Alex said grimly. "You're sure?"

"Yes, I'm sure. You know me, I done make mistakes like that. I know where I left that chair. But," she said, looking around, "they didn't do the wrecking job they did at Stephen's." Gwen's face wrinkled in concentration, still gazing at the apartment. "Why not?"

"I don't know, but I do think they gave Miss Bea something to knock her out." She hugged Bea to her. "It could have killed her. She's such a little dog, it could have killed her," and Alex held her tighter and tears ran down her cheeks, dripping on to the blanket-covered dog.

"I am not little," Miss Bea thought drowsily.

Gwen carried the tell-tale kitchen chair to the front door and put it under the knob.

"Come on now. Come on now," she said gently to Alex who was still heaving a few sobs. "We all need some sleep. We can talk in the morning."

"Okay," Alex sniffed, using the back of her hand to dash away the remaining moisture on her face. "And I have a lot to tell you."

"So do I," Gwen said in a low voice. "So do I."

"Me too," Bea thought. A vivid memory of the bad man's smell made her raise her head. "Puke and that stuff Alex uses to clean. He smelled of that." Then she lowered her head again and fell deeply asleep.

* * *

She was falling, falling, falling into a dark pit. Her hands reached out to grasp anything to catch herself, but the rough surface of the walls of the pit tore her skin and her flailing hands left bloody trails on the dark walls. She was shaking with fear, sure that at any minute she would be smashed at the bottom. Then she felt her face turn wet and cold, and she woke with a gasp.

Miss Bea was licking her face, frightened by Alex's moaning and trembling. Then she gave a sharp bark right in Alex's ear.

"Stop that! Wake up!" Bea insisted.

Alex opened her eyes. Her head was pounding and not just from the racket Bea was making.

"Okay, Miss Bea, okay. You can stop that now. I'm awake," Alex said, giving Bea a gentle pat. She had kept the little dog on the bed with her when she'd gone to try to get some sleep, wanting to monitor her breathing. Since Bea was standing with her front paws on Alex's chest and glaring at her with her black, shiny eyes framed by perked ears, Alex concluded Bea was fine.

Better than I am, she thought wearily. She moved the dog aside and swung her legs over the edge of the bed.

Alex pulled on old sweatpants and a baggy sweatshirt. Miss Bea jumped down off the bed and raced to the front door.

"Finally, a run," Bea rejoiced, dancing around in a circle.

"Oh, no, Bea. Just a walk, it's all I can manage," Alex said wearily, and she slowly got ready, pulling on outdoor clothes like she was moving underwater.

When they got back, Gwen was up, sitting at the little table with her head in her hands, and the coffee pot was percolating on the stove. Alex fed the disgruntled Miss Bea, got two of their chipped cups out of the dish drain and poured the coffee. Then she sat down opposite Gwen and for a few minutes they both drank their coffee in silence.

"So, Alex. What'd you think?" Gwen asked slowly, gazing down at her still steaming mug, her long fingers wrapped around its warm ceramic surface.

Alex stared into her own mug for a minute, pondering a reply. I'd better stick to what I learned, she thought. And for the rest, I really need to let it sink in.

"I met a couple of promising contacts for finding out about what happened to Stephen," she said matter-of-factly, and Gwen looked up.

"That sounds good," Gwen said in a neutral kind of voice.

"I think so," Alex said and started to summarize how Brownie had come over and chatted her up.

"A reporter?" Gwen asked in alarm. Her hands actually flew up and covered her mouth.

"No, no, Gwen. Really, I think she's okay. She knew Stephen, said she'd liked him, and said she can keep secrets." Alex paused. "I think anybody at that party is used to keeping secrets, right? I mean that was a room full of dangerous secrets."

Gwen took her hands off of her mouth and lowered them slowly to the table top, but her face shut down completely like a closed door with a "Do Not Enter" sign posted on it.

Alex just waited, sipping her own cooling coffee while she contemplated her roommate. I have no idea what is going through her mind, Alex thought, none at all. Then she realized Gwen was likely thinking the same thing about her. Alex looked down at her remaining coffee, but what she saw was the chasm between them. I don't know if I can bridge it, she thought anxiously. I don't know how.

She sipped her coffee again and the acid in it burned her empty stomach. She winced from the sharp pain, but it helped her focus. I won't try to fix that right now, she concluded. I'll just tell her what I learned and let her decide how much to tell me. She put the cup down on the table and tried for a matter-of-fact voice.

"So, anyway, Gwen, the reason you took me there I think will pay off. This Brownie person knows a lot of Washington gossip, and she's going to snoop around." Alex paused. "I have her card, and I think I should go talk to her this coming week. See what she's found out."

"Yeah, okay," Gwen said slowly, but in more of her regular tone. "You're right. It's why we went to the party, God's truth." She sat up a little straighter and then grimaced slightly.

Alex wondered briefly how much pain Gwen was still feeling from the beating by Hicks, but she didn't think she should ask.

"So, there's more on Brownie," Alex went on as calmly as she could manage. "She's married to an aide to Ambassador Adlai Stephenson, Bruce Reese Higgenbothem. Likes to be called Higgy."

"Yes," Gwen commented. "I know who Higgy is. I think he's one of Howard's good friends. Been around for years, working for Stephenson in one way or another." She paused. "I never knew he was married."

"Well, Brownie said they'd met in New York City during the war, got married and that helps them both. I mean, stands to reason, right?"

"Sure." Gwen took a sip of her coffee, seeming to relax a little.

"So," Alex went on, "did you see Officer Thomas?"

"Wait, what?" Gwen nearly spit the coffee out. "That cop that works with Hicks, he was there? No. Definitely not."

"Yeah, well he was. He was near the windows, away from where you were in that group of people. He was wearing an evening gown. I sent Brownie to go talk to him. That's another source for us, a good one."

"Well that's about right," Gwen said, recovering.

"So, that's about it for me. What did you learn?"

Gwen sat completely still.

She's wondering how much to tell me, Alex thought. How much she can trust me.

"Do you want some more coffee?" Gwen asked.

"Yes, thanks," Alex said, despite the fact that she was sure more coffee would give her more stomach pain.

Gwen came back with the coffee pot and filled both of their cups. Alex went to the refrigerator and got out some milk and poured it into her coffee. She normally liked it black, but she hoped the milk would cut the acid.

"Was kind of like the homegoing is going to be, I expect," Gwen said softly, and her brown eyes filled with tears. "So many friends, so much sadness and, truth be told, fear. They afraid. They always afraid but then this. Stephen murdered and cops coming around." Gwen put her thin arms around herself, self-comforting.

The fear, Alex thought as she waited. I have to remember the fear at all times. She sat back in her chair, jolted by a realization. That's why this whole thing feels so familiar. It's like being a socialist, secrets and fear and wondering all the time who you can trust.

"What?" Gwen asked, seeing Alex jolt back.

"Oh, just sympathizing with the fear," she said neutrally, but she thought to herself that she'd never trusted Gwen enough to tell her the real story of her family. She felt a pang of guilt. Should I?, she asked herself. But then suppose they catch up with me for all that? Investigate me and my family? Best she doesn't know all of that. It'll protect her some.

But even as she thought that, Alex knew it was mostly a lie. Hiding who she really was had become second nature to her.

"Well, anyway," Gwen went on. "Most important, I talked to Stephen's closest friend from State." She paused and her eyes narrowed as she looked directly at Alex. "You know what I mean by that? Closest friend?"

Alex just nodded. Gwen looked a little skeptical, but she went on.

"His name's Jack, Jack Karns. He's a lieutenant, works in that new department of Politico-Military affairs."

Alex started a little, but Gwen didn't seem to notice. She had retreated into her sorrow for a moment.

That's the department Frank Scott works in, Alex thought as some more tears pooled in Gwen's eyes. She kept quiet but was furiously thinking. Scott hadn't told her they actually worked together. Her unease about Scott increased.

"He was purely broken up," Gwen said with a heavy sigh. She impatiently dashed the tears away again and went on.

"Anyway, Jack said Stephen had told him he was really worried about something he'd found, and he had to figure what he was going to do with it. Jack said he asked Stephen if he could report it, and Stephen had said 'not without getting my ass kicked or worse.'"

"Well, that's really important, Gwen," Alex said.

"I thought so too. I'm going to talk with him again this week." Gwen paused, then went on slowly. "I got sort of real worried about him. You know, besides being a special friend of Stephen's and all that, he Jewish. So he's like got a target painted on his back already and then he could know more than he said at a party."

"I'm sure that's right, Gwen. And he wouldn't say too much, would he? Too many people, too many ears. So, speaking of ears, if you do that, when I go see Brownie, I'll also ask about Karns. You know, without letting on about what Stephen told him."

"Anythin' else you can think of?" Gwen asked.

"That Hicks. We need to know more about him."

"But how?" Gwen asked, tension in her voice. "We done want him to know we checkin' on him."

"I can call my family in New York. He came from there, and there are always rumors in the city about cops. Lots of the cops in New York are corrupt. Some of them are really just another criminal gang. Everybody knows it. I'll ask my mother and aunt."

Gwen sipped again and sighed.

"Okay, but tell'em to be careful."

"Yes, of course," Alex replied neutrally, but she thought to herself, when it comes to cops, they always are.

"And when are we going on a real run?" Miss Bea thought from under the table.

13

SUNDAY, JANUARY 29, 1961, MORNING

Alex gave the long distance operator her family's phone number and listened to the clicks as the call was put through. This Zenith service that still used an operator for long distance was cheaper than the new direct calling, and the only thing her family would accept when Alex insisted they get a phone. A party line was out of the question, she had told them flatly. She wanted to be sure her calls with them were not overheard, and especially their calls with union or party colleagues were private. Alex now paid the phone bill over their protests. She had argued she needed to be able to hear their voices when she'd gone away to college, and they had both agreed. Well, her aunt had agreed when her mother had teared up over being able to hear her daughter's voice.

A final click gave way to a buzz, and the phone was answered.

"*Mit*??" her Aunt Kitti yelled into the phone. Not "Hello" in Hungarian but "What??" Kitti still regarded the phone as a potential spy in their apartment. Well, Alex thought, with wiretaps possible she might not be wrong about that, but she replied in a normal tone of voice.

"Aunty, it's me, Alex."

"*Mi a baj*?" Kitti shouted back. "What's wrong?" Of course she'd think something was wrong. Well, in a sense, she's right to ask that, Alex thought as she translated the words to herself, but it's not a good idea to share too much about that right now.

"Nothing," Alex replied. "Speak English, okay? I am not so good at Hungarian anymore."

But Alex was speaking to dead air, and she could hear her Aunt explaining in Hungarian to her mother that "Alexandra is on the phone. I do not know what is wrong."

"Alexandra?" her mother's sweet voice came over the line like a balm to Alex. "*Mi a baj?*"

"No, Mama, nothing is wrong. *Semmi baj nincs.* Really, nothing is wrong. I called to tell you and Aunty I am coming home for a visit next weekend."

Dead air again. Alex sighed. She could hear the exchange clearly as her mother and aunt conferred in Hungarian.

"So, she say what is wrong?"

"No, she's coming home."

"Yes, but what is wrong?"

Calling was a mistake, Alex reflected as she waited, but she had been afraid a letter might not get to them in time to answer, and she had plans for her New York visit besides Stephen's funeral.

"Alexandra," her aunt began, coming back on the line. "Listen, Aunt Kitti!" Alex broke in with a louder voice before her aunt could get going again. "I am coming home to visit, but I do have a question. You understand? A question. And when I visit I want to find out more. *Megért?* You understand?"

"I understand. You no take that talk with me. English I speak all day. So what is question?"

"There's a cop here in Washington where I work. A bad cop. He used to be in New York. Peter John Hicks. When I come visit I want to talk to people about him. Find out what he did in New York."

"Ptui! Ptui!," Alex heard. Her aunt was spitting into the phone.

"You do know who he is?" Alex ventured.

"*Rohadék*!! Ptui! Ptui!"

Bastard, Alex translated in her head. Seems like she does know him.

"Okay, Aunty. Okay. I need to meet with some people who can tell me about him when I come. Next Saturday. Understand?"

"Yes, yes, understand. Two priests in Greenwich *falu*, you know, the what you call it, Vill-edge, and one of the mens writes for newspapers. They know. They know. I go see them. Tell them you come. Make a time for talking."

"Thank you, Aunty. I love you," Alex said, missing her terribly. "Let me talk to Mama too, okay."

"*Szerelmem*, you coming, see us?" Her mother always called her "my love" in Hungarian, and Alex's eyes welled up with tears. Her mother's

English was not as good as her aunt's as she preferred to stay quiet at the shop and make beautiful hats.

"Yes, *szerelmem*, I am coming to see you. Good-bye, darling."

Alex hung up, wrung out from the emotion of hearing their voices. Then she called out to Gwen who had gone to her room to give Alex privacy for the call.

"Gwen, Gwen, have I got things to tell you."

Miss Bea licked her lips, remembering the cream cakes Alex's Mama would give her.

"Let's go now!" Bea thought.

* * *

After the call with her aunt and her mother, Alex thought reading back issues of *The Village Voice* would be useful before she met with one of their reporters. The main Washington library might have those, she thought.

Alex consulted her bus guide and discovered on a Sunday she'd need to take three buses to get from her Georgetown neighborhood to Mount Vernon Square where the Carnegie Library, the beautiful, central public library in Washington, was located.

She also knew that the main library was open on Sunday afternoons. The guidebook she had bought when she'd moved to Washington had stated in its description that during WWII the main library had changed its hours to remain open on Sunday afternoons. The reason had been to provide a place for the thousands of servicemen who came through the city to have a place to go besides the bars. After the war, it still remained open for a few hours on Sunday.

After several hours, she alighted from the last bus and started walking up 9th Street. The striking, Beaux-Arts architecture of the main library building came in to view. It could have been picked up from a boulevard in Paris, she imagined and set down here. Large, curved top windows ran all along the façade, and a carved cornice topped it all the way around. The white marble looked stained in places, but it still dominated its surroundings like so many DC buildings did.

She walked on past the stately Victorians that lined the wide street. They had clearly become multi-family dwellings as the neighborhood had declined. The wrought iron fencing around what once must have been cultivated front yards was damaged in places, and most of the weed-strewn gardens had trash blowing around in them. The books had a far more beautiful place to live than the human beings, she thought with a rising anger.

You can build these imperial piles, she reflected grimly as she walked up the wide, marble stairs to the main door, but it doesn't help struggling people if they don't have a decent place to live.

Alex pushed on the huge, decorated bronze door and entered. She glanced around the dimly lit, cavernous space and then headed toward a desk clear across the room behind which an older woman sat stamping a pile of books. Then she flinched. The tap, tap, tap of the leather soles of her good pumps were loudly announcing her progress as she walked across what seemed to be a quarter of a mile of lobby.

There's no need to be nervous, she assured herself. It's just some research. But she felt the threat of Hicks with every tap.

The woman seated at the large desk stopped stamping and smiled at her and Alex smiled back. The name plate on the desk identified her as "Miss Cunningham." It should have said, "Typical Librarian." Grizzled, gray hair was pulled into a topknot from which several pencils poked out. Reading glasses on a chain rested on the front of a washed-out, flowered blouse with a high, Victorian collar.

Despite the welcoming smile, Miss Cunningham's faded blue eyes regarded Alex sharply. Probably assessing my capacity for damaging books, Alex thought wryly as she passed over her identification card. The reading glasses were immediately put to use.

"Miss Bell, welcome to the Carnegie Public Library. Just fill out this registration form, and I will give you a card."

Since there was no one else in the echoing space, Alex stood at the desk and quickly filled out the form and passed it back.

"Do you need any help finding things?" Miss Cunningham asked briskly.

"Yes, I do. Thank you. I would like to read back copies of a newspaper called *The Village Voice* that is published in New York City. Would you have those and where would I find them?" Alex asked.

"Yes, we do have bound volumes of those." Miss Cunningham did not even need to consult a card catalogue. "You'll find them on Lower Level Five. You can take those stairs over there," she said briskly and pointed.

Alex nodded her thanks and tap, tap, tapped her way across the marble floor toward the staircase.

* * *

The Village Voice had not proved difficult to find. The library carried bound copies of all the issues, back to the inception of the paper in 1955. There were six volumes in total. She carried over the dusty volumes one at a time, using a handkerchief to keep the dust off of her dark blue dress. She placed them on a table in the center of the stacks of other bound newspapers and periodicals. *The Village Voice* was a weekly, paid paper, Alex knew, but individual copies of the paper were passed around through many hands, including those of her family, since it had started.

Alex had assumed that *The Village Voice* publisher, Ed Fancher, was the newsman to which her aunt had referred. He was a crusader for workers' rights and the general well-being of people who lived in the city, especially in the Greenwich Village area.

As she pulled the first volume toward her and started to examine the headlines, she knew it was unlikely in the extreme that any police would be criticized by name in the paper. New York cops could be very vindictive when their bad behavior was brought to light. That was also true for any paper openly criticizing the Mafia. Not a good idea. And the rumors in her family's circle were that many of the really bad police were also "Maffia," the Hungarian word for Mafia. Still, there were ways journalists got around that, and Alex began to look for patterns in stories that somehow might involve the police.

Right away she began to see articles by Francher and others about the rise of drug addiction in the Village and calls for the city to deal with the problem of the huge flow of drugs coming into the Italian South Village in particular. Articles claimed that drug dealers "peddled their goods at Sheridan Square and at the intersection of Carmine and Bedford Streets" with impunity. What was not stated, but clearly implied was "Why don't the police arrest the drug dealers, not the addicts who are the victims?" A reader might conclude the police and the drug peddlers, and their suppliers, likely the Mafia, had an arrangement.

Alex made a note to ask her aunt's contacts about Hicks and the Mafia. Tricky subject, though, she thought.

She kept flipping pages and saw several pieces by a Reverend Howard Moody of Judson Memorial Church about the suffering of heroin users and addicts. I wonder if that's the "priest" my aunt was talking about, Alex reflected as she began to read the article. To her aunt, all clergy were priests, even Protestant ones.

Rev. Moody continually decried the punitive approach of city officials and police alike, and he advocated more treatment for addicts.

She also began to see some more recent articles about a "Captain Michael De Luca" who had just been promoted to Captain because of his work on the New York City police force as a "reformer." Alex wondered if the timing of Hicks's transfer from New York to Washington could have had something to do with the promotion of De Luca and his work on reform. She made another note on her pad. There was a recent interview with De Luca, and Alex made some more notes. He was "one of us," Harry Dowd, the interviewer, had begun the article. De Luca had been born in Brooklyn into an Irish Catholic family, the oldest of six children.

Lavish praise had followed. De Luca had been a "brilliant student' in high school, so much so that he had gotten a scholarship to Fordham University, a Jesuit school. His mother, in particular, had wanted him to become a doctor or a lawyer, De Luca was quoted as saying, but he had quietly taken the test for the New York City Police Academy.

"There was quite a row about that for a time, but I know they are proud of me," he was quoted as saying.

When Alex had finished reading, she carefully returned the volumes to the stacks. As she put on her coat and hat and gathered up her pad and pencil, she wondered how difficult it would be to get an appointment with Captain De Luca when she was in New York City. Could I pose as a reporter? she wondered to herself as she climbed the flights back to the lobby.

Alex stopped at the desk and thanked Miss Cunningham. As she tap, tap, tapped back cross the lobby toward the main door, she saw one other patron was now using the library. The man had glanced up as her footsteps echoed and then quickly back down to the reading table on the far side of the room.

Odd, Alex mused as she walked away. The man had still been wearing his hat and coat while he sat and read.

14

MONDAY, JANUARY 30, 1 AM, TIDAL BASIN

"Can't we f'kin meet in a coffee shop?"

"You are such a pussy. What did she do?"

"Went to the library for Christ's sake. I asked the old bat library lady what she'd looked up and the bat gave me this look like my old lady used to like I was dirt and told me it was none of my business. Wanted to reach over the desk and give her what for. Shit."

"How are we coming on that wiretap on their phone?"

"Gotta watch out for that damn dog. Barks like a machine gun when I come to the door. Figure when they go to work knock that dog out again."

"No wait. It could tip them off. Just watch them for now."

15

MONDAY, JANUARY 30, 1961

"Finally, a long run," Miss Bea thought as Alex cleaned her paws. They had run for miles along the canal path, but toward the north so there had been no chance for Bea to check out the place where she had uncovered what she still considered "her" find. She reminisced about that smell as she ate her dog food. "So interesting."

Alex sat by herself at the little kitchen table lost in thought while she drank some of the left-over coffee that Gwen had made at dawn. Gwen was gone now, but she had been up when Alex and Bea were getting ready to go for their run.

At Alex's questioning look about her being up, Gwen had hunched over her coffee.

"They'll purely let me go, if I done start workin' again. Get there early, make a show of catching up on work. It'll be hard, God knows, but there'll be talk and such, so I can listen, see if anybody knows anything."

Alex had nodded while thinking just how hard that would be for Gwen to try to listen out for gossip about Stephen.

But then Gwen's narrow shoulders had drooped even lower.

"I called Mama yesterday while you was out. She said she'd had a letter, come on Saturday. Stephen's body will be released, prob'ly Wednesday. Mama will have it sent to that church in Harlem so the homegoin' is gonna happen. Sunday. Like we thought."

"I'll come, Gwen, like I said."

Gwen had nodded, and a tear had appeared on her smooth cheek, a cheek that was visibly thinner than it had been only a week or so ago.

As Alex sipped the re-heated coffee after the run, she made a mental list of things she wanted to do before going to New York late Friday night. I should call that columnist and go see her was her first thought. Alex had felt very out of her depth with Brownie, but she had basically liked her. Truth be told, she smiled as she went to shower and then to select her armor for the day, she had liked Higgy too.

Alex chose a high-collared, long sleeved silk and wool shirtwaist. It was a silvery grey with tiny, pearl buttons down the bodice. A slim, black belt emphasized her very small waist, and the dress had a moderately full skirt. But when she looked in the mirror, she realized the dress hung on her.

My waist is getting a little too small, she thought. She took the dress off and with a few expert stitches, cinched the sides of the bodice and waist in.

I'd better eat something before I go, she thought. I don't want to have to alter other clothes. She went into the kitchen and fixed a piece of toast. She nearly finished it. She gave the unfinished piece to Miss Bea who appreciated the gesture.

Alex arrived at the Senator's office a little early, but like the previous week, while the door had been open, the office seemed to be empty. No Alistair, no Mrs. Anderson, and the Senator's door was shut.

She hung her coat in the closet, put her hat on the shelf above, and changed out of her low boots into her good pumps. There was a small mirror inside the closet door, and she used it to pat down her hair, though it scarcely needed it. She'd chosen to go with a chignon, a loose bun that gathered her thick hair down the back of her head, as it went well with the high collar of her dress.

Alex gathered up the mail from the box by the door and sat down to start opening it.

"Oh, very good Miss Bell, you're already here," crooned the Senator from behind her. Alex turned to see Senator Carpenter. She was speaking from inside her office, and the interior seemed dim. "Please let that wait and come in."

"Certainly, Madam Senator," Alex had said immediately. She grabbed her pad and pencil and walked briskly toward the voice.

Oh, I cannot stand it was Alex's first thought as she peered through the gloom of the office interior and saw what the Senator was wearing. Today she was in an eggplant purple suit, pearls in place but looking rather purple against the, heaven help it, purple, ruffled blouse that peeked out at the top of the suit jacket. Alex did not want to look down but could not stop herself. Yes, there were eggplant purple shoes. And why does she keep the overhead lights off so frequently? Alex wondered.

She stifled a sigh and again waited for the Senator to be seated before she took a chair. All that purple in the darkened room made the Senator hard to see. She appeared to be a white face with a brown helmet floating around the desk. When the white face lowered, Alex assumed the Senator had seated herself, and she sat down as well.

"Poor Mr. Carrington is ill again, I'm afraid," the Senator said without a trace of empathy. The tone indicated that Mr. Carrington was proving to be a disappointment.

I must not get sick, Alex said to herself, but she put a sympathetic look on her face.

"I therefore have another assignment for you, Miss Bell." She reached over to the side of the desk, snapped on a green-shaded desk lamp and pulled a file in front of her.

"I will need you to go to a hearing today of the Senate Subcommittee on the Investigation of the National Security Act. That is a subcommittee of the Judiciary Committee. It will be in the new Senate Office building at 10:30 a.m."

Alex could see the Senator was squinting down at a file. Then she raised her head and glared at her.

"Do you know what the National Security Act is?"

Well, Alex thought, my aunt has raged against it for a decade, but I'd better not say that.

"Yes, Madam Senator, I do. We studied that Act, passed in 1950, in my first government class. For example, that Act provided that an organization that has Communist leanings can be ordered to register with the Attorney General."

The Senator nodded approvingly and gestured with her plump, very white hand for Alex to go on.

"Of course, it made it illegal to establish a totalitarian dictatorship in the United States. That was a good step." And Alex actually thought that it was.

Another approving nod.

Should I go on? Alex wondered to herself. Probably best to at least bring up President Truman's opposition to parts of that Act.

"And finally," she went on in as neutral a voice as she could manage, "it gave the President the power to arrest and detain people who might be suspect of undermining the government," Alex went on without much intonation, rather like she was reciting in a class. "I believe President Truman opposed that provision that amounted to preventative detention, correct?"

"Well, yes, yes he did," the Senator concurred, but she didn't look happy about it. Her brown eyes narrowed in a frown that brought the many wrinkles on her face into play, creating craters of face powder, magnified by the greenish light from the lamp. Alex focused on those craters to try to keep from reacting to what she suspected might be coming.

"But, Miss Bell, it is extremely important with this awful Cuban revolution that we get even more tough on Communism here in our country as quickly as we can. Such things can spread, you know, and perhaps infect the Puerto Rican community, for example."

Infect? Alex thought indignantly, but she kept quiet.

"FBI Director J. Edgar Hoover is testifying, and as you know he has been very vigorous in rooting out secret Communists in our country and especially in our government. Very vigorous. Such an outstanding public servant."

Alex remembered First Lady Eleanor Roosevelt had forcefully disapproved of Director Hoover to the point where it became publicly known she thought of his FBI as the "American Gestapo."

So if it is such a treat to have Hoover testifying, Alex thought, still trying to tamp down her anger, I wonder why the Senator isn't going?

It was as though the Senator had read her mind, and she coughed a little.

"I would go myself, of course, but again I have important constituents visiting here." She paused and gave Alex what Alex assumed the Senator thought was an approving smile, showing her very even teeth. It did little to calm Alex, since her own fury at the idea of preventative detention was of long-standing.

"And you did such a wonderful job on your last assignment that I thought you would do wonderfully well on this one."

Wonderful, Alex thought derisively, but she tried to keep her face blank.

"So take careful notes and write them up. I do not know if I will do another letter to my constituents, but I think I will. The people of my state are patriots through and through."

Alex simply sat and said nothing to that.

Finally the Senator spoke into the silence, "Well, very good. You may go."

Alex nodded and left.

This is getting harder and harder, she thought as she returned to her desk.

* * *

Alex arrived much earlier at the Senate Office Building than the last time she'd been there, got her badge without incident and took the elevator to the top floor.

The cleaner who had helped her find the women's cloakroom the last time was again flicking a cloth at the window sills. She came down the hall as Alex got off.

"Hello, honey," was her cheerful greeting.

"Hello, ma'am," Alex said politely. "My name is Alex, by the way. Nice to see you again."

"I'm Maisie," the cleaner chuckled, her round face breaking into a lovely smile. Her wrinkles still seemed to radiate out like a star burst. Unlike the Senator's frown lines, Alex couldn't help thinking, still angry at the Senator for her attitude toward detention.

"You back again, hey? That's good." Maisie was saying approvingly. "But go on now, girl. Done be late."

"Thanks," Alex said, warmly. "I won't." And after depositing her coat and hat in the cloakroom, she took the elevator to the second floor and entered the assigned room a little more confidently than her last visit. Seeing one friendly face in the cavernous building had given her a tiny boost.

The room for this Senate sub-committee meeting was larger than that in which the committee had met. That's probably because of Hoover testifying, Alex thought as she looked at the set-up of the room. There was a dais at one end and a table with six chairs facing it. More experienced now, she chose a seat along the wall, but further toward the front so she would be able to see the FBI Director's face as he spoke.

She sat, got out her notebook and pencil, looked at the raised dais with the Senators' name plates and started writing them down. Many of the Senators had already taken their seats.

"Hello, your Highness," Frank Scott said, taking a seat next to her.

Alex wasn't as startled this time. She realized she had half been expecting to see Scott at this particular hearing.

"Hello, Mr. Scott," she said calmly.

"Frank, remember?"

"Yes, Frank."

Just then there was a minor commotion at the door, and Director Hoover and a contingent of what were surely FBI agents entered.

They are all dressed identically in the same ill-fitting black suits with the same haircut, Alex thought, chuckling a little to herself. All they lack is having "FBI" tattooed on their foreheads. She counted the number of men accompanying Hoover. Eight. Two of them took seats at the table in front of the Senators, one on each side of the Director. The others sat directly behind.

"First time you've seen Hoover in person?" Frank whispered into her ear.

She nodded, as the Chairman, Senator Hayden Bartlett, a Democrat from Minnesota, was gaveling the meeting to order. He then asked the Director to rise.

He's shorter than I am, Alex thought with some shock as Hoover stood for the swearing in. Hoover had loomed so large as an enemy in her childhood and youth that she had pictured him as very tall.

Not only is he short, Alex thought, he's also pudgy. She lowered her head so no one would see her smile. She made a mental note to be sure to tell her aunt all about that.

Hoover sat down, put on wire-rimmed glasses and started to read from a prepared document. Alex flipped open her pad.

"The Com—on—ist Party," he began.

Alex looked up. The what? she thought. Hoover had swallowed parts of the word "Communist." It was peculiar, but was it on purpose?

"Are far better organized than were the Nazis. . ." Hoover rolled on, offering absolutely no evidence that this was true.

"They want to weaken America, just like they wanted when they were aligned with the Nazis."

Good grief, Alex thought, raising her head from her pad and glaring at the round, self-satisfied face of Hoover as he bulleted out these lies. Some members of the Communist party in Germany under the Nazi regime formed part of the resistance to Hitler, Alex thought indignantly. He's lying, she thought, looking at Hoover's smug face.

Alex wrote Hoover's lying words down, but her hand shook a little. This was horrible.

"Com-on-ism," Hoover went on, "is not a political party. It is a way of life. An evil and malignant way of life more like a disease. It spreads like a disease, like an epidemic, and like an epidemic it must be contained in a quarantine to keep it from infecting this nation."

Alex's hand was trembling even more, but she wrote down the hateful words.

"America is still vulnerable to this infection with the Com-on-ist Castro right on our shores. At our very doorstep. And make no mistake. This is the same infection as the Fifth Columnists within our borders."

Hoover finished up his remarks by effectively repeating this string of lies several more times, varying the words only slightly. Alex concentrated on her pad, adding a few words to what she had already written, but her mind was in turmoil. There is no possible way I will write this up for the Senator, she thought. She realized she had no idea how she was going to finesse that, and she stopped taking notes.

The Senators began to question Hoover, and it just sounded like radio static to Alex until she dimly heard Senator Clarke, a prominent Democrat from New York, actually challenge Hoover. She bent over her pad again.

"Now, Director Hoover," Senator Clarke intoned in a carrying voice, "I read your confidential reports to the Congress and in fact your FBI has done a fine job of policing, either rounding up these Communists or driving them out of the country. By your own reports, there are very few if any organized Communist organizations remaining. Now, I don't think sending the American people into a panic, so they look for non-existent Communists under every bed is a good idea. I think the FBI should just continue its fine work and monitor the situation. What is your response, sir?"

Alex rapidly captured every word of what Senator Clarke was saying and knew she would use that for her draft letter for Senator Carpenter. The subtext was clearly that this Democratic administration did not want another Republican political witch hunt to get started.

Hoover coughed and leaned over to the man on his left, and they conferred softly before Hoover sat up and replied.

"Thank you, Senator Clarke, and yes, our agency has done fine work. We want it to stay that way and that means being more aggressive. You know we have rooted out many Com-on-ists in the government, and we have gotten rid of the kind of deviants vulnerable to Com-on-ist blackmail."

Oh, heavens, Alex thought. He means the homosexuals. She did not write that part of his reply down.

Senator Clarke interrupted.

"My point, exactly, Mr. Hoover. That work has been done. Policies on hiring and supervision have been firmed up. Again, I say the FBI should be duly proud of its work and not throw the American people into a panic when so much has already been accomplished. Just continue that good work, will you?"

The Chairman, another astute Democrat, Alex concluded, saw fit to gavel the hearing to a close at that point, thanking Hoover profusely for coming.

Alex kept writing in her shorthand, trying to get every word down accurately that Senator Clarke had said.

She was breathing like she had run five miles when she finished.

"Lunch?" Frank Scott asked quietly from her side.

Yes, I'd better talk to him some more, Alex thought, stopping her furious note-taking.

"Thank you, Mister, I mean Frank, I'd love to," Alex said softly and put away her pad.

Aunty is right. Hoover is a horrible man, Alex ruminated as she walked toward the door, Frank close on her heels.

And he's short and pudgy, she reminded herself as she saw the FBI contingent walking away down the hall in front of her. Hoover was in the center of the group of tall agents. From the back he looked like a garden gnome incongruously set down in a forest of sequoias.

But it doesn't make him less dangerous, she thought grimly.

16

MONDAY, JANUARY 30, 1961

Alex shivered as they left the Senate Office Building. She and Frank automatically turned west with the herd of staffers all headed to Ptomaine Row for a quick lunch. She felt chilled to the bone, and she knew it was not just the west wind carrying the raw, wet cold of DC winter weather that knifed right through any outer garment.

Alex was deeply afraid, and she wrapped her arms around her torso to still the shakes. Hoover, that boogey-man of her childhood and youth, she had just learned, was a real monster, worse than she had ever imagined.

Frank coughed, and Alex realized she had nearly forgotten he was there.

"So, I take it you want to just grab something at one of the sandwich places down the next block?"

His voice seemed carefully neutral, like he was trying not to spook her into running away. As he spoke, he moved slightly ahead of her and turned. Alex became aware he was using his broad, tall frame to shield her a little from the wind. He must have noticed the shakes, Alex thought. I better get control of myself.

"All I have time for, really," Alex replied, trying for a casual tone and at the same time catching up to walk next to him. "I have to get back and somehow make what we heard in that hearing into a letter the Senator can send to her constituents." She managed the semblance of a laugh. "It will not be easy."

Frank moved back to her side and silently took her arm. Alex managed not to shiver. Well, not much anyway.

The real problem, Alex thought, the hearing still on her mind while she and Frank walked in silence, is that Americans should panic at Hoover's views. He'd like to lock up anyone he disagrees with. Or worse.

They crossed the street and went in to the second, small eatery along the way. A sign over the door read "Pete's" in faded, red lettering. Frank held the door for Alex and, as she entered, the smell of frying onions nearly gagged her. The small diner was the width of about two train cars. A counter with stools ran all along the left side, and a row of small booths, upholstered in cracked and faded red vinyl, ran along the other. Every seat at the counter was taken.

Frank dropped her arm and moved swiftly toward one of the booths that was just opening up. His big body cut through the milling crowd quite easily.

Football player? Alex wondered as she watched Frank maneuver. Then he waved her over, and she walked toward him.

Alex looked dubiously at the small bench seat of the now empty booth, but to her surprise it did not appear greasy. The same with the vinyl covered table-top. She slid into the booth, still wearing her coat. She continued to feel bone-deep cold, but she did remove her hat and place it beside her on top of her handbag.

"Meet with your approval, your Highness?" Frank asked as he wedged his big body on to the opposite bench. He'd already hung his coat and hat on the coat rack at the side of the booth.

"It is perfectly fine, thank you," Alex said almost by rote and Frank huffed out a small laugh as he handed her a menu.

"The sandwiches are good. I'd recommend the grilled cheese," he said, putting aside his own menu.

Alex felt her stomach recoil at the idea of cheap, runny, yellow cheese on white bread. The smell of fried grease had only gotten stronger as they'd moved further into the small establishment, and she felt a rising nausea. She swallowed and then saw Scott looking at her in concern.

"Turkey sandwich for me," she managed to say softly, holding in the bile. "Just plain, please. No mayonnaise, tomato or lettuce. And no cheese." She thought she could just slide the turkey into a napkin when Frank wasn't looking and put it in her purse to take home for Miss Bea.

Frank gave their orders to the waitress who appeared almost by magic when he raised his hand. The more handsome the man, the quicker the service, Alex thought wryly and took a sip of one of the waters the waitress had brought them so quickly. It made her feel a little better.

"So, your Highness, how are you really?" Frank asked, bending solicitously toward her.

The table was so small that Alex felt trapped again. He really was so big. She leaned back before she could stop herself.

Scott must have sensed he was crowding her, and he sat back up straight. He took a moment to unbutton his suit jacket to give her some time.

Another bespoke suit, Alex thought involuntarily. Two-piece gray, wool herringbone. Focusing on clothes always soothed her. She took another moment to think how she could get information about him that was more than the cost of his clothes. And without giving too much away.

"I'm sad, really," she said slowly, putting her napkin in her lap and stroking it smooth. "I find I am so despondent about Stephen Gray and, really, how he died like that. I had only met him once, but he seemed like such a fine young man."

"We all miss him around the offices," he said, gazing at her with what appeared to be concern. His firm jaw was a little softer as he said this, but with a small jolt she realized the scar on his forehead was more visible, his hair having blown back in the wind, exposing it. It was much larger than she had originally thought. I wonder what happened? she mused, then registered that Scott was speaking again.

"Do you know when and where the funeral will be?" he asked.

No harm in telling him that, Alex reflected. Gwen will tell his colleagues at State.

"Yes, I do," Alex said. "It's this Sunday at noon at the 132nd Street Baptist Church in Harlem."

"Really?" Scott said, not managing to keep the tone of surprise out of his voice.

Alex frowned at his response.

He looked at her and seemed to register how inappropriate that must have sounded. He looked away and started feeling around in his jacket pocket for a little pad and pencil. He took time to write it down.

Alex watched him silently.

Where did he think it would be? she thought derisively as she watched him scribble down the information, the National Cathedral? But she quickly realized her real anger was still at Hoover.

Their meal was delivered, and she took advantage of the interruption to tamp down her irritation.

I need to get information at this lunch, not just some turkey for Miss Bea, she cautioned herself as she thanked the waitress.

She took another sip of water and waited until Scott had a mouthful of grilled cheese.

"I am sure his sister Gwen will let his colleagues at the State Department know, but could you make doubly sure both Duncan Connors and Jack Karns are aware? I am under the impression that they were particular friends of Stephen's. Well, in addition to you, of course," she said, giving him one of the "gaze up through your eyelashes while giving a tremulous smile" looks that she'd learned at Smith.

Frank just nodded, struggling to swallow the gooey cheese.

Alex really did smile then, but only to herself.

Frank took a sip of his own water, and Alex pushed ahead with her questions.

"I've never met either of them. What are they like?" she asked, watching Scott swallow his water and timing her next remark.

"They must be fine men to have been Stephen's close friends," she added.

"Yes, well, they are, of course," Scott fumbled a little.

"In what ways?" Alex gently persisted.

"Well, now, Connors, he was born in England. Parents immigrated here when he was a kid. Smart, smart guy. He and Stephen met at Harvard Law, I think. Funny pair, though," Scott said, reaching again for his sandwich.

"In what way?" Alex jumped on the remark, leaning forward a little, but careful to avoid leaning on the turkey sandwich with the clearly stale bread still sitting untouched on her plate.

"Well, I mean you know," he said, hesitating.

Alex just looked meltingly at him, saying nothing.

Scott put down the uneaten piece of his sandwich.

"I mean Connors, with that British accent, he's really a popular guy with the ladies around town, and Gray was you know, not like that. But they really got along."

Scott bent his head over his plate, and Alex took that moment to slide half her sandwich into the napkin on her lap.

More chewing from Scott.

Good, Alex thought. That awful cheese is helping me out here.

"And Jack Karns?" she asked sweetly, giving him a lower-wattage version of the eyelashes, tremulous smile routine.

Scott coughed and took a sip of water.

"Well, Karns, fine person of course. Fine military record. He and Stephen were, well, closer if you get my drift."

"I think I do," Alex said softly.

Scott turned his attention back to his plate, and Alex slipped the second half of the sandwich onto the napkin.

"Were there tensions around the departments that you heard about?" Alex asked as he was chewing again.

He coughed.

I better be careful, Alex cautioned herself silently. He could choke.

"What do you mean?" Scott breathed out when he could speak again.

"Oh, you know, I'm just curious about any tensions there." She paused and then looked up with a glare, clearly startling Scott.

"Somebody murdered him. Somebody knows why," she said coldly.

"Well, I don't know anything about any tensions," Scott said defensively. "Certainly none that would lead to murder," he said, but he glanced back down at his plate when he said it.

Alex just looked at him, but under the table she wrapped up the sandwich in the napkin. When she had it secure, she slipped it into her coat pocket, took hold of her hat and bag, and slid smoothly out of the bench.

"If you think of anything, please do let me know," she said evenly. "You can leave a message for me at the Senator's office."

She took out the correct amount of money from her purse for her share of the lunch and put it on the table.

"Good-bye," she said and immediately walked away.

Scott sat back in the booth, watching her back.

"Call you? Yeah," he said quietly. "Yeah. I might just do that."

But he was talking to himself. Alex was already out the door.

* * *

Alex was alone in the Senator's office, studying her notes from the hearing and wracking her brain for a way to draft the letter for the Senator's constituents without having her own head explode.

Mrs. Anderson had stood up at her desk immediately when Alex opened the door.

"The Senator does not like the office unattended, so I will get my lunch now," she huffed a little, and Alex had stood aside while she grabbed her coat and bag and departed rapidly.

Alex never thought she'd miss Alistair, but without him they were seriously understaffed.

"Dear Friends," she typed. "I am so pleased to write to you again with some more good news. Today at a Senate sub-committee hearing, our own Democratic Senator Clarke praised Mr. J. Edgar Hoover, the Director of the Federal Bureau of Investigation, who had been invited to testify, for his fine work in rooting out Communists and Fifth Columnists in our country over the last years. It is clear from the hearing that our country is very secure from any attempt to undermine our way of life. The Director thanked the Senator for his praise. 'Carry on the good work!' was the message the Director received, and I am pleased to pass that on to you. I am confident we have fine leadership protecting us in these times."

Alex paused and then started a new paragraph.

"I have been delighted to host a number of you here in Washington in recent weeks, and I would like to thank" and Alex stopped typing.

I will have to ask the Senator if she wants to share the names of the "important constituents" she's been meeting, of course, Alex thought, but she considered it a wise addition.

She carefully checked her document for errors and finding none she took it out, put the flimsy copy in a file along with the draft letter and took out a piece of notepaper. She wrote a note asking the Senator if she would like to thank the constituents who had been visiting, and she put the file with the attached notes on top of Mrs. Anderson's inbox for the Senator.

Alex turned her attention to the constituent letters and was amused that a couple of them were now addressed directly to Fluffy, asking questions about various pieces of legislation they had heard were being considered. Fluffy, of course, continued to be very knowledgeable and full of praise for Senator Carpenter.

Be careful, Alastair, she thought as she pulled another piece of the Senator's stationary toward her. You are in danger of being replaced by an ugly cat.

She was so engrossed in writing these replies that it seemed but a short time before a windblown Mrs. Anderson returned.

Alex greeted her and pointed to the file she had compiled. She explained the Senator would want it right away.

"Mrs. Anderson, do you mind if I run out to the ladies cloakroom for a moment?" she asked deferentially.

"No dearie, of course. Go ahead."

Mrs. Anderson was in much better mood having eaten.

Alex was not heading to the cloakroom, but to the pay phone on the corner of Constitution. She had placed Brownie's card and a suitable amount of change in her skirt pocket in preparation for running out when Mrs. Anderson returned. She was grateful for the skirt's flowing shape and for her forethought in putting nearly invisible pockets in the seams.

This phone booth was in better condition than the one in her own neighborhood, Alex reflected as she reached it. When she opened the door, it did not smell all that bad. She pulled the door shut to cut the wind. She had come out without a coat in order not to alert Mrs. Anderson of her true errand, and she was shivering again. She quickly deposited the coins and dialed the number on the card.

"*Washington Tattler*, how may I direct your call?" a harried voice answered. "Mrs. Brown, please," Alex requested.

There was a click, and she heard, "Brown here," as Brownie answered in about the same harried tone.

"This is Miss Bell," Alex said.

"Ah, sweetie, I wondered if I'd hear from you," Brownie said, her tone becoming much warmer.

Perhaps a little too warm, Alex thought warily.

"Brownie, I don't have much time. Could we meet for lunch tomorrow?"

"Good, good," Brownie replied quickly, but then went on before Alex could even reply.

"But don't come here to my office. I'll bring some sandwiches and meet you at the Lincoln Memorial around 12:15. That Lincoln, he'll keep us out of the cold, and we can talk."

"Well, alright," Alex concurred, a little taken off guard. But she was not unhappy to be meeting with the columnist where there would be less chance they'd be observed.

"Thank you. I will see you tomorrow," Alex replied. She heard a clipped, "Same here" and Brownie hung up.

When Alex got back to the office, Mrs. Anderson handed her back the file.

"Senator Carpenter approved your letter, and she dictated the names of her important constituents to me. I have them here for you."

Mrs. Anderson seemed pleased that the pecking order in the office had been restored. The message was clear that Mrs. Anderson should be the conduit to the Senator.

"Thank you so much, Mrs. Anderson," Alex replied, taking the materials. "I will have this finished very shortly," she said, and she returned to her desk.

I should have paid more attention to how Mrs. Anderson might feel a little displaced by me, Alex reflected as she rolled more paper and a carbon into her typewriter.

She re-typed her letter and added the constituent names. After a thorough proofreading, she returned the letter and the copy to Mrs. Anderson for the Senator's final approval and signature. Mrs. Anderson merely nodded her frizzled, gray head and took the papers to the Senator's door, knocked and at a murmur went in, closing the door behind her.

Alex returned to her desk and continued advancing Fluffy's legislative career.

* * *

Alex walked wearily up the darkened stairs of the apartment building. But when she reached the landing on the second floor, she heard shouting, and very faint barking. She ran up the next flight and, as she suspected, the noise was coming from their apartment.

The door was slightly ajar, and Alex recognized Hicks's loud voice, yelling presumably at Gwen. When she heard a sharp slap, she pushed open the door and walked in.

"Detective Hicks, Officer Thomas. Do what do we owe the pleasure of this visit?" Alex asked while calmly removing her hat and placing it on the table.

Hicks turned from where he had Gwen cornered on the far side of their small living area, next to the bookcase. She had her hand up to her left cheek where Hicks must just have slapped her, and her eyes were wide with fear. As Hicks turned toward Alex, she glimpsed Thomas, and he slowly shook his head behind Hicks's back, apparently signaling to Alex not to cross Hicks.

Too late for that, Alex thought grimly.

"Well, lookie here, the other slut has come waltzing in," Hicks said nastily, his florid face pulled into a grimace of pleasure as he took a few steps toward her. "Where have you been, you c***? Or should I say, who have you been doing?"

Alex did not reply immediately. She took off her gloves slowly, one finger at a time. Hicks actually stopped and watched. It was like charming a snake, Alex supposed. She placed her gloves next to her hat and turned.

"Actually, Detective, I have just come from a Senate Judiciary Sub-Committee meeting. I was representing Senator Carpenter. FBI Director Hoover was testifying," she said in a calm and measured voice. "I think you personally would have found it informative."

A spasm of rage passed over Hicks's face, though he did not advance further toward Alex. He turned his head and spoke over his shoulder.

"You see, Thomas. This is what comes of letting women off of their backs or out of the kitchen." He turned back to Alex, his enormous stomach heaving under his stained and wrinkled shirt. He was breathing hard. He looked exactly like a bull about to charge. But was he a bull with a leash on, afraid to physically harm a Senator's staffer?

Alex now slowly unbuttoned her coat, never taking her eyes off of Hicks. She took the garment off unhurriedly, folded it, and placed it on the nearest kitchen chair with one hand so she could still look at Hicks.

She could also see Thomas behind his back. His caramel face was mottled with red, and he looked anguished. He thought he knew what was coming.

Maybe, Alex thought. Or maybe not.

Alex had seen her ninety-pound aunt stare down a vicious cop in New York. She had been a teenager at the time, standing across the street holding a sign. She had been terrified her aunt would be badly hurt or even killed by the huge, angry cop who was yelling at her to get out of the street. But her aunt had not moved. Had shown no fear. She had just stood there, a small, immoveable rock. The angry cop had yelled some more and then turned away to yell at someone else.

"So, again, how can we help you, Detective?" Alex asked calmly.

Hicks took a couple of rapid steps toward Alex until he was about three feet away from her. She didn't move. The smell of whiskey proceeded him. He reeked of it.

"Who the hell do you think you are, you lesbo whore? I ought to give you both," and here he swung a big ham of a hand back toward Gwen, "what you should have from a real man."

"I am a legislative aide to a United States Senator, Detective Hicks," Alex said in measured tones.

Threaten me with rape, will you? Alex thought. You need to know you are not the only one with power here.

She went on, fabricating the rest.

"I asked Senator Carpenter if she knew of you, Detective. She said she did not, though she had added that she could ask colleagues should I require that.

"So I repeat, how can we help you?" Alex went on, her eyes never wavering from those of Hicks, though now she had to look up to do it.

"F*** it!" Hicks spat out, some of the spittle actually hitting the floor in front of Alex. She still did not move.

"Come on, Thomas. Total f***** waste of time," Hicks yelled over his shoulder, and he stomped toward the door. His sleeve brushed against Alex's arm, but she had been expecting that too, and she did not move a muscle. Thomas hurried across the room and out the door having wiped all expression from his face.

When Alex heard two sets of footsteps on the stairs, she went and closed the door and put the chain on. Then she collapsed on to the chair with her coat folded on it, not even caring she was wrinkling it.

"Oh, honey. You okay?" Gwen asked as she hurried over.

"I guess so," Alex said shakily. "I just stopped breathing for a minute there."

She looked up at Gwen's face, now swollen a little on one side.

"And you? Did he hit you any place besides your face?" Alex asked, concerned.

"No, I think he was just about to get goin' on me when you showed up. Oh, Alex, that was somethin'."

"No, Gwen. That was my aunt. I've seen her face down an angry cop, and I just did the same."

"Your aunt?" Gwen asked, curiously.

"I'll explain some time, Gwen. Just not now."

She heard another muffled bark.

"Where is Miss Bea?"

"Well, when they started poundin' on the door, that dog pitched a fit. I put her in the closet in your room. Ah thought they might just, you know, hurt the dog to make me talk."

"Oh, Gwen. Thank you," Alex said, a quaver in her voice. That was exactly what Hicks might have done.

Alex went to her room and opened the closet door.

Miss Bea stalked out, outrage in every step.

"I have never been so insulted in my life."

"I brought home a turkey sandwich for you, Bea," Alex said coaxingly.

"I will accept it," Miss Bea acknowledged, and she walked out to the front room with dignity and headed toward Alex's coat.

She could easily smell the turkey.

Oh, my. I sat on that turkey in my coat, Alex thought, and she hurried after Bea.

Miss Bea, as it turned out, did not mind a flattened turkey sandwich, and she ate all of it when Alex placed it in her bowl.

But Miss Bea could eat and think at the same time. "That bad man with the whiskey and the sharp smell of puke came here. I really should bite him."

17

TUESDAY, JANUARY 31, 1961

"A new run today," Miss Bea reflected as she and Alex sped over a long bridge that crossed the river below. Her nose quivered as it drew in the pungent odor of the river even though they were high above it. Most of the ice had broken up and mingled smells rose up to the bridge and clung like a low-lying fog of rotting eggs, dead fish, decaying trash and more.

They left the bridge and started to run down along the river. Dark patches on the water flowing out of pipes gave off a wave of such powerful smells that Bea, who was on a much resented lead, started to pull toward the river.

"No, Miss Bea. Leave it," Alex rapped out as she realized Bea was trying to get to where a pipe was disgorging raw sewage into the river. It smelled putrid.

Alex ran further up the slope, pulling a reluctant Bea with her to get away farther away from the disgusting smell. Really, Alex thought as she pulled Bea away. The farther south, the worse the river looks and smells. It really is just an open sewer.

They continued on the higher path for a short distance and went up a small rise. Alex stopped at the top. Bea looked up at her in surprise. Alex never stopped on a run.

There it is, Alex reflected as she gazed over at the distant Lincoln Memorial shining in the dawn light like an island of purity in the middle of a very dirty town. She thought about her upcoming bag lunch with Brownie in the shadow of Lincoln. She had read a lot both about Lincoln and by Lincoln in her studies, and she had continued to turn to his words when troubled. Lincoln thought that it might be better to live with a "pure" despotism, a government honest about its contempt for people's rights, than to live in a democracy filled with "the base alloy of hypocrisy."

She turned and ran back on the upper path, away from the stinking river, until they could cross the bridge. It seemed to her it was fitting that the stench of this river, a defining feature of Washington, became stronger the closer it flowed toward the capital.

Hoover reeked of hypocrisy, she thought furiously, and her renewed anger made her increase her pace. That was okay with Bea. She rarely got to run as fast as she knew she could.

* * *

Alex stood shivering in the vast, echoing marble chamber of the Lincoln Memorial, partly hidden by the columns that surrounded the great, seated figure. Brownie was not there yet, she had discovered. She knew her away around this building very well. She had visited a few monuments when she had first moved to Washington to share the apartment with Gwen, but visiting Lincoln had been her first stop, and she returned often. She was reading, again, the great words of the Gettysburg Address carved into the marble wall. She rarely bothered reading the Second Inaugural address that was also carved into the opposite wall. Too much wrestling with God, Alex always thought. Alex had given up on God as he seemed to constantly fail humanity. She admired Lincoln for giving it a try, though.

She read the words she always visited first. In a way, they were her substitute divinity, and she whispered the words she wanted to believe, "that government of the people, by the people, for the people, shall not perish from the earth." J. Edgar Hoover did not believe those words Alex was thinking when she heard heavy footfalls behind her.

"There you are, sweetie. Reading old Lincoln, eh?" Brownie said cheerfully as she came up to Alex. She had a kind of rolling walk like she was navigating the deck of a ship in a small squall. With her improbably red hair as smokestack, she could have been a little tugboat. Alex briefly wondered what it looked like when Brownie and Higgy walked side by side, one rolling side to side and the other bobbing up and down.

The rolling, rotund figure of Brownie was somehow reassuring. Alex smiled a welcome.

"Hello, Brownie. Thanks for suggesting meeting here. I like to visit Lincoln." Then she noticed Brownie was carrying a brown paper bag in one arm and a purse that looked big enough to hold her typewriter in the other.

"Here, let me take that," Alex said and reached out and hefted the paper bag. Whatever Brownie had brought for lunch, there was a lot of it.

"You are a nice child," Brownie said. Then she lowered her voice to a whisper.

"Now, follow me and don't speak here. These side corridors echo something awful."

She went on beyond the alcove with Lincoln's carved words and went all the way to the back of the building. There was another, less prominent alcove with a door at the back discretely painted the same color as the marble. Brownie fumbled in her cavernous purse and took out a large ring with some big keys. She inserted the largest key into the lock in the door and turned it. The door opened smoothly. She flipped a light switch on the inside wall, and a set of stone steps burst into view. Brownie started down the stairs, and Alex, totally bemused at this point, followed. The door closed silently behind them.

When they reached the bottom, Brownie turned right and flipped on another switch. It illuminated a relatively ordinary basement except there were dozens of squat pillars, not much shorter than those above, ranged as far as the eye could see, and the ceiling was very high. As Alex gazed up, she could see what she thought were drapes of cobwebs high above. There were cleaning supplies in one area and a card table and folding chairs along a side wall. Brownie moved toward the card table and put her big purse on a chair.

"Put that bag on the table, will you?" she said over her shoulder.

Alex did so, at this point simply shocked into silence.

Brownie turned and chuckled at Alex.

"Oh, honey, if you could only see your face." She held up the keys and jangled them for a moment. "You want to know how I was able to borrow these, right? Well, I did a big favor for a couple of the Park Service guys who keep Lincoln up there all clean and shiny. Those guys are not, shall we say, all clean and shiny. I found out and we did a deal. I can borrow the keys when I want to. They get to keep their jobs. It's a great place for me to meet people when we don't want to be seen or heard."

Brownie turned and tucked the big ring of keys into her giant purse. Then she lowered her bulk into one of the other folding chairs and gestured for Alex to take the one opposite.

"Sit down. Sit down. We don't have that much time. I imagine you need to be back pretty soon."

"Yes, I do," Alex said, amazed that she could form coherent words.

Brownie drew the paper bag toward her and pulled out two waxed paper wrapped sandwiches and two bottles of Coke. She handed a sandwich and a drink to Alex.

"Here. Tuna."

Well, Miss Bea likes tuna, Alex mused, but she did use the opener Brownie passed her. She flipped the cap off of the Coke bottle and took a sip. Her throat was dry. This basement had a lot of dust in it, she realized.

Brownie took a big bite of her own sandwich and started to talk at the same time.

"So, what have you and your roommate been able to find out, eh?" Brownie smiled a tuna fish smile, and Alex tried not to grimace.

She looked down at the cracked, cardboard top of the little table and pretended she was thinking, but she wasn't. She had already planned out what she'd reveal to Brownie and what she would keep secret. She would tell her nothing about the postcard or the photography equipment, or what Lt. Karns had said to Gwen. She would focus on Hicks first.

"That detective, Peter John Hicks, is really after my roommate and me too," she said, looking up, hoping Brownie had finished her bite of tuna.

Brownie nodded her head but kept on chewing.

"Stephen's funeral is in Harlem this weekend. Do you know that?" Alex went on.

Brownie nodded and added around another bite, "Yeah. Can't go my-self, but Higgy might."

"I'm going," Alex said, leaving out her family. "And when I'm in New York, I plan to try to talk to the editor of *The Village Voice*, and perhaps some others, about Hicks. He left the city right as a police reformer came in."

"I knew he'd left," Brownie contributed, "but I didn't know that timing. Good." She took a swig of her own Coke. "Good idea on contacting *The Village Voice*. They really stay on top of New York, especially New York dirt."

Brownie took another swig of her Coke and then cocked her head at Alex while giving her a penetrating look with her little black eyes.

"So, here's the deal," she said crisply. "I want you to come to a cocktail party tonight at the home of Phil and Katharine Graham. You know who they are?" Then she belched and took another bite of her sandwich.

"*Washington Post*, right?" Alex said slowly, hiding her shock at the invitation.

"Yeah. He really is the *Washington Post* now. Editor and publisher. Big deal with Kennedy in office. Wife's a big mover and shaker in her own right, organizing political parties and so forth. Washington runs on cocktail par-ties, really. That's where all the real power is brokered. You need to come and look at these guys with those innocent eyes while you flip that blonde hair around. They'll tell you all the secrets. Me? I listen to conversations, but the men look right through me. You can get them to spill it all."

Brownie crumpled her waxed paper and tossed it into the paper bag, obviously giving Alex time to think.

"So, can you come?" she asked brusquely, clearly a little put off by Alex's continued silence.

"All right," Alex finally said quietly, but she was thinking it was one thing to say she was going to find out who killed Stephen and quite another to actually try to do it.

"Okay then," Brownie said. "You got something to write on in your bag?"

"Yes," Alex said and pulled her pad and pencil out. She took down the address and time Brownie dictated to her.

"Now, lookie. We don't know each other, get it? Higgy arranged that you would get an invitation through Stephenson's office, but you don't know him either. That is, if he shows up. You show up and get those guys to talk to you."

"Which guys?" Alex asked, puzzled. She knew from her Smith days how to flip her hair and look at men under her lashes, but for what purpose?

Brownie sighed.

"You circulate, you listen, you figure out who's talking about the State Department, about tensions there, about DC police and maybe corruption, about Communists or homosexuals or both. But they'll likely not say Communist or homosexual. They'll say 'sympathizers' or 'card carriers' to mean Communists. They won't say homosexuals outright, it's more 'he's that way,' or 'a bit funny,' even 'batting for the other team'. Get it?"

Alex nodded solemnly.

Then Brownie looked at the uneaten sandwich in front of Alex.

"Hey, you gonna eat that or what?" she asked.

"I'll save it for later, if that is okay," Alex said having mentally promised the sandwich to Bea.

"Sure. No problem." Brownie stood up.

"Wait a minute, though," Alex said, and she caught a slight look of alarm on Brownie's face.

"How should I dress?"

Brownie looked relieved at the question and then she gave a small snort of laughter.

"How the hell should I know? Cocktail dress thing, like that. Not too fancy, but you know, elegant. Look up some pictures of Katharine Graham. Dress like that."

She hefted her giant bag on to her shoulder, and Alex picked up the wrapped sandwich and put it in her pocket.

"We gotta get out of here. I promised I'd have the key back before one," and she moved surprisingly quickly up the steep stairs. Alex followed, realizing she'd never look at Lincoln seated above without thinking of this subterranean area, filled with marble dust and Washington secrets.

* * *

Alex hurried back to the office and found Mrs. Anderson just hanging up the phone, her grandmotherly face drooping and tears swimming in her faded blue eyes.

She sniffed into a handkerchief while Alex hung up her coat and hat.

"Is everything all right, Mrs. Anderson?" she ventured, moving over closer to the woman's desk.

"Well, no, not really," Mrs. Anderson said sadly. "That was Alistair's mother. She said she came yesterday from Connecticut to take care of him, and she was alarmed at his condition. He is now in the hospital. They can't seem to figure out what is wrong with him."

She sniffed again.

"He was always such a polite boy," she added, unconsciously using the past tense. "My Jeffrey was taken young," she added and now her face screwed up with grief, the tears spilling over on to her soft, apple cheeks.

"Oh, my," Alex said, walking around the desk and lightly patting Mrs. Anderson on the shoulder. "I am so sorry."

"Well," Mrs. Anderson said, and she made a visible effort to pull herself together, "that was long ago. But it is hard. Just so hard."

Alex went back around the desk and stood silently for a minute, giving Mrs. Anderson a chance to pull herself together.

I should change the subject, Alex thought.

"Should we send flowers from the Senator?" she ventured. "And perhaps add our names too?"

"Oh, yes, of course we should do that," Mrs. Anderson said, brightening and pulling a pad toward her. "We always use that florist over on 22nd Street. And it is near the hospital where he is, too." She made a note.

"I will get the Senator's approval when she returns," Mrs. Anderson added almost to herself as the pencil hovered over her pad. Then she looked up and her gentle features curved into a small smile.

"That was thoughtful, Miss Bell," she said approvingly.

"Of course, Mrs. Anderson," Alex said softly. "Would you like to take your lunch break now? I can manage things here."

"No, no. I will just wait for the Senator to come back."

"Well, then," Alex said. "I will run out for a moment. I need to look something up in the library in this building for one of the Senator's constituents," she lied fluidly. "Am I correct in thinking the small library in this building is on the third floor, toward the back?"

"Yes, that's right," Mrs. Anderson said absently, writing again on her pad. She was muttering the names of various flowers to herself.

Alex was guessing the small library in the building would have back copies of the prominent papers. She needed to find pictures of Mrs. Graham in the society pages.

* * *

Alex had hurried home after work, given Bea a quick walk and then the sandwich.

"Mmm. Tuna," Miss Bea thought as she bent her head over her bowl.

Alex had done a quick wash and then contemplated her closet. The newspapers had not been much help, in the end. When she had looked at photos of Katharine Graham in the style sections, she had been disconcerted to find Mrs. Graham garbed in rather dowdy dresses that had a poor fit. She had wondered why. Mrs. Graham also had not looked particularly happy in any of the photos.

I don't own any dowdy, ill-fitting clothes, she thought wryly. Finally, she pulled out her ice blue, Duchesse silk and satin cocktail dress with the cap sleeves and a fitted waist with a small bow. Her dress was a Givenchy copy, similar to the dresses First Lady Jacqueline Kennedy favored. She couldn't copy Mrs. Graham, but she could copy Mrs. Kennedy.

Now she was on the sidewalk outside the elegant Georgetown home of Philip and Katharine Graham, her heart pounding in her chest. As she looked up at their enormous, ivy-covered, brick mansion, she hoped she had not made a mistake in perhaps being better dressed than her hostess.

She stood there, trying to still her breathing. Then she heard a car pull up on the street in front of the house. She turned and saw a chauffeur get out of the front of a long, black car. Important guests were arriving. She had better proceed, she thought, and get out of the way. She pushed the small garden gate open and ascended the steep steps to the front door. Before she could knock, however, the door was jerked open by a tall, pale, bespectacled man with President Kennedy hair and a wide grin on his face.

"Senator and Mrs. Fulbright!" he called out jovially over her head. "Saw you from the window. Come on in!"

"Coming, Phil," the measured voice she recognized from the Cuba hearing said behind her.

"Well, and hello," the man in the doorway now said, his grin still in place as he looked down at Alex. "And who are you?"

"I am Alexandra Bell. I work for Senator Carpenter and am a guest of Ambassador Stephenson," Alex managed to get out, but the beaming man she assumed was her host, Phillip Graham, just took her arm and partially led, partially pulled her inside, while saying "Fine, fine, that way, won't you?" as he quickly turned back toward his new guests.

"Bill, Harriet, good to see you!" he called boisterously out the door as Alex made her way alone down a long hall.

Harder and harder, she thought again and turned left into what she hoped was a cloakroom.

She was wrong.

Several men looked up from around a billiard table set under a green, rectangular chandelier in a smoke-filled room, but only one turned and came toward her.

"Well, little darlin', you lost?" asked a familiar voice.

It was Higgy.

18

TUESDAY, JANUARY 31, 1961 8 P.M.

Higgy took Alex's arm and guided her out into the hall, closing the door to the billiard room behind him. He kept hold of her arm and led her down the hallway, not speaking. His bouncing walk had disappeared. He handed her smoothly over to a uniformed, Negro maid who took her coat and hat with practiced efficiency, saying "Thank you, ma'am" as she carried them away.

He took her arm again and guided her silently through a swinging door and into a narrow pantry with high, glass-fronted cabinets containing glistening crystal and stacks and stacks of china. A countertop ran along below and below that were more cabinets.

"Butler's pantry," Higgy said shortly. He grimaced a little, his pink lips pursing. "This house was built before the Civil War, and sometimes it seems like the North didn't win, even among these so-called liberals out there," he said derisively, and he jerked a round thumb to indicate a door at the end of the pantry with glass panes in it that Alex had not noticed in the gloom of the narrow space. Now she could see figures moving beyond the door, distorted by the wavy glass.

Gone was Higgy's jovial manner, though he was dressed in a deep emerald velvet jacket trimmed with gold braid, black dress pants, a dark grey, almost black ruffled front shirt and another flag-sized tie. This one was striped green and deep gold. Alex knew something of how one used clothes as a shield, and that, she realized, is what Higgy did.

"You okay?" he asked suddenly, squinting his round eyes under his bushy eyebrows and peering up into Alex's face. She realized she had been staring at him, thinking.

"Yes, yes, I'm fine, really," she said softly.

"Well, you're not," Higgy said, a small smile appearing under his bulbous nose. Alex relaxed a little. The smiling Higgy was not gone.

"That's better," he said, patting her arm. "Now, I'm going to see if I can give you some tips before you head out there. Let's check out a few of the players, okay?"

Alex nodded.

"Good. Good. So be quiet, and we can see what we can see." Fitting words to action, he moved on tip-toe to right behind the wavy, paned-glass door. Alex followed. She was so much taller than he, she could just look over his head as he pointed.

"So, see the woman over there by the fireplace?"

Alex nodded, then realized Higgy couldn't see her.

"Yes," she whispered.

"That's your hostess, Katharine Graham. I'll introduce you when we go in around the other way."

"But," Alex breathed, "Brownie said you and I should pretend not to know each other."

Higgy gave a little snort that made a spot of mist on the glass of the door.

"That Brownie. She loves her cloak and dagger. No, no. It would seem odd if Ambassador Stephenson had put you on the guest list and I didn't know you, at least a little." He glanced over his shoulder at her. "It will be okay."

"But let's wait on that," he said softly, peering out again. "I see Philip has joined Katharine. That's Philip Graham, you know that." He shook his round head sadly. "Phil's got a little problem with being able to, how shall I say it, control his emotions. Up one minute, down the next. Takes it out on poor Katharine."

Alex looked out and saw a medium-height woman with light brown hair, a little overweight, wearing a shapeless, beige dress. She looked like she had dressed to disappear. That was how she had been dressed in the photos in the paper Alex had seen. Mrs. Graham was partially obscured by the tall man who had ushered her so unceremoniously in the front door. She could only see his back, but it was rigid, and his head bent down to his wife. He was gesturing furiously. Not a muscle in her face moved.

"Now, see those two guys over there, by the tall windows with those ghastly, brocade draperies?"

Higgy pointed a plump finger toward the other side of the room.

Alex peered across the sea of people milling around in the silk paneled and gilded room, the walls literally stuffed with gilt-framed paintings from the chair rail to the ceiling cornices. Yes, she mentally concurred when she located them. The draperies were ghastly. She saw two men, deep in conversation, one dark-haired and pinched faced, intensely smoking a cigarette. The other, a slim man with close-cut brown hair, had his back to her. He had his head cocked, listening.

"That's Edward R. Murrow and Eddie Follard. Both reporters. Stay clear of them. You'll get nothing and they'll get everything if you're not careful."

"Murrow," Alex thought. Another hero in her family. The broadcaster who had gone after McCarthy. Good heavens, they call this a party? she thought wonderingly.

"Now, now. That's just Washington," Higgy said, sensing her awe without even turning around. "Don't let it spook you." He peered out the door again and whispered, "Ah."

He pointed out a man standing on the far side of the room, an amber-colored drink in his hand. He had a shock of coal black hair brushed back from his forehead. His olive-toned face was striking, rather than classically handsome. Dark brows slashed below his smooth forehead and his deep set, dark eyes gazed intently at whomever was speaking to him. He was just medium height, but he had a wrestler's physique, very broad shoulders and a barrel chest. He was in a sharkskin, dark grey suit clearly tailored for him. His shoulders and the bespoke suit reminded Alex of Frank Scott.

"That's Captain Michael De Luca, the New York reformer cop. Getting a big reputation. He's here to speak at a DC cops convention on 'Combatting Corruption.'" Higgy snorted. "For all the good that's going to do. Anyway, he's also a big friend of the FBI Director, J. Edgar Hoover. You really need to talk to him. De Luca that is, not Hoover." Higgy's round shoulders shook with a little, silent laugh, then he sobered quickly. "Brownie says you think that De Luca drove that rat Hicks out of New York."

"Yes," she breathed. But she wondered how someone could be a reformer and a friend of Hoover at the same time.

"Okay now, one more," Higgy went on, nose almost pressed to the glass. "That's Lieutenant Jack Karns. The short, slim guy over there in the uniform?"

Alex squinted and saw the uniform. "Yes."

"Brownie says you know he was friendly with Stephen, so see what you can get there. He's with a couple of other guys I think are from State, but I don't know them."

Higgy turned and peered up again into Alex's face.

"So you ready now?" he asked kindly.

Alex realized she had calmed down with Higgy's tutoring, and she was sure that's what he had intended.

"Yes," she said and absently shook her hair back over her shoulders. She'd left it long, per Brownie's instructions.

Higgy chuckled a little at that, patted his own scrawny hair with a wry smile and gestured for her to leave the pantry the way they'd came in.

* * *

"So Katharine darling, how are you?" Higgy asked jovially of the still solemn-faced Katharine Graham. He had made a bee-line for Mrs. Graham when they'd entered the big room, and he had seen she was alone for a moment. He had taken Alex's arm, and she had felt his bouncing walk jiggling her arm all the way across the glittering room.

Katharine Graham gave Higgy a sweet smile.

"Fine, thank you, Bruce," she said warmly, clearly finding Higgy a welcome relief from her mercurial husband.

Higgy gave Alex a little nudge, and she stepped slightly forward.

"Katharine, I'd like you to meet Miss Alexandra Bell, a Kennedy campaign worker who now serves in Senator Carpenter's office. A Washington up-and-comer, I'd say," he said with a flourish of his free hand.

"How do you do, Mrs. Graham," Alex said quietly, but trying to match the older woman's warmth. She held out her hand.

"I am pleased to meet you, Miss Bell, and welcome to our home," Mrs. Graham said and briefly touched her fingers to Alex's. They were ice cold.

"Thank you, Mrs. Graham. Your home is so beautiful. It seems like a true Washington treasure."

Mrs. Graham looked pleased at the compliment, but it was clear to Alex she schooled her expressions very carefully.

"Katharine, I need to run," Higgy said lightly. "I leave Miss Bell in your capable hands. Her first Washington party, you know, but the work of the Ambassador must come first."

"Of course, Bruce," Mrs. Graham said with genuine warmth in her face.

Higgy turned sideways to face Alex and winked at her.

"See you around, Miss Bell." And he bounced away.

"Such a character," Mrs. Graham said, looking after Higgy.

"And very kind," Alex added unconsciously.

Mrs. Graham looked at her then, perhaps actually seeing her for the first time.

"Yes. He is." She paused. "And what are your hopes as you work in this administration, Miss Bell?" she asked, and her light brown eyes took on a shrewd cast that made Alex realize this was a very sharp woman.

Alex thought for a second.

"I would like to help our country become a better place for all its citizens, not just some. I believe President Kennedy is working for that as well."

Mrs. Graham nodded and then a short man with a narrow face bustled up and took both of Mrs. Graham's hands in his.

"Katharine, Katharine. Always wonderful to see you." He peered intensely into Mrs. Graham's face.

"Well, Bill, we only saw you two days ago, and I have not changed that much since then," Katharine Graham said in a dry voice.

Alex took this as her cue to fade away.

"Thank you for hosting me, Mrs. Graham," Alex said softly as she backed away.

"No, now Miss Bell, let me just introduce you to Bill Nelson here who is a painter and a friend of ours. Bill, let me introduce you to Miss Alexandra Bell, a legislative aide to Senator Carpenter. Miss Bell, this is William Nelson."

"How do?" said Bill Nelson, turning his intense gaze on to Alex for a moment, and then, to Alex's shock, he spoke to Mrs. Graham about her.

"I tell you, Katharine, if I didn't paint abstracts I'd be tempted to try to capture those eyes."

"Now, Bill. That's enough of that. Miss Bell, you had better escape."

Alex didn't hesitate. She turned and walked swiftly away, but she heard Mrs. Graham's soft voice behind her.

"Bill, why did you want to scare that innocent child?"

Innocent child? Alex thought indignantly as she hurried away, her spine unconsciously straightening.

She slowed down then and looked around the room for a moment, getting her bearings. Close to the archway at the entrance to the big room, she saw Brownie's shock of red hair. Alex tried not to flinch. Brownie was wearing a taffeta, maroon dress that was so dowdy even Mamie Eisenhower would not have deigned to wear it. She turned her head, giving no sign she recognized Brownie. Then she saw a dark blue sleeve with gold bands above the cuff through the crowd on the opposite side of the room, and she made her way toward it.

Lt. Karns was standing, facing her. He was short, probably a little shorter than she, and very slim. His trim, Navy uniform looked good on him, however, as it lent him some authority, especially with the rows of ribbons on his chest. She remembered his short brown hair, brown eyes and narrow face from the cocktail party at Howard's Georgetown home. How different were the two social occasions, actually, Alex mused. Not that much. Even some of the same people and most likely some of the same secrets.

Karns was listening intently to a tall man in yet another beautiful suit. Alex immediately assessed the fit over his broad shoulders and narrow waist and mentally applauded the tailor. It was not easy to get a smooth drape from cashmere.

She stood behind the cashmere suit, listening to the words being exchanged, but appearing to scan the room, looking for someone.

Cashmere suit had a clipped British accent. This must be Duncan Connors, she realized. He was supposed to have a British accent.

"Where the bloody hell do you get your information, Jack?" he was saying in a slightly annoyed voice. "It's positively inhuman the way you go nosing around like a bloodhound all the time. Give it a rest will you? I came here to get bladdered. So get off."

Just then Karns seemed to spot Alex behind cashmere suit.

"Miss Bell, isn't it?" he asked with a wry smile, signaling full well he knew she had been listening.

Alex moved slightly around cashmere suit so she could face him.

"Why, yes. And you are Lt. Karns, I believe. My friend Gwen Gray has mentioned you."

"Please convey to her my condolences on the loss of her brother, Miss Bell." He paused for a second, his dark brown eyes fixed on hers, and Alex knew then that he had seen her at the other reception and seen through her awful disguise.

"I will," Alex said solemnly.

"And let me introduce my colleague, Mr. Duncan Connors, also attached to the Office of Legal Affairs as Stephen Gray was. Duncan, this is Miss Alexandra Bell, a legislative aide to Senator Madeleine Carpenter."

Everybody knows everybody here, Alex thought trying to tamp down her alarm that Karns not only knew her name but also whom she worked for.

"How do you do?" Alex said formally and held out her hand to shake his.

Instead, Connors took her hand and held it, stroking the back with his thumb.

"I do very well indeed, little lady, very well indeed," Connors said, smiling down at her while still rubbing her hand.

"Delighted to hear it," Alex said in her Smith College voice that clearly conveyed "you are a boor" while jerking her hand sharply out of Connor's grip. He frowned at her.

Karns chuckled softly and took a sip of his drink.

Connors recovered quickly, Alex noted. I bet, though, he is not all that familiar with women pulling away from him was her next thought.

"I see you have no drink, Miss Bell. May I get you a small libation?" he drawled.

He's exaggerating the British accent, Alex thought. But if he goes away, I can talk to Karns alone.

"Thank you," Alex said, warming up her tone a little. "Yes, I would like a glass of white wine."

"Your servant," Connors replied, continuing to lay on the accent. And then he moved smoothly through the crowd.

Alex wasted no time.

"Lieutenant," she said quickly. "Gwen mentioned some concerns you shared, or rather, some concerns her brother had. I would like to know more about that."

"Not the place and time, Miss Bell," Karns said softly.

"When?" she followed up quickly as she saw Connors head above the crowd, moving toward them.

"Tomorrow. Noon. Steps of the Jefferson Memorial," he breathed.

Another landmark, Alex thought. I hope it doesn't have a basement. Then Karns looked over her shoulder and took another sip of his own drink. He must have seen Connors coming back. Alex had time to notice that the liquid in Karns's glass did not seem to diminish no matter how many sips he appeared to take. Very smart, she thought as she turned to smile at Connors.

Connors handed her a very full glass of white wine, and she had to take a sip just to keep it from spilling over.

"Thank you so much," she said after swallowing. That's one way to get me to drink the wine, she thought. This guy has had a lot of practice.

But before Connors could speak, they were all startled by a commotion at the other end of the room by the door that led to the kitchen.

"The President. President Kennedy is here," the whispers blew through the crowd like the hiss of steam from an approaching train.

Connors immediately brushed past Alex and moved swiftly toward where the President of the United States, John F. Kennedy, must have entered the room. Karns took time to whisper, "See you tomorrow," and then he too walked swiftly in the same direction.

Alex had the opposite reaction. She did not want to be seen by Kennedy, and she certainly did not want him to see her, but she was being pushed along by the press of the crowd toward him.

She felt a moment's panic and tried to stifle it. I just need to get to a wall, she thought, and she started to move sideways through the jostling crowd toward the fireplace where she had spoken to Mrs. Graham. Beside the fireplace were two alcoves with more of the draperies that Higgy thought were so ghastly. There, she thought and tried even harder to slide between the flow going cross-ways. The full wine glass was a hindrance she realized as the cool liquid kept sloshing over her hand. There was a break in the crowd for a moment, and she deliberately held her arm out and poured some more of it out on to what she belatedly realized was an Aubusson carpet.

Well, the white wine will not stain anyway, she thought, and kept moving.

Then she felt her stomach clench as she heard the distinctive drawl of the 35th President of the United States that carried over the buzz of excited guests.

"Phil, Kaaatharine, Ah was free, in a mannah of speakin," and here there was the expected titter from the crowd. "Ah hope it is fine for an old friend to craash your paaarty?" The drawn out vowels made Alex's heart pound.

She reached the far draperies and quickly slipped behind them.

19

There is no chance he would remember me, Alex lectured herself as she stayed hidden. She put the nearly empty wine glass on the floor, tried to still her racing heart and just listened.

The crowd was a like a single, living thing, panting and buzzing with excitement, but gradually it started to catch its breath and settle down. After a few minutes, Alex was considering slipping out from the alcove when she heard the President's distinctive drawl more clearly. He was moving toward where she was hidden.

"Now, Ah thought we could have a little chat here, Bill, about this Cuba situation."

"Certainly, Mr. President," William Fulbright responded in his deep, measured voice.

"Now, Bill, you see the threaat of force. . ."

Alex heard a door open and close, and the voices disappeared. She thought there must be a room of some kind beyond the alcove.

Of course, she realized. The President would not just drop in on a party. His appearance had clearly been arranged with the Grahams so that he could talk with Senator Fulbright outside the White House.

What a rabbit I am, Alex thought morosely. I run and hide at the first sign of trouble.

She exited the alcove and surveyed the room. There was just the expected murmur of conversation. She tossed her hair back over her shoulders, and it reminded her she had come with a purpose.

I'll get my own white wine and circulate, she thought, and headed for the bar area.

She asked the server behind the long table for a white wine and stood waiting quietly for it, trying to remember all Higgy's instructions and whom else she should try to find.

"Hey, fella, ya got any grappa?" a loud voice said from right behind her. "Brooklyn," Alex thought automatically.

"Grappa, sir?" the slim, Negro man behind the table said. "No, sir."

"Just yankin' your chain. Gimme some of that whiskey," said the loud voice with a guffaw.

"Here is your white wine, madam," said the server, holding out a glass, but to her astonishment a big arm reached around her and took it.

Alex turned abruptly, her shoulder almost knocking the glass out of the man's hand. He easily moved it out of danger, bowed slightly, and presented it to her.

"White wine, Miss?" he said, smiling down at her. "Now that's a lady's drink for sure."

It was De Luca, Alex realized, swallowing the curt retort on the tip of her lips.

"Thank you, sir," she said instead, taking the offered wine glass with a little smile.

De Luca reached over and took his whiskey from the server.

Then, to her shock, his big arm went around her back.

"Come on. Let's get outta here," he said, his loud voice next to her ear nearly deafening her.

Alex moved smoothly sideways to get out from under the sharkskin clad arm, and she walked quickly away from the crush around the bar area.

De Luca followed her closely as she moved toward the opposite side of the room from where she knew the President and Senator Fulbright were closeted.

She turned and smiled up at De Luca, giving him the full treatment of looking up from under her eyelashes and executing a little hair toss. And it was a long way to look up, Alex realized. He was very tall.

"How do you do?" she said formally. "My name is Alexandra Bell. I am a legislative aide to Senator Carpenter," she said, giving herself the small promotion that Higgy had given her earlier.

"Well, well," De Luca said, smiling down at her. "Not just a pretty face. A government pretty face." He took a sip of his drink and then went on.

"I am Captain Michael De Luca, at your service," he said and executed a little bow.

His Brooklyn accent had disappeared, Alex noted.

"Captain?" Alex asked innocently. "What service?"

De Luca chuckled, but Alex noted the humor did not reach his eyes. They were fixed on her.

"No, no, little lady. I'm not in the military. I'm a lowly policeman, workin' on keeping our cities safe for the likes of you." He raised his glass in a toast.

"Here in DC?" she asked, beginning to wonder why he seemed to be making it so hard to get any information out of him.

"The city of New York, I'm proud to say. I'm just visitin' here, doing a little work, takin' in the sights. And you are the best sight I've seen so far," he said, bending over her a little.

Alex resisted the urge to step back.

"Oh, that's interesting," she said and faked a sip of her wine. "I have met a Detective who said he had recently transferred here from New York. I wonder if you know him? Peter John Hicks?" Alex tried to watch for a change in De Luca's expression, but he showed no sign.

"Lots of cops in ole Gotham, sweetheart. I'm afraid I don't think I know him."

De Luca took a substantial swallow of his drink and then leaned even farther over her. She could smell the whiskey on his breath.

"How'd someone like you meet a police detective?" he breathed at her.

"Well, it's a sad story, really," Alex said nearly gagging from the smell of his breath, and this time she did take a small step back. "The brother of a friend of mine was killed and Detective Hicks is assigned to the case, apparently."

"Oh, that is too bad, too bad indeed," De Luca said, and now Alex was sure he was mocking her. "But I'll just bet Detective Hicks will get to the bottom of it. The very, very bottom."

And yet you just said you didn't know Hicks, Alex thought, and she realized how very drunk De Luca must be.

Then, to Alex's astonishment, De Luca reached out suddenly, took her nearly full wine glass out of her hand and put it with his empty one on a small side table by the wall. She stood still, shocked.

Then he came back and snaked a huge arm around her, trapping her.

"You and me, missy. We need to get out of here. Go someplace where we can have some fun. Not this stiff-shirt kind of thing. I bet under that silk. . ."

"Frank!" Alex called loudly, startling De Luca enough that he decreased the pressure of his arm, and she was able to quickly take several steps away from him.

Alex had spotted Frank Scott not twenty feet away. To her immense relief, Frank seemed to have heard her, and he started walking toward her. Alex sped up to meet him, leaving De Luca behind, or at least she hoped she was leaving him behind. She did not take the time to look back.

Scott seemed to sense her distress and walked faster.

"Hello, your Highness," he said to her, but he was looking over her shoulder to where De Luca must still be. "Peasants giving you trouble?"

"You have no idea, Frank," Alex breathed out, and she could not entirely hide her trembling.

Scott's lips narrowed into a thin line as he looked again at where De Luca must be.

"Take my arm, Alex," Scott said, his tone serious. "We'll walk well away. Well away indeed."

Alex did as he suggested and felt the warmth of his arm under his sleeve. It was immensely comforting. As she and Frank moved toward the far end of the room, she hazarded a glance back to where De Luca had been. But he had disappeared.

Alex looked back at Frank and thought, I'm going to trust him. It may be a mistake, but I think I have to risk it. I have to stop being such a rabbit.

"Frank, do you need to stay or can we just go?" Alex whispered.

"I can go, Alex," Scott said softly, looking down at her. "Let's get our coats, then, shall we?"

Alex just nodded, and they just left, stopping in the hall to get their outer garments without speaking to anyone.

They stepped out the front door and were instantly engulfed with a thick fog. The temperature had risen while they had been inside. In the enormous house, they had breathed in the thick air of the party, scented with smoke, perfume, and pretense. Now their nostrils were assaulted again as low-lying, yellow air carrying droplets with a hint of raw sewage from the river, noxious and cloying, engulfed them. The sky and even the street was hidden in the appalling gloom, and they had to carefully pick their way down the stairs and out the gate.

Alex covered her nose and mouth with a gloved hand, and she saw Frank had done the same.

Frank took her arm with his free hand, and they walked cautiously and silently along sidewalks that were nearly invisible. The globe-topped streetlights could illumine only a couple of feet below their poles, and the rest was filthy gloom. Then, after a couple of blocks, Alex felt the wind shift and the temperature start to drop. She took her hand off of her face and felt a tingle of icy air.

"Wind's coming from the north now," Frank said, also taking his hand away from his face and giving a cautious sniff. "The air currents are fighting for dominance, and I think the warm muck off the river is retreating as winter is winning again."

Alex felt Frank's body turn toward her as his arm moved over hers. But he said no more. She knew he was waiting for her to speak. Her habit of hiding was so strong, though, she almost longed for the privacy of the stinking fog to return.

Then she squared her shoulders and looked directly over at him. No more hiding in rabbit holes, she vowed.

"Frank, I want to thank you again," Alex began. "For helping me back there."

She paused and saw, remarkably, that now they could even see down the hill toward the illuminated Capitol dome in the far distance. "That," and she waved her gloved hand at the tiny, gleaming dome, "and all of this," and she gestured at the mansions that lined this Georgetown street that had suddenly sprung into view, "and the rest of it is so new to me. I feel like I am perpetually in that stinking fog we just encountered. I pretend I can see my way, but sometimes," and here she drew in a shuddering breath of the now frigid air, "I fear I will take a disastrous fall."

Scott stopped under one of the bulbous streetlights and lightly took hold of her shoulders. He was hatless and his hair blew away from his forehead as the glacial wind blew up the street. She saw his scar again, white against his reddening skin.

"Look, Alex, here's the secret. That's how everybody feels who comes here. I think this can be the most treacherous city on earth, especially now. Right now, navigating Washington feels just like navigating that unwholesomely thick, noxious fog back there. You can hear sounds that might be either talking or moaning, and maybe you can see the outlines of threat, but you can't know, most of the time, when hands might reach out from the fog, not to shake your hand, but to grab you and try to throttle you."

Alex shivered, but not from the cold. That's just what it feels like, she thought.

"I really think you're doing fine, though." He brushed one gloved hand against her cheek. "Your cool reserve works, you know. It makes people think you know more than apparently you do. It's not a good idea to be seen too well in a fog."

He dropped his hands but put one arm around her shoulder, and they started to walk on.

"So what got De Luca's blood up in there?" he asked conversationally, though Alex thought his question sounded a little forced.

His next words confirmed that. "I watched him with you for a while, and I started to feel concerned. It's why I walked over. He was threatening you, and he was getting less and less subtle about it."

Here we go, Alex thought and opened her mouth to speak. Then she stopped, mentally retreating a short way back into the fog. I can't say anything about Gwen or Higgy and Brownie, she cautioned herself. Those are not my secrets.

"I'm trying to figure out who killed Stephen Gray," she said bluntly, and Frank stopped dead and turned to face her, his mouth pulled into a grim line. But he kept silent.

I knew this wouldn't be easy, she thought, but soldiered on, talking to the front of his coat.

"The detective who is supposed to be investigating Stephen's murder is at best a violent, prejudiced thug. His name is Peter John Hicks and word has it he recently came from New York City when Captain De Luca started initiating his so-called reforms. I asked De Luca if he knew Hicks. He first denied it, but then I think he was so drunk he didn't realize it when he then implied that he did. I think that's what made him angry. He felt I had trapped him." She paused. "And I had. I learned there's a connection there."

"Are you out of your mind?" Frank burst out, his normally guarded expression turning thunderous. "Murder is done by dangerous, dangerous people. You have no idea, Alex, no idea at all how risky it is for you to try that. You have no palace guard to protect you in this swamp of a city, your Highness, and your elegant dresses and fine manner are no kind of armor against truncheons and bullets."

Alex felt her anger rising. Mrs. Graham took her for an innocent, and Frank seemed to think the same, though it jarred her to realize that he knew how much her clothing and her manners were her armor. She felt exposed. But she bit back an angry retort. Don't drive him away again, she cautioned herself.

"So help me, Frank," she said quietly, putting a gloved hand lightly on the front of his coat. "I know I can't do it alone, but I can't stand Stephen dying like that and no one brought to justice for it. Or worse still, his sister charged for it for no reason other than she's a Negro."

Frank sighed deeply and looked down on her, his face back to its normal, guarded expression. He put his gloved hand over hers.

"I will look into it, Alex, but you need to stay well away."

Alex's breath came faster, and she saw it form a cloud in the icy air. She turned that icy air on Frank as she looked up at him and held his eyes while she slid her hand out from under his.

"Don't you know me, even a little by now, Frank? Do you think I can just walk away and hope you will just take over finding Stephen's real killer?"

She saw the resignation in his eyes and was surprised. Maybe he is starting to know me, despite my protective armor, she thought.

She nodded.

"So that's settled then. We help each other."

Frank groaned a little and then took her arm again.

"I'll walk you to your door," he said stoically.

"Oh, no, that's not necessary," Alex demurred, not wanting him to see where she lived. "We're not that far now, and I can make it by myself."

"I'll say it right back to you, Alex. Don't you know me at all? I repeat, I'll walk you to your door."

They walked on in silence, Alex worrying about her roommate's response to her bringing Frank Scott to their apartment. But when she opened the door with her key, Frank behind her, it was clear Gwen was not there.

Miss Bea, however, was.

"And just exactly who is this?" Miss Bea demanded with a low growl as Frank crossed the threshold.

Alex stepped toward the little table where she saw Gwen must have left a note. She also wanted to see how Frank would do with Miss Bea.

She watched as he slowly shut the door, turned, squatted down, carefully pulled off his glove and stretched out a hand, palm down, for Miss Bea to sniff.

Bea narrowed her eyes for a moment, assessing the big man. The preliminary smells signaled no danger. She moved closer and sniffed his hand thoroughly.

"Some crab. Interesting. And whiskey. No pukey sharp smell like the bad men. Good." Miss Bea paused for a moment in her sniffing and clenched her teeth, remembering the bad men. Then she moved on to this man's shoes and trouser legs. "A little bit like the river with the dead fish," she observed, "and," she went as far as his knee, "some smoke and that smell of flowers that aren't flowers like Alex puts on sometimes." She sneezed and stepped back.

"He's okay," Bea concluded, "but he should leave." She sat down, clearly blocking the way to the rest of the apartment.

"What is her name?" Frank asked as he stood up. Alex noted he did not break eye contact with Bea, who was staring right back.

"Miss Bea," Alex responded a little absently, now reading Gwen's note through.

"I am at my sister's. Much to arrange. Back tomorrow. Gave that dog some water and food, Gwen."

"How do you do, Miss Bea?" Frank asked quietly.

"I am well," Bea thought, "and you should go away."

Frank turned and looked at inquiringly at Alex and at the paper in her hand.

"Note from my roommate," she said casually and put the folded note in her pocket. "She should be back any minute."

"I will be going then," he said quietly and turned toward the door. Alex had the distinct feeling he knew she was lying.

"I'm glad we actually talked, Frank," Alex said as she crossed to where he was now standing on the threshold.

"I am too, Alex, but," and he turned his head to give her a dark look, "this is only the beginning." He headed for the staircase without another word.

Alex closed the door and looked inquiringly down at Bea, still sitting sentinel facing the door.

"He is not a bad man," Bea conceded, and she got up and went to her basket.

Alex sat down at the little table still wearing her coat and put her head in her hands.

20

WEDNESDAY, FEBRUARY 1, 1961

"What is that smell?" Miss Bea thought, and she put her nose up and pricked her ears as she and Alex ran on a path by a tall fence. They were on a new run that so far had just been on sidewalks along regular streets. But now there was a dirt path with a few frozen puddles and this fence on one side with trees and bushes inside it. The smell got stronger and stronger. Miss Bea had never smelled anything like it. She was on a lead, but she pulled as close to the fence as she could. It was a heady mix of poo and pee and rotting grass and, she tensed, fur. Some kind of animal fur. She took a deeper sniff. Not squirrels. Something else. And then she froze. A huge roar, a deafening roar struck her ears so hard it was painful.

Miss Bea was terrified and so she reared up on her hind paws and barked her fiercest bark.

"It's okay, Bea," Alex said soothingly, patting Bea and easing her back on to all four paws. Then she pulled a little on the lead to start them running again. "It's okay," Alex said as they loped along. "That was a lion. It's like a big cat. We're just running by the zoo to get to Rock Creek Park. We'll be away from here in a moment."

"A cat? A cat made that noise?" Miss Bea thought with shock, and a vision of a giant cat leaping out from behind the fence spurred her to run faster.

They quickly crossed another street and turned into a park with a graveled path running along a rock-strewn stream.

It was peaceful. The air was cold and clear. Evergreens whispered in the slight breeze, shedding a little more of the snow on their needles. Tall trees raised their bare arms and they looked black against the rose-colored light of dawn.

"Now this is a run," Miss Bea sighed in contentment, the monster cat all but forgotten. If she could have known it, Alex was thinking the same.

A few roads ran through the park as well, Bea saw when the path they had been following came up to a two-lane road. There was only one car in the distance, so they ran across the street and on to a field dotted with some boulders.

Suddenly, there was another roar, but this was not a big cat. A car engine roared as it sped up behind them. There was a thud. Alex and Miss Bea both realized with horror that the car had jumped the curb and was chasing them in the field.

"Run, Bea, run!" Alex yelled. She dropped the lead, knowing Bea could get away faster than she could.

Alex had glanced behind her when she'd first heard the car engine roar and then scream as it accelerated. She thought she would never get the image out of her mind of the four, glaring headlights and the big, black bulge in the center of the car's hood bearing down on them.

She saw Miss Bea up ahead of her. Just ahead of Bea was one of the big boulders that dotted the field. It was surrounded by some smaller rocks, rocks that still probably weighed 500 pounds each.

"The rocks, Bea. Run toward the rocks. Hide in the rocks!" Alex yelled as she put on every bit of speed her years as a runner had taught her how to do.

"Rocks, yes," Bea panted. "Hide in the rocks."

Alex could hear the wheels of the big engine car throwing the dirt and dead grass up as it tried to carve through the thawing turf of the field. The wet ground was definitely slowing the powerful car, but it was still gaining on her. She didn't think she could make it around the rocks.

She saw there was a smaller rock in front of the largest boulder. Out of the corner of her eye she saw a piece of turf spin by, thrown up by the clawing wheels. The car was very close. She knew she had to chance it.

She ran for the smaller rock, jumped up and used it like an unyielding trampoline to launch herself up on to the giant boulder. She scrabbled for purchase. She got a small toehold and pushed up with all her strength as she heard the black car, unable to stop its furious acceleration in time, run up on to the smaller rock. A hideous, grinding noise followed. Alex found a tuft of grass growing in a crack near one of her hands and she grabbed it. She pulled herself up and on to the top of the boulder. She lay flat and peered back at the black car that was now limping away back across the field, one of its tires clearly out of align.

Alex squinted to see the license plate before the car disappeared. "DPL 8952," she read. A diplomatic plate? Really? she thought, shocked.

"Come down!" Miss Bea barked from behind her. Alex looked over the back edge of the boulder to the pile of smaller rocks below. Miss Bea had managed to climb up on the largest one and had her front paws up on the giant boulder, looking up. She was quivering from the tips of her ears to the end of her tail.

"Okay, Bea. I'm coming. I just have to figure out how to get down without breaking a leg or an arm."

"Good," Bea contributed, sitting down to wait for Alex. "And I want some water."

* * *

Alex and Miss Bea stayed on the sidewalks of main roads to get back to the apartment. Alex was tense, especially when they were crossing the now busier intersections. She could tell Bea was on alert as well, looking at the cars instead of sniffing at the tufts of dried grass pushing up from the remaining snow by the roads.

When they reached the apartment, Alex shut and locked the door behind them and then simply sat down on the floor of the entryway. She dimly felt that her hands and knees were stinging, scraped by her scramble up the boulder. But she could not summon the energy in the moment to stand up, let alone tend to them.

Miss Bea went to her bowl in the kitchen, drank thirstily and then came over and lay down beside Alex.

"Someone tried to kill us, Bea," Alex said dully.

Bea raised her head from where she had been resting it on her paws.

"I could not bite the car," she conceded, very irritated. Then she thought some more. "But I could bite that big cat," and with that satisfying image in her mind, she fell asleep.

Alex heard Gwen's bedroom door open behind her, but she could not yet seem to summon the energy to get up.

"Alex! Alex! What's wrong? Why you down there on the floor? You hurt?" Gwen cried out and Alex could hear her footsteps hurrying across the creaky wooden floor. She felt Gwen take hold of her arm.

"Come on now, honey. Can you get up? Let me help you," Gwen said, her soft voice and gentle hands helping to pull Alex back to reality. Alex stood up, wincing from the pain in her knees.

Gwen helped her sit at the little table and then she got the coffee pot and a cup and poured. She scooped two heaping spoonful's of sugar into the coffee, stirred it and pushed it in front of Alex.

"Drink it now, honey. Drink it," she said coaxingly, and Alex took a sip. "More. Come on now, drink up."

Alex did as she was told and took several bigger sips. She started to feel a little better.

"Thanks, Gwen," she said, sitting up straighter.

"So, what?" Gwen asked, tension creeping into her voice. "Was it that Hicks? Did he hurt you again?"

Alex knew Gwen was remembering her beatings at Hicks's hands.

"No. Not like that. Bea and I were running in Rock Creek Park and a car jumped the curb and tried to run us down," Alex said, remembering the noise of the big engine bearing down on them. She shuddered.

"We ran for some rocks. Bea hid, and I scrambled up a big boulder." She paused and turned her hands palm up. "That's how I got scraped, here, and on my knees. The wheel of the car hit a smaller rock and it damaged it. It drove away."

"Oh, my Lord, my Lord," Gwen said, and she patted Alex gently on the shoulder. "You see who it was?"

"No. Tinted windows. But the car had a diplomatic plate."

"Oh no," Gwen said.

"Exactly," Alex said.

* * *

Alex treated herself to a warm bath and then bandaged her scraped knees. She did not want to put big bandages on her hands and call attention to them, so she put small bits of tape over the cuts, and she chose a cream, silk georgette blouse with long ruffles instead of cuffs. The ruffles hung out at least three inches beyond the end of the sleeve of her navy blue wool suit and the fabric would tend to hide scrapes and tape. She did not want to get blood on her clothes, but she wanted no questions either.

She eased her gloves over her swollen hands and put on a close-fitting hat, her warm, tailored winter coat and pulled a thick scarf around her neck. She was still chilled after the warm bath. I still haven't recovered from the shock of being chased like that, she thought, but I need to meet that Lt. Karns at the Jefferson Memorial today at noon. She sighed at how cold that location would be. And what is with all these meetings at monuments? she wondered as she picked up her purse.

She patted the sleeping Miss Bea and left for the office.

* * *

Alex looked at her watch again. It was nearly one o'clock and Karns had still not showed. She was freezing. She had been standing inside on the side of the rotunda where the giant, bronze statue of Jefferson was located, but the wind off of the Tidal Basin just beyond swirled through the columns in icy streams, reaching Alex as she huddled by the wall. She wondered if Jefferson's huge statue, and especially the huge pedestal on which it stood, would be a better shield from the blasts of bitter air. She hurried toward it and felt the wind decrease as Jefferson and his pedestal cut the blasts from the body of water just beyond the entrance. As Alex scurried to get around behind the statue, she glanced up at Jefferson's grim face. Then she reached the pedestal, with Jefferson's back above. But she knew where Jefferson was looking.

Jefferson was facing toward his arch enemy, Alexander Hamilton, whose statue was directly across the city at the U.S. Treasury building. When Alex had first visited the Jefferson Memorial, a park guide had been there, rhapsodizing about how Jefferson was facing toward the White House. "Jefferson is guarding the people's house," the guide had assured the few tourists gathered around him.

I don't think so, Alex had thought at the time. She knew very well from her government classes that Jefferson would most likely be glaring at Hamilton. And only the Washington Monument stood between them. Washington had tried to pull the nation together, bridging the factions of Jefferson and Hamilton. But he could not overcome the enmity.

Washington had failed, Alex thought gloomily, wrapping her arms around herself as she huddled below Jefferson. Nothing has changed from then until now, she thought, except that it is worse.

Thinking of Jefferson's enemies made Alex think of her own. Who wanted her dead? Or, was it merely an attempt to scare her? The driver of the big engine car could have gotten out, tried to grab her or shoot her. But he hadn't. He had driven away with one wobbly wheel. She thought of the people to whom she'd spoken in the last few days. Had she angered someone? Appeared to someone to be a threat? But who? Not Brownie or Higgy, surely?

She shivered violently and not just from the cold. She decided to give up on Karns and splurge on a taxi to get back to the office more quickly. She stepped out from behind Jefferson into the cold wind that was swirling around the still empty rotunda and hurried toward the drive that led visitors to the monument. She could see a cab stand, and thankfully, a waiting cab.

Arriving at the old Senate office building, she wearily climbed the huge, marble stairs.

I wonder why Karns didn't show? she pondered as she labored up the steps that seemed steeper today, her skinned knees hurting her with every step.

Then she stopped dead.

I wonder if he didn't show because somehow he was the one behind the attempt to run me down this morning, she thought, horrified.

* * *

Alex trudged up the stairs to the apartment, worn out from the terror of the morning and the fruitless trip to the Jefferson Memorial at midday. Fortunately, in between, her work in the Senator's office had been light. Alistair was still in the hospital, Mrs. Anderson had reported in a worried voice. Senator Carpenter had not come in, and Alex had been able to sit quietly and slowly open the mail. She had discovered that by carefully holding the sharp letter opener using only the tips of her fingers, she could slit the envelopes without pain. Writing replies to the letters was out of the question, so she merely read the mail and sorted it.

As she put the key in the lock, she heard Miss Bea sniffing at the crack at the bottom of the door.

"Miss Bea, it's me. Move back so I can open the door," Alex called, puzzled by the dog's behavior.

She heard the scrabbling of nails and cautiously opened the door. Miss Bea was sitting in the little foyer in the middle of a bunch of shredded paper.

"I barked and I kept the man out. Then he pushed this paper under the door. I bit all of it," Bea reported.

"Oh, Bea, what did you do?" Alex sighed as she bent to pick up the damp shreds of paper and put them on the table. She could see there was a handwritten message, some parts blurred with dog drool.

"I protected you," Miss Bea barked, clearly offended.

"Yes, yes, I know you are a good watchdog," Alex said resignedly, reaching for a dog treat in an upper kitchen cabinet and handing it to Bea.

"Thank you," Bea conceded and took the treat to her basket.

Alex took off her coat and hat and placed them on one of the kitchen chairs.

Now, how to put this puzzle back together again, she wondered, looking at the pile of scraps on the table. She went to her room and retrieved two pieces of blank paper from her little desk. She flattened the shreds of the note between the pages and then put one of the encyclopedia volumes on top of it.

She realized she had a headache and then remembered she had had nothing since the sugar-laden coffee Gwen had fixed for her early that morning. She got out a can of chicken noodle soup and opened it. She ate it directly out of the can with a spoon while she waited for the scraps to flatten a little.

She threw the empty can in their bin under the sink and cautiously lifted the encyclopedia volume.

The note was not long, and she started to piece the scraps together. Finding a capital "K" and a small "a" on one torn piece gave her a jolt. She hunted for pieces that might fit with it. She found an "r" on a shred of paper, and an "ns" on a larger one that all fit together. She had the signature. Karns. A short time later she had it all. "Sorry. Held up. Be in touch. Karns."

She put her head in her hands. Karns knew where she lived.

21

THURSDAY, FEBRUARY 2, 1961

Alex and Miss Bea skipped their usual morning run by mutual consent. Alex's knees were still sore, and Bea would not even leave her basket.

Gwen was up early. She planned to meet her sister before either of them needed to be at work, she'd said. "I gotta talk to her. Mama wants us to say a few words about Stephen at the funeral, but she is makin' a fuss about it." Gwen's shoulders drooped. "As usual, and we can't have no nonsense like that. I don't want Mama upset by foolishness."

Gwen had jammed her hat on her head and left, clearly upset herself. Alex knew just to nod when usually calm Gwen got so troubled.

Alex took another bath, but she tried to use very little water. Just enough to cover her knees. Then she selected her dark maroon suit. She wanted to wear the blouse with the ruffles that hid her hands again and that suit would work well with that. Its sleeves were cut slightly short to allow for cuffs to be seen. And the flowing skirt hit her mid-calf so it would cover her knees and not pull when she sat down.

She put down Bea's food and filled her water bowl. The little dog was whimpering in her sleep, and Alex bent to give her a pat. Miss Bea started awake and looked up blearily at Alex. Then she shook her ears. She had been having a nightmare about a monster cat that roared like a big car. Then she put her paw over her nose and went back to sleep.

Alex hurried to the bus stop as gray clouds scudded across the sky. Their plump, dark masses flew over, blown by the gusting wind. The temperature must be below freezing, Alex thought wearily, and those clouds look like we'll get more snow. She saw her bus coming with relief and fit herself in among all the others jammed into the overheated vehicle.

Alex heard the sobbing even before she opened the door to the Senator's office. She went in quickly and saw Mrs. Anderson was crying noisily into a wad of tissue and rocking back and forth on her chair.

Alex threw her coat and hat on her chair and rushed over.

"Mrs. Anderson, what is it? What has happened?" she asked. She started to kneel by the older woman's chair and then remembered her torn knees. She crouched down instead so she could put her arm around the shaking woman.

Just then, the door to the office opened and Senator Carpenter came in. It took her only a moment to take in the scene, and then she walked briskly over to them.

"My heavens, Miss Bell, Mrs. Anderson, whatever is wrong?"

Alex stood up but kept a hand on Mrs. Anderson's shaking shoulder.

"I don't know, Madam Senator. I just arrived and found Mrs. Anderson very upset."

Mrs. Anderson did not even react.

"Help her into my office, will you, Miss Bell?" the Senator said firmly, and she walked quickly over to her office, unlocked the door and went in.

"Come on, Mrs. Anderson," Alex said softly, and she put her arm all the way around the shaking woman to help her stand. She supported her across the room and into the Senator's dim office and placed her in the nearest chair.

The Senator poured a glass of water and handed it to Mrs. Anderson.

"Here Agatha, drink this," she said. "It will help."

It did help, Alex saw. Mrs. Anderson stopped sobbing, took the glass and sipped. She hiccupped once and then sipped again. She held out the glass, and Alex took it.

"It's Alistair," she said, and tears pooled again in her faded, red eyes. "He died during the night. His mother called. Poor thing. She was so distraught. They will take him home to Con-nec-ticuttt," she hiccupped.

Alex put her hands over her mouth. She remembered Alistair's long, Airedale face and felt tears prick at her own eyes.

"Oh, my heavens," Senator Carpenter exclaimed. "That is terrible." She paused for a moment and then asked, "Did Mrs. Carrington say what the illness was?"

Mrs. Anderson sat up straighter.

"Some kind of infection in his bowels, she said the doctors thought. He had always had a weak stomach and intestines, and he'd told them on the phone he thought he'd gotten sick from something he ate in a restaurant that didn't agree with him. But it got worse, and well, then he ended up in the hospital, but it was no use."

Mrs. Anderson wept softly, her head bowed.

Alex and the Senator looked at each other over Mrs. Anderson's head.

"Miss Bell, Mrs. Anderson needs to go home and rest. I am going to order one of the cars from our Senate car pool to take her. Will you accompany her downstairs and settle her in the car?"

Alex nodded, but Mrs. Anderson's head came up.

"No, Maddy, no. You don't have to do that. I'll just take the bus," Mrs. Anderson said in a quavering voice.

Maddy. Agatha. Alex realized how long these two women must have known each other.

"Nonsense," the Senator said briskly and moved around her desk to pick up the phone.

"Now go fix your face and get your hat and coat. At this time of day, they should be here shortly. The guard at the entrance will ring when the car comes."

They were clearly dismissed, and Alex supported Mrs. Anderson as she stood up and walked slowly out to her desk. She got Mrs. Anderson's hat and coat and helped her into them. The phone rang once in the Senator's office and they heard a brief, "Thank you."

"Miss Bell, Agatha, the car is here," Senator Carpenter called out in her carrying voice.

Alex silently helped Mrs. Anderson to stand, walked her to the elevator and out to the waiting car. Alex murmured comforting words as she accompanied her, but Mrs. Anderson remained silent.

She returned to the Senator's office to find her standing by Alistair's raised desk. She seemed to be looking at his nameplate.

"I wonder if his parents would like to have this," she said quietly. Then she turned to Alex. "Please follow me into my office and shut the door, will you Miss Bell? You will need your pad."

Alex retrieved her pad and pencil from her desk and silently entered the Senator's inner office and closed the door.

* * *

The ominous black clouds had massed in the sky, darkening the city. The Senator had turned on her overhead light it was so dark, and the overhead fluorescent lights tinted her skin a ghastly yellow. She looked like a wax work figure of an old woman, Alex thought. No wonder she dislikes having the overhead lights on.

The Senator was standing, and when she saw Alex enter, she turned to look out her window. Alex could see it was sleeting. She was so glad Mrs. Anderson was safely in a limousine being chauffeured home.

"I will need to go to Mr. Carrington's funeral, Miss Bell. Please find out when it is and make arrangements for me to attend. His father is a prominent businessman and a donor to the Democratic party," she said tonelessly, still looking out at the sleet.

Alex winced a little but wrote it down.

"Flowers, of course. Ask Mrs. Anderson. She may very well want to do that herself when she comes back."

Alex nodded and then realized the Senator could not see her.

"Yes, ma'am," she said quietly.

"You know about her son, Jeffrey?" the Senator asked the window.

"Just that he died young," Alex replied softly.

"Quite so. Quite so."

"Anyway," and here the Senator turned from the window but remained standing. "We need to keep this office running." She paused, giving Alex one of her X-ray looks.

"You have done well in a short period of time, Miss Bell. Very, very well, I might say. I would like to promote you to be my new legislative aide. On a trial basis, of course. But I have no doubt you will excel."

"Thank you, Madam Senator, for your confidence in me," Alex said formally, her insides churning. "I will do my very best."

"I think you will, Miss Bell. At least, let's say I hope you will."

The Senator abruptly sat down behind her desk. Reaching over, she turned on her desk lamp, and the green shaded light did not combine well with the yellow overhead glare. Fortunately, she's wearing a rough tweed, brown suit, Alex couldn't help thinking. That weave and the brown color absorb some of this awful light. But she knew she was just thinking of fabric and how it absorbed light to calm her nerves.

Higgy had given her a false promotion and now she had it for real. At least, she thought with another lurch in her stomach, I have it if I do not make a mess of it.

"We will need to think of your replacement, then. Someone to open the mail, write the replies, greet visitors and so forth." She picked up a pencil on her desk and started tapping rapidly. Alex saw she was tapping on a file.

"I hope I am not making a mistake," she muttered softly, and Alex thought she was just speaking to herself. She stayed quiet.

"There is this young man," tap, tap, tap. "He is the son of a very promi-nent constituent in my state. In fact, he and my husband were great friends." She sighed and gave the file one quite hard tap. "His son has left college after only three semesters. His father, Norman Van Allen, invented some kind of part for a threshing machine and built a manufacturing empire in our state. His son, Reginald Van Allen," and here the Senator actually grimaced, "who likes to be called 'Reggie,' told his father he wants to 'take a year off and do work in the real world' or words to that effect." Four hard taps hit the file. "His father has asked me if I could 'find room' for Reggie in my office. Truly."

Alex could actually hear the quotation marks in the contempt the Senator could not fully hide that she could "find room" in a moment.

Alex wrote down "Reginald (Reggie) Van Allen" on her pad.

"So now, in fact there is a position he might be able to do. You will need to train him, of course. I think he's bright enough, really, but does seem to think a lot of himself." The Senator sat back out of the green light, and the grim expression on her yellowed wrinkles was truly frightening to Alex.

I hope she can frighten Reggie, Alex thought.

"What I would like you to do, Miss Bell, is first write a brief announce-ment of Mr. Carrington's death, our condolences to the family and so forth. Send that to the Congressional Newsletter. That one we get delivered here to the office every day. Then write a letter to the family from me, praising Mr. Carrington's accomplishments in his time as a legislative aide and so forth. That needs to get out right away. Then spend the rest of the day reading Mr. Carrington's files and educating yourself on what legislation this office will be pursuing during this Congress."

"Yes, ma'am Alex replied carefully, not wanting to reveal she feared she was way in over her head.

"I will close the office tomorrow and Monday out of respect for Mr. Carrington. And, indeed, there are no votes scheduled for either day. I think I will also fly back to my home state after Mr. Carrington's funeral and talk to Mr. Van Allen and Reginald myself." She paused, her yellowed face look-ing quite like the shrewd politician she was. "I think a rather large donation from Mr. Van Allen is on the horizon."

"Make plane reservations," Alex wrote on her pad. The Senator's plans should come first. Then she wrote, "announcement, letter, read."

"Madam Senator," she asked firmly, as a legislative aide should. "What airline and flights do you prefer? You will need a cars to and from the airport. Where shall the driver pick you up and I assume you will need a car when you arrive, both in Connecticut and when you go to see Mr. Van Allen."

Alex paused attentively, her pencil over her pad.

"Very good, Miss Bell," and the Senator outlined her plans. "And you will find the information on contacting the needed services, the airlines and so forth, in Mr. Carrington's files."

"Thank you, Madam Senator," Alex said. And when there were no more instructions coming, she stood up. She was not surprised to find her legs were shaking. She glanced at the Senator to see if she was noticing, but she had turned her chair to look out at the sleet sliding down her dirty window, making rivulets in the grime.

* * *

Alex just sat for a few minutes in the chair at the raised desk at the back of the office, looking but not touching anything. Then she picked up Alistair's desk nameplate and ran her fingers over it, remembering it was the first thing she had truly focused on when she'd come to the office for her new job. How long ago that seemed.

I will find a nice box and have this wrapped for the Senator to take to his family, she thought, as she opened a drawer to put the plate and its walnut stand away. There was a box in the drawer. It was clearly the one that fit the items. The box looked so new it was heartbreaking. Alex lifted the box, used the barely wrinkled tissue paper inside to wrap the items, and put the cover on. She tucked it away in a bottom drawer. She shivered. It felt like a tiny burial.

I need to get to work here, she told herself sternly and started looking through the other drawers.

Alistair appeared to have been very organized. The pending congressional bills were labeled and filed in one drawer. She would read them, but now she needed to find the information on travel for the Senator and enough information on Alistair to write the newsletter announcement as well as the Senator's letter of condolence. In the desktop rolodex she found the number for booking congressional travel and she called it. The woman who answered was very efficient and in short order she was told the tickets would be messengered over to the Senator's office. She would also arrange the cars.

Alex breathed a sigh of relief. One thing done.

She looked in the drawer and quickly found a file Alistair had labeled with his own name. There were three typewritten pages in the folder, the letter of application he had written to Senator Carpenter was one, and two other pages that listed his education, his accomplishments, the title of a paper he had published in his college journal, and his hobbies. Fencing and clarinet. And that was all. Not a lot to summarize a life, Alex thought sadly as she took a clean piece of paper from the center drawer and began to write.

She made short work of the announcement to the newsletter, saying only that Mr. Alistair Carrington, Legislative Aide to Senator Carpenter, had died after a short illness. She copied his educational information and then, after a little thought, added the title of the paper he had published in 1958 on "Stabilizing Commodity Prices." No wonder the Senator had hired him, she thought.

She brought the draft announcement in to the Senator who was reading from a file. She merely glanced and it and nodded.

"Madam Senator, your airline tickets should be here shortly," Alex added.

"Oh, very good Miss Bell," she said, and looked up with an approving smile.

Alright, Alex said to herself as she left the office. I can do this.

Alex called downstairs for a messenger, finding the number in Alistair's well-organized rolodex. She asked for the announcement to be delivered immediately to the newsletter office on K street.

The letter of condolence was more difficult. She had seen so little of the interaction between the Senator and Carrington. She decided to focus on his efficiency that she was deducing from his almost obsessively organized desk, and his sound preparation for what would have been a sterling legislative career.

Sterling? Alex mused as she read over the letter. Perhaps exceptional would be better. She hesitated. No, sterling was just a little unusual and would convey worth.

She had hand-written the letter, doing her best to mimic the Senator's flowing penmanship she had seen in other files. Is that wise? she wondered as she held the letter in her hand. Do I want to show I can easily forge her writing?

Don't guess, she warned herself. Go carefully now. Very, very carefully. I will merely ask.

She picked up the letter and went over and knocked on the Senator's door.

"Come in," she heard, though the normally carrying voice was muffled.

She opened the door and saw the Senator was on her private phone line. She waved Alex in.

"Yes, yes, it has been dreadful. And it will be so good to see all of you." She paused, listening. "That's correct." More listening. "Thank you. Good-bye."

"I'm sorry to interrupt, ma'am Alex said quietly.

"No, no. It's alright. What do you need?"

"I just finished the letter of condolence from you to the Carringtons and I wondered if you wished me to type it or write it out long-hand. My draft is in long-hand."

"Give it here," the Senator said briskly, holding out a hand.

Alex walked over and put the letter in her outstretched hand. She took it, placed it on her desk, turned on the dreadful, green-shaded desk lamp, and pulled her reading glasses out from among a mass of ruffles on her blouse. She peered at the letter for only a minute, took a pen and signed it with a flourish.

"Excellent. As always, Miss Bell. This can be mailed immediately," and she handed back the signed paper.

Alex nodded and turned to go.

"Oh, Miss Bell, before I forget. There should be some keys in the desk Mr. Carrington used. You should take them as you will need to be able to lock and unlock the office."

"I found no keys, ma'am, and I have looked in each drawer," Alex said. "I can look again, of course, but I do not believe there are any keys."

The Senator said nothing for a moment, clearly thinking.

"Yes, that would be the case, would it not? Mr. Carrington never returned to the office after he was taken ill. He would have had the keys with him." She sighed. "Well, if the Carringtons do not return them to this office, we will have to make arrangements. But for now, I do have an extra set."

The Senator rummaged in a left hand drawer of her own desk and pulled out two keys on a ring, one large and one smaller.

"Here," she said and held out the key ring to Alex who took it and kept it on her palm. "The large one opens the outer door. This will allow you to come and go as I need you to, or you need to do to finish work. Guard it carefully."

A key to a Senate office, Alex thought numbly looking down at the old-fashioned length of brass of the larger key.

"Miss Bell?" the Senator's voice interrupted sharply. "Do you need anything else?"

"No, no ma'am," Alex said, and she closed her hand tightly around the key ring and went back to the raised desk to start the reading files.

* * *

It was nearly nine o'clock in the evening and the Senator had long departed. Alex felt like she was studying for the Government major final exam in college. She had made a separate sheet for each of the Senator's two main committees, Foreign Relations, the one chaired by Senator Fulbright, and the Judiciary Committee. Alex had been to the meeting of the Foreign Relations committee, and the sub-committee of Judiciary on the Investigation of the National Security Act, the one where J. Edgar Hoover had testified. Those were major committees, the ones called "Class A" she knew, and she wondered how a newly elected Senator, and the only woman, had been appointed to those. Or had she inherited them from her husband?

Something to check out, Alex noted.

The "Class B" committee files were also clearly labeled. Post Office and Interior. She had put those aside for reading later, but she had flipped through them. There was an issue with "Indian Lands" apparently and she made another note to read up on the Indian lands in the Senator's home state.

There was one thin file labeled "State Department," and she placed it in front of her. I'll finish this and leave, Alex thought, expecting to find some pending legislation regarding State Department funding or the like.

Instead, she found a list of names headed "Security Protocols Enacted at the Department of State." These were all hand-written and not in Carrington's handwriting, nor Senator Carpenter's.

Were these State Department employees who had been terminated? Alex wondered. And why? Were these the suspected Communists or "deviates" Hoover had mentioned? Rolling her neck and shoulders to release tension, she took a blank sheet of paper and took another half hour to copy the names on the State Department list. She put that list in her purse and then put the original file back in the drawer.

Exhausted, she put on her outdoor things, locked the door behind her and walked through the echoing hall of the Senate Office building and down the stairs.

The Negro night guard greeted her with a "Workin' late, little lady" comment and a smile. She smiled wearily back. He unlocked the massive door for her and held it. She hesitated on the top step.

"Problem, Miss?" he asked, a little concerned.

Alex felt the list she'd copied was practically speaking to her from inside her purse. "Danger, danger," it seemed to say. She did not want to risk having her purse stolen.

"I was just realizing it was so late," she said softly. "Perhaps I had better take a cab."

"Now that is a good idea," he said firmly, and he raised his hand. A cab stopped quickly. Alex thanked him warmly and hurried down the steps to the waiting cab.

She still had a little money in her purse. Since she seemed to have stopped eating, there should be enough, she reflected. She slid into the warm vehicle and gave her address.

Only then did she think, I wonder if being a Legislative Aide pays more than being an Assistant? I should have asked. Really, I am the innocent Mrs. Graham called me, she berated herself as the cab drove down the streets glistening with a thin layer of ice as the sleet continued to fall.

22

FRIDAY, FEBRUARY 3, 1961, 1 A.M., TIDAL BASIN

Oh, for Chrissake. It's sleeting.

Would you stop talking about the weather? The kid died, you f**** moron. How did that happen?

I didn't give him much. I swear. Just sprinkled a little on his meatloaf. He was sittin' at a lunch counter. Leaned over for the salt. Just a pinch. Piece a cake.

I did not ask you how you did for him. I want to know why you were so incompetent you managed to kill him. I just wanted him out of that office for a week or two.

Well, shit happens, you know?

I do know. And what about your target? Who did she meet?

Nobody. I followed her real careful like and she waited around for an hour. Nobody showed.

You were made.

Nah. You know me. And hey, I heard your souped up fancy car got banged up. How'd that happen?

You heard that?

Yeah. Heard it.

No, you heard nothing.

Hey, is that a gun? Listen man, I heard nothing. Right.

Back up.

Waddaya mean back up? I'm almost in this freezin' water now.

Back up.

A splash.

Back up more. Stay there.

Silence.

*Christ. Christ. No more. My feet are freezing off. I'm getting'
outta here.*

Stand there and listen, you pikey bastard.

Moaning.

You never heard of my car, is that clear?

Yeah. Yeah. I get it. Lemme out.

You'll be more careful in the future now, won't you?

Sure. Sure. Can I get out? Oh man, please, please, lemme out.

Sobbing.

Footsteps retreating.

Splashing.

Oh God. Oh God. My feet.

23

FRIDAY, FEBRUARY 3, 1961

Alex flinched. Her footsteps sounded so loud in the empty, marble corridors of the Senate Office Building. She walked faster, trying to get warm. It felt nearly as cold inside this vast, empty space as it had outside. And she felt like she was trespassing, especially when she fitted the big key into the ornate lock of the Senator's office.

I have every right to be here, she told herself sternly as she heard the click. But she noticed her hand was trembling when she pushed the door open.

She had come in very early to continue reading the files in the desk. Since the Senator had closed the office Friday and Monday, she had realized she could leave earlier than she had planned to go to New York if she got to work very early.

She hung up her coat and then seated herself at what still felt like Alistair's desk.

This is my desk now, she firmly told herself, but her deepest fears of being an imposter could not entirely be suppressed.

Just get on with it, she told herself, like she always did when she feared her very carefully constructed life might be exposed, and she pulled open the file drawer in the desk a little harder than necessary. She took out the files she had not yet read. There were not that many she had not seen and soon she had finished notating what was in each one.

But is this all the files? she wondered as she put them back in the drawer in order. There were not that many in total for a year of work for a busy Senator.

She looked around the office. The only other place there could be files was in the credenza that sat under the window behind the desk. She went over to it and tried to open the one of the cabinet doors. It was locked. She got the keys out of her purse where she had put them after unlocking the main door. The second, smaller key looked like it might fit. She put it in the lock on the cabinet and turned it. There was a click.

She knelt on the floor and saw several boxes. They appeared to be taped. She pulled one out and placed it on the floor in front of her. The tape appeared to be still sealed and had "Property of Senator Edgar Carpenter" printed in ink. The box was quite dusty. Alex got up and took a handkerchief out of her purse to dust the top and then she lifted the box up to the desk. She took out the small flashlight she kept in her purse to use when the stairwell of their apartment had no light at all. She knelt down again and shined it briefly on the top of the other boxes. All of them clearly were labeled with the name of the Senator's husband. She sat back on her heels, thinking. These must have been moved to this office when Madeleine Carpenter had been appointed to fill out her deceased husband's third term and just forgotten. The tape on each seemed intact. The boxes seemed never to have been opened after they had been transported here.

Should I open them? she wondered. Well, I can at least see what is inside, she told herself, and then ask the Senator if she wants to continue to have them stored here.

She stood up and regarded the one box that was on top of the desk. I don't even need to slit the tape, she realized. It's so dried, I can just lift the lid.

She was right. The cardboard lid came off easily, and she placed it, with the tape still attached, on the side of the desk. She looked inside.

The box was filled with files.

She started to flip through them and her breathing became faster and her heart started to pound. Each file was labeled "FBI," but they differed by dates. The first one was dated from just after the war. She took the first few out and pushed the box to the side. She sat down and began to read. As she read, she became increasingly sick to her stomach. Senator Edgar Carpenter had detailed his concerns about what he seemed to regard as questionable FBI activities over the years. There were some flimsy copies of documents and a lot of handwritten material.

Why had the former Senator Carpenter kept this file? Alex wondered as she read further into what was clearly classified material. As Alex knew, there were no congressional committees that had oversight of the FBI, so this couldn't have been part of his committee work. Her Government 101 teacher had stressed repeatedly this was a major error and that the McCarthy debacle had shown there was a need for checks and balances when it came to the intelligence agencies. But she knew the FBI had continued to operate without direct congressional oversight.

She read further. Several pages were devoted to questions about investigations of the physicist Albert Einstein for "Communist leanings." Quite a few pages described surveillance and even informers on the "National Negro Congress" for unnamed "subversive activities." The names of several labor organizations were hand-written on one sheet with the names of FBI offices written below. Edgar Carpenter had put question marks beside some of them. She realized with horror that the International Ladies Garment Workers Union, the one to which her aunt and mother belonged, was one of those with an FBI office notation. Were all of these being surveilled? Infiltrated?

Alex sat back in the desk chair, shaking with fear and rage.

She thought of Lincoln and his contempt for hypocrisy. There was so much hypocrisy flowing through these documents with the handwritten notes it stank like the sewer flowing into the Potomac River.

She thought of her Smith major advisor and his suspicions about what really went on in government behind the scenes. He had pushed her to read that ethicist professor who wrote on public affairs and government, Reinhold Niebuhr, for her senior thesis. Even with her upbringing, she had thought Niebuhr far too cynical about government and in her thesis, she had questioned that. But now, she realized, as she made notes on these files with a quivering hand, he had not been nearly cynical enough.

Pain in her back and neck alerted her to the fact that she had been hunched over, taking notes for two hours. She leaned back in the desk chair to stretch and her gaze fell on the box in front of her.

The realization of what she had done, reading what were clearly classified files, struck her. Fearful questions broke over her like chilling, ocean waves, throwing up frightening questions one after another. Suppose Senator Madeleine Carpenter finds out I've read these files? Does she even know what's in them? Had Alistair read them? Why are they locked up here?

She remembered how dusty the boxes were. That calmed her a little. She doubted Alistair had opened them and read them.

Then she sat up straight like the desk chair had just given her an electric shock.

Oh, God. What could be in the other boxes? she thought, her anxiety returning.

She put the FBI files back in the first box and patted the tape down over the lid. Then she knelt on the floor again and pulled out each other box in turn. She carefully lifted the lids with their yellowing tape and peered in to each one. These seemed to contain files on Edgar Carpenter's regular

Senate committees and pending or approved legislation. Hopefully these were less alarming, but she had no time to examine them more thoroughly now. She finished her cursory examination and pushed the last box back in to the cabinet.

Then she took it back out and placed the box with the FBI files behind it. Then she shut and locked the cabinet and sat back again on her heels.

This is a ticking bomb, she thought. What do I do about it?

Well, first, I will not leave any of my notes here, she concluded. She got up and dusted off her skirt. Her notes about what was in the FBI files were lying on the blotter on the desk. She picked them up. She had written the notes in her special short-hand and they would look like gibberish to a casual observer, but she would not leave them. In fact, she was thinking about what she could do with them. For now, she folded them carefully and placed them in her handbag alongside the list of names she had copied the night before. She shut the clasp of her bag with a snap. That Niebuhr had had no idea what a sinkhole for virtue government really was, she though grimly.

Alex had already decided to take the list of State Department names with her to New York to ask her aunt and mother if they knew any of them. Now, she would ask them about some of what was in the FBI material. And they needed to know about the union being linked to an FBI office. Her aunt in particular knew far better than that ivory tower guy who taught up on Morningside Heights about how the real world actually worked. That would be a start.

She hurried back to the apartment to get Miss Bea and her small suitcase. She had spent far more time in the Senator's office than she had planned, but it had been eye-opening to say the least. She put Bea on her lead, and they dashed down the street toward the bus stop.

Alex and Miss Bea had perfected their way of bus travel during the campaign. Alex had altered a large satchel made of carpet fabric for Bea to ride in on the campaign buses without being seen. She had carefully cut out holes in the design and replaced them with mesh. Miss Bea had been frightened the first time Alex had placed her in the bag when she was a puppy. But she had soon settled down. It felt warm and safe, and Alex had put a small blanket in the bottom along with a bone and a couple of dog cookies.

Today, when they got to the local bus stop to catch the one that would take them to the main bus terminal, Alex merely put down the satchel, opened the top wide, and Bea jumped in. She smelled the bone and the cookies but did not touch them yet. She was an experienced traveler.

"I will stay still and quiet and wait until we are on the big bus," Bea told herself.

They caught the big, Greyhound bus to New York with not a minute to spare. Alex took a seat at the very back. She put her small grip on the rack above, but placed the satchel containing Miss Bea on the floor in front of her. Bea felt the big bus lurch and belch and then start to rumble down the road. She fell asleep immediately.

Alex stayed awake and looked blindly out the window. She did not see the white, marble buildings of Washington give way to scattered houses and then to farms. What she saw, as though it were printed on the glass, were descriptions of FBI agents or those they had bribed. She imagined their shadowy figures infiltrating groups, groups doing nothing wrong, just organizing for better wages and safer working conditions. What she saw were infiltrators coming after her family. And who had Senator Edgar Carpenter been, really? How had he had gotten such access to what surely had been confidential FBI memos and reports on their activities? Had he been spying on them, or spying for them?

* * *

Alex woke with a start when the growl of the big bus was magnified as it entered the tunnel that was the major conduit that ran under the Hudson River, connecting New Jersey to New York City. She could hear Miss Bea start to rustle around in the satchel.

"Just a few minutes more and we'll be there, Bea," Alex whispered. The bus would drop them near the Port Authority, about eight blocks from her family's apartment.

It was after ten at night when she and Miss Bea reached the stoop of the tenement off 42nd Street. Bea always enjoyed the smells of New York City, and she had happily walked along with Alex, who was struggling with her bag and the empty satchel. When Alex stopped to rest, Miss Bea would investigate the wonderful garbage smells New York City's sidewalks always offered up.

As Alex rested, she kept an eye on Bea. She knew New York sidewalks were a beagle nose buffet, but she didn't want Bea to nose out a chicken bone that could choke her.

They finally reached Alex's family's apartment building. Its ornate, brick and stone façade dated to the previous century, but it had held up surprisingly well, though the stone was now blackened with the smoke-filled, New York air. They climbed the steep, stone stairs worn in the center from thousands of feet over nearly a century. As they came up to the door,

Mrs. Bronstein, who had lived across the hall from them all of Alex's life, appeared.

"*Libling kind!*" she exclaimed, holding the street door open wide so Alex and Bea could come in out of the cold. "I no see you long time. Is good. Is good." Mrs. Bronstein spoke a lively mix of German, Yiddish and New York accented English, but Alex was always "darling child" in German.

She put down the brown paper shopping bag she had been carrying and quickly enfolded Alex in a hug that reached only to her waist. Mrs. Bronstein could not have been more than five feet tall when she was younger, and now she had shrunk several inches. But her apple-cheeked face, with black eyes that saw everything through thick glasses, was the same. Alex saw the glasses had become even thicker. They had become necessary as Mrs. Bronstein had labored over a sewing machine in a poorly lit, basement sweatshop most of her life.

Mrs. Bronstein then bent down and gave Miss Bea a thorough ear scratch, exclaiming, "*Sheyn hunt, sheyn hunt.* You take good care Alexandra, *nein?*" Alex smiled at Yiddish for "beautiful dog." Miss Bea did not speak either German or Yiddish, but she knew Mrs. Bronstein's kind hand, and she had already smelled the delicious kugel that was in the shopping bag. She politely accepted the ear scratches, while she hoped that some kugel would soon come her way.

"Come, come. I help you," Mrs. Bronstein said, standing back up and attempting to pick up Alex's grip.

"No, no, Mrs. Bronstein, you were just going out," Alex said, gently taking back the bag and picking up the satchel. She knew if she didn't immediately retrieve the bag, Mrs. Bronstein would start up the stairs, and it was three, long flights to her apartment and that of Alex's family. "I can make it just fine."

"Well, italics, I do need to get this to my Rachel down the block. *Leftovuerz* from Shabbat, and she forget." Mrs. Bronstein laughed, and her large, shelf-like bosom moved up and down. "Grantshildran they no forget," and she picked up her shopping bag full of leftovers from the Sabbath dinner and bustled out.

"Come visit, *libling!*" she called back as she bustled down the stone stoop like a woman half her age.

"Come on, Bea," Alex said wearily as she hoisted the bags. "We're almost home."

Bea took a last, long sniff of the lingering kugel smell in the small foyer and followed Alex up the steep, narrow stairs. As they climbed, the familiar smells of boiled cabbage, fried sausages and poor drains surrounded them, along with the sounds of babies crying, couples shouting and tinny music from ancient record players.

Home, Alex thought as she knocked on the third floor apartment door.

"*Mit??*" her aunt's voice came through the thin wooden door sharp and clear.

"Aunty, it's me, Alexandra. We got an earlier bus."

"Gizella, Gizella, it is Alexandra!" she heard. Chains rattled as they were rapidly pulled out of hooks and ancient locks clicked sharply as the bolts were released.

The door flew open, and her aunt flung her arms around her waist. Aunt Kitti was even shorter than Mrs. Bronstein. Her head did not even reach Alex's shoulder. She had no trouble seeing over her head as her tall, slender mother came hurrying down the narrow hall that ran through the apartment. Her mother's brown hair, now liberally sprinkled with white, was backlit from the light of the hanging bulb in the kitchen at the far end.

"*Szerelmem!*" her mother was calling, "You are here!" And suddenly Alex was embraced in a cloud of flour and roses and apples. Her mother always wore a dab of an inexpensive, rose cologne she brought at the local drug store, and its smell always calmed Alex.

Miss Bea's nose, however, focused on the smell of the flour and apples.

"Strudel," she thought and wagged her tail.

"Ah, and the *drágám kutya*," Alex's mother said. Alex was always "my love" and Miss Bea was always "darling dog." She immediately bent down to pet Miss Bea who wagged her ears and her tail. Alex's mother made delicious strudel. "And, I smell goulash as well," Bea thought happily and when Alex's mother stood up, Bea trotted down the hall behind her toward the kitchen.

* * *

Alex sat at the chipped, white porcelain table in the kitchen at the back of the house, a small glass of *Pálinka*, the Hungarian fruit brandy, in front of her. She realized she felt relaxed and full of food, an unusual feeling.

When she had come into the kitchen, the only room anyone used in the apartment apart from the tiny bedrooms, she had felt hungry for the first time in weeks and had eaten a small portion of the goulash and a larger portion of the strudel. All of this had been accompanied by the deep, red Hungarian wine her aunt and mother favored, and now there was the traditional fruit brandy.

It was a good thing she had eaten something, she reflected drowsily. Her aunt had made pointed remarks about how thin Alex had become, even bringing up Nazi prison camps as what those *szemetek* politicians in Washington D.C. were likely doing, working her so hard and not giving her enough to eat. "Garbage" politicians, Alex translated in her head. Not all of them are garbage, Alex drowsily thought, but a lot are. Her mother had just looked very concerned, and that had been worse.

Miss Bea had eaten heartily of her portion of goulash and strudel and had immediately gone to the basket kept for her in Alex's childhood room. She was now sound asleep.

Alex took a sip of the sweet, sweet brandy even though she knew she was risking falling asleep at the table. She looked at the dear faces across the table from her, their own brandy untouched. How she loved them.

Then she felt her mother take one arm and her aunt take the other and lift her gently from the kitchen chair and support her down the hall and into her bedroom. She felt them help her on to the bed, and she knew no more. She never felt it as they tenderly pulled off her clothes, and she never heard their whispered concerns.

24

SATURDAY, FEBRUARY 4, 1961

The smell of the strong, filtered Hungarian coffee sometimes called "black soup" woke Alex. Her head was pounding.

She got up and walked slowly to the bathroom. After she had splashed cold water on her face and dragged a comb through her hair, she began to feel a little more alive. No more brandy for me, she thought walking slowly down the hall toward the kitchen.

"*Kávé?*" her mother asked, holding out a cup to Alex as she entered. She took it and sipped a little of the hot, dark coffee before she even sat down at the table. Bright sunlight poured in through the window glass that her mother and aunt kept scrupulously clean, no small job in New York. The light stabbed at Alex's headache. She moved her chair so the glare would be at her back. She saw that Miss Bea had taken up a strategic position under the kitchen table.

Her aunt came bustling in to the kitchen, already dressed for work in the kind of tailored, shirtwaist dress she always wore. This one was a natty, gray wool that was clearly from one of the precious bolt end pieces her aunt loved. Alex smiled a little over her coffee cup rim. Her aunt was so tiny she needed very little fabric to make a dress for herself. She had a white cotton duster over her arm. She and her mother always wore the dusters at work, carefully hanging up their day dresses in the back, though in winter, if it was freezing, they wore both layers while sewing. But on the street, they wore their well-made coats and dresses with pride. And their hats, all made by her mother, were beautiful. They were of creamy, soft velvet or wool in the winter, and intricate, wrapped silk, sometimes beaded, for the warmer months. With gloves to hide their work-roughened hands, they could easily be mistaken for the very women whose clothes they sweated over creating in poorly lit basements. For many years, Kitti and Gizella had also marched wearing their beautiful clothes. That had not always protected them from police beatings, but Alex, as she had gotten older and gone with them, had seen the hesitant looks on some cop faces as they came upon well-dressed women marchers.

"Come, Gizella, we must go soon," her aunt said briskly.

Alex knew they worked most Saturdays until mid-afternoon.

"Y-es, Kitti," her mother said. Then she stroked Alex's hair, saying softly, "The Miz Bee walk with me. And she eat," her mother said softly. "Now you eat," and she turned and brought over some fresh bread, jam and a piece of glistening cheese and placed it in front of Alex. She patted her hair again and walked out.

"The cheese is excellent," Miss Bea contributed from below the table.

Her aunt was eating a piece of the bread wrapped around some of the cheese while standing in front of the stove. But her eyes were on Alex.

"Aunt Kitti," Alex said quickly while her mother was getting ready, "tonight I must show you some papers I brought with me. Some things I have learned that are very disturbing, you know, worry me."

Her aunt chewed her bread and cocked her small head at Alex.

"This work you do, much worries, I think."

"Yes, it is true, but this is worries for all of us," Alex said carefully.

Her aunt frowned.

"Okay. We talk." She put a hand into a pocket in her dress and took out a small piece of paper. "And here is place for talking man who writes for paper, and maybe priest too. They meet you, yes?" Her aunt put it on the table in front of Alex.

"Wastton sq pk, arc," was printed in a shaky hand. The number 1 was written below that.

"One o'clock at Washington Square Park Arch?" Alex asked, squinting at the scribbled words that were her aunt's version of English.

"Yes, yes. Says there," Kitti said impatiently and then gave her a little pat as she bustled out, calling, "Gizella, we going now!"

Alex heard the door close.

She got up and poured herself a little more of the strong coffee. Then she sat back down and nibbled a little on the warm bread. She passed half of the cheese to Bea who gobbled it up in two bites. She wrapped the rest in her remaining bread and ate it between sips of coffee.

"Excellent," Bea sighed, licking her jowls to catch any stray bits of cheese. Then she put her head down on her paws. They always ate so well when they came here.

* * *

Alex and Miss Bea walked the twenty blocks to the arch that was the symbol of Greenwich Village. By New York standards, a mere twenty blocks was not a long walk. New Yorkers walked everywhere when they could, and today, with the sunlight warming the sidewalks as it rose above the dark canyons of the densely packed buildings, many people were out walking.

Alex saw the tall, white marble monument as they approached from the north. It had been constructed to honor the centennial of President George Washington's Inaugural. As she and Bea walked through the center, she looked up at the intricate carving on the inside of the arch. The beautiful structure looked so solidly virtuous, so triumphant. But what had Washington's administration really been like, she wondered and realized her cynicism about government was growing every day.

Miss Bea stopped to sniff the grass that lined the path that ran through the arch and park. Alex looked around at the benches that were positioned along the sides. Only one bench was occupied with two men. One, who seemed to be in his thirties, had a raggedy beard and mustache. He wore glasses with thick, dark frames and a rumpled suit of a kind of hideous mustard color that bagged at the shoulders. He wore no top coat, only a thick, striped scarf. He was talking rapidly, punctuating his comments with a big cigar he kept punching out in angry gestures.

The object of his speech was a strikingly handsome man. He looked relatively young as well, likely also still in his thirties. Alex saw he was wearing one of those white collars priests wore, but with a tweed sport coat and an unbuttoned overcoat of black, slick, worsted wool. This must be the Protestant pastor, Howard Moody, she thought. No Catholic priest would dress like that. And oddly enough, he had an FBI type haircut, very short on the sides and top. While she watched, he took out a cigarette case from inside his jacket, extracted one, and lit it, all while looking fixedly at the agitated man beside him.

"Okay, Miss Bea," Alex said quietly. "Let's see what they can tell me."

She walked in the direction of the bench, taking her time. Neither man gave her any notice. She finally came abreast of their bench and just stopped and waited. It took more than a minute, but at last at least the man in the collar noticed her.

"May we help you, young lady?" he asked politely. His companion stopped talking in mid-sentence, looked up, and then took another long drag on his cigar.

"I hope so," Alex said quietly. "I am Alexandra Bell and my aunt is Magda Lacza of the International Ladies Garment Workers Union. She said we might speak of some things that affect both New York City and Washington D.C."

The bearded man, who had to be the editor, Fancher, looked up at Alex in frank amazement tinged with anger.

Alex thought she knew why. Fancher, and Moody too, had been waiting for the niece of a labor organizer. What they had gotten was a young, blond woman wearing a beautifully tailored, navy belted coat. Alex had borrowed one of her mother's black velvet, wider brim cloche hats with a jaunty feather in the band, and her hair was gathered into an intricate bun at the base of her neck.

The man in the clerical collar stood up politely, crushed out his cigarette under his foot, and offered her his hand.

"How do you do? I am Reverend Moody of Judson Memorial Church." He had a beautiful, clear voice. It was almost as musical as Senator Carpenter's.

"Hello," Alex said, shaking his hand and giving him a small smile.

The newspaper man remained seated, frowning and continuing to smoke his cigar.

Reverend Moody frowned down at him in return, but when the seated man still said nothing, he made a small gesture toward him.

"And this is Ed Fancher of *The Village Voice*. Wake up, Ed, and say hello to the nice young lady."

"Hello," Fancher said without rising. Then he turned to Moody and punctuated his words with the cigar.

"We're supposed to believe she's related to Kitti? I don't buy it. And what's with the dog?"

Miss Bea, who had been standing quietly beside Alex, clicked her back teeth at Fancher's tone.

"The 'dog'?" she thought, irritated.

Alex summoned her "you've crashed the sherry party" voice.

"I would think, Mr. Fancher, that surely a newspaperman would be able to see below the surface."

"Now see here," Fancher began, perhaps seeing Alex as a person for the first time.

"Now, now," Reverend Moody said in a soothing tone. "Let's all be seated and just talk over why you wanted to see us, young lady. Shall we?" And he made a courtly gesture toward the bench.

"Thank you, Reverend," she said as she sat down at the end of the bench farthest from Fancher, leaving a space for Reverend Moody to sit between them. "And please call me Miss Bell." I won't be politely dismissed as "young lady," Alex thought.

Miss Bea sat at Alex's feet, but she kept her eyes focused on Fancher and her teeth clenched.

Reverend Moody sat down and spoke to both Alex and Fancher. Fancher was still frowning deeply.

"Right, Miss Bell. How can we help you?"

Alex tamped down her irritation with Fancher. She realized he probably had very good reasons for his suspicious nature, given what his fledgling newspaper had been publishing.

"I am the senior legislative aide to Senator Madeleine Carpenter, but this really concerns a man named Stephen Gray. He is, or rather was, the brother of my roommate, Gwen Gray. He was brutally murdered nearly three weeks ago. He was a lawyer at the State Department. He was found beaten to death and wearing a woman's gown along the Potomac River." She caught her breath for a moment and plunged on. "He was frozen, and I found him while out on an early morning run with Miss Bea here." Alex patted Bea's head briefly.

"Oh, Miss Bell, I am so sorry," said Reverend Moody. Fancher said nothing, but he was clearly listening now.

"Thank you," Alex said, and she went quickly on to describe the actions of Detective Hicks, and then her brief introduction to Captain De Luca, but nothing more.

"I have read some of your reporting, Mr. Fancher, and also some of your stories, Reverend Moody, in *The Village Voice*. . ."

"I sincerely doubt you get the *Voice* all the way down in Washington, young lady," Fancher broke in, scorn evident in his tone.

"Please call me Miss Bell," Alex said firmly. "I read *The Village Voice* in the archives of the Carnegie Library in Washington. They have every issue up through December 1960."

"She's got you there, Ed," Moody interjected, chuckling a little. Fancher only frowned more deeply.

"To continue," Alex said, "it is clear to me and to Miss Gray that Detective Hicks is a violent bully and very likely corrupt. He is using the way Stephen Gray was killed, and how he was found, as an excuse not to actually investigate. In fact, I fear he wants to set Miss Gray up for the murder, as unlikely as that would seem. I know Hicks was here in New York for years and then suddenly left when De Luca was promoted with the promise he would 'clean up' corruption in the New York police department. I'd like to ask you, confidentially, what you know about that."

Fancher looked at Moody and then addressed Alex.

"I'd like to see some identification first."

Alex said nothing in reply but opened her purse and got out her wallet. She took out her congressional identification card and held it out to Fancher. It had a grainy, black and white photo of her on one side and "Office of Senator Madeleine Carpenter" and the Senate Office building address on the other.

Fancher put his cigar down on the pavement next to his foot, took the card, looked at it carefully and passed it over to Moody who merely handed it back to Alex. She put it away in her wallet and snapped her purse shut.

"So, what can you tell me?" she asked flatly.

Fancher did not pick his cigar back up, and he got a look on his face like he was about to have a tooth pulled. Then he spoke in a voice of barely suppressed rage.

"Hicks is scum. We both know it." He nodded at Moody who nodded back.

"Greenwich Village is crumbling from the inside because there are so many addicts now. It's mostly heroin, and it is packed up like so much cotton and transported on ships from Europe, nearly always Marseilles by way of Turkey. But it's not cotton. You don't even have to open up the big bales to know it's heroin and not cotton. Uncut heroin smells to high heaven, like vomit mixed with vinegar. Shit, you could stand on the dock and probably smell it on the ships out at sea. Doesn't matter though. The mob controls the ports, and the stuff is just unloaded and cut with God knows what. Talc and other crap that slowly poisons people even without the heroin mix. They're bringin' these poison pills here, and they are pushed out on to all the wretched slobs in this city. And a lot of the wretched of the city live right here." Fancher sighed and put his hands down between his knees and contemplated the pavement and his abandoned cigar.

Moody patted Fancher's knee briefly and took up the story.

"They give the heroin away first, Miss Bell. The East Village is probably half addicts by now, if not more. So, they give it away and when they have a sufficient number of poor souls who crave the heroin, they start charging for it. They stand around, brazenly selling it. You can even come by this lovely park in the evening and see the sales. Addicts lose their jobs, lose their families, commit petty crime to try to get the money to buy more. They will starve themselves to death for the drug. Starve their children. And the city just tries to lock them up instead of trying to help them recover from the addiction."

"And Hicks?" Alex asked, soberly.

Fancher looked up and spoke directly to Alex for the first time.

"This I don't know for sure, but what I suspect is that he was sent to down to Washington to start opening up markets there, getting the whole cycle of addiction going by giving the junk away first. This scum, they hunt out those on the fringes of society. Now that doesn't sound like your friend Gray, but certainly the homosexuals live in the shadows a lot of the time. Maybe this Gray got wind of that, who knows? Somebody took him out in that way to make him look like so much trash thrown away by the side of the river. Nobody investigates trash."

Alex nodded. Fancher's anger and compassion were coming through to her now, as was his journalist's ability to paint a scene. That was exactly how it had looked in the way Stephen was murdered. Was supposed to look, she corrected herself.

"It could be that, Miss Bell," Reverend Moody said, taking up the story. "Now it is not certain what Captain De Luca had to do with Hicks going to Washington. It might very well be that it was the threat of a reformer looking too closely into how things were being done in New York, but Hicks has been gone a while, and both Ed and I can tell you the tide of corruption among New York City cops has only risen since De Luca has been suppos-edly 'rooting out corruption.'"

Alex could hear the quotation marks in Reverend Moody's voice. He did not think much of De Lucas's reputation as a reformer.

Fancher nodded grimly, and Alex nodded at both of them.

That fit with the awful man she had met at the Graham's house.

She stood up.

"Thank you, gentlemen. Before I go, is there anything else you think I need to know?"

Reverend Moody stood as well and placed a hand gently on her shoulder.

"Be careful, Miss Bell. Be very careful. These men will kill you as soon as look at you if you get too close. God bless you and protect you." And he looked down on her in concern.

"Yeah," said Fancher. "Keep your head down. And tell your aunt I said hello. The last tip she gave me was gold," and he bent down and picked up his cigar. It seemed to have gone out.

"I will," Alex said, trying to hide her astonishment at his words. "Good-bye."

She and Miss Bea walked back up the path and under the arch.

Alex's head was spinning with questions. Had Hicks killed Stephen because Stephen had somehow found out that a new supply of heroin was coming into Washington D.C., and some drug dealers had been told to target homosexuals and get them addicted? She thought at least Fancher suspected that. Was De Luca a reformer or a criminal? Her encounter with him had inclined her toward the latter. He was certainly no knight in shining armor. And what kind of "tips" were her aunt passing to the reporter that were "gold"?

She walked along in a fog up 7th Avenue, thinking. Suddenly, she felt Miss Bea pulling hard on her lead.

Alex looked up. Bea was determinedly heading for a hot dog cart.

"I have had no lunch," Miss Bea commented with a not too subtle whine.

25

SATURDAY, FEBRUARY 4, 1961

As Alex and Miss Bea reached the landing on her family's floor, she saw Mrs. Bronstein's door was open. And within about five seconds, Mrs. Bronstein herself popped her small, frizzled gray head out the door.

"Ah, *libling*. I wait for you. Come. Come. I make *butterkekse* and have *kaffee*," she said, and she held her door wide.

Alex hesitated for a moment. She was tired, though more from what she had learned from Fancher and Moody than even the long walk. Miss Bea, however, immediately trotted toward the open door, and Alex followed, still attached to the leash.

"Sit, sit," Mrs. Bronstein said, indicating a small table in her tiny front parlor. It was covered with a lace tablecloth. A beautiful green and white porcelain coffee pot with what looked to Alex like a hand-painted, gilded floral design on the side sat on a little porcelain stand. Two matching cups and plates were placed beside it, along with a plate mounded with at least two dozen of the golden, German butter cookies.

Mrs. Bronstein bustled around, pouring coffee for Alex and setting down a bowl of milk for Bea and two of the cookies. Alex was touched by the lavish setting. This china was likely her most precious possession and the milk would be an extravagance. Add to that the amount of butter in the cookies, and Alex knew she was looking at Mrs. Bronstein's food budget for the week, especially since she had given her daughter and grandchildren the leftovers from Shabbat.

She sat opposite Alex and poured herself half a cup of coffee.

Alex took a cookie as it would have been impossibly rude not to, but she knew very well how to pretend to eat, and she would make the one cookie last.

Looking up at her hostess, she noticed she was looking uncharacteristically grim.

"Mrs. Bronstein, what is it?" Alex asked in concern.

"*Libiling*, I must tell you. I think man's follows you. A Mick, I think. You know. One of those Irish *gut-far-gornisht*?"

Alex knew "good-for-nothing" in Yiddish was often applied to those who appeared to be loitering. But she merely nodded, astonished.

"When I see you go out, I cleaning here, this room, windows there," and Mrs. Bronstein pointed toward the front windows of the little parlor, windows that rivaled her family's for their cleanliness. "So, can see street." She nodded vigorously.

"A man's, I see him and wonder what is this? Why he there? Just standing. Look building. I see him, stand over in shadow. Looks like Irish. What this Irish doing? I ask myself. Why watching? Then you come out and he follows."

Alex felt her stomach turn over, but she said nothing.

Mrs. Bronstein took a small sip of her coffee and then nodded.

"*Gottes Wahrheit*. And so I look and look and then I see you come back *mitt hunt* and the man's, he down the block, walking after you. I think still there." Mrs. Bronstein jerked her shoulder toward the front window.

"*Libling*, you go look there, yes? But you look but no let see you looking."

Alex nodded. She got up and stayed close to the wall so she could come up to the window behind the thick, lace curtain that was pulled to the side of the window. She looked out and there was definitely a man standing in the shadow of the stoop of the building across the street. In the early evening light, she could see him fairly well. He was smoking a cigarette. She saw he was actually looking up, and she shank back further behind the curtain. She stood there for a moment, considering. The man was young, probably in his early twenties. She could see why Mrs. Bronstein thought he was Irish. He had a typically Irish shock of black hair that fell untidily over his eyes. He wore a cap on the back of his head. He had a thin face with a sharp nose, and she could see a stubble of beard even from this distance. He slouched as he leaned against the fence that led down to the areaway below the stoop. He wore a dark jacket and pants, and she could see a sweater underneath.

"So, you know this man's? Who he is?" Mrs. Bronstein asked, studying Alex's face.

"I have no idea, Mrs. Bronstein, but it does seem as you say that he is following me."

Alex sat back down at the little table and sipped at her own coffee, thinking.

"I will be careful, Mrs. Bronstein, and I will look out for this man tomorrow when I go." Alex took a tiny bite of cookie. Time to change the subject, she thought. "So tell me, how are Rachel and Daniel and how are the grandchildren?"

Mrs. Bronstein launched into her favorite subject. Alex smiled, but she was thinking about the man across the street. Had he followed her all the way from Washington?

* * *

It had taken three tries before Alex had actually been able to extricate herself and Miss Bea from Mrs. Bronstein's apartment. Her mother and aunt had not yet returned, Alex was surprised to see. Wondering what was keeping them, she crept into the front room to peer out their front window. The man in the cap was still there, but he was clearly getting cold. He kept slapping his arms around him. Then she saw her mother and aunt coming up the street, carrying several shopping bags. The watcher looked at them as they came up the front stoop and into the building but did not show any special interest in them.

She heard the key in the lock and her mother and aunt bustled in with their bags. It was clear they had stopped to shop for food on the way back from work.

Alex took the bags from them and carried them into the kitchen.

"We make *csirke paprikás* for you, *szerelmem*!" her mother sang happily as she hung up her coat in the hall.

Chicken paprika. Chickens were not cheap. Another food budget strained, Alex thought guiltily, though her mother and aunt would eat the remainder of the goulash and the spiced chicken for the rest of their meals this coming week after she left. She worried again about Mrs. Bronstein having to subsist on cookies.

I will take her a portion of the chicken paprika after dinner as a thank you, she thought, and she made plans to give Mrs. Bronstein as much of her own meal as she thought she could sneak off the plate.

It seemed like only minutes to Alex, and the whole apartment smelled like onion, garlic and the sweet and spicy tang of Hungarian paprika. "Never dust!" her aunt would always loudly exclaim as though purveyors of stale, dried paprika lurked on the fire escape, waiting to sneak in and sprinkle their sawdust product on to her chicken.

Alex retreated quietly to the front room. The man was gone.

* * *

The dishes were cleared, but the warm kitchen still smelled of butter and chicken and spices. Alex still had a full glass of the potent, red wine in front of her. She had not drunk any yet as she didn't want the wine to befuddle her before sharing her notes with her aunt and mother. She had eaten a piece of the chicken and then managed to hide the rest under the egg noodles while they were clearing the table. She had scraped her portion and a little more from the pot on to a clean plate, covered it with a clean dish cloth, and just announced she was taking it to Mrs. Bronstein who had "treated me to coffee and cookies before you got home."

Mrs. Bronstein's whole, round face lit up as Alex handed her the plate. Alex gave her warm thanks for the coffee and cookies and her efforts to "watch that man." She told her the man was gone now, but she would be careful.

When she got back, she glanced into the kitchen. It sparkled. Slices of a rich cream and apricot cake were arranged on three plates on the table. Alex knew this dessert was Miss Bea's favorite and so did Bea. She was already sitting next to Alex's mother, giving her the melting, dark brown beagle eyes she could do so well.

Alex went to her bedroom and got her notes out of her purse before she joined her aunt and mother in the fragrant room.

"So, Alex," her aunt began before she could even sit down. "What is this worries you have, eh? We help. We fix."

"Worries?" her mother asked anxiously.

"Problems with her work," her aunt replied and then repeated that in Hungarian.

Her aunt took a swallow of her red wine and cocked her head to the side, fixing Alex with her shrewd, dark eyes.

Alex took the two sets of notes and patted them flat on the table. She started with the list of names at the State Department and what she thought they might mean. Her aunt listened and then translated for her mother.

"So, give here. Let me see," her aunt said.

"The notes are in my shorthand, Aunt Kitti," Alex said. "I'll have to read the names to you."

Her aunt and mother exchanged a smile.

Oh, no, Alex thought.

"So you think you so clever in school and your old aunt and mother know nothing?" Her aunt said, still smiling. "We look when you not here. We no so stupid. Girls can get problems. We check. Hah. But you no write boys, you write school studies. But we know how you write this," her aunt said, pointing to the pages.

Alex passed the pages over and absent-mindedly took a large swallow of her wine. Never underestimate them, she thought dazedly.

Her aunt put on her glasses and squinted at the first page.

"What is this, this word?" she asked in an irritated fashion.

Alex looked over.

"Protocols. That means rules, rules for how they are doing this thing about the people whose names are on the paper."

Her aunt read out the names one at a time so her mother could follow.

Alex passed a piece of her cake to Miss Bea who had moved over by Alex when she had gotten most of her mother's cake.

"So delicious," Bea thought as she delicately licked the cream off her whiskers.

When her aunt had finished reciting the names, she looked at her mother and then they both looked at Alex.

"Two. I think. We know two."

Her mother nodded.

"Harry Smeldkin," her aunt said pointing to the list. "And here, Joseph Lifton."

"Are they Communists?" Alex asked.

"*Kommunista?*" her mother laughed. "*Idióta.*" And her aunt laughed too.

"Harry, he not Communist, he not even good socialist. He from the Brooklyn. Bronx maybe. Join Socialist Workers oh like ten, ten or so, years. Come to few meetings. Not see what workers need. Leave."

Her aunt studied the paper some more and went on.

"Your mother right. Looking for Communists now is idiots. Mostly no Communists any more. And joke is *Kommunista idióta* also. What you got here, Alexandra, is *idióta* running after *idióta.*"

Her mother and her aunt both laughed hard and then toasted each other with their red wine.

So the so-called "Red Scare" is still just blowing political smoke, Alex thought wearily.

She got out her other papers.

"This worries me more. I copied these from notes the Senator's husband left. He had questions. Many questions about FBI. Things they do that are not right, I think. There are more files. I could not copy them all."

Her aunt's glasses went back on her nose, and she peered at Alex's shorthand. Then she started translating them into Hungarian so her mother could understand.

Alex was still trying to get her mind around the fact that her aunt and likely her mother too had broken her shorthand code years ago. She let the stream of Hungarian run over her while she tried to remember if she'd put anything personal in those high school notes.

Her aunt finished reading and translating, and her aunt and mother looked at Alex with almost identical faces, both fierce. Normally, they did not much look alike, except in certain expressions, and this was one.

"We know this about FBI and our union. They send FBI *kém*, you know word, means spy. He comes to our meetings," her aunt said. "Takes much time. We have meeting. End meeting. He go. Then we have real meeting. Stupid man, but we need be careful." She stopped, looked at her sister and then went on.

"You say there is more? Words you do not have here."

"Yes. Much more, I think," Alex said slowly.

"Cannot take, yes? Much, much trouble for you. You should see more, make your writings. Much bad things they do. Maybe use in work you do?"

"Yes, but still it would just be notes," Alex said, thinking aloud. "No one would believe me." She pulled the pages back in front of her and studied them. The meaning was there but not the shock of some of the actual memos.

I need the actual documents, but Aunt Kitti is right, stealing classified documents is a sure way to be sent to prison, she thought despairingly.

"Can you take some pictures?" Aunt Kitti said. "You know, with camera."

"That is a good. . ." Alex stopped. Pictures of documents. Suddenly the meaning of Stephen's Gray's case full of photography equipment flashed into Alex's mind like one of Stephen's flashbulbs had gone off in her brain.

Of course. That's what he had been doing, she realized, stunned that she and Gwen had not made the connection. He must have been taking documents from the State Department, photographing them and replacing them.

Her mind raced on. That's why he was tortured. Someone wanted to find the photos he'd taken. They'd killed him, but he must not have given in because they were still looking.

Alex put her hands over her face, horrible images coming to her. How he must have suffered, she thought. He had died for whatever secrets he had uncovered. And he had not given them away because whoever had searched Stephen's apartment and then mine and Gwen's was still looking, she thought. That is probably why that guy outside has been following me.

"*Szerelmem?*" her mother said softly, the Hungarian word for "my love" comforting her even as her mother's work-worn hand patting gently on Alex's arm did as well. She took her hands off her face and saw the two of them looking at her in concern.

"I was thinking of all the bad things these people do. It is truly terrible," Alex said slowly.

Her mother and aunt nodded solemnly. They knew very well what some people were capable of.

Alex drank the rest of her red wine and held out her glass for more. Her aunt filled her glass but made no comment.

I have to tell Gwen. And I have to photograph the FBI files, Alex thought solemnly as she took another drink of the blood red wine and felt the bite of the tannin and spices on her tongue.

"Are you going to give me the rest of that cake?" Miss Bea asked with a subtle whine.

Alex absently put her little dessert plate on the floor for Bea, but she was thinking about what documents Stephen might have taken out of the State Department and photographed.

Whatever they are, he died to protect them, she thought.

26

SUNDAY, FEBRUARY 5, 1961

It was barely dawn. Alex sat in a chair she had pulled over by the front window, the homemade, patchwork quilt from her childhood bed wrapped around her. She had been up all night, watching the street, but the watcher had not come back.

Last night, after Alex thought her mother and aunt had fallen asleep, she had gone into the small front parlor and begun her vigil. At first Miss Bea had jumped up next to Alex in the lumpy, oversized armchair, but she had not settled down.

"I cannot get comfortable. Why are we not in our beds?" Miss Bea grumbled.

Finally Alex had gotten Miss Bea's basket and placed it by the armchair. Bea had jumped down, circled a few times in her own bed and fallen fast asleep.

No so with Alex. Her anxiety about having brought danger this close to her family was high. She would keep vigil. She thought the watcher would return in the morning, but she didn't want to risk him coming during the night, perhaps trying to get in to their building and their apartment. But she hoped in the morning he would come back. She wanted him to follow her so she could draw him away from her family.

Stephen's funeral was at noon, and she had plenty of time. She was betting that whoever was searching for what Stephen had died to protect would think Alex would keep it with her.

Alex could hear her mother moving around in the kitchen. She quietly pushed the chair back to its normal position, woke Bea and carried the

basket and quilt back to her room. Bea went immediately to the kitchen and
Alex could hear her mother talking in Hungarian to Miss Bea, telling her
what a good dog she was.

Alex pulled on some old pants and a sweater she kept in the apartment
and grabbed Miss Bea's leash. She took her on a short walk, and when they
returned the watcher was still not there.

Her mother greeted her with a hug and a big cup of the thick, dark
Hungarian coffee. Alex sat at the table, sipping it, wondering where she
could get some of the Hungarian coffee beans in Washington. It was like
drinking straight caffeine, and she could feel it spreading throughout her
body, making her blood flow again through limbs cramped from a sleepless
night in a chair. She felt so much better after a few sips that she managed to
eat some of the fresh bread and cheese her mother put in front of her.

Alex washed in the apartment's tiny bathroom. There was no shower,
only a bathtub about the size of Miss Bea's basket. She carefully examined
her roots in the small, ancient, black spotted mirror, trying to see what
was actually a little of her dark hair and what was a mirror speck. I can see
some brown, she thought. I'll have to do touch-up color when I get back to
Washington.

For now, though, she'd borrow her mother's lovely, black velvet hat to
cover her hair. She would need a hat for the funeral in any case. Her mother
and aunt had stopped commenting on her hair when she visited, but she
knew they still felt it as a betrayal. She sighed.

She shook out her black silk and wool pencil skirt dress that she had
worn to the Senate hearing and hung it in the steamy bathroom to get out
the few wrinkles.

Finally, dressed and packed, she checked out the front window again.
The watcher was back.

She could hear her mother in the kitchen, and she looked into the
bedroom her mother and aunt shared. Her aunt was putting on a sweater
and looked up at her. Alex put a finger to her lips and beckoned her.

She led her silently into the front parlor and whispered.

"There is a man. He has been watching the building since yesterday. I
think he is a spy from Washington who followed me. Stay to the side and
you will see him. He's wearing a cap."

Her aunt went carefully along the wall and looked up briefly from behind the curtain.

"I see," she said.

"Watch to see he follows me when I leave, okay? I know what he wants,
and it is not here, it is in Washington. He will follow me back, I think. But
you make sure. If you see him again, be careful. Telephone me."

Her aunt left the window and came over to Alex. She took her by the arms and looked up into her face.

"You need we can call union men. They can come, make this man stop following you. You hear?"

"I understand. But now, it is not necessary." Alex paused. "But if he comes back here, call the union men, okay?"

Her aunt snorted but did not speak.

Alex turned and walked down the hall to the kitchen to begin the long, emotional process of leaving.

Her mother was standing by the sink and turned with a wax-paper wrapped package in her hands. She held it out to Alex.

"For you, *szerelmem*, and you, *drágám kutya*," and her mother bent to pat Miss Bea who was hovering by her mother's side, "to eat on bus." The sight of her mother's red rimmed, faded blue eyes as she stood up made Alex tear up as well. She reached out and hugged her mother with all her might, breathing deeply of the rose scent tinged with flour, and, she sniffed, some chicken. Oh no, Alex thought as she held on to her mother for another few seconds, they are giving me their chicken.

"Be safe, Alexandra!" Aunt Kitti instructed from the doorway, her voice gruff from tears she would not shed. "Never trust any of them, never!"

Alex went to the door and bent down to fold her aunt into a tight hug. She only met a little resistance.

"Too thin, too thin," her aunt said scolding her as she pulled away. "You give food, yes Gizella?" she demanded.

Her mother only nodded, drying her eyes with the corner of a dish towel.

Alex snapped on Miss Bea's lead at the front door and turned to face them.

"You call on telephone when you get home!" her aunt instructed.

"It will be very late," Alex cautioned.

"Is no matter," her mother said.

* * *

Alex and Miss Bea walked north toward Times Square where they would catch the train that would take them up to Harlem. Bea obligingly stopped to sniff at the curbside bundles of trash along the way, and Alex had several chances to glance back. The man was following.

Alex turned into a vacant doorway right before the subway entrance, put down the carpet bag, and Miss Bea hopped in. She hefted the bag and her grip and started toward the stairs to get down to the subway platform.

"Miss Bea, you're gaining weight," Alex whispered as she labored down the steep stairs to the subway platform. She went to the ticket window instead of using the tokens in her pocket only so she could check behind her using the reflection in the window. Good. The man was still there, following.

The subway ride up to the 135th Street station took only thirty minutes though to Alex it felt like hours. She could see the man who was following her in the next car. At every stop he glanced over at her. He is really quite bad at shadowing, Alex thought after a while.

She exited the subway station and released Miss Bea from the bag. She attached her lead and headed down the block toward the big YMCA building. The street was crowded with Sunday shoppers. Shops were busy and vendors with carts selling everything from vegetables and fruits to jewelry and records were lined up along the sidewalks as well. Alex and Bea navigated the crowds without difficulty. They were used to crowded sidewalks. Bea regularly stopped to sniff around food carts, and Alex could check on the man following her. He was having a little more trouble staying with them given the crowds.

This would be easier if I just gave him the address where I'm going, she thought, slightly annoyed at the incompetent shadow.

The crowds thinned out as they turned on to 132nd Street. This area was not far from the Hotel Theresa where Fidel Castro had stayed, Alex knew. In fact, she could see the tall, stately building with its distinctive spires in the distance. But she had never seen the 132nd Street Baptist Church before and as she and Bea approached, she had trouble believing it was a church at all. It looked like the kind of stone, gothic building that should be found on a New England college campus. Alex's limited experience of churches, all garnered from the outside, were the ornate, Catholic churches people in her family's neighborhood attended.

This has got to be the church, though, she thought as she could see a hearse and a group of about twenty people gathered outside a large, arched doorway. As she got closer, she made out Gwen standing in a group of women, likely her mother, her aunt and her older sister. Behind them, on the sidewalk, were men carrying musical instruments, and they were talking together. As she got closer, she could hear them humming and even singing a little, likely deciding on the music they would play.

Alex stopped walking, a vivid memory of Stephen playing on the old piano in the hotel lobby on the campaign trail holding her in place. That talent had been brutally destroyed, she thought, crushed and left to freeze by the river like so much meat in a butcher shop. Her grief welled up, fueled by her anger at the man who was following her until she felt she could not hold it all in.

She stopped walking and stood, her breath coming faster and faster. Then she turned and glared right at the man who was following her who had stopped at the corner, she saw, pretending to tie his shoe. She just kept glaring until he stood up and glanced her way. She held his gaze and tried to let all her fury show on her face. He stepped back, clearly startled that she was staring so angrily at him. Then he turned quickly, crossed the street and hurried out of sight.

Miss Bea pulled on the lead. She had spotted Gwen and was wagging her tail.

"Let's go," Bea whined.

Alex took a deep breath and let herself be led toward the group at the church door.

She went up to Gwen first.

"Thank you for coming, Alex," Gwen said in a flat voice. Alex could see she was shivering. She had pulled her brown wool coat around her instead of buttoning it and it nearly wrapped her small frame. But it wasn't keeping her warm. The cold came from inside. She's just holding on, Alex thought, her heart hurting for her friend.

Gwen introduced Alex to her mother, aunt, and sister. The two older women greeted her graciously, but they looked as drained as Gwen. Gwen's sister, however, was cool in her manner.

"You should put your bag and that dog in the minister's study before the service starts," she said with barely suppressed irritation.

"Thank you," Alex said simply, knowing full well that she too was just holding on.

"Alex," Gwen said softly, taking a few steps away from her family, "let me introduce you to my father's and brother's friends."

"I'd love to meet them, Gwen," Alex said and followed her over to the group conferring by the church door. She heard "So, 'Just a Closer Walk' to start then?" and there were sounds of agreement. "Then we got the sax, right, Len? And then John, he's gonna sing?" There were some nods and one "Amen."

"Gentlemen," Gwen said as they walked up, and the men immediately fell silent. "I'd like you to meet my roommate, Alexandra Bell. She also knew Stephen."

"Oh, Gwen honey, that's good, so good your friend here could come," a tall, thin man holding a trombone said, and he put his other arm around Gwen.

"Alex, this is Leonard Brown," Gwen said, smiling up at him. "He plays saxophone too, just can make you cry."

She stayed in the circle of Brown's arm but gestured to each one in turn in the small circle.

"Alex, this is Earl Jones," she said next, and a short, wiry man smiled kindly at her and nodded his grizzled head. "He plays about everything," Gwen went on. "He'll play the trumpet now, then piano and organ when we get inside."

"Early, call me Early, everybody does," he said, shaking Alex's hand.

"Early taught Stephen to play the piano," Gwen said with a little sob.

"Now, now, baby girl, your brother he catch on so quickly, it was hard to say who teach'n who," said Early, a little tear in his own dark eye, and he patted Gwen's arm.

"I'm Bud, Bud Silver," said a man with a drum sitting on the sidewalk next to him, putting out a hand. "So glad to meet Gwen's friend."

"Moses Sullivan here," said the last man, who was holding a clarinet.

"This was Gwen's daddy's piece," he said holding up the instrument. "I hope I can do it justice for his boy," he said mournfully. "Stephen gave me his daddy's stick before he went off to that college out West. Said this here clarinet was lonely just shut up in a case. Never wanted to play it himself. I told the boy I'd let his daddy's stick out to sing all the time." And he ran his hand lovingly down the well-polished instrument.

Alex and Gwen stepped away from the musicians.

"I'd better get Miss Bea and my case inside, Gwen," she said.

"Yes," Gwen said absently, her eyes going to the hearse where six men in dark suits were starting to gather.

Alex put down the carpet bag, and Miss Bea jumped in, though she was not happy about it. She was getting tired of being shut up in the narrow case.

Alex picked up the bag and her case and walked through the big doorway, up the six steps just inside, and then she hesitated in the gloom. The stone entryway was dim and very cold.

A very tall and quite portly man in a dark suit stepped forward out of the shadows.

"I'm Brother John, little lady, can I help you?" he asked in an astonishingly deep voice. It bounced off the stone walls, and Alex thought she could feel it reverberate in her chest.

"How do you do?" Alex replied softly. "I am Alexandra Bell, a friend of Miss Gwen Gray. I'd like to leave my things in the minister's office if that is alright."

"Certainly, certainly," said Brother John, booming the words at her. "Follow me," he said and turned immediately right and went down a dimly lit corridor toward a big door at the end.

"I'm the Minister of Music here and I will sing some in the service," he said as they walked along. He stopped before the large, wooden door at the end and reached into his pocket for a large ring of keys. He fit one in the lock, pushed the door open and flipped on a light.

Enormous bookshelves. That was Alex's impression. The room must have been fifteen feet high, and three walls had very tall bookcases in a dark, polished wood. They were filled with books, many with ornate spines. A desk was placed in the center. A couch and some chairs were the only other furnishings. For a book lover like Alex, this room was heaven. She put down the carpet bag and her grip and just gazed at the filled shelves.

"You got an animal in that bag?" boomed Brother John, startling her so much she jumped.

Alex realized Bea was sniffing the room through one of the mesh holes.

"Just my little dog," she said quickly. "She'll stay in the bag and be no trouble."

"Oh, I purely love dogs," said Brother John, bending down to the case, his voice softening so much Alex hardly recognized it. "May I pet her?"

"Of course," Alex said, and she opened the top of the carpet bag. To her astonishment, Brother John just reached in and lifted Miss Bea out with a big and very gentle hand.

"Hello, little one," he said, placing Miss Bea on the floor and squatting in front of her.

The touch of that hand had told Bea all she needed to know about this big man, and she wagged her ears in her most endearing way and then put her head right under that big, warm hand.

Brother John gave Miss Bea a thorough ear scratch as he spoke.

"Back on our farm in Mississippi, where I'm from, we had lots of dogs. Huntin' dogs and house dogs and dogs that been done bad and I fixed 'em up. No room here in this crowded city for a dog. I purely miss my dogs."

Brother John stood up and went to a small door that led off of the right side of the room. It seemed to be a bathroom as she could hear water running. Brother John came out with a large, ceramic cup filled with water.

"What's her name now?" Brother John asked as he placed the cup on the floor in front of Bea.

"Miss Bea," Alex said, thinking about how there were dog people and people who were not dog people.

Miss Bea lapped some water.

Suddenly, all three of them turned toward the window at the sound of a drum and a trumpet. The procession would clearly begin soon.

Alex went to put Bea back in her carpetbag, but Brother John just shook his head.

"No need, no need. She can rest here on the rug, and we'll just lock this door."

He bent down and gave Bea another scratch.

"She'll be a good girl, won't you, darlin'?" he crooned.

"Yes, I will," Bea thought. "But I will need my bone from the bag just the same."

Alex had already thought of that, and she reached down and got the bone out before she followed Brother John out the door.

"Be good, Bea," she whispered.

The sounds of the musicians tuning up got increasingly louder as Alex followed Brother John out of the church.

When they got outside, the hearse had moved down to the end of the block. Wooden barricades had been set up, and they blocked the street at each end. Many more mourners had arrived, and they lined the street on both sides. The six, black-suited men were standing at the rear of the hearse. The musicians had taken a position to the side, toward the center of the street. Alex could see Stephen's family standing closer to the side of the hearse. Some other men held crosses made of flowers, and she saw what looked like a keyboard made of white flowers and black ribbons. She hurried over to the mourners standing closest to her, and she took a position in back of them, next to the wall. Brother John stood beside the huge door of the church.

The rear doors of the hearse were opened, and the six men moved into position to take the casket as it slid out of the back.

Bud Silver, the drummer, hit his drumsticks together four times. The casket moved forward, followed by the men carrying the flowers and then Stephen's family. The drummer began to slowly hit the drum to match the pace of those carrying the casket and then the brass instruments began.

Two older women standing in front of Alex began to sing softly as the brass lifted the mournful melody. She listened to the words as the casket containing Stephen's body came closer and closer down the street. "I'll be satisfied as long as I walk, let me walk close to Thee."

And then the clarinet came in like it was crying with all the cries of all the people who had ever lost someone. Her chest hurt to hear it. "Daily walking close to Thee, let it be, dear Lord, let it be."

The casket was carried into the church. Alex could hardly bear to look at Gwen's face for all the suffering she saw there. Her mother, aunt, and sister had pulled dark veils down from their hats to cover their faces. But not Gwen. Her face was uncovered under her hat as though she wanted no barrier between herself and her grief.

The other mourners filed in slowly behind them, and Alex joined in.

Now I know why Gwen kept saying this was a homegoing, she thought as she matched her own steps to the heartbreaking melody. Stephen is coming home.

27

SUNDAY, FEBRUARY 5, 1961

Alex drew in her breath as she followed the mourners through the large doorway into the main part of the church. The church was so beautiful and so large. It was built in a semi-circle with balconies that soared above the main floor, seemingly floating there, connected by wooden arches.

It was the immense, stained-glass window at the front, however, that truly astonished her. Glistening, colored light spilled through the panels of intricate glass and reached for the altar far below. The men had placed Stephen's coffin in front of the altar on a white, cloth-draped bier and the whole was bathed in reds and blues and greens and gold. Alex hoped the sight would bring some peace to Gwen and her family as it really did look like Stephen could just travel up that light and head right into heaven.

I wish that were true, Alex thought sadly as she moved over to the farthest pew on the right and took the end seat. This was closest to the hallway that led to the minister's study. She hoped Miss Bea would not bark, but she wanted to be close just to check.

The musicians had moved up to the platform behind the coffin. Early Jones took a seat at a grand piano. Bud Silver sat behind a much larger set of drums than the one he had carried in the procession. Leonard Brown lifted a saxophone out of a case and spoke quietly to the other musicians. Then he turned, lifted the instrument to his lips and a sound so melancholy, so haunting came out that the mourners, who had been whispering a little to each other, fell silent and then, as the piano came in under the sound of the saxophone, they made sounds of moaning as another accompaniment.

All her life, Alex had heard jazz and blues in her neighborhood. Especially on hot summer nights, she would sit on the front stoop with her mother and aunt or play with other kids on the sidewalk accompanied by music coming from record players or radios with the volume turned high. And sometimes, an older man who lived up the block would bring out his trumpet and wail along, or challenge the music flooding the block.

But I have never heard anything like this, she thought. Never.

When Brown finished, the congregation fell silent except for a few "amens" here and there. Then Alex saw Brother John step up to the raised platform. He leaned down and seemed to say a few words to Brown, and then he turned and walked up to the front of the platform.

"Amazing grace, how sweet the sound" began in his big chest and came out his mouth, filling the huge space with a giant and yet gentle sound like kindly thunder.

The congregation sang too, and Brother John's voice led them up to the very top of grief and then back to comfort and assurance. Alex stayed silent, but her thoughts rose and fell with Brother John's voice. I have been blind, and I hope now I can see she said in her mind. Unfelt, a tear rolled down her cheek.

Brother John walked solemnly across the platform and down the stairs to a chorus of "amen" and "halleluiah" and "thank you Jesus." He took a seat in a pew just in front of Alex and sighed deeply.

Early Jones left the piano where he had been seated, picked up a trumpet and walked to the front of the platform and put the instrument to his lips. The congregation quieted and in that moment Alex heard a sharp bark.

Then the sound of the trumpet calling out a melody that the mourners instantly seemed to recognize and call out drowned out the barking.

Oh, no, Alex thought. She got up and hurried toward the hallway that led to the minister's study. She heard Brother John get up and follow her.

When Alex got entered the dim, stone corridor she could still hear Miss Bea barking. She was torn, wanting to yell at the dog to be quiet and not wanting to further disturb the service. Then she stopped cold in the middle of the corridor. Brother John nearly collided with her.

"Oomph," he grunted as he tried to keep his balance.

"Look!" Alex hissed. A man was kneeling at the door of the minister's study. She realized he was trying to pick the lock.

Brother John realized the same thing.

"Hey, you! Get away from there!" he called out in his booming voice.

Alex winced a little at how loud that sounded, though she could clearly hear the powerful sound of the trumpet still filling the church, and she hoped the intense music and congregational response would have covered Brother John's shout.

The man jumped up and turned. The cap was pulled down now and shaded his face, but it was the same man who had been following her for two days.

The minister's study was the only door at the end of the stone corridor, but he didn't hesitate. He must have already opened one of the mullioned windows that lined the corridor on the outside wall, and he jumped out the window. As Alex and Brother John reached the open window, they saw a large bush about five feet below the window with broken branches. The bush must have broken the man's fall. He was apparently unhurt as they could see he had already scrambled to his feet and was running toward the street.

"Well, I never," said Brother John as they stood watching the man disappear around the street corner. There was no possibility of either of them giving chase. Brother John could not fit through the narrow arch of the tall window, and in her pencil skirt, Alex could not climb or run.

Brother John locked the window and took out the ring of keys from his pocket. He made soft, soothing noises to Miss Bea as he unlocked the door and pushed it slowly open. She was standing right in front of the door, rigid with anger. She had stopped barking, but she growled softly.

"Bad man. Bad puke smell. He did not get in."

Brother John crouched down by the open door, using one hand to feel the scratches on the lock and the other to stroke Bea's fur that was standing up along her spine.

"We never seen such a thing here at the church," Brother John said, turning his head to look up at Alex. "Nothin' valuable kept in the minister's study 'cept the books." He gave Bea another long stroke.

"You good girl. You are a good watch dog," he said softly and stood.

"I barked at him, and he ran away," Bea thought, preening under the petting and the praise.

I know what he wanted, Alex thought grimly. He wanted to steal my suitcase.

"Brother John, you need to get back to the service. I will stay here with Miss Bea," Alex whispered.

"I purely hate for you to miss the rest of the service, chile. I tell you what. We lock this door, but you and little miss dog can sit down there near the end of the hall and then you can hear what's happening."

Brother John opened a closet door to the far right and extracted a folding chair. Alex snapped on Bea's lead and walked into the hall. Brother John locked the door behind them.

Alex followed him down the corridor, and he opened the chair for her and placed it near the open door leading into the main part of the church. She whispered her thanks and sat down. The trumpet was still singing its mournful melody, now accompanied by the full complement of instruments. The sound was incredible. And then it all stopped, except for some calls and crying. And the sound of my heart thumping in my chest, Alex thought.

Then she heard feet shuffling and a few muttered comments. And a voice she knew well came clearly into the corridor, exactly as though Gwen were standing there.

"My brother, Stephen Gray, was a brave, brave man. He was too young to have fought against the hateful Nazis, but he fought hate just the same, and he fought it bravely. The music our Daddy's friends are making for Stephen here today, that is brave too, and I think why Stephen loved it so much. Jazz is slave music, African music, and free music. Jazz just does what jazz needs to do to break with music that wants to keep you and me in our place, givin' us all those European classical chains when we can make beauty and rhythm that sings high and loud and free and that doesn't care what some think is proper and right. And Stephen Gray, my brother, was like that. And Stephen loved the law. He thought in his kind and generous way that if we could just change the law to be more fair then people of all kinds would be more fair and be more free. I loved that about him. . ."

Alex heard a little sob, and Gwen's voice started again, though a little higher as though she could keep the sadness in her throat by tightening it up.

As Gwen spoke more about Stephen and his love for the law, Alex wondered about breaking the law, photographing documents that proved some people were corrupting the laws and breaking them even in the government. How had Stephen Gray kept his love for the law and his breaking the law from pulling him apart? Except, of course, he hadn't been able to keep from being pulled apart, nearly limb from limb.

Gwen had finished speaking, Alex realized, as there was a smattering of "amens" and then silence.

Then there was the sound of 200 people rising to their feet and a creak. Alex risked a glance out of the corridor and saw that Stephen's casket was being lifted again. She saw the family file out behind the pallbearers. Then the drumsticks were knocked together four times and a blast on the brass instruments rang out the familiar "When the Saints Go Marching In."

Miss Bea, who had been dozing on the cold stone floor of the corridor, exhausted from her defense of the minister's office, started awake.

After the musicians and the mourners had walked up the aisle, Alex followed with Miss Bea. Alex stopped and turned back toward the altar before she exited the church. She let her thoughts embrace Stephen Gray. She whispered, "I hope you are at peace." Then she took a last look at the magnificent space, so different than the Catholic churches she had known in her childhood and youth with statues and plaques and rows of candles to be lit. This was so much more peaceful and, she realized, it didn't make her feel guilty and afraid.

* * *

Alex leaned back against the seat of the bus, feeling the pull of sleep. She and Gwen had managed to catch the 4 o'clock Greyhound bus back to Washington. Gwen looked exhausted, her face gray, and she was silent as the bus rolled along the highway that cut through the New Jersey farmland. The sun had set, and it was dark except for a line of red along the western horizon.

Gwen needs to eat, Alex thought. I should too, though the thought of the sandwiches in her bag made her feel faintly queasy.

"Gwen," Alex said softly, "My mother packed some chicken sandwiches for us. I think we should try to eat a little. I bet you've had nothing all day, right?"

Bea woke up in the carpet bag at Alex's feet.

"Some of that chicken is for me."

Gwen turned her head slowly toward Alex, like it was almost too heavy to move.

"Yes, all right. Yes," she said on a sigh.

Alex took her bag down from the rack overhead and set it on the empty seat beside her. They had the whole back row to themselves. She took out the sandwiches, grimacing a little. She had wrapped the wax paper package in a couple of clean kitchen towels to try to keep the food away from her packed clothes, but the whole bag smelled of chicken. She thought about how long it would take to get that smell out of her clothes as she closed and replaced the bag.

The small towels were helpful in protecting their dresses from the crumbs. Alex picked at her sandwich, passing pieces of chicken and bread down to Miss Bea in her carpetbag.

"What is this spice on the chicken?" Gwen asked suddenly.

"Paprika," Alex said. "It's a popular spice with Hungarians."

"It's good," Gwen said and took another bite.

When Alex, Gwen, and Miss Bea had finished the sandwiches, Alex folded up the wax paper, wrapped it in the towels and returned the now smaller packet to her case.

"We should get some coffee when the bus stops in Delaware," Alex said, sitting back down. "I'm so tired, but I have a lot to tell you."

Gwen looked over at Alex, determination replacing the lines of fatigue for a moment.

"I have a lot to tell you too," she said.

* * *

"He on this bus?" Gwen asked in an anxious whisper when Alex had finished telling her in a low voice about the man who had been following her.

"No," Alex said firmly. "I checked every man as we walked down the aisle. He's definitely not on this bus. He must have turned tail when Brother John and I caught him trying to jimmy the lock."

"I barked at him, and he ran away," Miss Bea thought sleepily from inside the carpetbag.

"They're still after something Stephen had, I'm sure of it," Gwen said, keeping her voice down.

"It's got to do with the photography equipment and somehow the postcard," Alex said softly back. "I had some thoughts on that," she began, and then she dropped her voice. "But first I have to tell you what I found in the Senator's office." Alex hurried through what she'd found in Senator Edgar Carpenter's files she'd read. "I thought about photographing the real papers, not just taking notes, and it came to me that could be what Stephen was doing with all that camera equipment in the case. He might have taken pictures of some documents or the like. But we still need to figure out what he meant on the postcard, break that code."

Gwen sat up straighter and turned toward Alex so she could speak almost directly into her ear.

"I done think it's a code," she whispered. "Remember I told you how that boy purely loved gadgets and pretendin' to be a spy and so on?"

Alex nodded.

"So when I was thinkin' about him, you know, to get ready to talk in the church, I thought about that. I agree. I think he musta photographed somethin' secret, somethin' bad. We know they want it. Enough to kill him for it. But they didn't get it 'cause he hid it on that postcard."

"On the postcard but not a code?" Alex asked, confused.

"No. Now listen. I know a professor at Howard. He works in photography and such. I'll go see him and ask. I think there's ways to take somethin' that's like the size of a piece of paper and somehow make it very small with the kind of cameras and all that Stephen had in that case. And he made somethin' small and put that on the postcard. Called a microdot, I think. Stephen and some of his friends were all up in that spy stuff, you know, like those James Bond books?"

Alex nodded, absently registering how Gwen sounded more like her mother now.

She leaned back against the seat, feeling her own fatigue. Could this whole thing be about spies? she wondered. I thought it was about drugs. Is that something else, or part of it? Her brain felt so sluggish, and it seemed odd somehow. Spies and drugs? She knew about the writer, Ian Fleming, and his spy hero. She thought the novels were about a British spy chasing Communists around in the Cold War. But now her mother and aunt were telling her there are almost no Communists left in this country. But there still could be spies. Or not. It could just be political fiction, like the novels. Her mind drifted. How hard is it to make one of these microdot things? she wondered. It would be a great way to keep pictures of those FBI files hidden. Except, she thought with a sickening feeling, Stephen had still paid with his life to keep whatever it was hidden. That was not fiction. That was fact.

* * *

It was nearly midnight when Gwen, Alex and Miss Bea reached the landing outside their apartment.

Suddenly, Bea started to sniff around the bottom of the door and growl.

"What's that dog doin' now?" Gwen asked in a grumpy voice.

"Someone has been here again, Gwen," Alex whispered.

"Oh, Lord You think they still in there?" Gwen asked in a shaken voice.

"I don't know," Alex said. "I don't think we should call the police though. Tell you what, I'll let Bea in and see if she barks like she's found someone. If she has, we can all run, I guess." Alex turned and looked down at Miss Bea. "You hear me Bea? If there's someone in there you bark and run back out."

Bea snapped her teeth together but did not comment. She didn't run from bad men.

Alex carefully opened the door and pushed it wide. There seemed to be no one lurking as Miss Bea did not bark. Instead, she kept her nose glued to the floor and sniffed around the little foyer. Then she ran straight to the bookcase by the window and sniffed there.

"Well," Gwen began, but Alex put her finger to her lips and stepped back out into the hall. Gwen followed, frowning.

"I wonder if someone has planted a listening device in our apartment," Alex whispered.

They both gazed through the open doorway. Miss Bea was now standing on her back legs, paws braced on the highest bookshelf she could reach.

"Stephen warned me about all that," Gwen whispered. "He was always checking in his office and even his apartment."

"Don't say anything about it, then, just go over and look while I talk about nothing important."

Gwen crossed the room toward the bookcase while Alex prattled about their trip.

"Oh, my heavens, I'm so glad to be back. I'm exhausted. I think I'll fix some warm milk and then just flop right into bed." She went on talking about how lovely the service had been, and Gwen peered behind the books on the top shelf. Miss Bea watched her.

Gwen turned and nodded to Alex.

Silently, they both walked back out into the hall. Miss Bea followed, puzzled.

"So we leave it, right?" Alex whispered.

"I think so," Gwen whispered back. "We'll have to just be careful until we can figure out who's after whatever Stephen has hidden."

"We need to check that his case is still hidden in that crawl space under the ironing board," Alex said quietly.

"Oh, Lord yes," Gwen breathed. "You keep talking and make some noise with a pan and such. I'll check."

"Okay," Alex said softly. "I'll also use the phone, call my family. Tell them we got here safely. They already know about my family, so not a big risk." But her stomach turned over in fear.

They went back into the apartment, softly shut the door and played their parts.

Gwen went to the little closet that held the ironing board, and Miss Bea followed her. Alex got out a pan. When Gwen nodded, Alex banged the pan on the top of the stove. Gwen opened the little door and peered in. She gestured okay.

Gwen looked down at Bea.

"You a good dog," she said.

"Yes, I am. I deserve some of that milk," Bea contributed.

When the milk was warm, Alex poured it into two cups and Miss Bea's bowl. They all drank in silence.

28

Did you get the case?

Ah, no. Not exactly.

What do you mean, not exactly?

I followed her up to the city just like you said to do. She stayed in a dump building, talked to a couple of guys down in the Village. Nothin' going on there. Didn't talk long. None of our guys. Next day she went uptown to that N***** f** funeral luggin' the suitcase and she left it locked up in a back room while they was carryin' on like they was back in Africa in the church. Shouldn't be allowed that.

And?

Well, you see, I got made when I was breaking in to get it. That dog made a racket. I swear I'm gonna kill that dog and then a big, huge N***** fella he chased me and, well, I figured she'd bring it back here and I'd get it.

You leave that animal to me. You failed again.

Well, now, we got a little time. And we know she brought it back here.

How exactly do we know that?

She brought it back on the bus. No sweat.

You were on the bus, you saw her bring it back?

Yeah. Yeah.

*You're lying. I met the bus. She and that N***** girl were on it. You were not.*

Well, I mean, I saw 'em get on in the city. Didn't want to risk being made and all so I just got a different bus.

You mean the earlier bus you took after you were made, don't you?

Ah, yeah. That's what I mean.

Sound of throat clearing.

So, did the bug get planted? Any trouble there?

No, actually. I did it myself. That's why it got done.

So, look. I'll get it that case. I'll go today get it this time.

Why should I believe you?

Well, 'cause, I mean, I will.

Never mind.

The sound of two pops.

You should not have lied to me.

The sound of clothes being searched.

You really were too stupid to live. You are carrying your real identification.

Sound of something heavy being dropped in the river.

With any luck you will float on down to the Chesapeake and the crabs will eat you.

Sound of chuckling and retreating footsteps.

I might even have you as part of a crab dinner some night.

29

MONDAY, FEBRUARY 6, 1961

Alex and Gwen shared a cup of coffee at their little kitchen table and made small talk for the sake of whoever was at the other end of the listening device that had been planted in their apartment. Alex had been too tired for a run, and Bea was still asleep in her basket when she and Gwen hurried out.

"I'll find a pay phone at lunch today, see if I can get a time to meet with Professor Lawrence," Gwen said softly as they walked down the street toward the bus stop.

"Good," Alex replied, grabbing for her hat as a gust of freezing wind tried to take it from her. "If I can make it, do you think it would be alright if I went along? I have some questions about how to photograph documents and shrink them down like that."

'I guess," Gwen said, holding on to her own hat as the wind gusts came faster. "You serious about making pictures of those files in the Senator's office? Kinda dangerous and all."

"Like you said, Gwen. Your brother was brave. I want to be brave too."

Gwen bowed her head and a tiny tear appeared on Gwen's wind-chapped cheek and trickled down. She just let it fall as she nodded her head.

"What is in those files is terrible, just terrible," Alex went on, trying to talk herself into going ahead with what she planned to do when she reached the Senator's office today. The FBI had their own secret operatives, spying on citizens who weren't committing crimes. It wasn't right.

"An agency of our own government has gone outside the law, again and again," Alex said in a whisper, walking closely beside Gwen. "I don't have any idea what I'll do with that information, but for now I know I have to make copies and hide them."

Gwen lifted her head, her face grim.

"I know, Alex. Lord, do I know."

* * *

Alex let herself into the dark, silent office. It was still far too early for Mrs. Anderson to come in and the Senator was traveling back today and had said she would not be in.

Before she had gone to bed the night before, Alex had sewed four large pockets inside her heaviest winter coat. Each pocket was the size of a document.

She took her coat off and lay it open on what was now her desk at the raised platform. Taking the little key, she opened the locked credenza and pulled out the box containing the FBI files. Nothing looked like it had been touched since she'd put it back.

Her plan was to take only the original documents to photograph, not Senator Edgar Carpenter's handwritten notes. Those she could hand-copy herself.

She went through the box, making two piles. One pile was the actual documents, though some, she now saw, were faded photostats, and one pile was the notes. As she sorted, she wondered how Senator Edgar Carpenter had managed to get these documents and actually keep some of the originals. And did Senator Madeleine Carpenter know anything about this? He had clearly been collecting the material for many years.

When she had extracted all the papers she was going to photograph, she divided them into four and inserted them into the pockets she had made inside her bulky coat. She quickly carried the coat to the closet and hung it up, buttoning the front and hanging it up at the far side of the closet. Then she hurried back and put the notes in the desk drawer where she could copy them in her shorthand during the day. She took the nearly empty file box, lay the tape back over the top and locked it back in the credenza.

Just in time. As she took a tissue out of her purse to blot her perspiring forehead, Mrs. Anderson opened the door. Alex quickly extracted her compact as well and began to powder her nose.

"Good morning, Miss Bell," Mrs. Anderson said wearily. Alistair's death had hit Mrs. Anderson hard, Alex realized, as it brought back memories of her son's death.

"Good morning, Mrs. Anderson," Alex replied, closing her compact and placing it back in her purse. She held her breath as Mrs. Anderson hung her own coat in the closet and placed her hat on the shelf. When Mrs. Anderson closed the door to the closet, Alex exhaled.

During the morning, Alex quickly copied Senator Edgar Carpenter's notes in her private shorthand. Not much of a secret way of writing though, she thought wryly as she scribbled, since her aunt and mother had been able to decipher it.

Mrs. Anderson spent the morning typing addresses on envelopes while also occasionally answering the phone and taking messages for the Senator.

Mid-morning, the mail was delivered, and Mrs. Anderson took it and brought it over to Alex. She managed to cover what she was doing with a blank sheet of paper, and she stood up to lean over and retrieve it from her. She noticed her hands were shaking slightly, but Mrs. Anderson did not seem to find anything amiss, and she returned to her typing.

Alex finished copying the notes slightly before noon. She put it all in the desk drawer and slid the pile of mail in front of her. She sighed. This was still her job, she supposed, until the dreaded Reginald who liked to be called Reggie showed up and was trained.

Precisely at noon, Mrs. Anderson put the cover on her typewriter and stood up.

"I'll be getting some lunch, Miss Bell. Can I bring you back anything?" she asked, her voice still slow and weary.

"No, no thank you, Mrs. Anderson. I have to run an errand during our lunch break."

"Very well," Mrs. Anderson replied, her voice now slightly muffled from inside the closet where she was retrieving her coat. "I will put up the sign that the Senator's office is closed for the lunch hour."

She adjusted her hat in the mirror that hung inside the closet door, pulled on her gloves, picked up her purse and the sign and departed. Alex could hear her placing the sign in the slot designed to hold it.

Alex started to breathe again.

She retrieved both Senator Edgar Carpenter's handwritten notes and her own copies from the desk drawer and quickly moved to the closet. She lay her coat out again, inside pockets exposed and put in her shorthand copies. Then she replaced the originals in the FBI file box. She took great care lifting the dried out tape over the top as it was getting more frayed even with her gentle handling.

She put on the coat, the inside pockets feeling impossibly heavy, got her hat and bag and locked the office door.

Alex's heart pounded. It was so loud to her own ears, it sounded like the drums in a Fourth of July parade. She walked as normally as she could, and she nodded pleasantly to the guard at the door. She walked carefully to the corner and when she was out of sight, she sprinted for a cab stand. One cab waited, and she got in.

The cab was quicker than the bus, but it still seemed like an eternity to Alex until she got to the building and raced up the stairs to their apartment. She had so little time.

Miss Bea stood in the foyer, puzzled by Alex's appearance.

"Much too early," she thought.

Alex flipped on the radio and under the cover of the sound opened the ironing board cabinet. She took out Stephen's case, opened it on the kitchen table and placed all the documents in a slot in the top that held photographic paper. She took out the camera and confirmed that as she had thought it was a 35mm Canon. She would need to buy new film in order to photograph the documents.

Alex had a working knowledge of photography from Harry Zimmerman, a union member and friend of her mother and aunt, who would take photos of the union job actions to document especially what the police did. The police would try to incite violence and then lie later about union violence and deny police brutality and even claim they had seen union members carrying guns to justify the use of force by police. Zimmerman was a short, wiry, grey-haired man with the piercing blue eyes. He liked to be called "Shooter," as, he chuckled to Alex, he was actually the only union member ever shooting. He had talked to the teenaged Alex about cameras and angles and how to frame a shot while she waited with him across the street, away from where the police might see him and break his camera. Though that had happened, Alex knew, and Shooter Zimmerman had been beaten up by the police more than once.

He had even let Alex take some photos when the police were not around. After a while, seeing her interest, Shooter had invited her to drop by his hole-in-the-wall photography studio a few times so she could see how photos were developed. Teenaged Alex was fascinated when she saw an image emerge as if by magic from the tray, especially when she had been the one to take the picture. Some of the photos she'd taken herself were now in her precious box hidden behind the wall in the front closet.

As she placed everything back in the case, she wondered about Shooter Zimmerman. Was he still taking pictures of what the police really did? She'd have to ask her aunt sometime. She was sure of one thing and that was that Shooter would have approved of her taking photos of these FBI documents.

Alex attached Miss Bea's lead to her collar and took her for a short walk outside. When they returned, Alex put down fresh water for Bea, turned off the radio and hurried out.

"What was that all about?" Bea wondered as she took up a vigil in the small front hall. Things were far from normal.

"I must keep watch."

* * *

Even taking a cab back, Alex was nearly an hour late getting back to the Senator's office, but Mrs. Anderson made no comment about that. She merely nodded to Alex while stuffing envelopes.

The afternoon dragged on. Alex opened and sorted the Senator's mail and began to answer a few. She did not bring up Fluffy in her replies even when one of the Senator's constituents mentioned him. She might be new to Washington, but she knew instinctively that more senior aides did not write in the voice of cats.

Finally Mrs. Anderson covered her typewriter again.

"I'm leaving, Miss Bell. I will see you tomorrow," she said wearily as she walked slowly toward the closet.

"You will lock up?"

"Yes, certainly, Mrs. Anderson. Have a good evening." Alex looked at the older woman's bent back as she went out the office door. It's like she's weighed down with grief, she thought.

But as soon as Alex heard Mrs. Anderson's retreating footsteps down the hall, she got up, checked again that the credenza was locked, got her own hat and coat, turned off the lights and hurriedly departed. She had a lot of work to do tonight, but first she had to stop and buy film.

* * *

"Wed 4:30 Tubman Hall room 460" Gwen had written on a piece of paper that she handed to Alex that evening while they made small talk for the listening device and ate their canned stew. Alex nodded and pushed away her nearly uneaten dinner. The oily gravy and the little chunks of unidentifiable meat turned her always difficult stomach.

Alex scraped the stew into Miss Bea's bowl and went to turn on the radio to cover the sound of her setting up the photography equipment.

Miss Bea bent her head over her dish and sniffed.

"I miss Mama's cooking," she thought as she licked up the congealing glop.

Alex retrieved the case, carried it into her bedroom, closed the curtains tightly and then set up the stand on her little desk.

There was a pamphlet of instructions in the upper pocket of the case where Alex had stored the documents to be copied, but she had not consulted it. Though the apparatus was clearly expensive, it was not at all difficult to understand.

She loaded the film into the camera, brought both of the lamps in her bedroom over and adjusted the light. She took the first of the FBI documents from the stack she had placed beside the photography stand, put it below the camera, adjusted the focus and snapped the picture.

Two hours and thirty-six photographs later she was finished.

30

TUESDAY, FEBRUARY 7, 1961

Alex and Miss Bea ran north along the canal path. It was still two hours before dawn and only the barest outline of the inky river was visible in the moonlight.

Despite her lack of sleep, Alex felt invigorated to be back on a run. The temperatures had risen during the last few days, and the path had only a few patches of ice. Her footfalls beat in a regular rhythm. It was soothing after the chaos of the last few days. She kept her flashlight pointed at Miss Bea who was off her lead ahead of her but staying mostly on the path. A few of the glittering patches of frozen grass tempted Miss Bea, but she mostly just trotted ahead, her nose taking in the myriad smells of river, small animals in their burrows, trash cans and especially the traces of other dogs that had come this way. She was content.

Alex was formulating a plan for the day. The Senator would be back, and she needed to have the documents replaced in the box before then. Last night, after she had photographed the documents, she had put on cotton gloves and carefully wiped each one clean of fingerprints before placing it on the stack. Now they rested snugly in her heavy winter coat that was hanging in the front hall closet of their apartment.

Even though she had plenty of time, she thought she should be getting back to shower and change so she could get to the office very early.

"Come on, Miss Bea," she called softly to the little dog who was minutely sniffing a portion of the frozen grass.

"What?" Bea thought, distractedly. Whoever this dog was he had been marking the glass along the path at regular intervals, and it had started to annoy her.

Alex ran up to the still sniffing Bea and snapped on her lead.

"Wait a minute," Bea growled, and she peed on the spot where that male dog had thought he was making a statement. "This is my territory," she remarked, and then she turned and trotted along beside Alex, satisfied she had done her best.

* * *

Two hours later, Alex was seated at her desk in Senator Carpenter's office, the FBI documents returned to their proper files, and the file box placed in its original spot in the credenza.

This was one of those days when her armor of exquisite clothing was essential to her. She had chosen a suit patterned on a Givenchy she had seen in Bergdorf Goodman. The fabric was a silk and wool blend in a deep, forest green. The jacket had three-quarter length sleeves, a standing collar that framed her neck exquisitely without being too dramatic, and it was fitted at the waist. The pencil skirt fell softly to below her knees. The shape of the collar really called for a choker necklace, but Alex had decided she wanted her neck to look vulnerable. She had to be very careful when she spoke to the Senator, and she wanted to seem to be no threat.

Mrs. Anderson had come in about half an hour previously, still looking very weary. Alex thought she was not sleeping well. Well, she knew a lot about that.

"Good morning, Madam Senator," Alex and Mrs. Anderson chorused, almost in unison, as the Senator entered.

Senator Carpenter smiled faintly at them and said "good morning" over her shoulder as she headed for her office. She shut the door firmly behind her.

Alex bided her time. She would wait until the Senator called for her. But the tension mounted as a couple of hours dragged by.

* * *

It was nearly noon before the intercom on Alex's desk buzzed.

"Miss Bell, please come in and bring your pad," Senator Carpenter said, her voice chopped up by the static in the instrument.

Alex replied in the affirmative and then stood. She shook out her skirt, straightened her jacket and picked up her pad. The next few minutes would determine a lot about her future in the nation's capital.

"Please sit down, Miss Bell," Senator Carpenter said, not even turning from the window where she was standing. Instead, she continued looking out through the streaks of grime toward the Senate office building opposite. The overhead lights were off as usual, though the desk lamp was lit.

"Thank you, Madam Senator," Alex said softly, settling her pad on her lap. It was a good thing she could take notes in her shorthand without even looking at the paper since where she was sitting was quite dim.

"Did you have a good trip, ma'am?" Alex finally asked when the Senator remained silent.

"Oh, I suppose so," she replied in weary tones. "The family was very upset, of course, and the funeral was lengthy. So many of Mr. Carrington's young friends spoke. It did go on for quite a while. I did have a satisfactory visit with the Van Allens."

The Senator turned from the window and moved toward her desk. As she came into the circle of light, Alex could see she was wearing a navy blue suit along with her trademark pearls. The dark fabric was rumpled, and Alex wondered briefly if it had been what she had worn to the funeral.

I need to focus, Alex thought, and she waited for an opening. It came right away, as she hoped it would.

"And you, Miss Bell. What were you able to accomplish in my absence?" the Senator asked, looking across the desk at Alex but somehow, Alex suspected, not really seeing her.

"I did the mail, of course, and then," Alex paused for maximum effect, "I decided to clean out that credenza along the back wall."

The Senator jerked back slightly. She sees me now, Alex thought, though there was still silence, so she went on.

"Yes, I found it contained several boxes, and I catalogued what was in them. I thought you might want to arrange to have them stored as they are notes and files of Senator Edgar Carpenter's."

Alex arranged her face to be as expressionless as possible. It was hard to see the Senator's countenance as she had moved back beyond the circle of light of the desk lamp. But her hands were clenched so tightly on the desk, Alex could see her white knuckles.

"How did you open the cabinet?" the Senator asked in a low, measured voice.

"You gave me the key," Alex said, again as neutrally as possible.

"Oh. Yes." A pause. "And what did you find?"

Alex took her time and started flipping pages on her pad. She had prepared for just this moment.

"I made a list." Flip, flip. "Yes, here it is," and she read off the names of the committees on the boxes containing those documents. Then she stopped.

She glanced at the Senator who was now gripping a pencil with both hands.

"Anything else?" the Senator gritted out, her tension palpable.

She knows, Alex thought as she bent back over her pad and pretended to consult it.

"Yes, there was one box that I thought at first also contained committee papers. It was labeled FBI, but then I remembered that there is no congressional committee that has oversight of the FBI." She paused and turned over a page in her notebook and then looked up. From what she could see, the Senator had leaned forward, into the light. Her normally pasty, white face was mottled with red, and it was rigid with tension.

After pausing a little longer, Alex went on calmly.

"So, I just closed the box, put the tape back on the top like I did with the others and thought I should consult you about what to do with all of them." Another pause. "We will really need that space for storage of your important committee documents."

"Indeed," the Senator said, sitting back again, out of the light.

Alex waited. The silence went on until Alex wanted to scream, but she held herself perfectly still. If someone saw us in this office now, she thought, we might be mistaken for two mannikins.

"My husband, Senator Edgar Carpenter, was a very idealistic man," the Senator finally said in a flat voice.

Alex waited.

"He saw a lot in the war, and he was devoted to preserving our democracy from what had happened to Germany."

She got up abruptly and went back to stand looking out the window, her back to Alex.

"I will arrange to have those boxes picked up and moved to a secure storage facility, Miss Bell. You will forget about them completely and get on with your work." Her back was rigid.

"Certainly," Alex said, using her same neutral voice, and she went on with barely a pause. "What would you like me to work on this week?"

"I would like you to read up on farm subsidies, Miss Bell. That is of prime importance to my constituents. There is a lot of information here in the library in this building, though you may also need to go to the Library of Congress for additional information. You know where that is, of course?"

She's getting me out of the office, Alex thought, even as she said, "Yes, ma'am. I do."

"That's all for today, Miss Bell," the Senator said dismissively, turning from the window to stand behind her chair. "You may go."

"Thank you, Madam Senator," Alex said, standing up and smoothing down her skirt.

She pulled her shoulders back and looked directly at Madeleine Carpenter, still standing beyond the circle of light.

"Senator Edgar Carpenter seems to have been a remarkable man and a remarkable patriot. His loss is a loss to our democracy, I think."

"Yes," said Senator Madeleine Carpenter, and she turned back to the window.

Alex stood up and started to walk toward the door.

"Miss Bell!" the Senator's sharp voice stopped her abruptly.

She had turned away from the window and was looking hard at Alex.

"Please get the key to the credenza and bring it to me immediately."

"Certainly, Madam Senator. Do you want the key to the door to the office back as well?" Alex asked, thinking, this will be the test of whether I will be able to keep my job.

Senator Carpenter did not reply for a moment.

Alex waited, trying to breathe.

"You may keep the key to the office as you will have need of it if you must get in early or stay late."

"Thank you, ma'am. I will get the credenza key immediately," Alex said softly, keeping the relief out of her voice.

Alex went out and took the small key from the ring in her purse and brought it back into the Senator's inner office.

"Here you are, ma'am," she said quietly, placing the key on the Senator's desk.

"Thank you. You may go. You should get started on that farm subsidy research right away. And write me a report when you finish. It will likely take you several days."

"Yes, ma'am, and thank you for the opportunity to do that," Alex said evenly, keeping even a hint of sarcasm out of her voice.

She is not her husband, Alex thought sadly as she headed back to her desk. She is keeping me on staff at least for now, wondering what I really know, but holding me at arms-length as well. I need to be careful. But, she thought as she sat down at her desk to get a new pad she would use for the library research, now she knows she needs to be careful of me.

She just doesn't know how careful.

Yet.

31

WEDNESDAY, FEBRUARY 8, 1961

At two o'clock, Alex shut the last, thick tome she had been reading on a history of American agricultural policy since the beginning of the twentieth century. The library of the Senate office building had been quiet, and she had made good progress on notes for the report. When she had arrived in the morning, she had let Mrs. Anderson know she would be spending the day doing research at the Senator's request and would leave from the library.

Being in exile from the office is a distinct advantage, Alex thought as she returned the books to the library desk. There was no need to make up an excuse to leave early. Gwen had let her know that the appointment with Professor Lawrence was in his office on the Howard University campus and she was determined not to be late.

She put on her coat and hat in the cloakroom on the first floor and hurried out to catch the first of the three buses she would need to take to get to the Howard University campus. The two mile distance was short, but the bus routes from the seat of government power to the historic university founded after the Civil War as a seminary to train Negro preachers were not designed for ease of access in either direction. And that was despite the fact that Howard University was now a world-class research and teaching institution. Or, Alex thought as she started down the street, perhaps that was still why.

As she walked toward the first bus stop, she registered how pleasant it had become outside. A watery sun had replaced the freezing gloom of the morning. She changed her mind on taking so many buses and decided she could just walk over to Columbus Circle, up Massachusetts a short way and catch a bus that ran north toward the campus along New Jersey Avenue. She could get off before the bus turned left at Florida Avenue and walk from there.

The walking feels good, Alex thought, as the tension from her confrontation with the Senator ebbed away. She ended up just walking the whole way and in a remarkably short time was nearing the famous university. She had never been to Howard, and as she headed north on the sidewalk, the campus came into view. She saw the immense lawn with its intersecting paths and the façade of Founders Library. It is stunning, she thought as she stood in what Gwen had told her was called "the Yard." The library and an historic chapel were arranged around the Yard, but it was the classical revival building, its red brick perfectly intersected by limestone, that drew her. Trees devoid of leaves dotted the Yard, and their empty branches seemed to be framing the library. It was too beautiful to be obscured in any way, Alex thought. This was her favorite kind of architectural style especially for a college or university campus. It looked so secure in itself. It would protect the knowledge it contained. She realized how much she missed her own college campus. There she had not been frightened all the time like she was now in Washington. Just some of the time, she thought wryly as she remembered keeping her identity a secret from her classmates.

Reluctantly she turned from gazing at the classical beauty of the architecture and asked a passing student to direct her to Tubman Hall. It turned out it was directly behind the magnificent library. It was a subdued version of the library, in the same red brick but without the stunning bands of limestone and the cupola. She entered and looked at the directory for Professor Lawrence's office.

Alex had done more than research agricultural subsidies in the library. There had been a catalogue for Howard University among the stacks, and she had looked up Professor Lawrence. There had been no photo, and she thought that a little unusual for a faculty entry for a photographer, but there was some information. Professor Lawrence had been born 1911 in Fayetteville, North Carolina, and he had attended Howard University at sixteen years of age, graduating in three years. He had planned a career in medicine but went to the New York Institute of Photography after graduation. He had lived and worked in New York City and had famously done a series of photographs on New York domestic workers for the Roosevelt era Federal Writers Project. Professor Lawrence had "served" in World War II, the biography said, but that was all that was said. Alex had speculated that was when Lawrence had learned to make microdots, but there was no way to know for sure. He had then been hired as an Associate Professor in the Arts and Science Department at Howard and was now a Professor.

Gwen could have told me most of that if we didn't have to be so careful about not talking in our apartment, Alex thought resentfully as she reached the third floor where Professor Lawrence's office was located.

She checked her watch and realized she was a little early. She walked down the long corridor to the large window at the end. It had a magnificent view of the Howard campus, and the library building was centered in it like the whole was framed for a photograph. Alex had never considered pursuing a career in academics, but given her short experience in government, she stood and pondered whether that would have been a better choice. It's not too late, she thought, and then she was startled out of her reverie by a deep voice calling to her from down the hall behind her.

"Miss Bell?" the voice repeated. Alex turned and saw a tall, thin man with copper-colored skin, high cheekbones and the most extraordinary eyebrows she had ever seen. They were coal black and reached across his forehead like two circumflexes that met in the middle, pointing down to his nose. A black mustache bent the other way so that the center of his face was framed by them. Dark, close cropped hair capped his head.

She realized she had not replied.

"Yes, I am. And you must be Professor Lawrence." Alex walked closer and saw two extraordinary dark eyes were twinkling at her from under those brows. She felt his own face might be his most interesting photographic subject.

"Indeed," said Professor Lawrence, his mustache curving up with his smile.

"Come in, won't you? Gwen has not yet arrived, but I think I can manage to fix us each a cup of coffee while we wait." He stood at the open door, beckoning her.

"That is, if I don't accidentally use developing solution instead of water to brew it," he joked as Alex entered the enormous office.

The lowering sun was sending such sharp shards of light through the tall windows on the west wall of the office, Alex was initially blinded as she entered. She turned away from the windows and saw Professor Lawrence had not turned away. He was gazing raptly at the approaching sunset.

"Light," he said softly. "It is everything." And he continued to face toward the window, clearly lost in contemplation.

Alex took off her coat and hung it on a coat stand by the door. She turned and saw that the Professor had actually picked up a camera and was pointing it out the window.

She stood quietly and just looked around the big space. There was an old, rolltop desk pushed against the wall to the right with a desk chair on wheels in front of it, but the room was dominated by several long tables that were piled with stacks of photos, papers, and some equipment such as a large microscope on a table opposite the windows. Some tall stools were pulled up haphazardly to the tables. To the far left there was a door with a light over the top. He has his own darkroom here, Alex thought wonderingly.

Just then she heard soft footsteps in the corridor outside. She turned toward the door to the hall, and Gwen appeared. She seemed to need a moment to catch her breath, and Alex saw her take in the scene. Alex could see Gwen register that her teacher was plainly deep in contemplation. They both stood silent, waiting.

The sun went behind a low-lying cloud, and Professor Lawrence turned away from the window.

"Gwen!" he said when he saw her.

"Hello, Professor," Gwen said, a smile lighting her face.

Alex realized with a pang how little she had seen Gwen smile recently.

Professor Lawrence walked quickly over to where Gwen was standing just inside the doorway, his long legs carrying him remarkably quickly. He folded Gwen into a hug.

"So, so sorry to hear about Stephen. It about broke my heart," Professor Lawrence said softly, and Gwen clung to him momentarily. Then she stepped back and gazed up at him.

"Thank you," Gwen said, blinking back the tears that came all too readily these days. "And you have met Alexandra Bell?" she asked, turning toward Alex, her voice a little hoarse.

"Yes, yes," Professor Lawrence replied, his own voice a little hoarse as well. He coughed.

"I was just going to fix some coffee, and then you can show me what you have brought for me to look at."

He turned toward the table along the back wall, and Alex saw there was a beaker full of water and a Bunsen burner below it. He turned on the flame and then bent his long back to reach under the table and bring up a tray with coffee cups, a French Press already prepared with coffee grounds with a little plate with cookies on it. Alex was touched, realizing that the professor had taken care to welcome his former student in this way.

After the boiling water was carefully poured into the press, Professor Lawrence turned from the table.

"Now, while that brews let me take you on a little tour, Miss Bell. Gwen is all too familiar with my office and darkroom here, but I am always happy to show it off," and he bustled over to the door that had the light over it.

Gwen had taken a seat on one of the stools at the center table. She hadn't even taken off her coat, Alex observed, just unbuttoned it. She was resting her head on her hand, leaning on the table. She's exhausted, Alex thought, but she resisted her impulse to fuss over Gwen, knowing she'd hate that.

"So, Miss Bell," Professor Lawrence was saying from the doorway of his darkroom.

"Go on," Gwen whispered, and Alex obeyed.

Alex went over to the darkroom door and looked in. It was nothing like the small, cramped space where Harry Zimmerman had taught her developing. There was a long processing sink, two holding sinks, a work area, a long counter for chemical mixing with shelves of chemicals above, and two enlargers.

Alex realized she was staring, but clearly Professor Lawrence was enjoying her gawking.

He smiled and began talking about the equipment and especially the enlarger, a new acquisition apparently.

Alex listened attentively, asking questions about the different developing tanks in particular.

Then Professor Lawrence looked out the door to where Gwen was still sitting, and his expressive eyebrows lifted as he took in her bent back.

"Ah well, perhaps coffee and then to work on what Gwen has brought, right? It is important."

Alex walked out into the main office, a little dazed, and Professor Lawrence snapped off the light in the darkroom and followed her.

The coffee revived Gwen a little, and Alex was glad to see her eat two of the cookies. She sipped her own coffee carefully. It was practically as strong as Hungarian coffee and that was saying a lot, she thought.

"Alright, Gwen, let's see what you have," Professor Lawrence said when they had finished their drinks. They had been sitting on the stools around the central table. Gwen turned away from the table slightly and pulled out the postcard from where she had clearly hidden it next to her heart. Alex noticed she had wrapped it in brown paper closed with tape to protect it.

She carefully pulled the tape off the ends of the paper and unfolded it. The postcard lay in the middle, and the crease where Gwen had hidden it in her shoe from the bully cop, Hicks, ran like a scar down the center.

Professor Lawrence picked it up and examined both sides.

"This," he pointed to what at first looked like an ink blot. "This is certainly a microdot."

Gwen swayed a little on the stool, and Alex stood up and moved next to her, concerned she might topple off it.

Professor Lawrence did not seem to notice Gwen's distress. He was peering at the postcard. Then he stood and went over to the large microscope on the far wall. Gwen got off the stool and followed him, Alex close behind.

Lawrence placed the postcard on the table and picked up a round lens like a jeweler would use. He bent and went over the card on both sides with the lens.

"Yes, it's there. I'll get it up and read it under the big microscope."

He reached up and took a very small tool from a box on the shelf above the microscope. Then he brought down another box that contained blank slides. And from a case adjacent to the big microscope, he took some glasses with magnifying lenses in the center. When he put these on, his dark eyes were so enlarged they looked like headlights.

He placed the slide on the postcard near the microdot, and, looking like a surgeon about to operate on a tiny tumor, he took up the small tool.

"Microdots have an amazing history," Lawrence said in a lecture voice while he bent over the postcard. "Been around for a long time, but it really was in the last war that the technique was improved with aniline dyes, the better to prevent counter-espionage."

He continued to talk, peering intently at the dot that he was transferring to the slide.

"That's not what we have here, though. Just an earlier method, what is erroneously called the Zapp technique. Nothing to do with anyone named Zapp, amazingly enough. An article by J. Edgar Hoover on espionage planted that lie in the American mind. He published that in *Reader's Digest*, can you believe it? Tissue of lies, of course. Hoover's way."

Does the FBI ever tell the truth about anything? Alex wondered.

Lawrence's bent back had obscured the operation, but within a few more seconds he was lifting the slide and placing it under the microscope. He carefully removed the magnifying glasses and returned them to their case.

Alex noticed Gwen was holding her breath and realized she was as well. It was likely Stephen had died for what was on that card.

Professor Lawrence turned on a light that was located at the bottom of the microscope, looked into the eyepiece at the top and turned a dial so that various lenses rotated above the slide. Then he used dials on the side to apparently fine tune the focus.

He let out a big breath and turned to them.

"Amazing. X marks the spot."

"What?" Gwen said shakily. Alex shook her head. It made no sense.

"It's a map. With an X marking a spot. And there is some text written on the map and a message for you, Gwen. Here, look for yourself," he said and stepped away.

Gwen shrugged off her coat and placed it over the stool behind her. But when she approached the microscope, she seemed to realize she was too short to see through the upper lens and stopped. Professor Lawrence was already moving a step stool over, and Gwen climbed up.

"It's a map, all right," she said in a whisper. "A map of Rock Creek Cemetery and, and, there's a circle around that Adams Memorial statue. It says, wait, this can't be, it says 'It is hidden between the seat and the wall behind the statue. Right side.' And there is an X drawn there." She paused, swallowing, and went on. "He wrote, "If I can't, you get it, Gwen, and do what you can."

Gwen looked up at both Alex and Lawrence, her face so drawn it looked like a mask.

"Here, Alex," she said, stumbling down off of the step stool. "You look. What does it mean? What did he hide?"

Alex dragged the step stool aside and looked into the lens of the microscope. It was a map of that cemetery, and she could see a jagged edge along one side where it had apparently been torn out of a book, perhaps a guidebook to Washington monuments. At the bottom it said, "Find a Grave" and sure enough there were little numbered squares among the paths. But there was a black ink circle around what was labeled "The Adams Memorial" on the map with an X. And in bold, black capitals was written exactly what Gwen had read off.

Alex looked up and shook her head.

"Adams Memorial," Professor Lawrence said slowly. "Astonishing place to hide something, and yet, very fitting." He looked at them with his piercing eyes. "You know its history?"

Alex shook her head and Gwen just stood, looking at him.

"Well, you know who Henry Adams was, right? The author and historian?" They both nodded.

"Well," said Lawrence, clearly back in lecture mode now, "His wife suffered from depression, apparently, and she killed herself by ingesting potassium cyanide, a chemical used to develop photographs. Adams commissioned Augustus Saint-Gaudens, the famous sculptor, to create a statue in bronze. The design is influenced by Buddhist philosophy, I believe, and he called it 'The Mystery of the Hereafter and The Peace of God that Passeth Understanding,' but the public commonly called it 'Grief.' Still do. Adams actually hated that glib, public name, but I have always thought it fitting. I have photographed it many times."

He absently nodded his head.

"There could definitely be a space between the rough-hewn chair on which the statue sits and the granite wall behind. Amazing Stephen would know that."

"But why just make a microdot of a map? Why not just do that to whatever he hid?" Gwen asked dazedly.

"Well," Professor Lawrence said slowly, clearly thinking aloud. "It could be he wanted to have the original document. I assume it is a document. And a photograph just wouldn't be the same as the original."

Alex thought of her photographs of the FBI documents. No, they were not the same, but Stephen had clearly run a horrible risk to hold on to an original document, if that's what was hidden.

Then she noticed Gwen had started to shiver. She went and got Gwen's coat where she had left it and put it over her shoulders.

"Come on, honey. Sit down again," Alex said and led the shivering Gwen over to the desk chair that would hold her better than a stool.

"Professor," Alex asked walking back, "is there any more of that coffee?"

"Yes," he said softly and poured what was left into Gwen's cup and added two tablespoons of sugar.

Alex carried it over and held it to Gwen's lips. She took a few sips and shuddered.

"Oh, Alex, what am I going to do?" she breathed.

"We'll do it, Gwen. We'll do it together. Whatever it is. We'll do it," Alex whispered back. Then she crossed back to where Professor Lawrence was standing, watching them.

"Thank you so much for your help, Professor Lawrence," Alex said, and he just nodded.

She glanced back at Gwen.

"We'll take the card and the slide with us."

"Certainly," he said and took the slide out of the microscope and put it and the card into a little box. He fitted some cotton batting over the contents and closed the box with a rubber band from the drawer below.

Gwen had gotten up and come over to them, walking slowly like someone determined not to fall down. But she pulled herself together and thanked Professor Lawrence warmly. And then she looked up into his face and said sternly, "For your own safety, do not tell anyone what you saw today."

"No, Gwen," he replied slowly. "I won't."

Alex and Gwen rode down in the elevator and did not speak.

When they reached the broad Yard, however, it was safe to talk. It was after six and clearly students had gone to the dining halls. There was no one in the area.

"We have to hide this," Gwen said in a whisper. "Before we go home. But where?"

"I have an idea," Alex said.

32

"We can hide it in my new desk in Carpenter's office," Alex whispered to Gwen as they walked along the path that led to the nearest street. "I can lock it."

Gwen nodded and then waved her arm to hail a cab.

"We can just take the bus," Alex objected.

"I don't want to take chances somebody could follow us from here on a bus," Gwen said firmly as the cab pulled up.

Alex gave the cab driver the address, and she and Gwen sat silently in the back of the cab. The streetlights of Washington came on as the dusk deepened toward night. Alex thought of Professor Lawrence and his love of light. Photography was certainly his passion as well as his field of study. Then her mind shifted to microdots. She hoped Professor Lawrence would be willing to show her how to create them on a return visit. She thought so. She smiled to herself. He liked to lecture so much.

As the cab pulled up to the Senate office building, Gwen and Alex dug in their purses and counted out the coins to the driver.

As they got out on to the sidewalk in front of the stairs, two young men in gray suits, identical maroon ties, and no topcoats came rapidly down the steps arguing about whether "S926" had a "snowball's chance in hell" of passing with "that idiot running the show." Young men in Washington were copying Kennedy's not wearing a topcoat in freezing weather. It's going to get a lot of them get sick, Alex thought. Then she thought of Alastair with a pang.

"I'll wait here, Alex," Gwen whispered as the young men hurried past them without a glance. "I don't want to have to show identification here."

"Yes, of course," Alex said and ran up the stairs. Good. One of the daytime guards she knew was still there.

"Forget somethin'?" he asked Alex as she dug out her identification from her purse.

"Boy, did I," she said confidingly. "If I don't finish writing up that summary for the Senator by tomorrow, I'll be in big trouble."

"You hurry, now. I'm about to lock up."

"I will, I will," Alex promised, and she ran to the elevator.

The long, marble hallway was empty, and her footsteps echoed alarmingly as she ran down toward the door of Senator Carpenter's office. She quickly unlocked the door and peered in. The office was dark and there was no light visible from under the Senator's inner door. She hurried to her desk, trying to avoid bumping her foot or hip on the desks placed around in front of her own raised one. The office was very dark, but she didn't want to turn on a light. She had put the desk keys on her personal key ring when she had found them in the center drawer. She fumbled for her keyring in her purse and finally pulled it out. She felt for the small key to the lower desk drawer. She had started to keep some personal items in there, and she lifted out her plastic makeup case. She took the box containing the postcard and the slide out of her purse and lifted the little tray that sat in the middle of the inexpensive makeup case. She removed some items in the bottom, and the box slid in. She replaced the tray and shut the plastic cover. She returned it to the lower drawer and locked it. She grabbed up the powder compact and the rouge she had taken out to make room and shoved those in her purse.

She hurried out, locking the door behind her. She raced back to the elevator. The guard on the door was looking impatient, and she gave him her nicest smile.

"Got it!" she sang out as she walked quickly past him.

He did not reply. He was already moving to close the big, metal inner doors.

"Gwen?" Alex called softly when she did not see her on the sidewalk.

"Here," Gwen said, coming out from behind one of the big, concrete planters that would frame the entrance with flowers in a couple of months.

"Ah didn't want any cops askin' me why ah was standin' around here," Gwen said when she reached Alex.

Alex nodded. Gwen had good reasons to hide from the police and not just because of what was happening now.

"Let's grab the bus I usually take and go to our neighborhood. We can get a bite to eat at that sandwich place. They have some tables toward the back," Alex suggested.

Their neighborhood had places that would serve the two of them together. That was rare, Alex now knew. Gwen had explained to her before how Washington treated Negroes. "Not like the South, where they just plain put up signs sayin' 'No Colored,'" she'd said flatly. "Here, it is oh so genteel and we're all sorry but there are no tables even when you can see plenty of empty tables." Not like around 42nd Street either, Alex had thought. There the small restaurants and delis just served whoever had the money to pay.

* * *

They both just picked at the turkey sandwiches they'd ordered. At least Miss Bea will enjoy the turkey, Alex thought, taking a sip of her coke. She felt a little better and took a bigger drink of the cola. I'm so tired, she thought, and I bet I look it too. She smiled a little with a memory. "You look like a rag went through the mangle the wrong way" her aunt used to say, with a little Hungarian thrown in, when she'd been up all night studying in high school.

She glanced over at Gwen who was frowning at her sandwich, clearly thinking.

"We gotta get what Stephen hid," she said, looking up at Alex, her smooth cheeks drooping like she had aged ten years in the last few weeks. Her eyes were red with fatigue.

"I know," Alex whispered, and she took another sip of her coke. "It's got to be explosive, whatever it is, and we know there are parties willing to kill to get it."

"Mmm. Mmm," Gwen muttered. "That boy and his spy stuff makin' this so difficult. Just like him." She paused. "And we get it? Then what?"

"Depends, I guess, on what it is," Alex said musingly. "One thing I do know is the ones who want it so bad are likely the ones who killed Stephen."

Gwen bent her head and nodded sadly.

"So, we get them to follow us when we go get it," Alex said. "We know they're listening to what we say in the apartment. We can draw them out, see who they are."

"We could get killed too. You think of that? Or they just plain jump us and steal whatever Stephen hid before we can do anything about it. And he died for nothin'," she said bitterly.

"You're right," Alex said, and took another sip of coke, thinking. Then she spoke.

"How's this? Whatever it is, Stephen hid it where Bea and I could go on a run. We've run in Rock Creek Park, and that cemetery is right next to it. I'll run before dawn tomorrow and get it, and I'll plant something else in its place. Then when we've got it safe, seen what it is, we can let them hear us planning to go there tomorrow night. We hide, try to see who they are."

"Maybe," Gwen said considering. "Just seein' somebody is one thing, but then what?"

"I think maybe we need someone else to come, someone in the government who could be a witness."

Alex paused, thinking. Lieutenant Karns had wanted to meet with her, but then he'd not shown up. He'd left a note, but she hadn't heard anything from him since then. Of course, I've been away for three days, but still. Then she thought of Frank.

"I'm not sure about this Gwen," she said slowly, "but I think I could have lunch with that guy, Frank Scott. You know, from State? He is a liaison to military affairs, and he knew Stephen and liked him. I could sound him out, see if he'd follow us and be another set of eyes. All this points to State and Stephen's work there."

But do I trust him? Alex asked herself silently.

"Do you trust him?" Gwen asked echoing Alex's thoughts.

"Not entirely, no," Alex said, considering. "But if we already have whatever Stephen hid, it's less of a risk. And I won't tell him we already have it."

"Still could get killed," Gwen said flatly, her face set.

Alex just nodded, knowing Gwen was right.

"I think I should try, though. I'll go for a run, look to see if I'm followed. If not, I get whatever it is, and we look at it. Then we'll know how much trouble we're in."

"We're already in plenty of trouble," Gwen said, handing her uneaten sandwich to Alex who wrapped it with her own in a clean handkerchief and put it in her purse.

They left the little restaurant, walked silently toward their apartment and up the stairs.

Miss Bea was standing in the entryway, rigid with anger.

"You are late, and I have not had my dinner," she growled.

"I have turkey for you, Miss Bea," Alex said, heading for the kitchen.

"Well, then, that will do," Bea thought, and she followed Alex.

* * *

Before dawn, Alex and Miss Bea were already running down Connecticut Avenue. Bea could smell the big cats even though they were several blocks away. She pulled to get across the street and Alex, remembering Miss Bea's reaction to the lions' roars, obligingly crossed over at the light. They were not heading for the big park in any case, but the cemetery a few blocks over.

There was almost no traffic at this hour, but she was very alert, checking frequently to see if they were being followed. The streetlights cast pools of light on to the sidewalk, but darkness stretched between them. Alex had her flashlight but did not want to use it until they got to the cemetery. No point in making it easier to follow me, she thought.

Even from a distance, Bea could hear the big cats start to make noise. It hit her sensitive ears like the rumble of thunder and she could smell fresh meat. She ran faster, and Alex kept up.

Rock Creek Cemetery was just ahead, and she and Bea ran into it, under the black, peeling wrought-iron arch at the entrance that gave them a grim welcome. The thin light of a half-moon came out from behind a cloud, turning the looming gravestones and statues ahead of them pearly white. Now that they were well beyond the smell of the zoo, Miss Bea had slowed down. She turned and looked at Alex. These lawns with lightly frozen grass and the big stones spread out everywhere were new to her and made her a little uneasy.

Alex ran ahead toward the dense grove of trees on the east side of the cemetery that she knew surrounded the sculpture. Like Bea, she felt a little unnerved by the moonlit grave stones and statues and the silvered grass. And she was hideously exposed if anyone were following her.

She plunged into the dark cavern of trees and stopped. Ahead, through the trees, she could dimly see the back of the stone slab of light-red granite that stood behind the statue. If the map taken from the microdot was right, whatever Stephen had hidden was between the slab and the stone chair on which the statue sat.

Alex stood stock still, listening. Miss Bea did the same and also sniffed the air for other humans. Bea had picked up on Alex's fear. Her beagle nose could even smell it, the sharp sweat that told her Alex was afraid. They stayed perfectly still, waiting.

Nothing, Alex thought. She carefully unzipped her jacket and took out the fake document she and Gwen had created last night. They had covered it with cellophane and taped it closed. They had debated whether to roll it first, but Gwen had argued that the hiding place would not be large and perhaps Stephen had left the document, if it was a document, flat. Alex had spare tape in her pocket in case the hiding place required their substitute be taped in place.

She crept forward toward the statue, and Bea followed quietly. Alex reached the back of the granite slab and looked out to the concrete platform on which the statue had been placed. A long, smooth stone bench was angled around the edges of the platform. There was still no sound.

Alex ventured out next to the statue, knelt down and reached into the small crevasse between the slab and the stone seat. She could feel nothing. Her groping fingers probed. Still nothing. She pulled her hand back and took out her little flashlight and put her face as close to the edge of the stone seat as she could. She shone the light into the space as far around as the light would penetrate. Still nothing.

She angled the light as far down as she could manage and saw a glimmer that was not stone. It was very low down in the crevasse, and only a corner was visible. She tried to memorize the location and withdrew the light. She lay her hand flat along the rough stone of the seat and pushed it down as far as she could.. Her bare finger touched something. She pushed her hand even lower and was able to pinch what was clearly something wedged there. She tugged carefully with two fingers, fearful of tearing whatever it was, though it felt like plastic, not paper. It slid up and then a larger part was exposed.. She was able to use her whole hand to pick it up and extract it from the small space.

She didn't waste time. She zipped the plastic rectangle into her jacket, took the cellophane-wrapped fake and used the flat of her hand to try to push it down into the same narrow crack. It was harder going, as the cellophane was stickier on the stone than the smooth plastic had been. Beads of sweat collected on her forehead and a few droplets fell into her eyes, stinging them. I don't need to see to finish this, she thought, and she just tried to blink the sweat away. Finally, she carefully withdrew her fingers and the cellophane-wrapped document stayed well down in the crack.

She stood up, her knees aching from kneeling on the granite and her face came nearly level with the bronze face of the statue. It was arresting. The bronze woman's eyes were closed and one hand was lifted to her chin. The face was riveting in its concentration even though it was supposed to depict quiet contemplation. The flowing, bronze cowl over the head framed the still face and gave some illusion of movement, or, perhaps, Alex thought, the flow of thought. It was almost hypnotic in its intensity.

Miss Bea tugged on the leash.

"We need to go" was the clear message.

Alex was startled out of her thoughts. Bea was right. They needed to get out of there.

Alex turned, and she and Bea ran toward the stand of trees, heading for the very center of the small wood where they had stood before, listening.

They listened again. Then Alex's heart nearly stopped.

Out in the cemetery, she heard a car. It was driving very slowly. Either the groundskeepers for the cemetery started work at dawn, or she had been followed.

She crept back toward the statue. She had seen that the platform on which it was placed was on the side of a hill. She hoped it would be possible to get away that way, around the concrete bench and down the slope.

She and Bea ran across the platform and scrambled between the end of the farthest bench and an encroaching bush. Thorns tore at Alex's sleeve, but she did not slow down. Bea was once again ahead, finding a path through the bare branches of the bushes that grew down the slope.

Alex could see the roofs of houses below. It was a long way down, but they made it without falling.

When they reached the sidewalk, they crossed the street and went down a quiet-looking, narrow side street. Alex knew they needed to keep heading downhill, and she guessed at the right direction. She kept them on dark and quiet side roads until she began to recognize the area.

Panting, they reached the apartment building and ran up the stairs.

Gwen must have been waiting by the door as it opened as soon as she heard them.

She stepped out and shut the apartment door behind her.

"Did you get it?" she whispered.

Alex nodded and unzipped her jacket. She took out the plastic rectangle and handed it to Gwen who opened it carefully. She held the enclosed document with trembling hands. Alex took out her flashlight to shine it on the paper so they could read it in the dim hall.

They did.

They turned to each other in horror.

It was far worse than either of them had imagined.

33

THURSDAY, FEBRUARY 9, 1961

Memorandum
To: Director FBI
Date: 1/15/61

INTERNAL SECURITY EMERGENCY

The danger of an internal security emergency is high in response to possible future military actions of the United States against the dictator Fidel Castro and his illegal regime in Cuba.

Known domestic security risks, especially homosexuals, Communist sympathizers such as members of the Socialist Workers Party, and Negro agitators must be identified now.

It is imperative that such potential troublemakers be confined before such plans regarding Cuba become known in order to prevent organized insurrection within the United States. These known and unknown domestic enemies can also include immigrants from Caribbean nations known to support the dictator Castro and his regime.

We are currently updating our existing lists of such internal enemies and potential enemies including current addresses and contacts.

After the inauguration of the president, these plans should be ready to be operationalized within weeks, site locations identified and methods for collecting and interning those persons who pose an immediate risk to the nation finalized.

There was no signature, Alex noted.

"Oh, my Lord, my Lord," Gwen mouthed as they both stared at the horrible memo.

Alex was finding it hard to breathe. Whoever had written this memo to Director Hoover was trying to once again set up concentration camps in the United States as had been done to the Japanese during World War II and as the Nazis had done to the Jews and those who resisted their murderous regime.

She shut her eyes in disbelief and saw her mother and aunt behind barbed wire behind her eyelids. She shuddered and opened her eyes.

"No wonder Stephen took this memo," Alex whispered. "And he must have known who wrote it."

Gwen nodded. Her rigid face looked like it had been cast in bronze like the statue in the graveyard.

"We have to do it," Gwen said softly, her lips barely moving. "Draw them out, find out who's behind this awful thing."

"I agree," Alex breathed. "So we go in now and talk about finding the map and our plans to go to the cemetery tonight. The place closes at six. I saw it on a sign by the front gate. So what do you think? Ten o'clock?"

"That's about right," Gwen said through clenched teeth, and Alex realized she was shivering in the cold hallway. So am I, Alex recognized with surprise. She had been sweating from fear and exertion from the run and now she was cooling off rapidly. Too rapidly.

"Let's get inside. I'm freezing and so are you. I'll start some coffee and we can talk about 'what should we do' and on, and then you can say 'we gotta go get it,' and I'll bring up the cemetery and so on."

"Okay," Gwen said slowly. Then she raised her hand that held the awful memo and held it at arms-length like it was a poisonous snake. "We gotta hide this too."

"I guess I can lock it in my desk in the Senator's office this morning before I go back to the library and finish that report." She paused, thinking. "But I'll have to call Frank Scott from the pay phone before I go in to the office. I'll ask him to meet me in Lafayette Park at noon."

"Good," Gwen said through teeth that were starting to chatter.

They went in to their apartment, closing the door silently.

"Do you want some coffee, Gwen?" Alex asked, trying to keep her voice normal.

"Sure. Yes," Gwen said shortly.

Alex put on the coffee pot and then picked up Miss Bea's bowls. She filled one with kibble, one with water, and put them down.

Bea ate her breakfast, having her own priorities straight.

"But you know, Alex, we have to go get this thing. Whatever Stephen hid," Gwen went on with only the smallest quaver.

"I know," Alex said. "But it could be dangerous, Gwen. Who knows what he hid in that Rock Creek cemetery? The postcard didn't say."

"We'll know when we get it, Alex. That's all. Tonight. It's got to be tonight. We can't let whatever it is just stay there. We have to go."

Alex poured the coffee and put out the cream and sugar on the table.

"Okay, okay. Don't get all upset. We'll do it. Maybe around ten tonight? Should be dark enough," Alex said and took a sip of her coffee.

"Right. Good," Gwen said. She went to their little kitchen table and nearly collapsed into a chair. She clenched her trembling hands together on the table near her coffee cup but didn't pick it up. Alex covered Gwen's hands with one of her own.

Had they been smart to do this, or were they playing right into the killer's hands?

Alex finished her coffee and went to her room, thinking about what she would wear to see Frank Scott.

It's hard to look like a princess in a winter coat and hat, she thought wryly. But she realized she cared more than she really should about what Scott thought of her and chose her armor of clothes accordingly. Besides, she thought as she put on the coat and hat she'd picked out, I want to disarm him.

* * *

Alex left the Senate office building and headed toward Lafayette Park. It was about a quarter to twelve, so she had plenty of time to walk the few blocks.

What a day it had been, Alex thought as she walked along. It wasn't even noon, and she'd found what Stephen had hidden, planted false clues with their listeners, and she had hidden the vile memo in her locked desk in the Senator's office. And she had made this noon appointment with Frank Scott. When she'd reached him in his office, he had just quietly agreed to meet her. He'd not asked any questions, but then, Alex reflected, perhaps he had not wanted to say more from his office phone.

Alex brought her thoughts back to the moment. She needed to watch to see if she was being followed. The sun was out, and the day was mild. Washington was having a February thaw. There were many people out walking and that made it more difficult to tell. She stopped several times and looked into reflections in shop windows, but she did not see anything suspicious. She was partly expecting the watcher from New York to be trailing her. He did not seem to be on the street, however, and he was so poor at following, she began to relax.

She still stopped at store windows to look back every few blocks, but she also started checking that her hair was still securely pulled up under the mink brown, brushed wool hat with the rolled brim she had chosen to go with a cream-colored cashmere, swing coat. She wondered if there might be a touch too much Audrey Hepburn in Paris look about it, but after all, she had copied the look from Givenchy, so it was likely. She smiled despite her tension.

As she approached the park, she looked for the statue of Lafayette in the farthest corner where she and Frank had agreed to meet. She could see Scott was already there, seated on one of the benches across from the statue. And she saw the moment he saw her as he stood up.

"Your Highness, you never disappoint," he said as she approached, and he took off his glasses and put them in his suit pocket. She wondered if he even needed them or if they were part of his attempt to divert attention from how intimidating his height and his shoulders could be. She registered he wasn't even wearing a coat.

"Hello, Frank," she said calmly, though her heart had started to race. "I am glad you could meet me."

"Here," Scott said, and he took out a clean handkerchief and spread it on the bench. Your throne awaits. We can't let that charming white coat get dirty, can we?"

"Thank you," Alex said primly, and she heard him chuckle as she seated herself.

"I brought some sandwiches and coffee," he said conversationally when she had seated herself. He lifted a paper bag from beside the bench.

"Just the coffee, I think," Alex said.

"That's right," Scott said, nodding. "You don't actually eat, do you?"

He handed over one of the coffees and took the other for himself.

"Frank, what I have to say does not go along with a picnic in the park," Alex said, turning so she could look at him more directly on the bench.

"Really?" he replied, noncommittally.

"Yes, really," Alex replied, and then she paused. She'd tell him the truth, up to a point.

"I need your help," she began, and his green eyes narrowed immediately.

"What's wrong?" he asked, and he turned and put his arm along the back of the bench. It felt like he was shielding her. Or trapping her.

"Stephen Gray sent Gwen a postcard. On it was a microdot, giving the location of something he had hidden. He left Gwen instructions to go get it if he could not. He had mailed the postcard the day before he was murdered."

Scott frowned, but said nothing, and Alex went on.

"Gwen and I think that Stephen was tortured and killed for whatever he had hidden. Our apartment has been searched, his apartment has been searched, and I've been followed. Whatever it is, they have not found it. But now she and I know where it is. We want to go get it, and we think whoever is behind this will follow us. We can surprise him or them and find out who killed Stephen."

She paused, breathing hard like she had been running, but then she rushed on, anxious to get it all out.

"We need someone else to see who it is, someone in government. We can't go to the police. That Detective Hicks is not only a bully, he's a criminal, a drug dealer."

"Drug dealer?" Scott interrupted, leaning forward. "Do you have information on him, or are you just speculating?"

"No, I'm not speculating," Alex said between her teeth, annoyed at the interruption. "I'll tell you what I know about Hicks from my trip to New York, but not now. Please just listen."

"Okay, okay," Scott said, and he moved closer to her on the bench.

"In any case," Alex went on, "Gwen and I don't think Hicks is the one who murdered Stephen. All of this seems to point to the State Department."

Scott leaned even further over her so he could speak almost into her ear.

"Look, Alex, I'll take it from here. Just tell me where Stephen hid whatever it is, and I'll draw them out and figure out how to prosecute. You need to stay far away from this. You're even too close now. Princesses don't go around capturing murderers. They'll snap you like a twig."

He was so close, she had felt his breath on her cheek when he spoke.

Alex sat still for a moment, looking at Scott's frowning face. Even at this time of the day, she could see the dark shadow of his beard returning. She registered he needed a haircut. Then she gave herself a mental shake. She needed to focus. She'd worked to get this knight in shining armor response. Now she had to use it without letting him take over.

"Don't be fooled by my clothes and manner, Frank. It's a disguise, just like your professor glasses and beautiful, bespoke suits are a disguise." She pulled back a little on the bench and gave him her iciest look.

"You need to do it our way. Gwen has had her brother brutally murdered, and she's been beaten up. We won't stand by and let you take over. We need you as a witness, but we'll do it without you if we have to. Besides, whoever they are won't follow you. They'll follow us."

Scott sat back and looked at Alex like he'd never seen her before. But then, instead of replying, he tensed and put both arms around her. He bent his head to hers.

"Hey," Alex said, trying to pull back out of his embrace.

"Be quiet," he whispered. "I think someone is watching us from that stand of trees over on the right. Just play along with me here, okay?"

Alex gave a tiny nod. She knew she should be afraid that they were being watched, but the circle of his big arms made her feel safe. She realized how rare it was for her to feel safe, especially here in Washington. Instead, she constantly felt on the edge of exposure. She relaxed slightly, leaning in toward him. She smelled the starch in his shirt. Let me take just this one moment, Alex thought.

Scott tightened his arms and moved even closer to her. She could feel the tension in his body, and his head was angled toward the trees. They stayed like that, a frozen tableau, for a couple of minutes. Alex just breathed and tried not to think.

"I think he's gone," he whispered, and he moved his head so his face was inches from hers. She closed her eyes and felt his lips on hers. She felt his hands move up under her short coat toward the center of her back, his fingers moving gently over places she had never considered had that many nerve endings. She had been kissed before by guys from the Ivy League colleges, but never like this. They were boys, not men, she thought vaguely, and kissed him back.

Scott lifted his head, and she opened her eyes.

"Well," he breathed and sat back a little.

Alex felt like she was surfacing after a deep dive into a warm pool. She looked at Scott's face, still only inches from hers, and then she registered he looked a little smug. She stiffened. She knew he could feel it.

"This doesn't change anything, Frank," Alex said firmly. "Gwen and I are going tonight to get what Stephen hid, with you or without you."

He moved his hands to her shoulders and for a moment she thought he might even shake her. But his hands only briefly tightened on her shoulders, and then he pulled back.

"What a damned mess," he groaned. "Tell me what you have in mind."

* * *

Alex walked slowly back toward the office, but she was so preoccupied she gave no thought to whether she was being followed or not.

Frank had agreed to hide in the trees that lined the cemetery and watch for her and Gwen to walk through the gates at around ten. He'd try to identify anyone who might be following them, and, if possible, detain them.

Alex had said she and Gwen would get what Stephen had hidden, even though she had already retrieved it and planted a fake. She felt no guilt about deceiving Scott about that as she was certain he was withholding information from her as well.

The problem is, Alex mused as she walked along, he had been too cooperative. He had thought a couple of kisses would turn my brain to mush. The kisses had been nice, well, more than nice, but a girl had to keep her head, especially when some people wanted to kill her. She knew Frank was planning something that he wasn't telling her.

Alex went directly to Senator Carpenter's office. She had finished her research that morning and had a solid draft of her report on the outlines of a "New Frontier in American Agricultural Policy." That is what Alex had titled her report.

It was inspiring language, Alex thought as she typed up her handwritten draft. Kennedy had used the term "New Frontier" in his acceptance speech at the Democratic National Convention when he had been selected as their nominee for President. It had stuck as a campaign slogan, and she had learned from reading the congressional weekly newsletters it was now being used to describe policy for upcoming legislation.

She typed the document. It was good. She had emphasized the expansion of President Eisenhower's "Food for Peace" program in the Kennedy policy. Many Latin American countries were included, but Cuba was specifically excluded, and she was again reminded of the horrible memo. There would be no "Food for Peace" for the Cubans in the new program. She dared not leave that out of her report for the Senator, but she relegated it to an endnote.

The scope of what was being discussed to be included in this omnibus bill was immense, and Alex had summarized as best she could. She did smile occasionally as she typed "supply adjustments" and "price supports," concepts that were functionally democratic socialism. But she did not add the latter.

The proposed cut in wheat production, in exchange for price supports, would be controversial in the Senator's state. She made a mental note to draw that to the Senator's attention.

She was just pulling the last page of the report and its carbon out of the typewriter when she became aware the Senator was standing behind her. It was disconcerting, but she tried not to show it.

She stood up and turned.

"Hello, Madam Senator, I have just finished my report for you on the upcoming agricultural legislation," Alex said. She turned back to her desk, separated the last typed page and the carbon and added them to the pages already stacked there.

The Senator still did not speak.

"Would you like them now?" she asked into the silence.

The Senator nodded and held out her hand.

Alex handed her the sheets and just stood there. The Senator began to read aloud.

"The outlook for American agricultural expansion has never been greater. . ."

The Senator paused and then read silently for a few more minutes.

Alex stood perfectly still.

"Miss Bell, you write very well. Very well indeed," Senator Carpenter said, looking at Alex with almost no expression on her face. Under the brighter, overhead lights of the main office, she looked older. And her face seems a little thinner, Alex thought. She had on a flamingo-pink suit. The color did not flatter the Senator's pasty face. Overall, she did not look well.

"Thank you, Madam Senator," Alex said quietly.

"Those boxes have been moved to a secure location," the Senator went on, now watching Alex's face closely with tired eyes.

"That is good," Alex replied neutrally. "There will be more storage for your own papers."

"Yes," said the Senator. She turned and walked toward her own office, carrying Alex's report.

Alex sat down in the desk chair.

She doesn't know what to do about me, she reflected soberly.

Then she felt a jolt of alarm. I hope she doesn't have a key to this desk.

34

THURSDAY, FEBRUARY 9, 1961

At just after nine in the evening, Alex, Gwen and Miss Bea left their apartment building and started to walk the two miles to Rock Creek Cemetery. Alex and Gwen were dressed in black watch caps and dark, heavy overcoats. Alex had sewed interior pockets into both. Gwen's pocket held her brother Stephen's baseball bat that she had retrieved earlier in the day from his apartment. Alex had placed the long pocket down the inside side seam so Gwen could keep it from swinging by pressure with her arm.

Alex had two interior pockets, also located under the arms. Hers contained two heavy flashlights she had purchased on her way home from work. They could double as clubs if necessary. Like the police use them, Alex had thought grimly as she had selected the two longest and heaviest from the hardware store. And, just before they had left, Alex had given Miss Bea a good sniff of the listening device planted at the top of their bookcase and then led her immediately out into the hall and shut the door.

"Find the bad man, Bea. Find him," Alex had whispered to the little dog.

"Cigarettes, a little puke, sharp smell," Bea rehearsed in her mind.

"You think that dog understands what you're tellin' her?" Gwen asked curiously as they walked along the sidewalk, close together.

"I do," Alex said.

Bea shook her ears, the closest a dog comes to a shrug, but did not take her nose off the job for a second.

The night was damp and cloudy. A light ground fog started to rise from the patches of wet grass they approached the cemetery.

Oh, great, Alex thought, seeing the white mist, as if being in a dark cemetery at night with the prospect of actual killers lurking isn't bad enough, now there's fog. Very atmospheric fog, she told herself, trying to keep calm. She tried to look objectively at the coils of vapor rolling along among the tombstones, an occasional gust of wind blowing them into white streamers that could be taken for horizontal ghosts.

Searching for a thought that would give her courage, she recalled when some of her classmates at Smith had dragged her along to a horror movie about graveyards junior year. What was it called again? "Burying the Living" or something like that. The graveyard scenes with bodies rising up, surrounded by fog had been so obviously faked that Alex had chuckled a little. This is just like that, she lectured herself. Toughen up. It's so creepy it's almost a fake.

"Alex," Gwen whispered, and Alex jumped nearly six inches in the air. So much for being tough, she thought.

"Yes, what?" Alex whispered back as they made their way toward the stand of trees where Frank Scott should be hidden.

"Nobody followin' us that I can see," Gwen hissed.

Just then the thick, black clouds overhead parted and a sliver of moon appeared. The moonlight it cast was reflected off of the fog, and the many white marble tombstones were lit up like hundreds of searching flashlights had hit them. And, they both realized with a start, they were lit up too. Anyone in the trees could pick them out in an instant.

Alex tried not to panic. She looked around and saw some of the tombstones were actually large memorials. There was a huge one right to their left.

"Let's run," she hissed to Gwen. "Let's get over behind that big memorial over there so we can't be seen from the trees." She put action to her words, and she and Miss Bea sprinted for the big rectangular block of stained stone that was more in shadow. She felt Gwen close behind.

As they crouched behind the stone, Alex peered out around the carved stone corner and looked out toward the trees that were now farther to their right. She began to draw her head back behind the memorial that was, this close up, sizeable, but she glanced at the name carved in large, Gothic letters on the side. "Coffin," it said. And come to think of it, Alex shuddered, this huge grave marker was shaped exactly like a coffin. A really big coffin. She shuddered.

"How about this?" Gwen asked in a low voice. "If any creep's here, they must be in the trees, waiting for us. And your friend, that Frank, he must be too, I guess. So we split up. I go left and get in the trees from there." She pointed. "You go right. That's where that statue is where Stephen hid his paper, isn't that so?" She glanced up. "That moon should be back behind the clouds in a minute."

Alex nodded.

"Give me some time to get around through the trees and then you and that dog move toward the statue. Any luck, I can bring this bat down on somebody's head before you know it." Then Gwen unbuttoned her coat and got the bat out and gave it a little shake. Then she held it down by her side.

"Gwen, I don't get how I'll know you're in position," Alex said, thinking out loud.

"I can make good bird calls," Gwen said, and immediately the sound of a crow came out of her mouth.

"Good heavens, Gwen," Alex whispered. "That really does sound like a crow."

"Goin' south, visitin' family in the country, you can learn a lot," Gwen whispered back. "Besides, that dog will smell me, right dog?" Gwen said, looking down at Bea.

"Certainly," Miss Bea thought. "You smell like that soap you use."

"Okay," Alex said slowly. Then she looked toward the copse of trees that loomed along that whole side of the cemetery. The trees were thick, and their black trunks looked like prison bars from this distance, but Alex knew it was penetrable from her earlier visit. They had to stay off the gravel path that led to the Adams Memorial.

"Let's go," Gwen hissed as the moon went behind a cloud. They left the shelter of the big coffin and ran in opposite directions toward the trees.

A light rain began to fall as Alex and Bea approached the first trees in the thicket. The bare branches above them were so intertwined, they actually blocked the rain a little, but the drops pattered on the matted leaves on the ground.

Good, Alex thought. That muffles our footsteps a little.

It was much harder to see now under the trees and without the sliver of moon. Alex did not dare to use her flashlight. She had to follow Bea. She crouched down so she could speak directly into the little dog's ear.

"Miss Bea, find that place where I pulled out the paper. Find it."

Bea did not hesitate. She put her nose to the dripping ground and then started to trot forward. Alex followed, hoping Gwen could find her way without Bea's help.

Suddenly, Bea stopped and sniffed in a small circle.

"Here. Cigarette and sharp smell. Bad man." Bea started to pull forward, but Alex bent down again and whispered.

"No, Bea. We need to stay behind these trees until you can smell Gwen."

They waited, the rain pattering down on the leaves. Alex looked out from behind the tree where she was hiding. She could just see the bronze statue and the rain running in rivulets down its flowing cowl.

Miss Bea raised her head. There was a low sound like a twig breaking, but then a scuffle and the sharp crack of a baseball bat.

"Come out, girlie, or I'll hit this N******* again," a harsh but oddly deadened voice said.

Miss Bea stood rigid. "Stay here, Bea, but if you see a chance to bite, take it," Alex whispered. She let go of Bea's leash and stepped out from behind the tree.

"That's it. Come over here and get what that Nancy-boy hid," said the same harsh voice, now closer.

Then Alex saw him. He was standing in front of the statue. He was a tall man with a black ski mask obscuring his features. He held a large, black gun, and it was trained on her.

"I will," Alex said firmly, though her fear for Gwen and her anger at Frank Scott for not showing up warred inside her and made her legs shaky.

She went to the back of the statue, knelt down and pulled at the corner of the cellophane covered document she had hidden there. The tape gave way easily, and she took it out.

"Don't get up. Hand it here," the harsh voice said.

Still kneeling, Alex turned and handed what she had retrieved to the man who was now only feet away from her.

"Turn back around," he hissed, and she heard a click. He was going to shoot her.

"Oh, Christ. God damn this dog," the man yelled, and Alex heard Bea's growl.

She stood up and turned.

Bea had a tight hold on the man's ankle. The gun was not in his hand. Alex looked around frantically and saw its glittering outline on the wet leaves. She lunged for the gun and got her hand on it.

Bea yelped, and there were no more growls.

"Hold it right there," a gruff voice said from behind Alex, coming from the trees. She turned to look for the source of the voice, and the ski-masked man kicked at Alex's hand. The gun she'd retrieved flew up in the air. The man in the ski mask caught it and in the next second had run behind the thick granite slab at the back of the statue.

The man from the trees, a scarf over his nose and mouth and a hat pulled low, ran after him. Is that Frank Scott, Alex wondered, or are there other players in this?

"You okay?" asked a frail voice from the opposite side of the statue.

Gwen was walking slowly toward Alex, blood dripping down the side of her face.

"Me?" Alex choked out. "What about you? That's blood, you're bleeding."

"That idiot tried to put me out with the bat, but I jerked away, and he just clipped me. And the hat protected me some."

Gwen came up, and Alex could see she was dragging the bat down by her side, and her watch cap was sticking out of her pocket.

"Where's that dog?" Gwen asked when she got closer. "Chasing that miserable creep, I hope."

Alex looked around for Bea and was horrified to see her lying still a short ways away on a pile of sodden leaves.

"Bea, oh Bea," Alex cried out and ran over to her and knelt down.

Miss Bea started to stir even as Alex put a hand gently on her side to see if she were breathing.

"Lie still, Bea," Alex said in a tear-choked voice. "Just rest for a minute. You'll be okay, you'll be okay" she kept repeating, trying to reassure herself.

Bea struggled to get up, and Alex picked her up and held her on her lap. She gently felt Bea's ribs, and Bea did not react so Alex was reassured that she didn't have internal injuries. But she had certainly been knocked out.

"You are such a good dog. You bit the bad man. You are the best dog. The very best dog," Alex said softly.

"Yes. Bit him. Hard," Bea reflected and then closed her eyes.

Gwen sat down on the granite base of the statue, took a tissue from her pocket and held it against her temple where blood was still running down the side of her face.

"What happened?" Gwen asked. "Where is that creep?"

"I'll tell you, Gwen, but I think we need to get away from here," Alex said, getting carefully to her feet while still cradling Bea. "Another guy with a gun tore off after that guy in the ski mask, but God knows where they are now. I think the second guy was Scott, but he'd hidden his face and I think disguised his voice."

Gwen stood too, and Alex was glad to see she was steady on her feet.

"Let's go see if we can get a cab. I'll hide Bea in my coat, and you can pull your cap back on."

They walked slowly down the gravel path toward the cemetery entrance. The drizzle had stopped, and the sliver of moon made a reappearance that helped them find their way.

As they got to the edge of the trees, they checked to see if they could see Scott or the ski-masked guy or both. The sweep of grass and mass of tombstones was vacant.

"You know, Gwen, our clever plan seems to have been a bust," Alex said in a whisper as they reached the sidewalk and began scanning the road for a cab.

"I know just what you mean," Gwen said, and then whether from exhaustion or the crash after adrenaline or just because it just hit both of them what they must look like, they started laughing.

A cab got by them.

"Oh, shit," Alex said, looking at the taillights of the receding cab.

And they laughed some more.

* * *

They finally flagged down a cab and reached their apartment. Gwen unlocked the door as Alex was still cradling Miss Bea in her coat.

Then they both stopped stock-still in the little hall.

Frank Scott was rising from their little couch. The listening device was lying on their little coffee table. The wire had been cut.

"Get out," Alex said angrily.

Scott said nothing.

35

FRIDAY, FEBRUARY 10, 1961

"I said, get out!" Alex gritted out coldly, and she carried Miss Bea directly to her basket in her bedroom, came back out, and shut the door.

"Listen, Alex," Scott said, making no move to leave. "You were never in any danger. I had him covered the whole time."

"Really?" Alex said, and her voice was so icy, Scott felt the chill from across the room.

"Gwen was hit on the head with a baseball bat. She could have been killed," Alex went on in the same cold voice. "And Miss Bea was kicked unconscious," she added through her teeth.

"I'm sorry about that. Truly. And I just did not expect you and your roomate would split up like that," Scott managed.

Alex opened her mouth to retort, but Gwen got there first.

"Did you get him? Did you get that man that killed my Stephen? Did you?" she said, moving closer to where Scott was standing by the couch. "Did you?" she persisted getting right up to him when he did not speak.

"I already knew who he was, at least I thought so. I confirmed it to-night." Scott said, and both Gwen and Alex gasped.

"What?" Alex asked in a choking voice. Gwen made a sound like she had been hit in the stomach.

"His name is Duncan Connors," Scott went on, though he turned slightly toward Alex.

"You've met him, Alex, at that party at the Graham's house."

Alex said nothing.

He turned toward Gwen.

"He's an immigrant Brit, works in the State Department. I don't know if you've ever met him, Miss Gray, or if Stephen ever mentioned him."

Gwen shook her head no.

"Well, his family came to the States when he was eight. His father worked for a British-American company. He applied for citizenship when he was eighteen. He met Stephen in law school. They were never close friends, but they knew each other." Scott paused and looked at the silent women standing in front of him.

"The fact is, Connors is a Communist. He's a plant in the State Department for the Soviet Union. His job, I think, is to try to bring about war between the United States and the Soviet Union by fomenting conflict. There are those in the Soviet Union who seem to think a U.S. invasion of Cuba could be the match that ignites that war."

Alex remembered her aunt and mother telling her there were no Communists any more. Apparently, they were mistaken, she thought dazedly.

Scott cleared his throat.

"Anyway, Connors wrote that memo to Hoover about putting certain groups of people in concentration camps. It's part of their plan to create civil unrest along with the invasion." He paused as he saw their look of surprise, and then went on.

"Oh, yes, I know what's in that document. Stephen told me. He stole it so he could have the original as proof of what Connors was up to. He wanted to expose him as a Russian plant at State. He hid it and then Connors and his henchman, Aiden McCaffrey, an Irishman who jumped ship in New York and worked for the mob for a time, was recruited to help him get it back."

He looked at Gwen. Alex saw there were actual tears in his eyes. "They tortured and murdered Stephen to get the document, but he didn't give it up."

Alex thought of the incompetent idiot who had been following her. He was one of Stephen's murderers.

"Have you arrested this Duncan Connors?" Gwen asked, wringing her hands together. Alex could tell she was using all her will power to stay on her feet, and a trickle of blood ran out from under her dark cap.

"No," Scott said, looking grim. "I followed, confirmed it was him. I made him think he'd lost me, and I saw him take off his ski mask to look at the document. He knew immediately it was a fake, by the way. But we need to keep Connors in place and watch him and intercept other plans. That's my job."

"No," Gwen said, anguished. "No, you can't do that. He's a murderer. Just no," she whispered, and her legs started to give out from under her. Alex saw her start to collapse and rushed over to her. She was able to help lower her to the floor. Gwen just sat there, slumped. It seemed to Alex that the stone of grief in her heart was weighing her down so much she couldn't seem to hold herself up.

"You need to give me that original document," Scott said, looking at Alex.

"Not a chance in hell," Alex said angrily.

"You do, Alex. Connors knows you have it."

"It's well hidden," she replied curtly.

"Here?" Scott asked, casting a glance around the small apartment.

"No," Alex said.

Scott stayed silent but did not stop looking around.

"So what about Gwen?" Alex hissed at him. "Hicks is fitting her up to pin Stephen's murder on her. Are you just going to stand by and let that happen too?"

Scott turned back. His face was stony, but she knew she'd scored a hit there. She was glad. She wanted to hurt him. She'd started to care about him, and she was kicking herself for it.

"No. Connors shot and killed McCaffrey and dumped his body in the Potomac. He was pulled out by an early morning fisherman. We made sure enough evidence got to Hicks to prove that McCaffrey killed Gray, so he'd quit there. Hicks's a lazy son-of-a-bitch, and he took the easy way to say he'd solved a case. Gwen is safe."

Gwen didn't even raise her head at his words.

Scott paused and then went on in a deadpan voice.

"We think McCaffrey also killed that kid Carrington in your office."

"What?" Alex said, her mind reeling from all that he was saying. "Killed Alistair? Why?"

Scott walked a few steps over to the window and spoke over his shoulder.

"Connors wanted me to chat you up, get to know you and eventually recruit you. Apparently Senator Edgar Carpenter had compiled some confidential files on the FBI, and he wanted to get his hands on them." He paused, but he still didn't turn around. "I think McCaffrey was told just to give Carrington something to make him sick for a week or two so you'd have to take over his work in coming to hearings and so forth, so, well, so I could meet you and recruit you." He sighed. "Apparently the Carrington kid had had digestive troubles from birth, and he developed a hole in his intestine. He died from sepsis."

Scott turned around to look at her, his face unreadable.

"I didn't try to recruit you, of course. I just said I would to play along with Connors to keep an eye on him. My boss in this is Lt. Karns. He's in

charge of this operation, but he has been devastated by what Connors and
McCaffrey did to Stephen. He thinks he should have been able to prevent it,
talk Stephen out of stealing that document even if he had to break his cover.
He's in a lot of mental pain."

Scott paused and looked at Alex, watching for a reaction to his next
words.

"But, I expect you know nothing about those FBI files." He paused,
watching her.

"Or do you?"

Alex felt ice cold fear fill up her chest. She tried to resist it, and she
tried hard not show any trace of what she knew about those files, or that she
had copies hidden, hidden right here in their apartment.

She focused on the faces of Stephen and Alistair, dead because of the
stupid secrets people in this town hoarded like a misers. She started to
tremble with her rage and grief, and she turned a furious face toward Scott.

"I don't know what you are talking about, Frank, except that you seem
quite comfortable with covering up murders, and now you're telling us you
are going to let one of Gwen's brother's murderers go free," Alex said in a
dead voice.

"Give me that document, Alex, and those files." Scott replied.

"No," she said.

"You must," he replied.

"The answer is no, even if you torture me to get their location out of
me." She regretted the words as soon as they were out of her mouth, but she
just stood there and glared at him.

Scott strode over to her, grabbed her by the shoulders and pulled her
in so that her face was inches from his. She could feel him breathing hard.

"For the love of God, Alex, I'm trying to keep this country safe. I'm
trying to keep you safe." He kissed her hard and then released her like she
was scalding him.

"That's what I'm trying to do too," she said fiercely, but also feeling like
his mouth and his hands were still on her.

I won't give in to him, she thought. I won't, even though I want to, and
then she heard a soft moan from Gwen, and she turned away from Scott to
her friend.

"You need to go now," Alex said over her shoulder as she bent over to
help Gwen to her feet. "I don't want you here."

She braced Gwen under her arms and half carried her to the bathroom. She only flinched slightly when she heard the front door slam.

* * *

"Oh, Alex, what are we gonna do? Stephen's murderer just runnin' around free? That's not right," Gwen said at the breakfast table, her hands cupped around the mug of sweet, hot tea Alex had made for her.

They could speak freely, Alex had told Gwen when she had come out of her room. The first thing she had done at dawn was to wake Miss Bea, who grumbled about it, and she and Bea had done a thorough search of their apartment for any other listening device. She worried that Scott could very well have planted another spying apparatus when he had broken in before they had arrived last night. Alex hadn't seen anything, and Miss Bea had not seemed to smell anything, Alex had informed her.

She looked over at Gwen. She really did not look well and had already admitted to Alex she had a splitting headache. Alex had put two aspirin next to the tea. Thank heavens it was the weekend, Alex thought, so Gwen will have some time to recuperate.

"Well, we have got to get that Connors arrested, Gwen. I mean, you know it, and I know it. But we'll have to do it in another way. I don't know how much you were able to get last night, but Scott is keeping him at State so he can watch him and look for treachery. But he can't watch him every minute. Connors could kill someone else, for God's sake."

Gwen nodded her head and then looked like she regretted it.

Alex poured herself some coffee and sat down opposite Gwen. She had been up early, worried about Miss Bea. She'd actually checked her twice during the night, but Bea responded normally by waking up, growling in an irritated fashion and then putting her paw over her nose and going back to sleep.

They had gone out earlier for a short walk, and Bea had eaten a little of her breakfast. She was back in her basket, asleep.

Showered and dressed in her most severe black suit, Alex was ready for the day.

"So, Gwen, here's my idea. Tell me if you agree," Alex said, and she outlined what she had been thinking about since before dawn.

Gwen listened intently.

"I think so, Alex. I think so," she said, and she put the aspirin tablets in her mouth and took a sip of the cooled tea.

* * *

Alex had hoped journalists worked on weekends. It turned out they did.

"Brownie," Alex said briskly into the pay phone receiver when she recognized the journalist's gravel voice at the other end of the wire. "Don't say my name," she followed up immediately.

"Okay," Brownie said laconically. Alex guessed she had plenty of phone conversations that began like that.

"Can you meet me at noon at that place we had lunch underneath the old gentleman? It's important."

"Sure, kiddo."

"And Brownie, if Higgy is in town, could you ask him to come too?"

"Yeah, he's here for the weekend. I can do that."

"Thank you," Alex breathed.

Brownie just hung up.

* * *

"Oh, my stars. No, no," Higgy said as he read the original memo and passed it over to Brownie whose lined face froze in horror as her eyes traveled down the page.

They were in the basement underneath Lincoln again, sitting around the card table. Brownie had brought some cokes and a bag of sandwiches, but Alex cautioned they should look at the memo first and not risk getting any food or drink on it. She had given them the background on Duncan Connors as the author and how Frank Scott was spying on him at State, not willing to have him arrested for murder just so he could continue to spy on him.

Brownie and Higgy looked at each other, stone-faced, and then Higgy spoke.

"I've been in politics a long time, Alex, but I have never seen or heard of anything so diabolical." He paused, his whole round body seeming to deflate like a birthday balloon with a small leak. "And this Soviet plan, you know. It could very well work, as all of the people Hoover hates and fears are on this list." He shook the paper a little. "And I've heard rumors that the CIA is pushing for an invasion by U.S. troops of Cuba. But there's another half-assed idea of training Cuban exiles to do it. Those fools think the Cubans, and the Soviets too, won't think it was us anyway?" He shook his round head so vigorously his large bowtie flapped around.

"They could put us in one of those camps, Brownie, if they knew about us," Higgy said, and he reached over and touched his wife's cheek where a little tear had escaped from her eye. She put her hand over his.

"I know, Higgy, I know," Alex said slowly. "You both are at risk, but it's my family too." They both looked at her in surprise.

Alex took a deep breath. They had trusted her, and they were vulnerable. She had to tell them.

"My aunt and my mother are Hungarian immigrants. They work in sweatshops in New York City and are members of the Socialist Workers Party. Have been for many years. And they're union organizers. They would be targets too. Probably me too for lying about my background."

"No kidding, sweetie," Brownie said softly, and her big hand patted one of Alex's that was resting on the shaky card table. Brownie's pat made the rickety table do a short jig.

"So this is the original memo, correct?" Higgy said briskly, still holding the paper. It wasn't immediately obvious that Higgy was a lawyer, but now Alex saw his legal brain at work.

"Yes," Alex said, and she held out her hand to take the paper back and put it in the plastic sleeve that had protected it at the Adams Memorial.

Instead, Higgy reached over and took the sleeve and slipped the memo inside it himself.

"Stevenson," he said to Brownie.

"Right," Brownie replied. "Only way."

"I don't speak your shorthand," Alex said, a little miffed that they were talking around her. "What are you suggesting?"

"Ambassador Adlai Stevenson," Higgy said. "He hates Hoover, and he agrees with what Mrs. Roosevelt had the guts to call Hoover's FBI, 'the American Gestapo.' And he'll hate that a Soviet spy has killed a fine young man like Stephen Gray and is still allowed to stay in place at State. Oh, yes. He'll hate all of this."

"Yes. And he'll do something about it," Brownie contributed, nodding her head. "That's what he's like."

"You agree? And you'll give me the memo? He'll need the original," Higgy asked Alex sharply, all trace of the jocular personality gone.

Alex sat and thought. Should I let go of the memo for which Stephen had been tortured and murdered, she asked herself. Do I trust them?

Trust came hard to Alex, but she thought of Brownie and Higgy, and her aunt and mother behind barbed wire and realized they were in this together.

"Yes, I agree. And I discussed it with Gwen this morning. I'll tell her this part."

Higgy put the plastic-covered document into his briefcase that was sitting on the side of the table. Brownie reached for the food bag and handed out sandwiches.

"Turkey okay?" she asked Alex. Alex nodded. Miss Bea liked these turkey sandwiches.

Alex reached for her coke and took a big drink. The basement walls and floor were covered in a fine layer of plaster dust, but she knew her dry mouth was from fear.

Frank is really going to be angry, she thought. Too bad.

But then she picked up the cellophane wrapped sandwich in front of her and pulled out one half. She ate it slowly.

I'm through being afraid all the time, she mused, and she bit off another bite of sandwich.

36

THURSDAY, MARCH 2, 1961

It had been three weeks since Alex had talked to Higgy and Brownie about Connors, and she had heard nothing. She'd been anxious but kept telling herself and Gwen it would take time. Finally, this morning she had gotten a typed note addressed to her from a "Miss Brown." It had been hand-delivered to the Senator's office. The note had suggested they meet this noon "on the lower floor of where we met before."

Just like Brownie, she had thought.

So now she was sitting in the dank basement under the Lincoln Memorial, thinking.

Perhaps there was finally some news about what Ambassador Stephenson was doing about that awful Connors, she thought as she waited. Just from reading the news, Alex realized these past weeks had been a very busy time for the Ambassador. There were mounting tensions between the United States and the Soviet Union over the Congo, and a UN resolution had been adopted about preventing civil war in that troubled nation. And, President Kennedy had just announced the creation of a "Peace Corps," and there had been a lot of hoopla about that. But still, she fumed as she waited for Brownie, there's a murderer walking around free.

The door to the basement of the Lincoln Memorial had been ajar when she'd arrived, and the lights were on in the stairwell, so she had just walked down expecting Brownie already to be there with a greasy bag of sandwiches and some cokes. But the cavernous space was empty, so she had sat down to wait. It was taking her a while, Alex thought, getting more chilled by the minute.

Then she heard the upper door close and footsteps coming down the stairs.

Oh, finally, she thought, and rose from the folding chair.

But it wasn't Brownie.

Duncan Connors appeared on the stairs, and he was holding the same black gun he'd held on her at the Adams Memorial.

Alex was frightened, but not all that surprised. Then she saw Lt. Karns coming quietly down the stairs behind Connors. She thought for one second he was there to capture Connors, but then he looked directly at her and said and did nothing.

Oh, God, no, she thought. He's one of them.

Connors turned and nodded to Karns and then turned back to her.

"Well, girlie, I bet my British colors you'd fall right into my lap," he said with a smile that did not reach his icy blue eyes.

"Those are the wrong colors, aren't they Duncan?" Alex replied, stepping around behind the folding chair. "You mean the Soviet colors. You're a Red through and through." She looked at Karns, partly up the stairs, with contempt.

"And you too, Karns. You stink. And to think Stephen cared for you."

"Not that hard to fake being a fag, sweetheart," Connors said contemptuously, and she thought he was also digging at Karns. Karns's face was still a blank.

"Not hard to fake being loyal to America either, is it Connors?" she said, matching his contemptuous tone.

"I'd so love to do you, you bitch, right here, right now," Connors growled, and he walked closer to her, licking his full lips. "But I don't have the time." He waved the gun at her, and she could see his hand trembling slightly. Underneath the bravado, he was scared to death.

Karns came further down the steps.

"I need Carpenter's FBI files," Connors snarled. "They're on to us, and we need something to bargain with. That boyo Hoover will cover our escape if we've got those files."

"Files?" Alex asked, putting as much sweet confusion into her voice as she could.

She had already gone back to Professor Lawrence, used his darkroom to make prints, and gotten a lesson in how to make microdots. She had used Stephen's equipment at night to convert all the FBI documents she'd photographed into microdots that now sat in a safe deposit box at the local bank. She had burned the printed photos in the kitchen sink. It had taken hours for the smell to clear, even with opening the windows.

"I want to smash that mouth of yours until the blood pours out and you choke on it, you lying bitch. I want to so much, but I need that face of yours to look all pretty." He stopped and licked his lips again.

"But there are parts of you that can bleed, and nobody will see it. So quit lying. I know you rented a box at the bank. I been following you. We're going to take a little car ride. The ole lieutenant here will drive us, and you're going to get those papers for us, or I will kill everyone in that bank, you understand me, you filthy slag," he spit out, his face contorted with rage. He was practically frothing at the mouth, still waving the gun around.

Behind him, Alex saw Karns pull a gun out from inside his jacket and point it. For a moment she thought he was pointing it at her, but then it moved with Connors as he took a step to come even closer to her. Then they all heard the noise of a door opening at the top of the stairs, and the two men glanced away from her up the stairs.

Alex stopped caring if she'd be shot by two men or just one. While they were distracted, she pulled up on the back of the folding chair, shut it and swung it at Connor's head as he turned back. It connected, and he staggered back but did not fall. He still had hold of the gun.

Karns fired at Connors, but Connors didn't go down. He screamed in rage or pain, and he shot Karns point-blank in the chest. The noise in the hollow space was deafening.

Connors swung back around toward her, and since he was still between her and the stairs, she ran the other way, toward the pillars in the dim reaches of the huge space.

As she rounded the first pillar, a roar and a ping of plaster over her head told her he had recovered and was shooting at her.

"Stop right there, Connors," she heard echoing off the stone walls.

It was Frank Scott's voice.

"There are dozens of FBI agents behind me. You'll never get out of here alive unless you surrender."

"You bloody bastard!" Connors yelled, and she heard another gun shot.

"Frank!" she screamed.

"Oh, la di dah, it's Frank is it?" said Connors, savagely. "Well, you bitch, your precious Frank is in this with me. Him and me and Karns. He's me boss, or did he leave that little tidbit out when he was doin' you?"

Alex crept to the next pillar back, trying to make no noise.

"Don't believe him, Alex," Scott called out. "Karns is a double agent, working with me. Connors is a Soviet spy, and we've learned he also deals drugs here in the District. He's connected to Hicks. We have him cold."

Alex shook with fear but still said nothing. She crouched behind a pillar. Was Connors right? she wondered. Was Frank in it with him? What about Karns? He shot at Connors. Was Karns dead? Was Frank trying to capture Connors? Unless he meant to kill him and have him take all the blame. Dead traitors can't implicate others.

"I knew that Karns was really a fag," Connors bragged. "You both think I didn't know that? But you won't take me if I have the little beauty here as my hostage." Alex could hear him moving closer to the pillars.

"Stop right there!" Scott yelled. "Alex, don't come out from behind one of those columns!" And immediately she heard another shot.

Alex used the noise of the gunshot reverberations to cover the sound of her tread as she ran three pillars to the right, further into the darkest reaches of the basement.

But she wasn't the only one who had run for cover during the noise of the gun discharging. A flip of a suit jacket showed her Connors had gained the pillars and was moving along them. Then she heard footfalls and a scrape, and she realized Scott had also gotten to the first of the pillars.

"Alex, don't answer me. He'll know where you are. But I want you to know I've told you the truth. Karns and I work together. Connors is the spy, and he's been exposed. He'll go to prison on the drug charges. We got Hicks to roll on him, but that's only what we'll tell the press. He'll pay for what he did to Stephen and the kid in your office. He will pay."

"Shut up, you bloody bugger," Connors yelled from deep in the basement. "I took my orders from you. Don't believe him, girlie. He just wants to kill me and get his hands on the files. He'll kill you when he does."

"Alex, I swear to you he's lying. You have to trust me," Scott called out, and a derisive laugh echoed from the back of the basement. Scott fired his gun toward where the sound had come from.

Do I trust him? Alex thought, anguished. But then she chose, and she ran around two pillars toward the front where she thought Scott was standing.

She had miscalculated. He was one pillar further to the left, but they saw each other. He gestured for her to stay where she was, and she nodded.

He went around the pillar and ran forward, ducking behind a pillar two rows down as another shot rang out from Connor's direction.

Alex could not see what was happening, but it sounded like Scott had run forward again.

Then there was another gun shot, and a man screamed.

Had Connors shot Frank, or was it the other way around? Should she run for the stairs? She trembled with indecision and then heard a commotion as a dozen feet tramped down the stairs. She turned and held her hands in the air.

"FBI!" yelled the lead man as he ran up to Alex. "You Bell?" he asked in a gruff voice.

She nodded.

He turned and gestured to an agent.

"Take her up now."

But before Alex and the agent could move, Frank Scott came around the last pillar. He was covered in plaster dust.

"Connors is back there. I shot him, but he'll live. I have his gun here," and he handed it butt first to the lead agent.

Another agent was bending over Karns who was partially sitting up, leaning back on the stairs. His jacket was open and Alex could see the tear Connor's bullet had made when it had torn into what she thought was called a flack jacket Karns had apparently been wearing. He looked up and gave her a wry look that turned into a grimace as the agent moved to help him stand.

More agents spread out and moved quickly among the pillars in the direction where Alex could now hear muted swearing.

Scott came over and folded Alex into a tight embrace.

"I thought he would kill you," she whispered into his dust-covered jacket front.

"I was terrified he would grab you and use you as a hostage. He'd have finally killed you when he got what he wanted."

"I know," Alex said, and burrowed tighter into his embrace.

"You're not safe while you have those files," Scott said into her hair.

"What files?" Alex said, not raising her head.

* * *

Alex and Gwen each had a glass of wine. It was not their first. Alex was recounting what had happened in the basement of the Lincoln Memorial.

"So he was a drug dealer too?" Gwen said, amazed. "Just like that Hicks."

"I knew it," Miss Bea commented, raising her head from the soup bone Alex had given her. "Smelled like puke and that stuff that hurts my nose." She resumed chewing.

"You know, Gwen, I think that Captain De Luca is in the drug dealing up to his neck," Alex said slowly, thinking aloud. "I have a few ideas how we might be able to get him."

Bea raised her head again and sighed. Then she resumed gnawing. She'd do what she could to keep Alex safe.

"That's not gonna be easy," Gwen said slowly.

There was a knock on the door.

Alex went to open it. She was not surprised to see Frank Scott standing there.

"I have some news for you and Gwen," he said solemnly. "May I come in?"

"Yes," Alex said and stepped aside to let him pass.

He greeted Gwen and refused Alex's offer of wine.

"Duncan Connors was murdered in the hospital following the surgery. He had been given cyanide, but it was not self-administered. There was a guard on the door, but he'd been hit over the head. The guard's conscious now but remembers nothing."

Alex said nothing, shocked and yet somehow not surprised.

"So, he's dead? The man who murdered my Stephen is dead, just like that?" Gwen said, sitting down hard on the little sofa.

"What can I tell Mama?" she asked, looking up at Scott's face. "She needs to know Stephen's murderer is dead."

"You can tell her that her son's murderer was a drug dealer who was shot by the police and who died in the hospital of his wound," Scott said flatly.

"No," Alex said, frowning at him. "You can't leave a mother to think her son had anything to do with drugs. Just no."

Scott turned toward Gwen and said in a soft voice, "Tell her that her son died a hero for trying to protect his country from those who would betray it to foreign powers."

Gwen nodded. She took the phone with its long cord, carried it into her bedroom and shut the door.

"Thank you," Alex said quietly. She sat down on the sofa, and Scott sat in a chair opposite her.

After some silence, she asked, "And how is Lieutenant Karns?"

"He'll be okay. There's a lot of bruising and two broken ribs, but the jacket kept him alive and breathing, though I think he's taking some leave." Frank paused. "He really did love Gray, I think. And let me tell you, Alex, being a double agent tears you apart." He stared at the floor.

Alex picked up her wine from the little coffee table and took a sip. Scott just sat there, looking down.

"Ah, Alex, sometimes I hate the job I do," Scott said after a while, and he went over to the couch, put an arm under hers and pulled her to her feet. He folded her into his arms.

"I know, Frank," Alex said, and she raised her head to his and kissed him. "I am beginning to know just how that feels."

37

FRIDAY, MARCH 3, 1961

"So, dish," Brownie said over her plate of fried eggs and hash browns. They were in a back booth of the diner "Pete's" on Ptomaine Row where Frank had first taken her for lunch. Alex had just ordered toast and coffee, but she had eaten most of the toast. She took a sip of the coffee and then leaned forward.

"Well, I'll tell you what you may not know from Higgy and then what you can print, okay?"

Brownie nodded and dug out her notepad from her huge purse while she chewed her forkful of eggs and potatoes.

"Shoot."

"What you can print is the drug angle. And it's a good one, as that ghastly police detective, Hicks, was up to his jug-handle ears in bringing drugs to Washington."

Brownie wrote furiously.

"Can't implicate that New York so-called reformer, Captain De Luca, directly, but put in some speculation about whether the police in New York have perhaps been 'lax,' and they should have let cops in the District know of their suspicions of Hicks. Duncan Connors was in on the drug distribution with another guy from New York City, Aiden McCaffrey. Irish immigrant, worked for the mob in the city. He's dead too, so no problem saying that." Alex paused. "But you better not say 'mob.' I don't want you fitted for, as we say in New York, 'a pair of concrete overshoes.' Better say 'criminals.'"

"Yep," Brownie said, not raising her head.

"Now, Duncan Connors was the author of that ghastly memo, and he and McCaffrey tried to torture the location of it out of Stephen Gray. They didn't get it but killed Stephen in the process and tried to make it look like it was a homosexual encounter that had gotten violent."

"Can't print that," Brownie said, raising her head. Her wrinkles drooped into a deep gloom.

"I know. But now at least his mother knows the truth."

"Well, thank God for that," Brownie said. Then she looked up at Alex.

"So Higgy said the Ambassador was on to that memo like white on rice," she said. "Took it to some of his pals in government who actually care about things like the Constitution. They cottoned on to Connors and got some FBI pals to start investigating the 'Commie traitor' in the State Department. Higgy heard third hand that Hoover wanted to know if Connors was also a homosexual. Ironic, isn't it?" Brownie gave a combination groan and chuckle.

"Anyway, how'd that Connors die?" Brownie asked. "I'm sure it wasn't from his so-called wounds."

"Somebody poisoned him in the hospital," Alex said grimly.

"Oh, man. But I can't print that, right?"

"No, you can't, but I've been thinking about that. It's clear that somebody pretty high up is planning some kind of military action regarding Cuba. That's a story worth following. You could also speculate about whether Connors represented 'foreign interests' in the State Department. That should be okay. And then it is crucial to keep our noses to the ground about Cuba. There's US-Soviet tension in the air."

"Yeah," Brownie said, scribbling away. "I could talk about the Congo and then kind of imply that's not the end of it, maybe just the beginning."

"Good idea," Alex said, and absently took her last bite of toast. She chewed while Brownie kept writing.

"So I think I have the gist of it here," Brownie said as she tapped her notebook with her pen. Then she put them aside and picked up her fork.

"There could be several stories there, Brownie," Alex said consideringly.

"You think?" Brownie said.

* * *

Alex arrived at the office and put away her coat. Mrs. Anderson had not arrived. She took the time to fix her hair back in its French twist that went so well with the high collared, navy blue fitted dress with the medium flair to the skirt. Professional and yet feminine.

She went to her desk and started working on the file of letters from Senator Carpenter's constituents that she had been unable to finish yesterday given the incredible events. She had used a phone in Frank Scott's car, an absolutely amazing thing to her, and called the office to say she had was feeling unwell and would not be returning.

My God was that the truth, she thought as she sorted through the remaining mail.

What was also the truth was that Alex was getting very tired of having to do all the Senator's Senate committee work along with the correspondence.

Then she heard Senator Carpenter's key in the lock of the office, and she entered quickly having realized the door was already unlocked.

"Good morning, Madam Senator," Alex said briskly. Their relationship had settled down to treating each other with cool formality.

"Good morning, Miss Bell. I see you are here early."

"Yes, Madam Senator. I had to catch up on my work since I did not feel well yesterday."

"That was too bad, yes," said the Senator, absently pulling off her gloves as she headed for her office.

"Madam Senator, if I may?" Alex said sweetly. Senator Carpenter turned but did not speak.

"I'd like to know when the young man who will be joining us in the office as an assistant will arrive."

"Today, I think, Miss Bell. He took his own sweet time about getting here," she said, but Alex thought that was more to herself than to Alex.

Mrs. Anderson arrived, but was immediately called into the Senator's office and then she left to go on an unnamed errand.

Alex sighed as she now had to do three jobs, answer the phone, attend to the mail, and work on another briefing paper for the Senator.

The door of the office opened with a bang, and a young man with blond hair that was too long, a two-day fuzz of beard, wrinkled khaki pants and an even more wrinkled collarless shirt strutted in. Alex noticed he wore dock shoes with no socks.

"Well, hello, beautiful," he swaggered. "Where is Aunt Maggie? I've got a job here, doncha know?" and he gave Alex what she was sure he thought was a winning smile. And it probably was with some undergraduate girls.

This must be Reggie.

Alex stood up behind her raised desk. This gave her several inches on old Reggie, and she used every one of them.

"You are Mr. Van Allen, I presume. First, I am your direct supervisor, Miss Bell. You will only refer to Senator Carpenter as Senator Carpenter, Madam Senator, or rarely, ma'am."

"Hey, wait now," Reggie began.

"No," Alex said sternly. "Be quiet."

"You are unsuitably dressed for the office of a United States Senator."

Reggie sputtered a little, but Alex ignored him.

"You will leave immediately and see a barber for a haircut and a shave. Then you will go to this person at this men's haberdashery," and Alex paused to scribble the information on a piece of paper. The name was of an old friend from New York who knew tailoring was an art form. She leaned over her high desktop and handed the paper to Reggie.

"You will need at least three suits, preferably with vests. Subdued ties, button-down men's shirts, dark socks," and here she glared at his bare ankles and dock shoes, "and men's leather shoes."

"Hey, lady!" Reggie protested.

"Do not interrupt, and when you address me, you may only address me as Miss Bell or ma'am."

Reggie glared but was silent.

"You do not have employment here. Not yet. I will decide on that based on your ability to carry out these few, simple instructions." Alex knew she was going out on a limb here, but she'd never have control of this idiot unless she took a firm stand now.

"When you return, suitably attired, Mr. Van Allen, I will begin your training."

Reggie just stood there, his lightly tanned, freckled face looking dazed. His blond hair seemed to be drooping.

"Go," Alex said firmly. "You don't have much time if we are going to get any training done today."

"Yeah, well, okay," Reggie mumbled.

"Mr. Van Allen," Alex said coldly. "Say 'yes, ma'am.'"

"Yes, ma'am," he replied.

"Very good. Now you better hurry, and please close the door quietly."

Reggie did as he was told, and Alex took a deep breath.

"Very, very good, Miss Bell," said the Senator's voice from her doorway. Alex turned.

"Thank you, Madam Senator," she replied.

Then Alex heard a subdued meow just before the Senator's door closed. Oh, she thought grimly. Fluffy is back.

Then she smiled. Fluffy was Reggie's problem now.

The phone on her desk rang.

"Hello, Alex," Frank said when she'd identified herself. "Can I take you to dinner tonight? Pick you up in the lobby of the Senate office building at 7 o'clock.?"

Alex considered, and then she spoke softly into the receiver.

"Yes, thank you, Frank," she said formally.

She heard a subdued chuckle.

"No, thank you, your Highness," she heard and then the phone disconnected.

But I'm still not giving you those FBI files, she said to herself.

38

MIDNIGHT, ROCK CREEK CEMETERY, AT THE STATUE "GRIEF"

A figure sits on the stone bench, facing the statue.

I don't even know where your grave is, so I came here. I miss you so much, and I want to kill you. Why didn't you give it to me, you total idiot?

Silence, then a deep sigh.

You didn't have to die like that. I could have given it to them, saved you all that pain.

Sobbing.

You suspected me, didn't you? For all we were to each other, you still didn't trust me.

Oh, Stephen.

HISTORICAL NOTES

It is, of course, crucial in writing an historical novel to do research in the period. The "Sixties" has fascinated historians for decades, and there is a library's worth of material to consider.

I recommend the following books, articles and videos for those who would like to read some of what I read to write this novel. All the references may be found in the bibliography.

While historical novels are fiction, it is important for verisimilitude to have the broad outlines correct. Otherwise, the world created by the novel will not seem real and the reader will not enter it, but stand back.

Location is crucial in historical fiction writing, and given the intersecting racial and sexual contexts of this novel, getting clear on those constructs and their impact on where characters could and could not live was important. *African Americans in the Greater DC Area: 1930 to the Present* by Leah Brooks and Caitlyn Valade was invaluable in its detail.

The 500-page book by Chris Myers Asch and George Derek Musgrove, *Chocolate City; A History of Race and Democracy in the Nation's Capital*, is a sociopolitical history of race in Washington, D.C. from colonial America through the present. The sweep of the narrative helps the reader understand the first majority African American city in the U.S., and it is supplemented with maps, charts and photos. There are some good journal article length summaries of this book, but the length of the book itself should not deter you. It is fascinating, especially in light of current events.

The landmark U.S. Supreme Court decision, Brown v. Board of Education of Topeka in 1954 that ruled racial segregation in public schools unconstitutional, even if the segregated schools are otherwise equal in quality, reverberated through the country after that date. In 1960 and 1961, when my main characters travel by bus, or attempt to stay in a hotel, the continued resistance to desegregation is all too clear.

While many Americans know about the "Red Scare," the persecution and purging of suspected Communists by Senator Joseph McCarthy and his ilk, far fewer know about the on-going discrimination against LGBTQI persons in government and private work called the "Lavender Scare." As he was about to leave office as Secretary of State in 2017, John Kerry issued an apology for this persecution. Secretary Kerry wrote, ""In the past—as far back as the 1940s, but continuing for decades—the Department of State was among many public and private employers that discriminated against employees and job applicants on the basis of perceived sexual orientation, forcing some employees to resign or refusing to hire certain applicants in the first place," Kerry wrote. "These actions were wrong then, just as they would be wrong today."

Despite this persecution, Washington D.C. had a vibrant Queer culture and I found Genny Beemyn's book, *A Queer Capital: A History of Gay Life in Washington D.C.*, very helpful in constructing the fictional world that my characters inhabit in D.C.

You can learn about how deeply this persecution was embedded in the FBI by reading the extensive book by Douglas Charles, *Hoover's War on Gays: Exposing the FBI's "Sex Deviates" Program.*

J. Edgar Hoover features in this novel not only for his persecution of LGBTQI persons, but also for his strident anti-Communism and his racism. And, I believe, these tended to merge in Hoover's mind as he saw LGBTQI persons and African Americans as inherently security threats. In effect, for Hoover, a white, heteropatriarchal society was synonymous with national security. Again, the seeds of today's conflicts were widely planted and cultivated by Hoover and his FBI.

The scene in the novel where Hoover testifies relies on a video from the 1950s. It is clear, however, that Hoover never changed his views on Communism and his use of a "disease" metaphor is quite instructive.

Central to the plot is the actual war on American political freedom conducted by Hoover's FBI over many years. For this, be sure to read Nelson Blackstock, *Cointelpro: The FBI's Secret War on Political Freedom*, as it is based on actual documents obtained through the Freedom of Information Act on this long-term attack on American freedoms and especially on the civil rights of African Americans.

Fidel Castro and the Cuban revolution feature in the novel, and Cuban foreign relations debates in 1961 were contentious and ultimately gravely misguided. These can be read in the originals.

John Fitzgerald Kennedy has had thousands if not millions of words written about him. Many regard Ted Sorenson's *Kennedy: The Classic*

Biography, as exactly that, the classic biography. While slightly worshipful, it does document the history well.

I also read Katharine Graham's book, *Personal History*, for crafting the brief appearance she makes in the novel. The book is a very informative read.

Finally, I did read many articles in the archives of *The Village Voice* for the scene in Greenwich Village and found it engrossing. You might as well.

It should be clear both from the novel and from these historical sources how much the "Sixties" has shaped our current context. From concentration camps for those seeking asylum from persecution, to putting children in cages, persecuting racial/ethnic minorities for standing up for their civil rights, denying equal rights to LGBTQI Americans to political intrigues of all sorts, the decade of the 1960s is the past that is still present.

Discussion Questions

1. Alexandra Bel changes the spelling of her name, her hair and skin color, and hides her immigrant background. Why do you think she does this and is she justified?

2. How do you see Alex changing throughout the novel?

3. The relationship between Alex and Gwen Gray is central to the narrative. Why do you think they became friends?

4. The persecution of LGBTQI persons has been called "The Lavender Scare." It followed the "Red Scare," the witch hunt for Communists that subverted American freedoms. Had you heard of this before? If you have, what was the context? If not, why do you think this period is not well known?

5. Mrs. Eleanor Roosevelt was a strident critic of J. Edgar Hoover and what she called his "American Gestapo" tactics in gathering information on citizens through wire-tapping, surveillance, and other dubious methods. Hoover looms large in the formation of American attitudes and values, having run the FBI and directed its methods for nearly four decades. What was your impression of Hoover before reading this novel? Has it changed?

6. Alex Bell is skeptical of religion, but her roommate Gwen Gray seems to be a person of faith. What are your own views on faith and how do they compare and contrast to these characters?

7. "Washington runs on cocktail parties," Alex is told. Is it your impression that is the case today? Why or why not?

8. Alex creates an image of herself by using her training in fine tailoring to dress in designer clothes. Why is the Senator so frumpy by comparison, or is she too creating an image? What is it?

9. Alex's aunt and mother work for labor rights through their union. They are hassled and even beaten by police for this work. What are your views on unionization?

10. The relationship between Alex and her little dog, Miss Bea, is central to the novel. What do you think that represents for Alex?

BIBLIOGRAPHY

Asch, Chris Meyers, and Musgrove, George Derek. *Chocolate City; A History of Race and Democracy in the Nation's Capital.* Chapel Hill: University of North Carolina Press, 2017.

Beemyn, Genny. *A Queer Capital: A History of Gay Life in Washington D.C.* Milton Park, Abingdon: Routledge, 2015.

Blackstock, Nelson. *Cointelpro: The FBI's Secret War on Political Freedom.* Atlanta: Pathfinder, 1975, 1988.

Brooks, Leah, and Valade, Caitlyn. *African Americans in the Greater DC Area: 1930 to the Present.* Center for Washington Area Studies. https://cpb-us-e1.wpmucdn.com/blogs.gwu.edu/dist/7/677/files/2017/09/Final-Version-Mapping-Segregation-Policy-Brief-1tjali5.pdf.

"Brown v. Board of Education of Topeka (1)." *Oyez.* www.oyez.org/cases/1940–1955/347us483. Accessed 17 Jan. 2021.

Charles, Douglas. *Hoover's War on Gays: Exposing the FBI's "Sex Deviates" Program.* Lawrence: University Press of Kansas, 2015.

Daley, Jason. "State Department Apologizes for the 'Lavender Scare.'" Smithsonianmag. com (January 10, 2017). https://www.smithsonianmag.com/smart-news/state-department-apologizes-lavender-scare-180961746/.

Foreign Relations of the United States, 1961–1963, Volume X, Cuba, January 1961–September 1962. "206. Memorandum for the Record." https://www.foreign.senate.gov/imo/media/doc/CDOC-105sdoc281.pdf.

Graham, Katharine. *Personal History.* New York: Knopf, 2002.

"Hoover on Communism." YouTube. https://www.youtube.com/watch?v=UDCVdho8TYM.

Sorenson, Ted. *Kennedy: The Classic Biography.* New York: Harper Collins, 1965, 2009.

The Village Voice. Openculture.com. https://www.openculture.com/2017/08/read-1000-editions-of-the-the-village-voice-a-digital-archive-of-the-iconic-new-york-city-paper.html.

www.ingramcontent.com/pod-product-compliance
Lightning Source LLC
Chambersburg PA
CBHW051146030726
47504CB00004B/1068